MUSE

ALSO BY MARY NOVIK

Conceit

MUSE

a novel

MARY NOVIK

DOUBLEDAY
CANADA

Doubleday Canada and colophon are registered trademarks of
Random House of Canada Limited

Library and Archives Canada Cataloguing in Publication

Novik, Mary, 1945-, author
Muse / Mary Novik.

Issued in print and electronic formats.
ISBN 978-0-385-66821-7

I. Title.

PS8627.O9245M87 2013   C813'.6   C2013-902626-6
C2013-902627-4

Text and cover design: Kelly Hill
Cover images: (woman) Malgorzata Maj/Trevillion Images; (Avignon) created from
a photograph by Richard Susanto/Shutterstock.com
Printed and bound in the USA

Published in Canada by Doubleday Canada,
a division of Random House of Canada Limited

www.randomhouse.ca

10 9 8 7 6 5 4 3 2 1

For

Keir, Karen, Alexander, and Matilda

Clairefontaine

1309–1324

1

Avignon

1324–1341

79

Palais des Papes

1342–1348

195

The Vaucluse

1348

277

Clairefontaine

1309–1324

One

FIRST HEARD my mother's heartbeat from inside her dark, surrounding womb. It mingled with my own heart's rhythm, then changed to a harsher, more strident beat. It was then that I had my first and most famous vision of a man kneeling in a purple cassock and biretta. I could see him as if I were looking out a window made of glass. He was framed by curtains that fell in crimson folds around my mother, who lay beneath him on the bed. His face was as clear to me as the blood vessels inside her womb, his skin foxed with a tracery of veins. I looked straight into his eyes and they were as hard and blue as lapis lazuli. I kicked with all my might to drive him off.

When I was older and further from my mother's heartbeat, I told her this vision to bring her close to me. After my grandmother Conmère left to boast about me to the cloth-workers along the canal, my mother picked me up to kiss behind my ear.

"It was the eightieth day of your life, Solange, the day your soul entered your body. You moved inside me, telling me that I was carrying a daughter. This means we will soon have a finer place to live, a bed of riches in another chamber. Now that the Pope and his men have come to Avignon, Fortune will spin her wheel to raise us up."

Before long, my mother had a visitor, a priest whose every act was full of kindness and ceremony. After his first visit, he came each week. I would run to him and call him Papa, and would receive three kisses on my cheeks. Then I would unburden his arms of gifts: honey, wax candles, an apple or a plum, the almonds I craved, sometimes a length of cloth or lace. He gave Maman a perfume bottle and a bracelet wrought of silver, with a shank of his hair embedded like a relic.

When the Rhône flooded and the water spilled across the low road beside the canal, Papa arrived with wet shoes, carrying a wooden box under his arm. He let me open the clasp to take out the alphabet letters stacked inside, then spelt words on the hearth for me to read. *Mater.* Maman. *Pater.* Papa. Conmère did not leave her corner that day, but rocked back and forth, crooning oddly.

"What is wrong with her?" Papa asked.

Maman said, "This happens when the canal floods. She thinks the water is rising up to choke her and complains of prickling in her arms and legs."

"I have prickles also," I said, but they were paying more attention to each other than to me.

"Perhaps Conmère has second sight like Solange, but lacks the clarity to speak of it," Papa said. "Your gift is in your face and chestnut hair, but Solange will speak in many tongues. Look how she reaches for the wooden letters! When she is of age, I will give her a dowry so she can enter a great abbey or wed a man of noble birth to have fine sons."

On All Saints' Day, Papa did not come as promised. Instead, another priest arrived in a black cassock to announce that Papa had left this world to find a better one. My mother banged on the priest's chest with her fists and refused to talk or eat all day. After a week our fuel was gone and Conmère walked beyond the cemetery to gather wood. She returned with a faggot of sticks and a sack of coarse flour.

"No more white bread for you," she said crossly, tying a shawl around me for warmth. "The fire is only for cooking now."

Our clothes and bed-linen became damp over the winter. When our food ran out, Maman would descend into the tavern to beg food and ale from the drunkards, who followed her upstairs to climb behind the bed-curtains with her. In the spring, Conmère opened the shutters so we could hear the water rushing over the paddle-wheels, and not the sound of my mother's frequent visitors. At night, I slept with Conmère on her paillasse of straw in the corner made fragrant by her herbs and salves, and in the day, I trailed after her along the Sorgue, cutting willow shoots to weave paniers to sell in the market. She told me that her father had been a cloth-dyer with a thriving business where the tavern stood now. The tavern was the Cheval Blanc. The street was the rue du Cheval Blanc. The city was Avignon, the home of the Pope. I was to remember these things if I was separated from her in the busy streets like a lamb torn from the side of a ewe.

Conmère boasted that her name was Le Blanc and that she had once owned the whole building and a milk cow in the shed besides. Most of her stories were dark and wild, told in a tongue that I could scarcely understand. I believed little that she said, least of all that she had owned a cow, but I knew where I lived—at the sign of the white horse along the Sorgue canal. Here, the water spun out of the paddle-wheels into the vats where the dyers worked the dye into the cloth, staining their arms and legs dull purple.

At Pentecost, the anniversary of my birth, Conmère kneaded lard and coarse flour into a flatbread, pressed rosemary and salt into the crust, and laid it on the fire-grate. As it baked, she rubbed my legs with fragrant oil, stopping at the birthmark on my thigh. It looked like the chalice I had admired in Notre-Dame-des-Doms, but I knew it wasn't, because it was too small.

"What is it?" I asked, as I did each year.

"A thimble. The mark of the cloth-makers, who are your kin and mine."

She whetted her knife, tested the blade on her thumb, then scored a gentle line, the width of a thread, beside the thimble. I scrambled onto the bed next to Maman to show her the newest mark.

She kissed the beads of blood away. "Another thread to bind you to me. Now, count how old you are."

I touched a finger to each mark in turn. "Five," I said, and was rewarded with a chunk of bread.

Boots arrived, a fist beat on the door, and I leapt off the bed as a man came in from the tavern. He spat a mouthful of ale at me and deposited his sloshing flagon on the floor. Then he tugged off his hose, climbed on top of Maman, and jerked the bed-curtains closed. Conmère sat on a stool, carding fleece, her eyes flicking between her spindle and the swinging draperies. At first, the sounds were the usual ones made by male visitors, then Maman begged him to stop, and I became afraid for her. Conmère clapped her wool-cards while I thrashed the draperies with the broom, striking him on the leg.

"Get off my mother," I ordered.

The knave emerged with a red face. "Having another of your famous visions?" he yelled, wrenching the broom from me. "Who do you see this time? Another bishop? The Pope himself?"

He chased after me, hitting the floor more often than he hit me as I scurried to escape his blows. Conmère kicked his shins, swearing at him in the old tongue until the broom cracked against her skull. As he raised it again, I clasped my hands as though I saw the Virgin before me and chanted the Alma Redemptoris Mater as fast as I could in Latin. I chanted it over and over until he dropped the broom, crossed himself, took a fortifying drink from his flagon, and said, "Get rid of this filthy saint, or else you'll lose your trade. Hardly any men come up here as it is."

Maman dove at him with the pointed spindle and it was his turn to scuttle, half-running, half-tumbling down the flight of steps. I threw his boots and hose after him, sat on the top step, and listened to him spill his tale to the men in the tavern. It pleased him to leave out the spindle and to make much of the little virgin with her gift of tongues to conceal his own cowardice in running from us.

By Michaelmas, my reputation as a prodigy had spread throughout the cloth-makers' quarter, though truly I was no child wonder but had only learnt some Latin from Papa. By Martinmas, the tavern louts stopped coming upstairs because Maman was with child by one of them. We had no tallow to make soap and candles, and little fuel. When the mistral hurled itself against the oiled cloth windows, we stuffed rags into the shutters and darkness descended in the daylight hours. The smell of meat rose through the floorboards from the tavern's spit, making me nauseous with hunger. My bones did not grow and Maman, her face pocked and her breath sour, seldom got out of bed.

I lay beside her, spinning Papa's bracelet around her wrist bone. "Look out the window," I begged, pulling on her arm. "The moon is red and the water is racing through the paddles."

"This infant refuses to be born, Solange. Use your gift to look into my womb to see what evil is within me."

I pressed my eyes against her bare skin, but could not see the child or feel it move. "It is dark as night inside."

In the morning, Maman's belly jumped beneath my hand. The bold kick told me it must be a boy. Soon he was battering her with his fists and knees, and Maman clutched her sides with each new spasm. Why would he not come peacefully into the world as I had done? Instead, he tore his way out of her womb in a fury of blood. Conmère caught him as he emerged. Once out, he fell quiet, his flesh curiously blue as Conmère pushed him from my sight. When her poultices could not stanch the river of blood between Maman's legs, she broke the broom across her knee.

Maman told her, "Go at once for Father Arnaud at old Saint Martial."

I stroked Maman's cheek until a blow sounded on the door, knocking it open. It was Papa's friend in his priest's cassock, with Conmère behind him. He did not sit, but stood swinging his arms at his sides impatiently.

"You agreed that this would be best, Madame," he said. "It is better done quickly for her sake and for yours."

I crawled onto Maman's bed to lay my head against her middle, which now felt cold and dead. She drew me towards her and wept, her fingers tangled in my hair. When her silver bracelet caught my eye, I gave it a spin.

"May I have this, Maman?"

"No, little one, for I am dying. I will need it to bring Papa to my side."

"Why must you die to make him come?"

"When you are older, you will understand." She felt for the empty perfume bottle on a ribbon around her neck, caught some of my tears in it, then her own, then pressed my fist around the bottle. "When the last trumpet sounds, I will fly to you to collect my tears. Now leave with the good Father and do not look back. Mind the nuns and learn your letters as Papa wished. I will be well where I am going." She squeezed the breath out of me, then released me so abruptly that my feet shot down to the floor. When Conmère lurched towards her, wailing, Maman grasped her hand. "The Virgin will take better care of Solange than either you or I can do. Let her go where she will be fed and clothed."

Conmère uttered a charm in the old tongue as the priest swung me onto his hip. He carried me screaming down the stairs, through the tavern, and across the plank over the canal. When he paused on the other side, I squirmed out of his arms, but got no further than his broad palm allowed.

"Let me go to Maman!"

He pressed me against the earth so I could not kick him. "Avignon is a city of men. It is no place for a young girl. Your grandmother is herself no better than a child. If you stay here with her, you will both starve."

With his free hand, he dug in his alms-bag for a dry cake. I bit off a piece, tasting white flour, honey, raisins, and almonds. I shoved the rest in my mouth with two hands before he could take it back. After I had choked it down, his iron grip closed around my wrist.

"There are more cakes like that in the abbey where I am taking you."

He stood me on my own two feet and gave me his wineskin to suck on. The cake was making its way into my stomach, where it filled the hollow that had ached for days. As we walked alongside the canal, the great wheels of the cloth-workers turned in a frenzy, driven by a river enraged and swollen by the full red moon.

Two

WE FOLLOWED the angry river on foot as it left the city, and met the freedom of the paths and fields upstream. Slowly, the ramparts fell behind in the distance. As Avignon disappeared into a cloud, the night bell of Notre-Dame-des-Doms rang out.

The priest crossed himself. "Your mother's soul has left her body now."

I knew this meant that Maman was dead, but I hoped to see her before long. I clutched her perfume bottle in my hand so her soul would know where to find me. The priest entered a borie at a junction and reappeared with a sleepy donkey. He hoisted me on the front, then mounted, his legs almost dragging on the earth. As we left the river on a well-trodden path, the donkey's swaying lured me into a half-sleep. After a while, the priest climbed off to make the going easier. Then he made me slide off to walk as well, so he could lead the donkey along a narrower track. My toes were raw from pushing against my shoes by the time I saw the church tower ahead. Soon the abbey itself appeared, like a walled city with outbuildings scattered in the fields around it. My nose caught the scent of thyme—like Conmère's skin, but bitten and sharpened by the frost—and I slipped my hand out of the priest's to run towards the high gates. There were no sounds but a night bird calling and twigs snapping underfoot, until a nun came out of the gate-house to greet us, her keys clanging at her waist.

The priest said, "This is the child I told the abbess I would bring."

"Leave her with me. You will be fed in the almshouse." The gate-keeper pointed him towards a shadowy building outside the wall.

A water kettle was steaming on a fire near the gatehouse and the gatekeeper threw on vine cuttings to build up the heat. Then, with only the moon for light, she took out her knife and sheared my hair close to my skull. I squeezed my eyes shut, but she did not nick me once. She left to fetch something and I dug a hole in the soft earth to bury the perfume bottle so she couldn't take it from me. I had just covered the hole when she was back with two buckets of cold water, which she poured into a tub.

"Take off your clothes."

Since I didn't move, she stripped the clothes over my head and lifted me into the cold water. I looked down at my naked body with its ice-blue veins, wondering if I would die like my blue brother. Even the kettle of scalding water she poured around my ankles barely took off the chill. I bottled up my tears and cursed her as fiercely as Conmère would have done.

"That is the last time you will speak in the old tongue," she said, running a brush over a soap cake to scour the words from my mouth.

The soap stung so much I was afraid to say another word. She scrubbed my body, dried me, and clothed me in a homespun tunic, which had been warming near the fire. Then she threw my old gar-ments on the flames, sparing my shoes to put back on my throbbing feet. Only now, with the stink of burning wool in my nostrils, did she unlock the abbey gates to push me through.

As the sun rose, bathing the sky in gold, bells rang like hammer-blows and nuns hurried into the cloister, forming a black line that snaked past me into the church. A large girl with flying hair skipped after them, leaving the door ajar for me. Some words were spoken by an important woman in the chancel, then the nuns' voices lifted in song and I was fed with joyful sound.

The girl was at my side as soon as the chanting ended. "Your fingers are white. Do this to heat them." She crossed her arms over her chest and tucked her hands into her armpits. "I will show you how to do everything. We must be seated before Cook finishes beating the gong one hundred times."

My arms folded like bird wings, I followed her into a refectory with trestle-tables at which nuns sat in complete silence. The sweet aroma of the food drew me forwards in spite of my fear and I climbed on a bench beside the girl. With gestures, she demonstrated how to tip the pitcher and how to fill my trencher from the vessels of savoury food. I was an apt pupil, eager to learn. When my face was greasy, she wiped her lips with her hem and I did the same. I gestured towards the single abbey cake on our small table. She broke it in two and served herself the bigger portion, but I ate my part gladly, for there were raisins in it.

Once the meal was over, she led me back into the empty church. She told me that her name was Elisabeth and that the nuns observed the rule of Saint Benedict. The abbey was Clairefontaine, after Agnès de Clairefontaine, the abbess. The long words came out oddly from Elisabeth's mouth. Perhaps she had never had her mouth washed out, for she spoke almost as roughly as Conmère. She showed me where the ashlar blocks had shifted in one of the chapels, making a crawl space for an animal to climb through on all fours.

"This is how I go out after curfew," she said, "but you are not allowed to." From the church, she went ahead of me up the inner stairs to the lay dormitory. We entered a cold, dark cell, where Elisabeth pointed out a small bench hewn from sturdy oak, which would be mine, and a bed that was hers alone. At last, she noticed that I hadn't spoken.

"You can talk now. The nuns must be silent after compline, but here we can make as much noise as we wish."

I took the coarse blanket she gave me and laid it on my bed, well satisfied with my small empire. The bed was low and hard, little more than a straw pallet in a wooden frame, but I would be safe here until Maman came for me. My stomach was full and I was warmer than I had been for months. Although Elisabeth pretended not to want me, I could see that she had prepared for my arrival. On my lopsided bench sat a new candle, shorter than hers but just as useful. Beside it she had stacked some garments she had outgrown. She showed me how to fasten my new cloak to ward off draughts, then tied the cap snugly beneath my chin for me. What did I care that the cloak dragged along the floorboards? It had a wide, deep pouch to carry abbey cakes in.

When I thanked her, she reached for something on a ledge. "The abbess told me your mother is dead, like mine," she said. "I use this sponge to collect my tears when I am sad. Would you like one too?"

I could only nod because my tears were already unbottling themselves and spilling hotly down my cheeks. She held out a little sponge that was almost as nicely rounded as hers.

"This is how you do it." She dabbed my eyes and cheeks. "We will be sisters, but you must do everything I say because I am three years older. One day I will be a Benedictine, but you will not, for you are too small to be given to God. The abbess took you as a kindness, since you have no dowry to give the abbey."

It was true I had brought nothing of value, only the perfume bottle that I had buried in the soft earth by the gatehouse. All that long day, I spoke only to Elisabeth, but learnt fifteen useful hand signals, mostly for food. That night in our beds, I listened to Elisabeth sucking noisily on her tongue until she fell asleep. Then I crept down the inner stairs into the north chapel and wriggled through the gap in the tumbled ashlar into the darkness. I sought my hiding place near the gatekeeper's fire and dug until my fingers hit glass, unearthing the perfume bottle.

Safe in my splendid new pouch, it climbed up the stairs and into bed with me, where we waited for Maman together.

In the morning, the abbess sent for me. I opened the door of her house to find her sitting on a cushioned chair, eyes closed and lips moving as she worked her fingers along her beads. She was the important woman who had led the singing in church. I looked for something to do until she finished her paternosters. On a stand beside her was a curious box covered in leather, which I managed to slide over the edge of the stand and catch just before it banged against the floor. The hasp was locked, probably by the key I saw hanging from the abbess's belt. The noise had jarred her from her prayers and I shrank into myself, hoping she would not rebuke me.

"What do you think it is?" Her words were sharp and clear, like nothing I had heard alongside the canal.

I made my mouth as round and red as hers and spoke as crisply as I could. "A box of alphabet letters."

"You are not far wrong." She was smiling at me. "It is a book of words made up of letters. When you are older, I will teach you how to read them. You must address me as Mother Agnes."

"You are not my mother."

"My child, your mother is dead. You will never see her again."

My lip trembled. "That is not true. I will see Maman when her soul comes back for this." I took the tiny bottle from my pouch to show her.

She pulled out the stopper, sniffed, then held the vessel to the light. "Are these your mother's tears?"

"Yes, and mine too. I waited all night, but she did not come."

Mother Agnes was silent for a time. "She will not come for many years. First, you must grow old, much older than I am. Hide this in a secret place and think no more about it." She tucked the bottle back into my pouch. "What did your mother call you?"

"Solange," I said. "*Sol*, like the sun." I saw that she approved, which gave me courage. "I was born at Pentecost and thus my hair is red."

"And *ange* for angel. It is a good name, for you are said to speak with the tongue of an angel." She stood up to examine a map nailed to her wall. Her wooden stick pointed to the walled city of Avignon, then tapped along the winding blue river. "Your reputation for clairvoyance has travelled upstream along the Sorgue as far as our abbey." The pointer caressed a little abbey painted brown and green. "Here is Bingen in the north"—the pointer tapped on another painted abbey—"where Saint Hildegarde resided. When she was three, Hildegarde was given to an abbey as an oblate, as you have been. She was so famous for her visions that she became the abbess and was consulted for her prophecy by popes and emperors." The pointer stopped. "Do you know what prophecy is?"

"It is second sight," I said, but she wanted more from me. I tried to think of something worthwhile. "Before I was born, I had a dream about a bishop."

"Tell it to me now."

I scratched my head with both hands, without finding anything to tell. "It's gone now. How can I remember what I see inside my head?"

Her tone sharpened. "When you have a vision, you must remember it."

She was not acting like a mother now. I threw myself on the floor beside her, burying my face in my arms. "This abbey has too many rules and I am too small to learn them!"

The pointer reached over to tap my skull gently. "You will, my child, for it is your destiny. You have the gift of clairvoyance like Hildegarde."

"I don't want to have a destiny!"

"Do not worry. Your head will grow bigger to understand these mysteries."

She put down the pointer and chose another book, this one with a scarlet cover. Then she sat on her cushioned chair, spread the book across her knees, and beckoned me closer. I slid across the floor and raised my head to see empty lines as neat as shelves. After a while, I stood up beside her to feel the small, even ridges with my fingertips.

"How did you make the rows so straight?"

"With a stylus. Each of these lines must be filled with words. This is where we will write down your visions." She lifted the page to my nose so I could sniff it.

"It smells like a barn."

"This is vellum, Solange. Never forget the scent, for only the rarest books are made from it."

Three

DISCOVERED THAT the nuns rose with the sun and retired when it set. Eight times a day the bells called them to the divine offices, first prime, then terce, sext, and none. Vespers were at sunset, compline at nightfall, and in the full of night nocturns and lauds.

The bells chimed slowly for the hours to give the sisters time to gather from the hives and the vines, the kitchens and the scriptorium. I watched them brush earth or flour from their palms, then hurry breathlessly towards the church, never running, yet never late, their feet moving invisibly under their black habits. In the dark of night, they stumbled down the inner stairs like sleepwalkers. At that hour they seemed to find chanting a penance, because they slurred words and sang out of tune. I trailed behind or escaped outside, alert to every night sound, hearing owls screech and pebbles shift under the feet of mice or squirrels. Sometimes, in the distance, I heard the deeper tones of the bell I had left behind at Notre-Dame-des-Doms.

Elsewhere in the abbey, speaking was frowned upon, but the church burst its walls with holy sound. It smelt pleasantly of cold, damp stone and beeswax tapers lit for departed souls. Before long I was climbing onto a bench beside Elisabeth so I could sing when she did.

"O Lord," I chanted. "You will open my lips and my mouth shall declare Your Praise."

Though I sang lustily, I could not make my soul go where my mother's had gone. My spirit spiralled upwards with the high notes to the vault, then tumbled to the pavingstones alone. After a time I began to lift my voice to the Virgin, but not to the bloodthirsty god who had taken my mother from me. In the triptych he hung like a skeleton from his wooden cross. I knew that the church wine was his blood and the bread his flesh, but to me he looked no different than the men who had climbed on Maman's bed with their flagons and loaves. Each day I longed for her perfumed heartbeat and her kisses beneath my ear, but at night I missed the pungent odour of Conmère, who would have comforted me on my sparse bed of straw.

After my first mass the abbess allowed me to light a taper for Maman. I chose a tall one, which with luck would burn until day's end. Though my eyes were wet, I held my head high, as Maman would have wished. I fingered the sponge in my pouch, waiting for the nuns to leave.

Elisabeth arrived to stand an even taller taper next to mine. "This is for my mother," she said. "You can dry your eyes now if you want."

I dabbed my eyes with the sponge and wiped my nose on my sleeve. "Where do you think their souls are now?"

"Haunting the abbey somewhere. The stockbreeder says the souls of dead nuns come back to inhabit the heifers and ewe lambs."

"Why not the new pigs?" I asked.

"Too ugly." Laughing, she abandoned me, for she was old enough to have chores around the abbey.

That first summer I learnt to be content with my own company. I ran from one end of the grounds to the other and lay exhausted in the moist, fragrant hay, listening to the golden hum of bees mingling with cicadas. I rested on the bank of the Sorgue to listen to it rush over rocks as it used to rush over the cloth-workers' wheels. If the hens were laying, I dug my hands into the straw and ran with new eggs as a gift to the abbess. These were my territories—the hives, the vines, and the fields. I inspected my ewes and my calves, and my grapes ripening on the vine, and helped the stockbreeder carry pails of mash to the animals. The ewes trusted me to feel their bellies to see how many lambs they were carrying. When I told the stockbreeder that the black ewe was carrying three ewe lambs, she did not believe me, but after all three were born safely and named after dead nuns, she sent me to the beekeeper for a reward of honey.

By Pentecost, the day of my birth, my feet had so outgrown my shoes that Elisabeth gave me her old sandals. In return, I took her to see a wooden post dark with mildew, where the snails swarmed over one another, fighting their way to the top. We lay on our bellies, observing ants marching in an orderly row like Benedictines filing into church to say the hours. This reminded me of a trick that Conmère had played on me.

"Watch me bewitch them," I said.

I polished a stone, uttered one of Conmère's spells, and placed it in the ants' path. When they scattered and knocked one another down, I told Elisabeth that I had the power to command hordes of insects— ants, beetles, whatever I wished. As we lay side by side, we picked the burrs and foxtails off each other and told stories about our dead mothers. Because Elisabeth was nine years old, she remembered more than I did, and since she was old enough to help in the kitchens, she had a knife of her own, which I coveted.

I folded up my tunic to reveal the age marks on my thigh. "Lend me your knife to carve a line." I scored the sixth line so neatly it produced only a single bead of blood, which I licked off so she wouldn't see it.

"Why didn't you bleed?" She grabbed her knife back, unhappy with how it had turned out, since she did not wish me to have magic powers.

That night I dreamt of a butcher pinning down a lamb, then drawing his blade over the yearling's throat. The lamb jerked, spurting blood all over me. It ran over my toes, down the gutter, and into the canal, where the paddlewheels churned the writhing red pus towards the city moat. When I had wrenched myself out of the hideous dream, I prodded Elisabeth, who let me crawl beneath her blanket for the first time.

After I had related the dream, she said, "Tell me again. How long did the lamb jerk after it was dead?" She squirmed with pleasure as I described it once more.

"Is it a vision?" I asked hopefully.

"No, you are not important enough for that. It was only a dream about a butcher who slaughters animals for winter meat. You must have seen him at Martinmas before you came to the abbey."

Upset with me now, she punched me in the belly—not too hard, because I had told her a good story, just enough to send me scuttling back to my cold pallet. Mindful of the lines waiting in the empty ledger, I took my tale to the abbess in the morning just the same. It must have been a real vision, because Mother Agnes bade me sit on the stool to tell it to her. When I was done, she reached for the scarlet book, dipped her quill into her ink, wrote some words, then dunked the quill again. From where I sat, I could not fathom how the ink got up inside the abbess's pen. I walked the legs of my stool closer, but was too late to see. She made her flourish, blotted the page, returned the book to the shelf above my head, and gave me a pickled egg to chew on.

Four

I N MY SECOND YEAR in the abbey, the abbess ordered me to run errands for Madame de Fores, a widow from Les Baux-de-Provence, who had just arrived to take her vows and work in the scriptorium. Nothing about Madame looked like a nun, not even her fine cambric wimple. In procession on Ascension Day, she walked a step behind the abbess, who wore the crest of the Clairefontaines and a heavy chain of office to assert her precedence. Behind the two of them came the obedientiaries—the sacristan with her holy book, the librarian with her quill, the cellaress with her keys, the gardener with her shears, then the others in order of rank. After them flocked the familia: the lay sisters, Elisabeth and me, the servants, and the farm-workers.

One day I took Madame a piece of honeycomb dripping sweetness through my fingers. She surprised me by taking a bite straight from the comb. Afterwards her dainty tongue darted out to lick her lips.

"Are you not afraid of the bees' sting?" she asked.

"They seem to like me."

When the sacristan rang the bells for sext, Madame wiped the residue from our hands with a scented cloth and drew me close to read her book of hours. We bent over the book together, breathing on it while we turned the pages, and the parchment became warm beneath our hands. On each page were miniature paintings of a tiny, perfect world. Did God dwell in such a book? Surely a saint had created such glorious pictures.

"How did each one get so small?" I asked.

"The illuminator looks through magnifying glasses to paint with a brush of fine hair, even finer than yours. I copied this book for my own use and told the miniaturist to paint what I like best. See how each letter is perfect, yet alive? Each word is like a ripe fruit eager to be bitten into." She showed me how to take the words and roll them in my mouth. "This is our language, la langue d'oc, which the troubadours used for their love songs."

I touched her hand, fascinated by its pallor. If my mother had lived, would she have been so soft and fragrant? "My mother spoke like you, but not so sweetly."

"Yesterday I heard you talking in the old tongue with Elisabeth. Do not let the abbess hear you, for it comes from a low, dark place."

She combed the sticky honey from my hair, and I told her what I knew of my lady-mother, the little I could remember. "My mother died bearing a child. I do not know why she bothered, for my brother was dead when he came out. I have not lit a taper for her since Lent," I confessed.

One hot tear dribbled from my eye, then another. Soon I was clutching Madame and sobbing. When at last I stopped, she rubbed the furrow from my brow with her scented cloth and asked me whether I would like to listen to her favourite book, *Le Roman de la Rose*. Over the summer, she read it to me. As we neared the end of the poem, I puzzled over the roses and bushes, gardeners and shears. The rose was a lady and the lady was a rose. Beyond that, I was uncertain, for there was also a knight lurking behind the rosebush, wary of her thorns.

I fingered the coat of arms on Madame's habit. "When will I be a lady?"

The leaves of the book fluttered shut. "How old are you now?"

I raised my tunic to reveal the newest mark on my thigh.

"You are seven years, like a page," she said. "But next year, do not score your leg, for it hurts me to see your flesh so scarred."

"When I am fourteen, will I be a squire?"

"No. You are of the nuns' keeping. Here you are fed when you are hungry and physicked when you are ill. You will become a novice, then a nun. Or, if God wills it, you will marry and go to a fine estate as I did. I doubt you will make a good nun, for you love poetry too much, but it is better if the abbess thinks you will. She believes you will bring renown to her abbey."

"I have visions like a saint," I said stoutly.

"So I have heard, but when did you have your last one?"

A year had passed since I had dreamt of the slaughtered lamb. I inspected my dusty toes, now sticking so far out of Elisabeth's sandals that they sometimes tripped me. "Will the abbess send me back to Avignon?"

"Not if you have another vision soon," Madame advised.

That night, I dreamt of a lady and her lover in a walled garden with roses, peacocks, and the scent of mille-fleurs. Was this my own future spinning out before me, eager for me to catch up to it? The next day, while Madame wound wool from the skein I held across my hands, I told her my dream.

"That will do very well," she said, when I had finished. "However, leave out the part about the knight. That will not do for the nuns." She tucked the end of the yarn into the finished ball. "Now, go to the abbess and tell her as you told me."

I went to the abbess's house to recite my vision. When I came to the knight, I reluctantly gave his part to a unicorn, which rested its head in the lady's lap. After I had described her wide fur sleeves, fine wimple, and pleasing fragrance, Mother Agnes nodded with satisfaction and reached for the scarlet book with the prepared lines. She dipped her quill, tapped once, scrutinized the nib.

"Are you sure it was a unicorn?" she asked.

The unicorn was false, for I had added it myself. I did not wish to disappoint her, so I described the unicorn I had seen in Madame's book in all its rich detail.

"It is well that we have taken you into our custody. The lady is Notre Dame and the unicorn is Our Lord. This is the story of how He took on flesh and was born to the Virgin. It is allegory, one of the figures of rhetoric."

"Why can't the unicorn just be a unicorn?"

"Because everything we apprehend on earth has spiritual meaning. Our microcosm is a pale double of the macrocosm."

"Why does it have to be that way?" I rubbed my eyes, angry at myself, and at this double world, and at the abbess.

"The enclosed garden you saw is Our Lady's womb, the hortus conclusus that has never been entered by a man. Now we must record your vision. You may hold the ledger steady as I write."

I gripped the book with both hands while the abbess wrote laboriously, keeping to the lines. Each time the ink ran out, she dipped the quill and tapped it briskly. The letters appeared one after another in a squashed, unhappy row. At last she made her flourish. This time I was close enough to see that it was her Clairefontaine crest.

"That is a good start," she said, "but it is only a single page. You must try harder to have visions."

Having visions was too much trouble. I had just given her one vision and she was demanding another. But writing—that would be easier! As soon as she dropped the quill, I had my fingers on it.

Seeing it in my hand, she offered, "You may sign your mark next to mine."

I wrote *Solange* with my left hand, then added *Requiescat in pace*.

"Why did you write that?"

"It is on the wooden cross by the cypresses, where the nuns are buried."

"I see we have given you too much freedom. You have learnt too much of the wrong sort of thing. It is time for you to enter the work of the order. We have a new pope, John XXII, who will live in Avignon, which will bring many commissions to our scriptorium. Madame will need to assist with the copying every day."

As Mother Agnes lifted the scarlet ledger back to its shelf, I slipped the quill up my sleeve where she could not see it.

"You must start the trivium with me at once, learning grammar, rhetoric, and logic. You may also help in the scriptorium," she added in a kindly voice. "From tomorrow, Elisabeth will fetch and carry for the lay sisters."

"She will not like it."

"Elisabeth will do as she is bidden," she said sharply. "She was kept out of charity when her mother, who was a kitchen servant, died."

I sat on my stool with the quill stabbing my arm while the abbess told me the story of Mary and Martha from the Gospels. They were sisters who were as different as salt and sugar.

"When you have taken your vows," she said, "you will be Sister Marie-Ange and Elisabeth will be Sister Martha. You have received the better part, Solange. Now strive for the obedience to play it well."

The pain in my arm had somehow travelled to my belly, where it was taking root like a great hunger. The abbess seemed to have forgotten that I, too, had been accepted out of charity. If I did not produce more visions, I was in danger of being sent back to the tavern to starve with Conmère, who might be dead herself by now. I must learn to write as quickly as I could to help with the new commissions. Surely being a good scribe was more useful than having feeble visions?

Five

N OW THAT I WAS helping in the scriptorium, my life fell into a different rhythm. I outfitted my corner with useful things—like the stub of red ochre stolen from the librarian—for the day that I would become a scribe. If the scribes needed books to copy, I fetched the psalters, Gospels, and other manuscripts blackened by frequent handling. When the scriptorium was tranquil, I looked at them myself, tracing unknown words to memorize their lineaments and studying the playful woodcuts made by monks hankering for a fuller life. The big abbey cat often sat upon my feet. I named him Ambrose because honey-sounds purred from him like the honeyed words of Saint Ambrose. A working cat, not a pet, he kept the scriptorium free of mice, while I kept it free of dirt and insects. Whenever the copyists signalled—for talking caused mistakes—I ran for parchment, ink, and feathers, or swept quill-shavings out the door, chasing Ambrose off the porch-stone where he lay sunning his fat bottom. Soon he was back to pounce on the spiders I had flushed out.

In spring the mistral blew across the fields, whistling soil against the scriptorium. I was tired of running for parchment when the scribes drew a rectangle in the air. Everyone else in the scriptorium had an important job. The librarian was the master scribe, who mapped out the folios for the others, though her decorations were simple and without taint of pleasure. Along the wall, the scribes were seated according to diminishing rank and window light, with Madame in the first position, followed by a pair of novices, both eighteen, who were apprenticing as copyists. Two grey-bearded monks from a kindred monastery worked in a shed at the rear, one as a parchmenter and jack-of-all-trades and the other as a bookbinder.

One day when the scriptorium had emptied for the divine office, I climbed onto the librarian's chair to peer through her magnifying glasses at the merchant's bestiary she was repairing. She came back early to find me touching the paint-strokes on the ferocious crocodile. I sprang down with her glasses still hugging my nose and she plucked them off me in such fury she almost crushed them.

"You've smudged the page with your fingerprints. You are no better than the merchant's children, who tore this exquisite book." She threw a fistful of scrubbing sand on the pavingstones at my feet. "Kneel on that until I tell you to get up."

The scribes were now returning, stifling their conversation as they crossed the threshold, first Madame, then the novices, all three casting glances of pity my way. The coarse sand dug into my knees. At last, through red, stinging eyes, I saw the librarian leaving with the bestiary beneath her arm, probably to lock it in the armarium. Madame waved an empty ink-pot in my direction. I picked the sand out of my knee-caps, ferried the pot to the ink-well, and hobbled back to her.

"The librarian doesn't want me here," I said. The blood came back into my legs, attacking them with pins-and-needles.

"I will tell her I need an assistant."

All of a sudden, the sand torture was worth it. "Will you teach me to be a scribe like you?"

"Yes." She pulled me onto her lap to rub the stiffness from my legs. "I will keep your hands and feet busy. First, you must choose the best materials and treat them with respect." She unstoppered the ink-pot beneath my nose so I could smell it. "This is made from oak-gall, with a trace of wormwood to discourage mice. The ink is thick enough to adhere to the quill but thin enough to slide onto the parchment. Ink should never drip or blot the page, or stain your fingers."

She strapped her copybook to the upper half of her desk, placed the new quire below, then trimmed her quill and dipped it into the ink-pot not once but twice. Instead of tapping the quill, she let the excess ink run off the nib in its own time. With her left hand, she pressed her penknife against the margin to hold the parchment taut. I watched the line fill with delicate words, much easier on the eye than the abbess's plodding script. She inked her family coat of arms at the end of the quire.

"I don't have one of those," I pointed out.

"Then you must earn a Benedictine colophon like the librarian's."

As the days shortened into autumn, the copyists began to skip the divine offices to make better use of daylight, since candles and lanterns—with their risk of fire—were prohibited. The librarian enforced absolute silence, for each scribe was copying one of the Gospels for an overdue commission. The librarian had completed Luke in her swift purposeful hand and the novices were on the last chapters of Mark and John. By Seven Sorrows, Madame was still labouring on Matthew. The librarian circled, her bony frame bent at the waist as she inspected Madame's spidery letters, her stylus tapping on errors I had not detected.

Madame arrived at her desk late one morning, cradling her writing arm against her chest. "A stroke of apoplexy in the night," she whispered to me. "It weakened the entire right side of my body."

It frightened me to see the ink staining her skin because she was brushing her fingers instead of lifting them, as she had taught me. Worse, she did not appear to care. Each day, each quire, her arm became more limp and disobedient and I did more of the work for her. When she was on the last page of the last quire, I pinched my fingers to warn her that she needed to squeeze in two more verses of Matthew. She did not compress enough to make both verses fit and had to rotate the quire to write the last one in the margin. She drew her coat of arms so ineptly that it leaked into the page, and left the scriptorium abruptly.

What should I do? I could not give the quire to the librarian, as was usual, for she would not have to squint to see its obvious faults. Instead, I ducked into the shed to entrust it to the kindly bookbinder. He took one look and put it into the sewing frame, placed the earlier quires of Matthew on top, added the other three Gospels, and tightened the clamps. He threaded his needle to begin stitching the quires together.

By the time the four Gospels had been bound in covers and the librarian saw the errors in Matthew, it was too late for her to demand corrections. She galloped towards me, her wrath so thunderous the water clock trembled, its escapement slowing almost to a halt, and I raced out of the scriptorium, cold with fear.

Some days later, I was chasing Ambrose through the cloister garden, his feet churning like a Benedictine late for prayer, when I ran into the abbess, who was inspecting the books in the armarium beside the church door. Her key made two *clinks,* one in the lock and the second as it fell back against the other keys hanging from her belt.

"Have you read your Latin psalm for this week?"

"Not yet." I dug my toe into the soil to stir it around. "Why must I learn so many psalms?"

"You must know them all before you take the veil. When you are a choir nun, you will sing one hundred and fifty psalms every week, each with its own prayers and antiphons. I have explained this to you before." Her eyes checked me up and down, from untied cap to dirty shoe-leather. "You are meant to be in the scriptorium at this hour. Instead, your laughter was echoing through the cloister, disturbing the nuns at their work."

I hung my head, my fingers clasped behind my back. Surely she knew that the librarian was out of patience with me? If she didn't, I was not about to tell her. I kept my eyes fastened on my shoes. "I am sorry."

"Say it in Latin."

"Mea culpa."

"Have you been to the river again? As well as neglecting your duties in the scriptorium, you have soaked the new shoes you received at Michaelmas."

"I swept the scriptorium floor this morning." This was not a lie. I had done it before the librarian arrived, so she could not thunder at me again.

"And what else have you accomplished?"

"The librarian will not give me any other jobs."

The abbess walked me out of the cloister into the scriptorium, past the novices' flying hand signals, and up to the librarian, who was writing as if her commission had come from God Himself. "This child is now eight, old enough for useful work," the abbess said. "She is tired of scouring floors. Give her a quill."

Only the abbess dared speak so loudly while the scribes were writing, for errors with the pen were costly. The librarian's face, when it rose from her quire, was the yellow of old tallow.

"A scribe cannot be left-handed," she said. "The ink would smear as her hand crossed the page. Enough parchment has been ruined by Madame de Fores."

"Madame's arm is withering. I have put her into the guest-house, where she will have some respite from the rules." The abbess squeezed the librarian's elbow to stop the motion of her pen. Her voice lowered a notch. "This child has the gift of clairvoyance."

The librarian was having none of it. "We have no use for visions here."

"But with Madame gone, you do have need of an apprentice. There are three books in the armarium waiting to be copied," the abbess said. "With so many new commissions, our abbey will soon be as well known for our books as for our honey. Teach this child good penmanship, for she is quick to learn. Let her begin by copying a psalter for her own use. Give her a large quill that will be easy for her small hands."

Before the abbess swept out, I was in my corner to collect my bag of pumice, the red ochre, a goose feather, and the dog's tooth from a skull I'd found bleaching in the sun. Thanks to Madame, I also had a blade for shaping quills, since she had given me her penknife with the ivory handle. When I had visited her, she told me the knife was called a miséricorde, because it would protect a woman's honour if a man attacked her.

I sat on Madame's chair, arranging my tools and an old sheet of parchment where I wanted them. I pruned barbs from the shaft of the goose feather, sending out a spray of quill-shavings. But only when I took a sliver off my knuckle and slid to the floor yelping did the librarian take notice of me. She wrenched the bloody, half-whittled quill from my fist, grasped the waist of my tunic, and hoisted me back onto Madame's seat, where my shoes dangled a foot above the floor. She trimmed my quill, then made a row of perfect letters, with the descenders barely clearing the ascenders below, all stopping precisely at the margin that the bookbinder had ruled.

She arranged my fingers around the nib. "Now, complete the page without a blot, or you will never touch parchment again."

Each day I filled the same unforgiving sheet with letters, then scraped them off to write new ones, until the sheet was soft and ragged. I could read Latin thanks to the abbess and had long since learnt to write the paternoster and Ave Maria. I had watched Madame's quill flash along the line, dispensing ink firmly but lightly. Now I learnt that each letter was penned with an exact number of strokes at precise angles—doubly hard to execute with my left hand. I wrote painstakingly, keeping my wrist straight and my fingers curled so I would not smudge the row as my hand passed over. I danced each page to the librarian, who inspected it before she let me scrape off the ink to move to the next letter.

When I reached z and she told me to go back to the beginning again, I protested. "I heard the abbess tell you that I could make a psalter."

"First you must master black-letter."

"My black-letter is as good as the abbess's."

Her mouth relaxed into a half-smile. "That may be true, but yours is too big. Come to me when your letters fit between the lines."

Beneath her stool, in the pile of discarded scraps and threads, I spotted a punctured sheet—not just parchment, but womb-vellum. I carried it back to my desk to begin writing at once. To hide the hole, I created an ornate capital such as I had seen on the finest manuscripts and decorated it until it became the thicket of brambleberries near the river. Beside the capital, I began to write The Lord is My Shepherd, one of the Latin psalms the abbess had taught me:

> Dominus regit me et nihil mihi deerit. In
> loco pascuæ ibi me collocavit. Super aquam
> refectionis educavit me. Animam meam
> convertit.

Alongside the verses, I drew the stockbreeder standing in the pasture with our grey mare and her new foal. I used the red ochre I had stolen from the librarian to put a blush of shame into the mare's cheeks and to give the foal a rosy glow. To encircle them I drew more vines, thickly black over the cream vellum, with dramatic flourishes all round, until I came to the bottom of the page, where my mark should go. Since I did not have a colophon or coat of arms, I inked a design of my own: a big S with a crowned image of me holding my scale of justice and my sword aloft.

I waved my masterpiece in the air to dry, rattling the stiff new vellum so the novices would stop their copying to see what I had done. I had completed my first commission and I wanted everyone to know it. I jumped down to parade my psalm in noisy triumph around the scriptorium. The novices made approving signals and clapped each time I passed them, but the librarian kept writing. At last, she laid down her quill, threw out an arm to halt me on one of my circuits past her desk, and took the vellum from me. She scratched off a small blot with her fingernail.

"Your letters are still too large," she said, "but they are well formed. Even more surprising, every word of the Latin is correct. Now, scrape off the psalm and write it again, only smaller. Tomorrow I will give you a quire so you can begin your psalter."

Six

At noon on All Saints' Day, the abbess entered the church in her full regalia as Agnès de Clairefontaine. She was limping slightly in her pigaces, the newest shoe fashion from the northern fairs. On her hip was the Clairefontaine sword, entrusted to her by a brother who had travelled east to fight for Christendom. The obedientiaries and choir nuns followed in order of precedence and took their places in the stalls, where their new Michaelmas shoes lined up precisely.

Abbot Bernard emerged from the sacristy, tapping his crosier across the flagstones. His voice erupted into song, so deep and stirring that it roused the nuns. Their throats opened, their voices doubling and trebling as they competed for his ear. Stationed at the rear was the dark-skinned Benedictine who had arrived on horseback with the abbot. Even with his travelling cowl pulled over his forehead, he was unmistakable, the only monk in a sea of chanting women.

When the office was over, the abbot struck the brass bowl with the mallet. In crept the pale novices from the scriptorium. He asked them the question—*Voluntateque agitis? Are you willing?*—and they prostrated themselves on the cold stones, their palms whiter than white, scrubbed clean of every ink stain. They professed their vows so quietly that only the abbot could hear whether they truly meant them. He sprinkled too much holy oil and gave them their new names jovially, Sisters Blanche and Ursula.

Afterwards the abbot escorted the abbess to the refectory, talking to her loudly. Once they had sat down at the high table, the obedientiaries took their seats around them, their bottoms swathed in cushions and their backs supported by the wooden carvings of the virgin martyrs. His mouth resentful, his eyes as shadowed as an infidel's, the monk carried in the abbot's bulging saddlebag. The nuns gathered to look, forming a black curtain with their habits. I elbowed between them to see the abbot extract a book a psalter wide and two psalters thick, which he laid open in front of the abbess. As we watched, she fanned the pages, rich with miniatures, then scrutinized the coat of arms pressed deeply in the binding.

The abbot pointed out a detail on the crest. "A bear—the blazon of Cardinal Orsini. Your scriptorium is to make his nephew a copy more splendid than this original." He gestured towards his companion. "This is Tommaso Tarlati, a master illuminator, who will paint the miniatures. Master Tarlati will travel to Avignon to choose the folios for the copying, along with the gold leaf and paints that he requires for the illumination."

The abbess's sleeves fluttered. "All this for a nephew?"

"His son." The abbot's sotto voce was easily heard. "It is not a time of piety, Mother Agnes. This John, who calls himself Pope, is making his relatives officers and cardinals. He has moved into the bishop's palace and is buying up all the buildings on Doms rock. Avignon has become a vassal of the Holy See. The spirituals call her a whore for welcoming so many men, five hundred in the papal court alone."

The abbess wet her lips. "And their libraries?"

"Full of books that need copying for the young men in their retinues. There will be much work from Orsini if we please him."

The abbess's fingers twitched as though she were counting the new commissions. She signalled for the meal to begin and said something to the sacristan.

"The abbess wants you at her table," the sacristan said, pushing me towards her seat at the end of the carved bench.

The sacristan climbed up the stairs inside the wall and appeared in the falcon's nest above our heads, where she opened *The Golden Legend* to read from the Life of Saint Cecilia. The words mingled with the sweet aromas of meat and piecrust, butter and garlic, salt and oil, and a peace fell upon the room. I put my knife on the cloth as the obedientiaries did. This end of the refectory was magnificently hot, but I would have been better fed in my regular place next to Elisabeth, since none of the bowls of food made it past the librarian, who steered them back to the abbot before they reached me.

The sacristan had arrived at the part where Saint Cecilia was jailed in the public baths, withstanding seven times the usual heat. The neophytes dipped their sponges and veils into her blood. I normally enjoyed such bloodthirsty details, but the fire had overheated me and hunger made me dizzy. How long would I have to wait to eat? To get closer to the food, I ducked under the table to wriggle between the long black habits until I reached the abbess's pointed shoes. The abbot had kicked off his riding boots and wore only his stinking buskins. As I squatted between them, he lifted the table covering to see who was treading on his toes.

"This must be the child oblate," he said to the abbess.

"She has had few visions since coming to us. Perhaps we were wrong in taking her. Can a child lose her clairvoyance?"

They dropped the cloth to cover me, muffling their voices. What if they turned me out to send me back to the Cheval Blanc? I was only a child—how could I find the friars' path to Avignon on my own? What if I slipped from the muddy track and tumbled into the rushing Sorgue? In my cramped grotto beneath the table, the abbot's dirty buskins brought back a little something from my past. Cradled in my mother's womb, I had seen similar buskins, but they were clean and of a bishop's purple hue. Now, crouched in this sweating caldarium on All Saints' Day, I was as hot as that child inside her mother, awaiting birth. Surely, tested by being roasted like Saint Cecilia, I had earned a real vision. I pushed my fists into the hollows of my eyes and sat stone-still, expecting a revelation, but instead of a Voice from afar I heard a forlorn sob from right inside me. All at once, a long-forgotten vision popped out and I scrambled onto the bench between the abbot and the abbess to tell them.

"When I was in my mother's womb, before I was born," I declared loudly, "I saw a priest like you on top of my mother in her bed."

The abbot reared up, his hands spread across the table. The obedientiaries looked from my face to his, anticipating a display of temper that would crush me. The abbess pressed her finger to her lips. She had drunk deeply of the wine—a deep, dark red, undiluted by a drop of water—and so had the abbot.

I would not be silenced. "His eyes were not brown like yours, but as blue as the Virgin's mantle, and from his belt hung two big rusty keys."

"Forgive her, she is yet small," the abbess begged. "She was eight years old last Pentecost."

The abbot dropped back into his seat, his voice low. "She was born at Pentecost, you say? Eight years ago? Then the man she saw with the tarnished keys must have been Saint Peter warning of the Pope's corruption, since he had just arrived in Avignon." His tone was urgent now. "Mother Agnes, this girl will be the making of your abbey. The sacred wells up in some infants, then submerges itself for years, only to fountain up—like this—on solemn feast days. When she is older, men of rank will travel the breadth of Europe to consult her as a visionary. Think of the fame she will bring to Clairefontaine, the gifts of wine, the banquets!"

This was all very well, but my stomach was empty *now*. I shouted, "I cannot wait that long to eat!"

The abbot was startled. "My child, have they let you go hungry? Feed upon whatever you like best."

He gestured to the vessels of food spread across the board. I saw milk curds and honey, roasted almonds and chestnuts, a stack of honey cakes, and plump yellow plums well soaked in spirits. Standing on my knees, I seized an abbey cake, plunged it into a pool of cream, and shoved it into my mouth with both hands.

"There is no need to spill, child, or to choke. Sit down and we will pass the dishes to you. Which do you wish first? I suppose the platter of stewed figs and fowl. If she is well fed," he confided to the abbess, "she will grow rapidly and be of more use to the abbey. There is no sin in eating richly. Only eight years old, you say? Such zeal in one so young must be commended."

Seven

WHEN ADVENT ARRIVED, so did a donkey cart with Master Tarlati, the Florentine illuminator, along with his spacious desk. In a second cart was a glazier with barrels of sand, which cushioned panes of glass for the scriptorium's first glass window. After the glazier was finished, the Florentine set up his desk in the flood of light, placing his tools on wooden rests near his right hand. The librarian spread her plan for the psalter-hours in front of her window of oiled parchment and the Florentine gave his approval, pleased that she had provided so much space to display his art.

"When will you begin to paint?" the librarian asked.

"Not until the scribes have copied the full year's calendar."

"That will take weeks!"

"Better that I spoil their work than that they spoil mine. You must do all the borders yourself to save me time. Like this." He ran his pencil around the perimeter of January, adding bare branches with winter birds. "All the decorations must be done before you pass the folios to me."

The librarian pushed Blanche's and Ursula's desks together and strapped the Orsini psalter-hours between them. They would write side by side in scripts that had grown so alike one could scarcely tell them apart. As the two settled themselves, their joyful hand signals hung in the air like musical notes. I brought two pots of the new ink for them and placed a third one on my own desk.

I asked the librarian, "Where shall I begin?"

"Finish copying the breviary you are working on, but not with that," she said. "Continue with the old ink and used parchment."

Disappointed, I whetted my knife, sharpened my quill, and practised working the same number of letters into each line as Blanche and Ursula were doing. The librarian would soon need to call on me to help.

Over the winter, the rhythm became second nature—the scratching nib, the oaky scent of the ink, the parchment moving beneath my hand until it was warm and slippery. The ink flowed dark and alive from the well-cut quill. I was putting more words on each line, with grace and ease, but still the librarian withheld her praise.

Instead, she danced attendance on the Florentine, doing the pen flourishes for him with a peacock quill and allowing him to go to the warming house as often as he wished. Even so, he complained that his fingers stiffened at night in the cold almshouse where he slept with the other monks. I was not surprised when the abbess gave him one of her own blankets and told me to bring him eggs, fresh from her henhouse, for his glair and glues. When he let slip how much he liked a good fat hen, she ordered seven preserved in an urn of grease for him. Soon he was eating as often at the abbess's table as with the monks in the almshouse.

As Dame Fortune spun him to the top of her wheel, Madame plunged. She no longer had any strength in her right side, not enough to stand or even sit. When the fasting began in Lent, I held a lamp while the strong-limbed gardener, Sister Raymonde, carried Madame from the guest-house to the infirmary, where she would be permitted meat. I stuffed straw into the cracks in the old wall to keep out the wind, but even so, she suffered from the draughts. At compline each night, I lit her lamp against the dark and lay beside her if she wanted company.

Madame's arm began to give off a sickening odour, which no amount of honey sweetened. One night I found the arm tightly bound and Madame in a fever. Falling asleep beside her, I became mired in a brightly painted miniature in which saints were displaying their amputated arms and toes as proof of being tortured. I was still there at dawn when Raymonde fetched me. She lifted me into the mare's saddle with her to ride beyond the garrigue to forage for the morels Madame liked. Some hours later we rode back through the abbey gates. Cold, filthy, and out of sorts, I clambered down from the mare to charge into the infirmary, where I was terrified to find Madame in a death-sleep, her arm shortened to a throbbing, bandaged stump.

I yelled at her and tugged on her good arm to wake her, but Raymonde caught me by the waist and removed me to the floor, howling like a wounded animal. Since she would not let me go, I bit her fist to get away from her. She twisted my arm behind my back and forced me to look at Madame. When I stopped howling, Raymonde's grip slackened and she held my hand over Madame's nostrils so I could feel her breath.

"She is not dead, Solange. She is still breathing."

"Why did this evil attack her?"

Her face closed in on itself. "You must ask the abbess questions like that."

"You took me out of the way on purpose!"

"It would have been worse for you if you had stayed. I made Madame an opiate to drive away the pain so Cook could amputate the arm with her meat-saw. Madame will not know her arm is gone until the morning, unless you jolt her awake with your screaming."

How could Madame not know? My fists pounded at the stupidity, pounded, pounded against Raymonde's stomach, until I fell upon the cold stone floor, my arms and legs flailing, and she grabbed my wrists to pin them together, my boots kicking helplessly against her solid legs.

At my next lesson with the abbess, I leaned against the wall with my hands shoved up my sleeves and my head buried in my cloak. The abbess motioned me to my stool, but I refused to sit. She stood eye-to-eye with me and folded back the cowl to see my face.

"Why was Madame's arm sawn off?" I demanded.

"It was putrid with infection. She is suffering less now than before." Her fingers milled gently through my hair. "Whenever I need courage, as you do now, I take down the Clairefontaine sword."

She stood on the stool in her bare feet, the whites of her toes puffy from her ill-fitting shoes. She unhooked the sword, then handed it to me pommel first, so that I could see Saint Peter's toenail gleaming like a jewel.

"My brother was one of the Knights Templar who took flight from Philip the Fair and Pope Clement V, leaving this sword in my keeping. I sold some of the abbey lands to send him to safety—all the woods between the old quarry and the mill—but I could not send him far enough. He was killed not by the infidel but by King Philip's men. My brother's last sight was the cross-hilt of his common sword, a reminder of Our Lord's martyrdom. We came from the same womb at the same time, but he died before me in a foreign land."

We balanced the weight of the sword between us, then she let me stand on the stool to put it back myself. Her tears glistened on the silver scabbard, making the sword feel lighter. My face was also wet, but my tears were for Madame, who scarcely recognized me anymore. The abbess drew me towards her map of Christendom with the pilgrimages and holy sites. The cathedral with the word *Rome* showed that it was the proper home of the popes, not Avignon.

"Where did Hildegarde live?" I asked, though I knew it as well as the abbess did now.

Her pointer tapped over to the little abbey labelled Bingen-on-the-Rhine, where popes as well as emperors had consulted the saint. I would never tire of hearing how she had been given to the abbey as an oblate, as I had been.

"From the age of three," the abbess said, "Hildegarde saw visions with her immortal soul. A Voice addressed her from the sky, *O homo fragilis. O fragile man, ashes amongst ashes and dust amongst dust, say and write what you see and hear.* One day, Solange, you will be as great as Hildegarde, the sibyl of the Rhine. I have decided that you will take the veil at fifteen, as she did."

The abbess arranged herself in her chair to begin the lesson and I moved my stool to its usual place beside her. Despite the abbess's faith in me, I knew I was not living up to my promise. I was nine now, but had heard little from on high, only a faint croaking from inside her wall, where Elisabeth and I had trapped a frog. The abbess unlocked her great psalter. Together we marvelled at the miniature of the Last Judgement. The illuminator had well captured the rapture of the saved flying up to join the cherubim and the agony of the damned sinking into the murky depths of hell.

A fear struck me like one of Elisabeth's belly punches. "Will Madame die?"

The abbess's cheeks became red and shiny. "Per fretum febris. Through the straits of fever she will attain God."

But what about Madame's arm? What if Cook had tossed it on the dung heap behind the kitchen? If so, the grey mongrel might have carried it off, with wasps still clinging on it, to devour the flesh and scatter the bones. This dog was so desperate to get a taste of meat that I had seen him chewing on parchment shavings outside the scriptorium.

"How will her soul know where to find her arm?" I asked.

"The soul will know where to go, like the dove returning to the dovecot." The abbess dipped a cloth in lavender water to cool her temples. "The soul will bring the arm to the body and Madame de Fores will be whole in paradise."

"But God said, *Ashes amongst ashes and dust amongst dust.* What if Madame turns to dust before her soul arrives?"

"This is a good question," she said, stroking my hair, "for the prophet Ezekiel wondered the same thing. *Son of man, can these bones live?* And lo, God breathed into the bones and they stood up and walked."

Still, she was not addressing the problem of how body parts could get out of a man-eating crocodile or a cannibal or a starving dog. Patting me on the head did not help. I was tired of being put off with flimsy answers. After all, my mother had not come to collect me, although I had slept with her perfume bottle for almost four years. I had added so many tears to that small bottle that my grief had run over the rim.

"But what if it is only dust from worms or moles, not from Madame?" I asked. "How is the soul to know? What then?"

"The soul will know," she said, locking the hasp on the psalter. "That is enough for today. Do not trouble yourself any further, my daughter, for the health of your soul is in my hands. Since you appear to have mastered grammar and rhetoric, in the next lesson we will work on logic. I am persuaded you have much need of it."

Eight

OUR YEARS AFTER Madame's death, the Orsini psalter-hours were finally completed. On the day the last quire was entrusted to the bookbinder, the nuns started the pruning of the vines and snow appeared on Mont Ventoux to the north.

At Epiphany, Elisabeth dug her thumb into the hollow of my shoulder, urging me awake for nocturns. Now that I was twelve, our cloaks were the same length, though mine was new and made of finer wool. I flung it on to follow her down the night stairs into the church. The abbess began by consecrating the bound psalter-hours. She prayed that it would meet with Cardinal Orsini's approval and acknowledged the toil of all the scribes and monks. Even I was thanked, though I had only ferried supplies to the scribes. After the first psalm had stirred and lifted me, I escaped into numb sleep until the sacristan's roving lamp attacked my eyes.

"Where is she?"

I sat up straight. Nocturns were still underway, but Elisabeth was gone. What perverseness had made Saint Benedict put the longest service at the darkest time of night? As soon as the office was over and the nuns had gone up the stairs to their beds, I crawled through the broken wall in the chapel to search for Elisabeth. The snow was thin and old, a crust that made noises underfoot. The owl had left his perch in the yoke of the pine to hunt for prey. I knew him by his call, *who-looks-for-you, who-looks-for-you-all*, though sometimes he barked like a dog to fool the nuns.

A light emerged from the sacristy—Mother Agnes fastening the door behind her, her gilded crosier spraying lamplight into the dark as she set out along the path towards the woods. She paused near my hiding spot beside the pine to look for something. When the snow crunched, she deposited her lamp so she could grip her crosier with both hands. A twig snapped and a moving shape sank into the darkness of the outbuildings.

"Quo vadis?" the abbess called, brandishing her weapon. *Whither do you go?* Then, more imperiously, "Who?"

This much Elisabeth understood, for she stepped out of the shadows with a knife in one hand and a carcass dangling from the other. A stoat, but I had seldom seen one this colour—white except for its black-tipped tail. A deep scratch ran from Elisabeth's thumb up her forearm. Her cloak was also torn, probably from the barbed thicket near the garrigue.

"Why are you scavenging in the woods?" the abbess asked.

Elisabeth swung the carcass, admiring the drops of blood fanning across the snow. "Ermine for the Florentine. He said it makes the finest brushes."

"Your work is in the kitchen and almshouse, not waking men at night."

The wind rose, dusting up the snow, which allowed me to shift without being heard. I had come out in my inside shoes, no better than gloves on my feet. The stoat's blood had already frozen on the snow and I could no longer feel my toes.

"I will be sixteen soon."

"Too old to be crawling through the hole in the north chapel. I am surprised you can still get through it. I trust my familia to obey me without locks and chains." When Elisabeth swore in the old tongue, the abbess's response was swift. "If you talk like a servant, I will put you outside the wall to eat and sleep with them."

"Why not, since you refuse to let me become a novice?"

"You scarcely know a single psalm."

This was not true, as I had discovered by sitting beside Elisabeth in church. She could chant many, though she could not read or write them.

"I have read my Latin book from Lent."

"You mean that Solange read it to you. You spend your time skulking about the woods while she copies the church fathers for her own instruction. In a few years Solange will be made a master scribe and take her vows as Sister Marie-Ange."

Elisabeth swung the carcass again. "She has not had a vision since that one about the unicorn."

There was a whiff of envy about Elisabeth tonight, but as the moonlight touched the abbess, I saw no surprise on her round face. She turned away, and planted her crosier firmly with each step towards her flickering lantern. Elisabeth reached it first, blocking the abbess's route.

"You said I would be Sister Martha."

"So you will." The abbess was staring at the crimson snow, as if just realizing that the blood was dripping as much from Elisabeth's wrist as from the dangling stoat. "Perhaps you *are* ready for new duties in the abbey. You may begin your year's novitiate as a lay sister. You need not study Latin or concern yourself with the business of the abbey."

Elisabeth made a rude sound through her nose. "The lay sisters are no better than servants. I wish to be a choir nun and attend meetings in the chapter house."

As much as I knew Elisabeth, slept and ate beside her, I had not guessed the heat of this ambition within her.

"You must do as you are best fitted, Elisabeth." Mother Agnes was calm, yet resolute. "Tomorrow I will travel to Avignon to claim the final payment from Cardinal Orsini. The cart would get mired in the snow, so I must ride the mare. I need someone to accompany me and you are the only one who can cling to the mule. Put that knife away. Your skill with it may prove useful if thieves should beset us. First light will be upon us soon and we will be better for some rest."

At this welcome news, Elisabeth was quickly gone, and the abbess poked her crosier into the long shadow beside the pine where I stood.

"You may come out, Solange."

I moved into the light. "How did you know I was here?"

"Who else could it be? You and Elisabeth are seldom far apart. However, that must change. What I said was as much for you as for Elisabeth, for you are destined to take different paths. You must begin to use your education to glorify the abbey."

The abbess's gentle wing had spanned my life all these years. Under her direction, I had completed logic and embarked on the quadrivium. Nevertheless, in all my lessons with her, the scarlet ledger had sat on her shelf above me as a silent reproach, for I had not given her what she most wished: a vision as great as one of Hildegarde's. The time had now arrived when she would demand more from me.

Nine

THREE DAYS LATER, I was keeping watch from the top of the bell-tower, when I saw the abbess and Elisabeth returning to the abbey, their cloaks as black as the ermine's tail against the snowy fields. Elisabeth was riding in front, her head driving into the sleet, her heels digging into the mule's flanks to keep him pushing forwards. The abbess was close behind, hunched over the mare's pommel in the shelter of Elisabeth's broad back.

I rang the bell to alert the abbey and met the riders at the gates. Elisabeth leapt from the mule to help Mother Agnes down from the saddle. When her feet touched the ground, she stumbled and gripped Elisabeth for balance.

The librarian hurtled towards the abbess, her cloak unhooked and sleeves flying. "Did Cardinal Orsini pay in gold?"

The abbess halted the questions. "Send for meat and drink at once, then assemble the scribes in the scriptorium. I will be there as soon as I have eaten."

The abbess walked stiffly towards the cloister, while Elisabeth,

tired but proud, gathered the reins of the two mounts. The mare whin-
nied and reared up, smelling the stable, and it was all Elisabeth could
do to hold her. I hauled on the mule's reins until he settled down. As
soon as we had stabled the animals and filled their buckets, their noses
were buried in the oats.

I asked, "What did the cardinal say?"

"I did not hear, because the abbess sent me on an errand to the
street of the goldsmiths. I found the door with the compass on it and
delivered her letter to a man of science."

"What was the message?"

She shrugged. "It was in Latin."

I threw up my hands in exasperation. "She should have taken me!
I can ride the mule as well as you."

This outburst made her laugh. "He handed me this." Elisabeth dug
in her cloak for a tooled leather case. "The abbess said it was for you."

I unfolded the clever instrument of bone and glass—magnifying
glasses for close work on parchment! Elisabeth's face shone with pleasure,
giving me her blessing in my rôle as a scribe. Mumbling my thanks, I folded
the glasses and stowed them in my pouch. I hoped she did not know how
much the abbess had paid. The abbess was not only generous but also wise,
for she had allowed Elisabeth to take most of the credit. Together we shut
the stable doors, placed our hands on the bar, and forced it down.

As we walked arm in arm, she told me about the trip. "Avignon is
full of strange customs and foreign goods. The quarters are so crowded
with travellers and pigs that we could not ride. And the stench! The
streets are slippery with dung. The abbess could barely keep her footing
in those boots she wears."

A bell pealed far off to the west. Was it the cathedral? A long time
had passed since I had thought of Notre-Dame-des-Doms and the
press of faithful on their knees inside it.

"You'll be hungry," I said, waiting until she was half-way to the
refectory before I turned towards the scriptorium.

Mother Agnes was on a soft chair, her cloak still pinned against the cold. A lay sister lowered a basin of hot water to the floor and tugged off the abbess's boots as anticipation built amongst the scribes and scriptorium monks. The abbess grimaced as she immersed her feet.

"We knew the Orsini livrée by the arms carved on the arch," she began. "I gave the cardinal the psalter-hours at once. He praised the miniatures, one after another, until his tongue grew tired of praising and he began to pick out small faults. Finally his hands rested on the despoiling of Christ in the hours of the Passion."

His eyes must have caressed Mary Magdalene, so carefully worked in crimson, gold, and purple. The Florentine had counted on another man's appreciation of her beauty, for he had lavished his skill on the Magdalene, painting the slyness of Eve into her. To my eye, she had Blanche's face grafted onto Ursula's body, and stood between the Virgin and Mary of Bethany like a blood-rose between two white ones.

The librarian prompted, "How many florins did he pay?"

"Five." The abbess leaned her head back, closing her eyes.

"So few? How can that be?"

"He said that the three Marys are not in that Bible verse."

If the Florentine had any shame, his face would have gone as bright as the Magdalene's hair, for he had blithely painted over the librarian's cartoon and added more faces to the crowd to entertain himself. But no, he was not humbled. He was on his feet, rocking confidently from heel to toe.

"Mother Agnes," he said, "why not offer the psalter to another prelate, one who would pay more?"

The abbess grasped her calves, one at a time, to ease her feet from the basin, although they had not been in long enough to get relief. The water streamed onto the flagstones. The lay sister stooped to dry the blistered feet, then backed out eagerly to tell the cloister of the stingy payment.

"Because you worked the Orsini bear so cleverly into the minia-tures," the abbess said wearily, "as the cardinal was delighted to show his kinsmen, who were gathered around." We had all watched these bears becoming smaller and more witty, the last no larger than a grain of rice. "It seems, Tommaso Tarlati, that as much as I dislike the double plough, we are yoked together, for the cardinal prizes the indelicacy of your art. He has awarded us a commission for his nephew's marriage and given you licence to let your fancy roam this time."

The Florentine took the book that she held out to him. "*La Vita Nuova—The New Life*—by Dante Alighieri. Another Florentine, who writes in my native tongue."

He read a few pages to himself, then translated. The poet Dante, he explained, fell in love with Beatrice when she was only nine. Nine years later he had a vision in which Amore, the god of love, appeared to him carrying Beatrice in one hand. In his other hand Amore held the poet's burning heart, which Beatrice, naked except for a wisp of scarlet, devoured.

The Florentine sniggered as he handed the book to Ursula. "It is a bedchamber gift to stimulate the bridegroom's heart and body."

"A book we cannot read cannot corrupt us," the abbess asserted.

Ursula was too red-faced to open it. I reached for the book, but she passed it behind my back to Blanche, who passed it to the librarian. I had grown a hand's-breadth in a year, but still no one took any notice of me.

The abbess said, "The copying will take a twelve-month, but will fill our cellar with salt, spices, cured fish, and dried foodstuffs." She upended a purse of gold florins. "The first payment—to buy the finest vellum. If we scrape it ourselves and do not blot the pages, we will have enough left over to build a new infirmary."

"But our vows!" Ursula protested. "Saint Benedict enjoined us to read holy works, not pagan ones."

I stood up quickly, as tall as Ursula was. "I will do it."

The Florentine agreed. "Solange's writing is slanted in the Italian style. She has not taken her vows and need not know what she is copying. I will check her pages each day at dusk to spare the librarian."

Before the scribes could object, the abbess carried the manuscript to my writing desk and helped me bind it with leather straps.

"Bless your work, child," she said, covering my fingers with hers. "The fate of our infirmary is in your hands."

In the morning, I placed my new magnifying glasses on my desk. Blanche noticed them at once and sent Ursula a jealous signal, but I steadied myself to face the task before me. On page after page, I saw the intriguing words *Beatrice* and *Amore*. The lean, graceful script ran in one unbroken line. I practised on used parchment while the librarian and the Florentine mapped out the folios and illuminations. Each of the forty-three brief chapters would have a miniature—but this time the Florentine would draw his own cartoons. Once my wrist was supple and my letters sloping and continuous, I called for a folio of perfect vellum.

At dusk, after the scriptorium had emptied, the Florentine leaned over my shoulder to read my first flight of cursive script, letting the words roll richly off his tongue as he warmed himself against my back. Big as a bull, he stank of drink and something rancid, like oil gone bad, but perhaps this was how all men smelt. It was the first time one of the monks had touched me and it made me feel more womanly, almost as unclothed as Beatrice.

"The other scribes are envious," I said.

"Leave them to me. Your letters are finely wrought, a joy to the eye. However, to be a scribe who copies the most prized books, you will have need of Italian. I will teach you the Tuscan dialect from my own lips, Gentilissima."

"The abbess has forbidden it."

He lifted me down from my chair lightly. "Your little ears did not hear correctly. She did not actually forbid you to learn Italian."

He had twisted her meaning, yet where was the harm? Up to now, the abbess had encouraged my passion for learning, and all day I had been hungering to know the words instead of blindly copying them. The poetry had teased my ear with sweet, long syllables of love and I yearned to discover the fate of Dante and his Beatrice. I would soon be thirteen, old enough to please myself. Besides, how could the abbess discover my furtive pleasure if neither of us told her?

Ten

THE QUIET IN THE scriptorium sped my work and I feasted on Dante's words, picking up their meanings quickly with the Florentine's help. Even when folios awaited him, he hovered over Blanche and Ursula, chivvying them along with bawdy hand signals, finger-milking, and ear-pulling. Sometimes he spent more time teaching Ursula to illuminate than wielding his own brush. He used our faces in his miniatures and gave his females tall, high-waisted forms like ours, to which he added rounded, fecund bellies. He had become a Solomon with his harem, hornswoggling them and cuckolding God.

In the gutters of the folios he prepared, I found Italian phrases that I erased briskly, although their coarseness was indelible. He made his cartoons deliberately lewd. But when he dipped his brushes, the miniatures became as luminous and spiritual as Dante's love for Beatrice. There had never been a girl like Beatrice, never such blandishments of brush and colour as the Florentine lavished on this pair of lovers. It made me wish that I could draw.

While I waited for another folio to work on, I visited Sister Raymonde in her gardening shelter, observing her load her brushes for the showy petals of the opium poppies. Ever since her opiate had eased Madame's pain, Raymonde had been trying to get their shape and colour exactly right. I leaned into her as she painted a new one, soaking up her body heat and the earthy scent of furrows after a rainfall. From her, I learnt how to sketch outlines in ink, then fill them with brushstrokes, one colour at a time. I washed an old book clean of ink to create my own hortus deliciarum, my garden of delights, drawing flora and fauna and the daily life of the abbey. Over the months, as Raymonde's poppies turned to seed, lost their petals, and died, I brought her specimens from my rambles in the fields, Lady's bed-straw or devil's paintbrush, only to see her open her record book to find them already there. Her science was so exact it extended to the furthest corner of the abbey grounds.

"Goosefoot," she'd say, turning pages, "yes, here it is. From the river— amongst the willows. But this wort is unusual." She picked up a specimen I had brought. "I haven't seen blue flowers on this before." She sketched it briskly in ink, then dipped her brush into the lapis lazuli, which I had stolen for her, to paint a brilliant wash over the flower.

One dusk, when the scribes had left the scriptorium and the Florentine read my Dante pages to check them, he found only a single wavering end-stroke to correct. After he had complimented the vigour of my pen, I asked, "Will you teach me how to draft cartoons?"

"Show me what you can draw." His big hand splayed across my desk, oddly inviting to the touch. When I had inked a cornflower with deft strokes the way Raymonde had taught me, he tilted his head, acknowledging its merit. "But can you draw a man?"

After shaving my quill to an exact point, he drew a heap of straw next to my cornflower, a peasant girl lying back against the straw, and on top of her a monk, his habit flapping to expose his hairy buttocks. Then, slyly, he wet a brush on his tongue, loaded it with madder, and reached across me to colour the girl's hair and cheeks a brazen red, like mine. Ashamed that I had encouraged him, I thrust his cartoon beneath my other papers and cleaned my tools with extra care. I was waiting for him to leave so we did not walk out together, but he was in no hurry to go.

"Can you imagine what it is like to work in this scriptorium, with its moist and tempting females?" He circled my writing desk, swaying, eyelids almost shut. In his fist, stained with the Virgin's blue paint, was a flask of eau-de-vie, but his words had never been more sober. "Like me, you crave a love akin to Dante and Beatrice's, but human love is not found in abbeys. Think what you must forfeit to become a nun, Gentilissima. Be certain before you prostrate yourself on the church pavement, for a chill goes through you that lasts a lifetime."

I was stripped to my shift before Abbot Bernard and all the abbey on the day I became fourteen. Pentecost was early in 1323 and I shivered in the nave as the sacristan clothed me in my new habit. The abbot asked me whether I offered myself willingly and with an open heart, and I answered in the correct Latin. I was then accepted into my novitiate and he advised me, as he advised each novice, to keep my secular garments so that if I did not espouse obedience and chastity, I could climb into them once more. Otherwise, in a year's time, I would profess my vows as a choir nun.

When all was done, the nuns embraced me and bade me welcome. The abbot put his arm around my shoulder and walked me to the cloister. "You answered very capably today," he said cheerfully.

"I am grieved I have no dowry, Father Bernard. I hope my talent as a scribe will bring income to the abbey."

"No, no, no—your gift is your clairvoyance, my dear."

"I have had few visions."

"We will not trouble her for more, shall we?" He looked conspiratorially at the abbess. "Do not press her, Mother Agnes, do not urge, but send me word by a quick horse as soon as she has one."

He drew me apart from the abbess. "Now, tell me, because the abbess refuses. How far has the Florentine progressed with illuminating the Dante?"

I knew the abbess was afraid to inform him because we had already taken more than the twelve-month expected by Cardinal Orsini. "Half-way," I said, though it was half the truth.

The abbot weighed a purse on his palm and dangled it in front of the abbess. "Then I am commanded by Orsini to give you half a payment."

The abbess loosened the string to fish out a coin. "Pope John is minting his own florins?"

"Such are the times. Let us hope his gold is as pure as the King's. Now, Mother Agnes, stop scrutinizing your coins and escort me to the refectory. Where is the banquet you promised me for receiving this child into her novitiate? Your abbey is renowned for its table and this is Pentecost! I insist on sampling your eau-de-vie, though the Florentine says it is fiery. No, dear abbess—do not deny you distilled your rotting fruit! I will not object if a flask finds its way into my saddlebags. But pity my poor horse. Put a jar on both sides to balance his load."

It was just past midsummer when the stockbreeder discovered me lying in the pasture, reading one of the finished Dante folios while I waited for the Florentine to prepare a new one.

"Watch Emmanuelle for a sign she is ready for breeding," she said.

"What should I look for?"

"You'll know. She'll start acting oddly."

I continued to read, glancing over at Emmanuelle frequently. In cow years, Emmanuelle was no older than I was. She was one of the more intelligent heifers, with soft, begging eyes, though I could never tell exactly what she wanted. In the afternoon, her tail stood strangely erect. As I approached, she swung about, knocking me to the side, then trotted towards a cowardly heifer to leap on her back, forelegs dangling as she pumped up and down. I pulled Emmanuelle off, yelling for the stockbreeder, who shouted that I should halter her and lead her to the small field. By yanking and scolding, I got her into a corner. I was tying the rope to the fence just as the stockbreeder led in our brown bull by the ring in his nose. Once she let him go, he lumbered over to Emmanuelle to sniff her hind parts, pawing a hoof and snorting, pawing and snorting. He took a violent leap on top of her and began making quick, clumsy jabs. Then he wandered off, no doubt trying to recall what he had left off doing. I ran to Emmanuelle to console her, for I felt upset myself. I led her back to the pasture with her tail crooked a little to one side, and as we walked, it fell by stages until it hung softly, as was usual.

I retrieved the folio and lay back on the sweet hay, watching Ambrose, the big abbey cat, prowl for mice and feeling the sun-drenched earth through my novice's habit. Two of the cows peered at me curiously, but I had seen enough of cows. When I waved a dandelion at them, they took flight. I was glad I was not as timid as a cow, though I regretted teasing Elisabeth for having udders. My fleurs had arrived, heralded by sore breasts, cramps, and shooting pains. Everything about me was changing. Even my hair was darkening to chestnut like my mother's. What if I went into heat like Emmanuelle and courted suitors on the neighbouring farm?

The dandelion fell onto the folio and I licked the page to remove the stain. It tasted alive, like the side of a cow. It seemed unfair to calves to end up as leaves in books. I did not want to read a book made from the womb-vellum of Emmanuelle's calf, not after what the bull had done to her today. Could I see inside Emmanuelle if I pressed my eyes against her belly? I was too lazy to try, but the more I ruminated and sank into myself, the more I fancied I could see through her hide like calfskin oiled for a window. Tiny but well formed, the bull-calf ripening inside Emmanuelle was not brown as she was, but white with black spots. The spots inflated inside my head to merge into one terrifying blotch, until a carcass the size of a cow sat rotting on my legs, turning them green from toes to waist. The weight and the stench were pulling me downwards. Before long, I would be suffocated by earth. At last the foul odour penetrated my trance, and I sat up to find Ambrose squatting on my feet. Emmanuelle was grazing companionably nearby. The stink came from the fresh cow pie she had deposited beside me.

I could recall my trance clearly, even to the seven spots on the calf. All this time I had been waiting for a vision from above, when I had been seeing into bellies all along. I decided not to tell the abbess, since I did not know what good she could make of it. However, I would tell the stockbreeder in case it was a bad omen for Emmanuelle's calving. Small for a heifer, she might have a hard time of it. In no hurry, I lay on the nymph hay, rich in clover and cat's tail and smelling of midsummer, until the sun set and the bells sang out for vespers.

Autumn arrived, the nights became cooler, and the cicadas stopped whirring. One morning I stumbled upon an egg in the rere-dorter, where a wandering hen had sought warmth to lay it. I carried it to the scriptorium and cracked it on the edge of my desk to make glair. I separated the egg white and strained it into two shells, one for me and a larger one for the Florentine, which I glued to his desk. He had set out his Dante folios, cartooning on his left and illumination on his right, but had made little progress from the previous day.

I had been having strange dreams since I became a novice—dreams of Dante embracing me, dreams of a life beyond the abbey—which made no sense, for Fate had decreed that I would never marry. The end of my apprenticeship was nearing. I had completed the trivium and quadrivium and mastered the church fathers. I did not think I would make a good gardener, or beekeeper, or cellaress. I knew I would never be a stockbreeder—I might as well have been born a cow—and I would never be as devout as the sacristan. Most likely, I would continue in the scriptorium. In time I might become a librarian, distributing Lent books to the nuns to read, mapping new folios, and doling out copy work to the scribes. However, my heart was set on something more. I wanted to be sought after across Europe as a scribe, to copy the finest commissions in the finest script, perhaps even to be a painter-scribe so I was not dependent on illuminators like the Florentine.

The librarian had been urging him to take an assistant to hurry his work. Hoping to be chosen, I was drafting my own cartoons, imagining the colours I would pick when I was allowed to dip my brush into the most costly paints—vert de flambe from wild irises and azur d'outremer. Each day, the Florentine found fault with my sketches, amused at a misshapen skull or a left arm longer than the right. He had not yet allowed me to illuminate even a hair of his divine Beatrice or a laurel leaf in Dante's crown. But at night—at night I dreamt of gold and silver foil beaten to supreme thinness and the manuscripts that would spill from my pen in the years to come.

At Candlemas, the Florentine placed the last folio of *La Vita Nuova* before me with a smirk, opened to his final cartoon. An erotic triumph, it illustrated, far too carnally, Dante's hoped-for reunion with Beatrice after death, a fitting wedding gift for Cardinal Orsini's nephew. As soon as my work was done, a few more days at most, the librarian would assign me a more mediocre task, but I could not bear to part with Dante and his Beatrice. *La Vita Nuova* would be in the scriptorium for a few more months while the Florentine painted the full-page miniatures. While he painted, I decided, I would make a second copy of *La Vita Nuova* for myself, penning it at night when the scriptorium was empty.

Eleven

IT WAS SHROVE TUESDAY, it was cold, it was the middle of the night, and my stomach was queasy from the delicacies of the abbess's table. I sprang awake to find Elisabeth on her knees on the floorboards, her face mottled and her eyes red. She was scraping all her belongings into her cloak. I stayed silent until I saw that she was fingering my paternoster beads.

"What are you doing with my paternoster?" I caught the string of agates flying past, just before they hit the wall.

"I took it to pray with, but it did no good."

"Where are you taking those things?" At my question, she doubled over, head to knees, and sobbed. I got out of bed to see what was wrong, and discovered that her tunic was stained with blood. It seemed to be coming from between her legs, although it was not the right time for her fleurs. I tried to speak slowly, although my thoughts were racing. "The blood will slow if you lie down."

"It cannot be stopped, for I have sullied Our Lord's bridal chamber." She showed me an ugly wart perched on her middle knuckle. "The devil's mark."

"You also have welts on your wrist, Elisabeth, but they are from the hot kettles in the kitchen, not the devil. Where do you get such ideas?"

She began to chant a crazy sermon. "The cow that leads the herd has a bell at her neck, so likewise the woman who leads the song and dance has the devil's bell bound to hers, and when the devil hears the tinkle he says, 'I have not lost my cow yet.'"

"The bell you hear is in Gadagne. It always rings before ours here."

"Do you not see? I am with child! Enceinte."

So that was why her back was bent and her hands pressed on her belly, why she had lost her chaste odour and smelt of a man. Over the past months, Elisabeth had grown so big from overeating that I had not noticed this infant taking root.

"Who has done this to you?"

She shook her head, refusing to answer. One of the travelling friars, I guessed. He had taken her roughly, given the welts on her wrist, which were not from a kettle after all. But why was she bleeding? Her raving had reached such a pitch that she might disturb the nuns—sound sleepers, but not *that* sound. She was on all fours when the next pain caught her. I crouched beside her, afraid that she might die, as Maman had done, in the agony of giving birth. My courage had turned hollow, a horrid, wretched hollow deep within me.

I got to my feet. "I am going for the infirmarian."

"No."

"Then the stockbreeder."

"Not her, not anyone."

For once, Elisabeth was wiser than I was. If she was exposed, she would be cast out. How many times had we been told that maidenhood had its fruit a hundredfold in heaven and that carnal love was licking honey from thorns?

She clutched my ankle to stop me leaving. "Stay with me. You help the stockbreeder bring forth young."

"I have never done it by myself. This is a child—what if I fail?"

I held her as another pain seized then released her. I helped her lie on her back so I could pull her tunic up, applying my ears, eyes, and fingers to her womb. The infant was tiny, but it was coming now. Could a child so small live? At the next contraction, she braced her feet against me and we slid, clinging to each other, against the wall. The infant surged out between her thighs in a river of running blood, with solid chunks like chicken livers. I picked the infant up gently—one heartbeat, two—then it became quiet in my hands. I choked on my sobs, too affrighted to look closer.

Elisabeth curled on the floor, moaning. Her eyes closed, she was spared the pain of seeing her stillborn infant cupped in my blood-streaked hands. Before she could look, I swaddled the fœtus and shoved it out of sight behind me.

I choked out some words to comfort her and calm myself. "You have lost your child. It is quiet and at peace."

The nocturn bells began to toll, mourning our loss. I had to think what to do. The afterbirth had been expelled cleanly, instead of staying inside to poison her. I suspected she had done more than climb over night fences to rid herself of this burden. Perhaps she had swallowed some ridding potion that had savaged her. I took her hands in mine to say the Latin of the absolution. Her mind was shaken, but her whimpering told me she had heard.

"I have been your confessor, Elisabeth. You will do three times forty days of penance. You will go faithfully to all the hours. Above all, you will remain silent. No one need know what has happened. Listen to me!" Her shoulders, when I put my arms around them, were wet with perspiration. "Your maidenhead is gone, but you may still be celibate. You must learn to read and write, and you must obey the abbess in everything."

I hugged her tenderly. In me was a sadness, for this stillbirth had driven her where I could not follow. "These are now yours," I said, twisting my paternoster beads around her wrist to hide the welts. "You will be a good novice and then a good nun, and you will forget the sad outcome of this night. I want your solemn promise."

"Yes, yes, I will," she said, as the agates dragged down her arm.

It was a honeyed lie, given as sleep claimed her, but this promise was all she had to give. I accepted it from her, the only sister I would ever have, knowing that even a lie could guide a life aright. I held her until she stopped shuddering, then sponged the blood from her legs and drew her blanket over her.

I was ill to my stomach waiting for nocturns to end, rocking back and forth as uncontrollably as if I had given birth myself. At last, I heard the nuns mounting the stairs to return to sleep and took grim courage for the task ahead. I could now carry the tiny corpse through the tumbled ashlar in the chapel. Outside, I would dig a grave with my bare hands so no one would hear the scrape of the spade or its bitter clang as it hit rock. The softest earth was in the abbey's churchyard, but only hallowed corpses rested there, after their souls had been saved.

Had this infant been ensouled? I lifted the swaddled fœtus into my lap and touched it tentatively. It felt older than the forty days at which the soul entered a male child. If male, it had died without being baptised and would be eternally damned. But what if it was female? The soul would not arrive until the eightieth day. My tears had fallen on the bloody swaddling, moistening it enough for me to peel it from the tiny corpse. It was a girl, perfectly formed, with every limb exactly as it should be, as much a part of me as of Elisabeth, yet none of her looked fully human. I had seen animals born before time, but never had such fierce grief assailed me. She was the size of my trembling hand—certainly older than eighty days, a fœtus animatus. Even now, a soul was fluttering inside her, an anima preparing to take flight. I gathered the bundle to my heart to baptise her myself, saying every word of Latin I could remember from the liturgy—one wild, unstoppable, crazed word after another. Then I lifted my eyes to witness her soul's escape. After I had swaddled her in clean linen, I cradled her in my arms and carried her outside, beneath the cypresses, to give her a home in the soft earth of the hallowed graveyard.

Twelve

A T DUSK THE FOLLOWING DAY, Ash Wednesday, I took
Elisabeth through the silent darkness to the bathhouse after
the nuns had bathed. When she undressed and I saw her still-swollen
belly, I ached for her travail, knowing the agony she had gone through.
I helped her climb into the barrel, soaped her, and poured rinse water
over her. Then I took her back to our cell and made sure no one came
near since her flesh was frail and her thinking unstable.

In the following days, her disquiet grew. She was sure that the wart
on her finger was getting larger. Although I doused it with eau-de-vie to
stop the oozing, two more warts sprang up and soon an army marched
across her knuckles, broadcasting her guilt to the whole abbey, or so she
believed. Elisabeth was attending all the hours to chant the Latin
psalms almost word for word. Even more unsettling, she was haunting
the church at other times, saying prayers tearfully for her dead. Why
had I ordered her to do penance? Now she could not be stopped, and
the nuns might guess the reason.

Lent, with its rigour and deprivation, was a blow to our appetites.

By the second week, the nuns squabbled over what they might and might not eat. I was drawn in, and heard myself argue the merits of almonds over walnuts, for I was fasting for the first time and crossing off the days until Easter.

As the weeks passed, the chapter meetings became unruly, stirred up by papal letters warning against sorcery and malfeasance, for Pope John feared an attempt upon his life, a fate the abbess welcomed. Ever since her brother, the Knight Templar, had been despoilt and hounded, she had hated the French popes. On Palm Sunday, she reported, the Pope preached a sermon in Notre-Dame-des-Doms denying that the souls of the just saw God face to face, as former popes had promised. The Pope stood accused of heresy for this assault on the Beatific Vision and the abbess was not sorry for it. Such large transgressions had made her more attentive to the souls in her own keeping. Her eyes fell upon Elisabeth—her newfound piety, her surprising knowledge of the Latin psalms—and she announced that Elisabeth would be allowed to become a choir nun, as she had wished, instead of a lay nun.

Overnight, Elisabeth's warts became enflamed. I was awake all night contriving remedies to treat her hand. Nothing—neither a hot poultice nor cool salve—would calm the itching. When the sun rose, I went into the pasture to pick Saint John's wort to soothe the warts. I had no sooner cut a few stems than the stockbreeder called out to me.

"Is your knife sharp?"

At my nod, she hastened me to the cow-shelter, where Emmanuelle was struggling to give birth. "She will be calmer with you. Hold her head and talk to her while I try to get the calf out."

I had assisted many times, but today my heart was uneasy. I did not wish to attend another difficult birth, and was shaky and out of sorts from lack of food and sleep. When Emmanuelle could not deliver on her own, we had to push her onto her side and tug out the calf by ropes tied to his ankles. As Emmanuelle licked him dry, I saw he was not brown like our herd, but white with black spots. I did not need to count them to know that there were seven. The stockbreeder gave Emmanuelle a pail of mash and measured a length of twine. Because the newborn was a bull-calf, she would castrate him so he would fatten quickly.

"Get your knife ready," she said. "Your hands are steadier than mine."

The stockbreeder tied a lace knot around the scrotum to lessen the bleeding, then held the calf's legs apart while I went in swiftly. I cut cleanly with my knife and dropped the severed testicles on the straw, feeling unhappy about my part in it. Now that the calf was up, the stockbreeder was counting his spots, and I regretted telling her about my prediction. I shaded my eyes from the sun as I hurried through the ploughed field. I was not fast enough, for she spurted past me. Her skirts caught on a deep furrow, she stumbled, dropped to her knees, raised her arms, fell again, her shouts getting louder as she approached the abbey, the calf draped over her arms with its afterbirth dripping tissue and blood. The nuns emerged from the cloister, debating the cause of the stockbreeder's fit, and soon her voice, shrieking that I was a sorcière, was joined by the dissonance and buzz of rumour.

It was true that the calf was not brown like Emmanuelle or the bull that had bred her, but spotted as I had foreseen. But how was this sorcery? I hid in my cell to order my thoughts. It did not take the abbess long to find me. She sat on the bed, speaking to my back, since my head lay buried in my arms.

"Some of the obedientiaries are accusing you of misconduct. They are demanding a meeting."

No longer under her protective wing, I must answer to the chapter. For years, she had warned me this day would come. I had reason to fear their sting. Now that I was a novice, I had seen hardened nuns reduced to tears in chapter. Worse—it was the sixth week of Lent. The nuns were weak from eating lentil soup with only a few spices to enliven it. The quiet nuns had become more listless and the quick-tempered even more quarrelsome than usual.

"Can't we wait until the nuns are eating meat once more?"

"The cloister has erupted in a fury of grumbling, Solange. There will be no end to it until you take the stand."

The abbess entered the chapter house as Agnès de Clairefontaine. Moths had attacked her fur-trimmed robe, and the toes of her pigaces were bent and tired, but her brother's sword rested proudly on her hip, with Saint Peter's toenail shining in its pommel. Behind the abbess came the sacristan, the librarian, the other obedientiaries, and the choir nuns, who positioned themselves in tiers beneath the ribbed vault. Since it was Elisabeth's first chapter meeting, she sat in the upmost tier, her hand tucked up her sleeve to hide the warts. My mouth was dry and tasted of copper as I took my place in the stand. According to the rule, I must listen but not speak. Each of the nuns had the right to testify.

The stockbreeder spoke first, her fingers knotting and unknotting. "Solange is in the habit of touching the wombs of ewes and cows. I have heard her talk to the unborn. I am convinced"—her voice climbed shrilly—"that she caused the bull-calf to burst out in spots by casting a spell upon it."

My hands still smelt of the birthing stall, where we had brought a life into the world together. How long had she been envious of my ability to comfort her beasts? Her testimony had barely finished before Sister Raymonde rose. Large and solid, she rooted her feet on the pavingstones.

"This is not necromancy or a virgin birth. The calf is a product of its parents. The heifer did not conceive this calf by herself. The facts are clear. God bids us use our eyes. We must look about us for a spotted bull!"

This caused a stir amongst the nuns and the sacristan jumped up to respond. "I suppose we must look for a natural father for the Virgin Mary? And for Our Saviour? I have seen you consorting with Solange amongst your poppies and nightshade. You have taught your pupil well. You should be banished to practise your science amongst heretics."

Raymonde's thighs landed on the bench with a heavy slap. I steadied my thoughts. If I let them stray, I would become as overwrought as Elisabeth, whose eyes skipped from one nun to another, resting only a few seconds on each face. Next, one of the nuns might suggest striking me with reeds and driving me into the wilderness, or dragging me in a spiked box, then flaying me alive and hanging me from a post. Their common sense had taken flight on hooves of envy. Soon they would stampede towards the nearest bucket of warm mash.

The stockbreeder was still on her feet, in full cry. "Perhaps the spell Solange cast is part of a general maleficium she has caused. What if the other cows in our herd break out in spots? Emmanuelle and her calf should be taken to Avignon to be exorcized by Pope John."

This allusion to her great enemy the Pope brought the abbess to her feet amidst much rustling of black taffeta. I smelt the faint odour of lavender, a sensible fragrance, and took heart.

"It was not a spell, but prophecy," the abbess said. "Have you forgotten that Solange was accepted as a child oblate because she has the gift of clairvoyance? Since then, she has mastered the seven liberal arts and shown remarkable skill in the scriptorium. So much so that the abbot has just granted her a colophon as a master scribe, the youngest in the abbey's history."

I was not the only one knocked astride by this announcement. The librarian took a step towards the abbess, saying, "O prophecy, here is thy sting! Mother Agnes, you have always believed that honey drops from Solange's lips. However, no honest scribe writes with her left hand, nor so accurately and well. Your favourite has a devil's paw."

In the highest tier, Blanche gave Ursula a push. As Ursula rose, her hand grazed the rail, flying out to command the room's attention. I had never heard her speak in chapter before. "Mother Agnes, we are ten years older than Solange. Why have you given her a colophon before us? She already thinks herself superior because she knows Italian and we do not."

The abbess made an impatient gesture. "She only copies it. She does not understand."

"She converses in that language with the Florentine!" cried Ursula.

I stared at Ursula, whose eyes evaded mine. The abbess began to cough—violent, wrenching spasms—and now *my* eyes fled in remorse, for I had disobeyed and wounded her and was ashamed. Further quarrelling broke out amongst the nuns, who deserted their orderly rows to debate heatedly with one another. At last, the abbess managed to subdue her cough. She drew her sword and held it aloft to quiet the uproar.

"You bicker one minute and are tight as thieves the next," she said. "With hysteria such as this, the holy Templars were hounded to their deaths, my innocent brother amongst them. Women accused of sorcery have had their tongues extracted with hot tongs. Would you wish this torture on Solange?" She paused to survey the shamefaced chapter. "There will be no talking in the cloister until Easter Eve. We will all be better for some medicinal silence.

"Listen to your abbess. Solange has had a vision, but not a simple one like her unicorn with his head in the lap of the Virgin. When Saint Hildegarde was a girl, she could also tell the colour of a calf inside its mother's womb. This is a prophecy about the future of the Roman church. Our heifer is Holy Mother Church and her bull-calf is the French pope. The seven black spots are a blight on the papacy. This means there will be seven popes in Avignon, each afflicted with one of the seven deadly sins. Only when the last pope is hanged for a heretic will the church return to Rome."

Mother Agnes had so amplified my prediction about the spots that it was unrecognizable, even to me. Yet an aura of startling truth illuminated it. Perhaps it *was* a prophecy. The serious faces of the nuns in their tiers, their awed silence, their transfixed eyes—this was more worrisome than any accusation they had levelled at me.

The chapter house began to swim and my legs buckled in a giddy heap. I knocked my forehead on something going down and lightning flashed across the vault. My eyes turned back into my head and the tiers of nuns became a choir of saints and cardinals, toiling upwards against the prevailing air currents in which seven French popes were spinning. From their mouths, banderôles unfurled with the words *Superbia, Desperatio, Dolor, Discordia, Stultitia, Avaritia,* and *Luxuria.* Angels with heaving bosoms and tiny legs hovered on rapid wings in an azure heaven dotted with gold-foil stars that must have cost a dozen florins. The illuminator's true skill, however, was revealed in his portrait of hell, enriched with swirls of ebony, ormolu, and ver-milion—colours I had been coveting in the Florentine's miniatures. The faces of hell's sinners were grotesquely familiar. The Florentine was positioned upside down in flames, his feet a lurid blue. The stockbreeder was in an ecstasy of swollen nudity, a hideous serpent writhing round her hips. Hell's mouth gaped below, a scarlet orifice sucking the affrighted clerics towards it. It was a Last Judgement worthy of the Florentine's own brushes.

Then the spectacle faded, leaving a dull ache in my skull. The numbness crept down my left arm into my fingers and the flying nuns reverted to a swarm of women buzzing about my ears. I found myself lying flat on the cold stone floor with my eyes closed. The abbess was beside me, giving an order to someone.

"Fetch my scarlet ledger. I must record what Solange is uttering."

"No, don't." Even as these words—and more—escaped my lips, they sounded foreign. I stared at the infirmarian, who had pushed up my eyelid with her thumb.

"She is in delirium."

"No," said Elisabeth, shoving in. "She is speaking in the old tongue."

The nuns edged closer. Several crouched to minister to me and I was relieved when Elisabeth elbowed them aside to gather me into her strong arms. My eyelid dropped as the infirmarian was thrust away. Elisabeth cradled my head, whispering, "Forgive me, Solange, I did not believe you had second sight until this day. Tell me what you saw."

I babbled for some time, grateful that only Elisabeth could understand. "I must be light-headed from fasting. Say nothing to the others, for it was a foolish, hungry vision—a vapour that escaped as swiftly as it came."

But I knew it was more than that. I had never had a vision so profound and the dark, intransigent power that had gripped me could return at any time. I did not wish to tell the abbess, for she would twist and transform my ravings into a prophecy that bore no resemblance to what I had seen. Soon she would be redrawing the map of Christendom on her study wall, making Clairefontaine-on-the-Sorgue equal in size to Hildegarde's abbey at Bingen-on-the-Rhine. Elisabeth was caught up in the same excitement, translating far too eagerly, making my vision of the Last Judgement sound so rare and glorious that the abbess's face became red and shiny with anticipation.

"Elisabeth, stop," I said, but she was too wound up to hear.

"Do not strain yourself," the abbess advised. "You will remember more in time. And you may tell us in whichever language springs to your lips, for Saint Hildegarde also spoke in tongues. From this day forth, you must dedicate yourself to cultivating your gift of clairvoyance. The time has come for you to embrace your destiny."

Thirteen

AFTER NINE YEARS TOGETHER, the abbess had separated Elisabeth and me. I was as lonely as an anchorite in the guest-house, where the abbess had put me to have freedom to reflect. Elisabeth was faring better than I was. Her warts had shrunk and she was now the cellaress's assistant, a fitting job for someone quicker with weights and measures than with words.

The inquisition in the chapter house had sobered me and the solitude had given me time to think. The animosity of the nuns had been replaced by indigestion now that they were eating meat and cream, but those who had called me a sorcière might do so again. What would the future hold now that the abbess had elevated me so far above the others? The nuns were already lowering their voices as they passed me in the cloister. The abbess had set me to reading the mystics, schooling me to be a visionary. Before long, she would send for the abbot to profess Elisabeth as Sister Martha and me as Sister Marie-Ange. Once we had taken our vows, we would be wedded to both Christ and Clairefontaine, yet I felt less fitted for this rôle than ever. Even Elisabeth seemed to have more of a calling than I did.

Each evening after vespers, the old abbey cat and I sought comfort in the empty scriptorium. I was staying late in the summer light to finish my own copy of *La Vita Nuova* and Ambrose was curled up on the warmth of my toes, too indolent these days to chase marauding spiders. In here, the soothing water clock still regulated time. The rising moon spilled through the glass window, giving me enough light to copy Dante's final lines. The familiar words enfolded me, but the nib was flooding with ink and needed shaping.

I carried my knife to Ursula's desk to sharpen it. Tomorrow, at Pentecost, I would use it to cut a fifteenth stroke into my thigh. I ran Ursula's whetstone along the blade, noticing that she had begun to decorate a small book of hours. A nobleman astride a white stallion, a clerk in particoloured hose, a stocky tradesman with a hairy chest— youths she must have known before she entered the abbey. Why had she turned her back on the world of men? In one miniature, a tall, high-breasted girl combed her tangled hair in front of a mirror. On the girl's bed, ready for her vows, lay a Benedictine habit and a pair of shears. A basin and chipped ewer, night shoes by the open door, worn stairs winding down to church—all had come skilfully alive without an extra stroke. I realized that when the Florentine finally took an assistant, it would be Ursula, not me.

But I was a better scribe. This was my vocation and I embraced it passionately. I intended to become a renowned scribe, one of the few Benedictines known across Europe by their signatures at the end of exquisitely penned manuscripts. I returned to my desk to copy Dante's last words and ink my colophon for the first time. I drew it painstakingly, an act of love. As I blew it dry, I heard a curse. The Florentine had entered the dark scriptorium, banging into one of the writing desks. Deafened by his own noise, he did not sense me until I spoke.

"You will see well enough when your eyes adjust."

"Ah, it is our new master scribe. I hear you are adept at changing the colour of calves inside the womb. Why don't you try your charisms on me and see how you fare? I will be a willing vassal." His big hand descended on my colophon. "Signing your work already?"

Why was everyone envious of me? When his hand shifted, I closed the folio, corked my ink-pot, and wiped my quill. His habit stank and he was more than commonly drunk.

"Stay and talk to me," he said, "or I will tell the abbess that I taught you Italian."

"She has found out already." I placed my knife in its groove and squared my folios, then weighed them down with a piece of slate.

"And if I tell her of Elisabeth's sin?"

"What do you mean?"

He spat out some vulgar Tuscan that disgusted me. So he was the one who had held Elisabeth down, causing the vicious welts. And I was caught alone with him, as Elisabeth had been. There was no use calling out, because the bells had rung for compline and the nuns would be singing lustily, drowning out all other sounds. I took a few steps backwards, away from him.

"You used her, then cast her off," I accused.

He scraped some blue pigment from the back of his hand. "She came to me, begging for companionship. Her thighs fell open readily."

I knew this was a lie. Perhaps Elisabeth had gone to him one time, hoping for affection, but she would only have returned if he had threatened to report her to the nuns. "You made her big with child," I said, regretting my words instantly.

"If that is so, where is it? Her belly is no bigger than it always was." He considered this almost meditatively. "I suppose you two got rid of it. What coin will buy my silence now? Will you pay as Elisabeth did, opening her legs at my bidding?"

My knees almost buckled beneath my habit. "So you admit you forced her?"

"Once a woman has tasted a man, she hungers for him. I will be gentle if you do not anger me." One hand fumbled inside his scapular near his groin and the other pushed against the wall to block my way. "I hear that your mother had a talent in this also. All the monks in our monastery knew of her—one of the best whores in the Cheval Blanc."

Everything I had eaten was jostling and heaving inside me. "I have had enough of your lies!" I shouted.

"It is no lie. You told everyone in the refectory yourself when the abbot attended the feast of All Saints. Do you forget? You said that when you were still inside the womb, you saw a priest lying on top of your mother in her bed in the tavern."

So I had, but I had not realized what my vision meant. Nor did I wish to think about it now—all I wanted was to get past him to the door.

His words trickled out, oily and black. "The abbess has the wrong idea about your destiny. It is in your blood to be a whore."

I spat at him, unable to speak two angry words together. This seemed to excite him, rather than the reverse, and he stepped towards me. He dropped his cowl and his scapular, and loosened the cord at his waist. Then he stripped off his robe and posed naked, bold with drink. He plunged his hand into the librarian's almond oil to grease his phallus. He was lecherous and hell-bound for it, and I grew weak with fear. Ambrose rubbed against his leg, as if trying to distract him, but the Florentine kicked him aside and the cat hit the stone wall with a lifeless thud.

The Florentine backed me up against my writing desk. Every part of me was trembling now. Even if the nuns heard me scream and came running, they might misinterpret what they saw. After calling me a sorcière, the chapter could easily condemn me as a whore. He was now so close that I could see his bloodshot eye and smell his fœtid breath. Taking a blow from my elbow, he shunted a little to the side, then twisted my hair about his fist, wrenched me around, and slammed my face onto my writing desk. He groped at my tunic, pulled it over my head, and bent my wrist behind my back to pin me down. His hand gained strength, became a hoof, a claw tearing at my flesh. His thigh jammed me against the desk, lifting me and splaying my legs. He entered me from behind, as large and brutal as a bull.

Unable to move, I could only weep until it was over. I freed my arm and reached for my hem to wipe the vomit from my mouth. He withdrew and let out a burp of satisfaction. This small, strange act of rudeness brought me back to life.

Like the night, I was dark and cold. Like the rat, I was swift.

I was blind with rage. I could not see. I could not speak. But I could still feel.

I felt for the knife on my desk and turned towards him, his naked body sagging against the wall, his lips slack, his eyelids half-closed. With my right hand, I seized the sac that hung between his legs. Sensing the warmth of my fingers around him, he hesitated, hopeful. I readied my knife. I knew that when I jerked it through the layers of skin, his testicles would fall into my palm as cleanly as the calf's.

But he caught on too quickly. At the knife flash, he grabbed for his scrotum to protect it and took the blade across his wrist instead. My knife scored deeply, severing tendon and bone, and the blood sprayed over his chest. He bellowed and fell like an ox onto the pavingstones, pressing his mutilated hand between his thighs to stop the bleeding.

The moon was high above the scriptorium, my only witness. He was in a raving fit. From the way the blood was spurting, I knew he would never paint on vellum again. I had to get out fast or he would kill me.

I could take no more. I was done. I must leave the abbey, but I meant to leave by my own power, not be driven out. Within minutes, I gathered a few belongings and was gone.

Avignon

1324–1341

Fourteen

RACED BY THE STING of my injuries, I travelled behind
a clutch of friars on the night path to Avignon—more men
than I had encountered in ten years at the abbey. If they had turned to
look, they would have seen a wandering friar with his head cowled and
his hands tucked into his scapular. After two leagues, where the friars'
path met the Sorgue once again, we were joined by journeymen and
artisans seeking labour in the city. Fate had directed my hand when I
maimed the Florentine, for ahead of me were the well-built towers of
Avignon, twice as many as when I had left. At cockcrow, I dropped
further behind to discard my outer habit, then followed the river downstream past farmers' fields, past dwellings and small bourgs, until it was
tamed into a canal by the cloth-workers.

I entered the outskirts of Avignon just as the bell at Notre-Dame-
des-Doms rang out to signal Pentecost, the day of my birth fifteen years
earlier. Soon the folk would throng the streets to celebrate the feast day.
Here, beside the busy paddlewheels on the rue du Cheval Blanc, where
the dyers' waste spilled into the canal, I recognized the Cheval Blanc with

its ancient sycamore. The tree had been there before the canal was built, before the dyers and their wheels. Underneath it was a squatting beggar, her eyes vacant, her grin unmistakably Conmère's toothless grin. When I greeted her with affection, offering her the remains of my food, she did not recognize me, but she would not let go of the cheese I gave her or the crust. Her joy was terrifying because it was the joy of greed, not of love.

"Look, I'm Solange!" I bared my thigh to show my birthmark and threw my arms around her.

Only then did she understand who I was. She muttered some words in the old tongue and led me up the stairs to our chamber, which looked unchanged. Someone lay in a heap on the bed, breathing loudly. I banged the shutters open in a spray of dust to let in the odour of the dye vats and the canal.

The bed groaned. "Go away. It is too early."

"The bells have rung for prime."

"What do I care for bells?"

A woman the same age as Maman when I had last seen her and just as brazenly dressed. When I told Perrette—for this was the harlot's name—that I was Conmère's granddaughter and that I had walked from Clairefontaine abbey, she was up, cursing, and I was in the bed with a cool compress on each foot. My courage drained and I felt the pain caused by the Florentine's rough treatment. I slept all day, ate well, and slept again with my back to Perrette, soothed by the familiar creaking of the paddlewheel.

In the morning, Conmère rustled in the corner with her herbs and ointments, talking to herself. Perrette held out a handful of small coins, but Conmère went down the stairs without them.

"She'll get bread at the Pope's almonry," Perrette said. "We won't see her again until dark."

"What happened to her?"

"She lost her daughter and her daughter's child on the same day. Over the years her wisdom has turned simple."

"That must be why she never searched for me."

"This is your bed now, the only thing of value in the chamber."

"I have no need of such a large bed." I ran my hands across the wooden table to locate the childish letters I had carved, *Le Blanc*. My name, though I had not thought of it for years. "I will take this table instead, for it was also my mother's. This is my métier." I unrolled my knife, quill, and ink-horn, but she waved them off.

"The clerics need courtesans more than scribes."

I showed her the bundle of Dante quires I had carried from Clairefontaine. "Where can I find a bookbinder?"

"North of the butchers, near the tanners. Take this for food." She tossed me a coin.

I looked at the denier. "How much should I get for this?"

"Enough for a meal. Go to the rue de l'Épicerie near Saint Pierre. I suppose you remember where that is?"

"If not I'll ask."

She gave me a gat-toothed smile. "Cover your hair. And stay away for a few hours. I have a visitor coming."

As I crossed the plank over the canal, she stuck her head out of the casement to yell at a boy, who withdrew his purple arms from a dyer's vat. I walked north along the rue du Cheval Blanc, following the canal until it flowed into the moat around the wall. Once I was through the southeast gate and inside the city wall, I found people fighting for direction, no one willing to give way. For every woman wearing pattens to protect her shoes, I saw a score of men in colourful garments. Merchants or clerics? I could not tell the difference.

The buildings were blackened with smoke and unclean commerce, and the jutting overhangs cut out the sun. Past the turning, the street broadened to reveal newer structures faced in stone. Men in livery guarded a courtyard, from which clerics emerged, talking loud, stiff, schoolbook Latin. This was the first time I had seen a cardinal other than in a book of hours. The street narrowed and changed again. Dogs, pigs, men—all moved too swiftly and made too much racket. I rounded the corner to be hit with a horrid stench, and pinched my nostrils. I spotted the youth with purple arms leaning against a wall, a smile on his face.

"Did Perrette ask you to follow me?"

He nodded, falling into step with me. "You'll get used to the smell. Today is not bad. It's worse when it's windy. *Avenio cum vento fastidiosa sine vento venenosa.*"

So he knew some Latin. *Avignon—with wind terrible, without wind venomous.* "Is this the street of the bookbinders?"

"Not yet. That stink is the butchers," he said. "It's carcass-burning day." We jumped clear as a meat-cutter threw entrails into the centre gutter. "All the leather-workers are in this parish. Not that way." He stopped me. "That leads to the goldsmiths. And not across, because buildings are being linked for a cardinal's household. They are taking over the houses of the old Avignonnais."

I ducked after him into a workshop where parchmenters, book-binders, and scribes laboured in near darkness, all the instruments and actions of their trades jumbled. No one was bantering with hand signals, no one decorating or illuminating, for their product was too crude to require it. My nose, so clever at picking out a single herb from the surrounding countryside, was defeated by the clashing odours. Swabbing brushes, animal glue, gelatine, book covers bent and burnt into shape, uncured parchment. At any moment, I expected to see the skeleton of the cow from which these by-products had been carved.

"Take me to a better place," I said to the youth.

"All the booksellers are the same." He tapped my elbow in warning. "Here comes Belot, the owner."

Belot's fleshy red face thrust up to mine. Hands scraped raw, a brace of knives on his belt. I unwrapped my bundle, and stacked the quires on his messy desk. He turned the leaves, rubbed the parchment with his thumb, checked the catchwords.

"*La Vita Nuova* by Dante Alighieri," I told him. "Every word is there."

"Where did you get it?" Suspicious. Loud.

I plucked a quill from his ink-pot, skewered some cheap parchment with my knife, and wrote Dante's final sentence in Provençal, Latin, and Italian using increasingly elaborate scripts, then inked my colophon at the end, proof that I had apprenticed under a Benedictine master. Again that pause, that red face sizing me up, throughout which the dyer's boy stood resolutely by my side.

"Ten sous," Belot announced.

"*La Vita Nuova* is not for sale. I want it bound, plain leather, no tooling." I did not tell him that I planned to make copies of it—for surely the Italians pouring into the city wanted to read their greatest poet, Dante. "Plus I need parchment, good ink, and a commission to take with me." Before Belot could laugh, I added, "I was told there is a shortage of scribes in Avignon. When my colophon is better known, I will seek employment in one of the private libraries."

Belot spat close to my shoes. "This is the only work you'll get in this city. You'll sit here." He banged his fist on the only empty table. "One denier a gathering."

I stood my ground. "That will not feed a dog! How much for Latin and Italian?"

"The same. You'll use black-letter. The faster the script, the more we both earn."

I looked at the cramped desk, without even a stool to squat on. I thought of my wide desk in the abbey, my cushioned seat, the fine parchment and oak-gall ink, and said, "I will do the copying in my own workshop."

He leaned on the stack of Dante quires. "It's still piece-work. And you must sell me the Dante outright."

"I want it bound for my own use."

"No one in the confraternity will bind it for you. We all worship in the same church and abide by the same rules. You deal only with me, not other booksellers or buyers. And if I hear of you selling your copying, bound or unbound, inside the city wall . . ."

The dyer's boy wrested the quires from beneath Belot's monstrous hand. For someone so young, his voice was firm. "I'll return for the commission and the materials she needs to do the copying. Put them in a parcel for Luc."

As we walked towards the rue de l'Épicerie, Luc pushed a leering monk out of my path. "How old are you?" I asked.

"Old enough to apprentice with you. I saw your colophon. In seven years, I want to have one myself."

Fifteen

WITH MY FIRST COINS from Belot, I rented the chamber next to Perrette's with a low window that opened over the canal, and moved in my table. Soon the base of my thumb ached from making ink strokes at top speed with Luc standing ready to run the gatherings back to Belot. It was hasty work and there was no time for rubricated capitals, or even a brushful of colour.

I bought an apprentice's cap and gown for Luc and told him to put about that a scribe had come to the quarter who would copy documents for less than the going tariff. In the day, I could scarcely hear the hours ringing through the city noise, but at night, the nocturn bells broke through my sleep. I would rise, search anxiously for my night shoes, then remember that I did not need to attend the divine office. Missing Elisabeth's back against mine, I would lie down again with the casement ajar and listen to the rushing of the Sorgue over the paddle-wheels as I had heard it as a child.

By autumn Luc was bringing me a steady flow of copying from men outside the city wall who could not write for themselves. I taught

Luc black-letter and before long he was doing enough plain work to keep Belot off our backs. Soon the quarter's merchants were bringing longer documents and letters up the stairs for me to copy. While I worked, they studied my countenance, my speech, my scholarly gown, unable to deduce my status. *Where has she come from?* they seemed to ask. The French thought me Italian and the Italians, French. My skill at languages set me apart, but mostly I copied in the local Provençal, for I had not found anyone to pay me to copy *La Vita Nuova* in Italian.

I had been in Avignon over a year, when a message requested that I wait upon two students who had arrived from the University of Bologna. I found the run-down dwelling near the rue de la Change. A crooked, slender building, but better than one of the shanties that students had erected in the graveyard. My knock was answered by a tall, lanky gargoyle, whose stained tunic revealed him to be more of a gourmand than a scholar. His chin peppered with hair like a half-plucked capon, he stared at me until I shook my leather quill-box.

His Provençal came out in a rush. "I don't suppose you speak Italian. My brother calls this city a god-forsaken Babylon, but I think it should be called a Babel for all the silly tongues that wag in it." He led me down a corridor past a pail of slops and up a flight of stairs. "We are being robbed of a florin a month for this hovel. I am Gherardo and *that*"—he pushed me into a murky chamber—"is my brother, Francesco, who hopes to be a famous poet one day. Get out your quill to record the most execrable nonsense that ever man has composed to earn a soldo. Checco, here is your scribe!" Then, observing me bleakly, he asked, "I suppose you have a name?"

"Solange Le Blanc."

I shoved the untidy pile of documents to one side so I could write at the desk. Gherardo sank onto some cushions and closed his eyes. Only then did Francesco, who had been gazing out the window, turn towards me, with the sunlight flooding his face. So this was what an Italian poet looked like: younger and more handsome than I had imagined Dante.

Francesco hovered as I arranged my tools. Once I'd uncapped my ink-horn, he began to dictate in Latin, addressing the letter to Cicero, a writer who had been dead for fourteen centuries. Francesco was already a seasoned orator, though he was only a few years older than me. His voice was a joy to listen to and he paced to the rhythm of his own sentences, his movements elegant, as spare as his brother's were gauche.

After he had finished dictating, he looked at me to see if I had kept up. I allowed myself a final whiff of Paris ink and held the parchment out to him. He studied the text, nodded approval, and snatched the quill from my hand to sign his name, *Francesco di Petrarca de Florentia*. I noticed a glimmer of respect in his eyes. And why not? I had made his Latin appear more polished by recording it in a formal running script.

He began pacing again, dictating a second letter in surprisingly good Provençal to Guido Sette, a friend in Bologna who had written to borrow money so he could join the brothers in Avignon. For this letter, I chose a more familiar script. After Francesco had reminisced about shared pleasures, he turned the tables on his friend, for whom I began to feel sorry.

He prodded his lounging brother with his boot. "Gherardo, how shall I describe my financial state to Guido?"

"Like a nanny goat that hasn't been bred," offered Gherardo, rising on one elbow. "If she is bred, there will be an ongoing supply of milk and a kid to sell at market. The poet, likewise. Once bred by a little money, he can be milked of verse for years to come."

"Perhaps I need a muse like Dante."

"Even better," Gherardo said. "He milked Beatrice of poetry for twenty years."

"Dante did not think of Beatrice so vulgarly," I protested.

Gherardo seemed surprised to hear this. "If Francesco does not get a patron, we will be sleeping in the cemetery, for we have both given up the law. We have already spent the patrimony our father left us and we need new cloaks and hose to make a showing in the city. I cannot strut in these ill-fitting shoes."

I said, "I doubt that any patron will pay for a letter to Cicero."

"You may be right. Is there a demand for poems here?" Gherardo asked. "Read her the one you are writing, Francesco."

Francesco came over to the desk to shuffle through the array of documents, nudging my arm several times, most likely on purpose, before he extracted one. "At prime, the sun enters the power of Taurus," he read. "Quickening the earth with heat and colour."

"Now, that is subtle," Gherardo said, "for Taurus is a lusty bull."

"There are some more verses, equally silly, which I will spare you," Francesco said to me. "I have crossed out more lines than I have kept. Tell me, Solange Le Blanc, what does an Avignon lady wish to hear from a courtier?"

"Put yourself at her mercy and beg for her love," I suggested, a little too quickly. "Say you will die if she does not pity you."

"Now, Checco," Gherardo said, "here's a young woman who can write love poems as well as you, like one of those figs that are sweet when green." His thumbs split an imaginary fig, which he pretended to eat.

"Don't mind Gherardo's high spirits." Francesco's eyes were on me now. "Would a lady give away her heart so readily?" When I reddened, realizing what I had let myself in for, he answered for me. "I suppose no woman could resist the idea that she has such power over a man! I will give you whatever you wish in your sonnetto. I will be hot one moment and cold the next. Fevers and chills, whatever you command, but after my poem is finished, you must consent to write the fair copy for me. Your penmanship is exceptional and you are schooled in two languages."

"She appears to like you, Checco," Gherardo said in Italian. "Perhaps she is fond enough to do it for nothing."

This was annoying. "You must pay me for the materials that I used today," I said. "Coins, not on account, and the same again if you wish me to buy parchment."

"*Three* languages," Gherardo corrected his brother, "since she has just understood my Tuscan. Taught by an old husband, I wager."

I forced my writing tools back into the leather box, damaging a quill. I should not have insisted on payment since I might have spoilt my chance to assist a man of letters, the only one I had met since arriving in Avignon.

"You are wrong, Gherardo," Francesco said. "See how she lowers her eyes? She is no married woman. This maid was not raised in a city, but in seclusion. Her voice has a resonance, like a plucked lute." Then to me, "Perhaps your father was a learned scribe who taught you all he knew?"

I made no answer, for he had arrived at one that suited me better. His skin, so close now that I could sense its warmth, had the bloom of dusky, ripened grapes.

"Why do you speak Italian in such a way?" he asked. "Even our grandfather was not so formal."

"I learnt Italian while copying Dante's work. *Da questa visione innanzi cominciò lo mio spirito naturale . . .*" My ears grew hot as I listened to myself. Why had I chosen to recite that intimate line? *From the moment of the vision, my natural spirit was enamoured by that most graceful lady.*

A dark, poetic eye met mine as he completed the passage, "*. . . ad essere impedito ne la sua operazione, però che l'anima era tutta data nel pensare di questa gentilissima.* It is Dante's description in *La Vita Nuova* of the effects of love. You have shown yourself to be wiser than I am. That is the kind of poetry I wish to write, not this."

He crushed his poem in his fist and threw it on the floor. I had put my foot wrong again, for I had not meant to shame him. I retrieved the sheet and smoothed it so it could be reused.

He laughed. "Don't pick that up. It's only paper—something new for drafts and ephemera. You are delightfully archaic, Solange Le Blanc, but I believe I like you that way. You cannot say *no* to me! I am determined that you will be my scribe."

Some days later, a hot, dry day without a breath of wind, I was heading towards the public baths on the rue de la Madeleine couchée when I encountered the Petrarch brothers, who were cooling themselves at the quarter's fountain. Francesco's hair was streaming with water, and his skin was darkened to olive by the dunking. Gherardo sat on the lip of the stone basin, shaking the moisture from his hair. They had tossed aside their long gowns, the badge of the law student, and now wore only loose shirts and hose that clung to calves still muscular from their ride from Bologna. I wondered whether to pass without speaking, as a well-bred woman would do, or ask Francesco if he had any copying for me.

Francesco made the decision for me, calling out, "Solange Le Blanc! It is too hot to walk about the city."

Gherardo sprawled on his back on the stone basin, legs astride, ignoring me. Francesco sprang up to counter his brother's baseness, and pulled me into the shade of the basin, where we could talk without being observed.

"Sit here with me. I haven't sent for you because I have yet to find a patron and, until then, I cannot pay you." His eye lingered where the thin wool of my surcoat gaped just below my shoulder. "Your sleeve is untied."

I held still—my throat hollow, my eyes soft, my breath free—as he slid a finger into the gap to fish out the loose end to tie it. Where was that scent, like a patch of wild mint—was it on his hair, his shirt, his mouth? His lips neared, perhaps to kiss, perhaps to speak some intimacy out of his brother's hearing.

Gherardo's eyes shot open and he sat up. "I am sweating again."

"Why not go to the public baths," I suggested. "I was going there myself."

Gherardo put on his long gown, cuffed the dust from his hat, and lurched in the direction I pointed. Why shouldn't I go with them, when I had already broken decorum by walking out without a servant and sitting close to a man? Francesco retrieved his gown and we went along the street and up the stairs to the baths. In the antechamber, a giant eunuch stood with arms crossed to bar our way.

"Wife or harlot?" he asked Francesco, although I was wearing my scribe's gown. "Wives through the main door, harlots through the curtain. If she's neither, you cannot bring her in."

Why didn't the gatekeeper speak to me directly? "You have seen me here before. I am a citizen of Avignon, a public scribe."

"A public what?" Then, out of the side of his mouth, he told Francesco, "There are better wantons to be had inside."

Francesco kept his face turned from me as he fumbled to get his coins back into his shirt. Clearly, he was not going to challenge the eunuch for insulting me, and I was too humiliated to stand up for myself. I ran down the steps and back into the street. I did not slow down until Francesco caught up and took my elbow to guide me along the rue de la Bouquerie, where the stalls were opening after the midday rest. We said nothing, as if we had agreed to forget the painful incident.

At last he spoke. "What I would give for a freshening wind! The heat sucks the worst odours of the buildings onto the street."

It was a relief to criticize the city. "Now you know why Avignon is called a sewer," I said. "But be careful when you wish for wind. Soon enough, the mistral will drive the dust into the creases of your face as fiercely as into the cracks in the masonry."

The alley was knotted with people. Ahead of us, some spiritual friars and nuns, mostly barefoot Franciscans, trudged with their heads down and their hands tucked into threadbare habits. Outside the Pignotte, the spirituals joined the line of lame and poor, beggars of all kinds, even peasants in village costume, who were queuing for the Pope's free bread. The city marshal's men prodded the line to flush out troublemakers with strong opinions. A white friar dressed like Christ must have said something heretical, for a sergeant knocked him face first into the dirt.

"News of this attack on the spirituals reached us in Bologna, but I did not believe it," Francesco said. "I must report this to my friends."

"It is dangerous to write such letters."

"Perhaps, but they must be written, and I need someone I can trust to copy them for me."

He seemed to be suggesting that I do it. Did that mean he considered me a friend? "Don't slow down," I warned, as we approached the Matheron gate, which had a human leg nailed to it. "Keep moving. This is what happens to heretics. After they are tortured, they are beheaded, drawn, and quartered, then nailed to the gates to warn new arrivals to the city."

Made grave by this display of cruelty, we walked until we met the Rhône, where we found a poplar offering shade. We sat down together, close but without touching.

"This is a vulgar river," I said. "I much prefer the Sorgue."

"At Fontaine-de-Vaucluse, the Sorgue issues from the sheer rock in a pure cold stream. Someday I'd like to take you to see it. Eventually, I wish to live there to dedicate myself to study and reflection. First, I must endure this horrifying city, since Pope John and his cardinals are here. I must earn their attention or be invisible to men of culture."

"You are in exile like Dante."

He seemed grateful for this comparison. "Yes, I believe I am. I would like to read his *Vita Nuova* again, if you'll lend it to me."

I hesitated. "I can't risk damage to the unbound quires, but I will make a copy for you."

"That will take too long. Lend it to me as it is."

"I am hoping to receive a commission to copy it."

"And I cannot pay you . . ."

Was it a statement, or the sharp edge of an argument? I waited to hear what he would say next. On his feet now, he twisted a branch until it sprang back viciously. I saw how it was: he had asked for something and I'd refused him. He noticed a wasp's nest spun around one of the branches and broke into it with his fingers, daring the wasps to sting Francesco Petrarch.

"In this shapeless gown, I am a student, nothing more," he said.

"First that oaf in the baths mistook me for a rogue the equal of himself, then you remind me that I have no coins to pay for copying when my profession demands a scribe."

It was my turn to speak. "What about my humiliation when told I had to enter that narrow door for harlots? There was another door for wives, but you—scholar, courtier, man of such great talent—were not willing to let me pass as your wife, even for an hour. Instead, you let me stumble back into the street alone."

In a surprising gesture, he dropped to a knee. He took my hand and rubbed his thumb across the ink stains on my palm. "You are as you should be—a scribe's daughter in a scribe's garment."

Arguing had hurt my throat and I was glad to let the matter go. "My father was no learned man, Francesco. Such a man would never leave his daughter on her own in Avignon. I was trained in an abbey and came here to earn a living with my pen, just as you did. I wish to work on manuscripts in a good library, a merchant's or a cardinal's, French or Italian, I care not which."

"Your ambition is unusual for a woman." He was still kneeling beside me, coupling my fingers with his. "But grant me this—the man should lead the way. Once I have made my name as a man of letters, I will reach down to pull you up beside me." Demonstrating, he lifted me to my feet. "First, serve me as a scribe so my writing can be properly presented to men of wealth. As soon as I have found patronage, I will double your investment."

Our hands were still linked, and I longed to keep them that way. "How will you do so?"

"Through loyalty, Solange—great loyalty, such as no other man will ever pay you."

Sixteen

ON THE SUMMER SOLSTICE, I was at the ostler's at daybreak to choose two horses. Today, Francesco and I planned to ride to the fountain of the Sorgue that he found so occult and stirring. The horses stood saddled and ready, and I was irritated, by the time he arrived.

"We agreed to meet here at the first hour," I said.

"But what is the first hour in Avignon—the hour after midnight, or prime? There is no logic to it. I waited until the town crier called it out."

"The first hour is always at dawn."

"Making the hours twice as long in summer than in winter."

He boosted me into the mare's saddle and she headed of her own will towards the nearest city gate. Sturdy but unloved, she trod as if her hooves pinched, and Francesco had to slow his gelding to her pace.

Today we spoke Italian, for it was rich in echoes and big, soft rhymes. We discussed the poems he was struggling to write and the verse letters he was having more success with. I was making the fair copies of his work in my best script with decorated capitals. These he presented to important men—cardinals, bishops, anyone who would give him an audience—in the hope of receiving honorariums. At other times, I worked in my chamber in the Cheval Blanc for tradesmen who needed documents copied, and from this plain work I earned my living, since as yet I had taken no coins from Francesco.

After two leagues, the terrain became so familiar that I hoped for a glimpse of Clairefontaine. At this time of year, the nuns would be out thinning the shoots in the vineyard. I would not be welcome after maiming the Florentine, but I hoped to observe the nuns from afar and recognize each by the way she stooped with her shears or wiped her brow in the heat.

"Shall we ride upstream along the Sorgue?" I asked. "We may be able to see the abbey where I was raised."

He dismounted to unroll a map against the mare's neck, so I could see it. "Show me where it is."

"About half-way between Avignon and Fontaine-de-Vaucluse. Somewhere near Gadagne, for we could hear its bells just before ours."

His thumb landed on a village. "We are nearly at Gadagne now. Was your abbey to the east or west?"

On the map, one bell-tower looked much like another. I ran my finger across the sheet, unable to identify the Sorgue's twists and turns.

He laughed at my difficulty. "Your Sorgue is not one river, but many. After it leaves the source at Fontaine, it splits into separate channels that flood the delta." When I said no more, for fear of revealing further defects in my education, he shoved the map back into his saddlebag. "We'll ride to Le Thor to meet the Grande Sorgue, then continue to Isle-sur-la-Sorgue to cross the bridge there."

We arrived at Fontaine-de-Vaucluse as the sun was reaching its peak. Francesco pointed to the house that he hoped to own beneath the towering cliff where the Sorgue began its journey. We walked our mounts up the incline towards the source, watered them, put them in the wild hay, and scrambled over the rocks to see the river surging from a black, bottomless cavern in the earth. We climbed back down, coated by spray and grime, and Francesco cut our spiced sausage into neat rounds. We ate the peppery meat while a heron fished in the river beside us.

The long ride had made us carefree and I hoped that it had made us something more, for my affection for Francesco was deepening. He propped himself against an umbrella pine, closing his eyes. Exploring the river, I discovered an inviting pool, formed by some giant boulders heated by the sun. I removed my outer clothes, loosened the veil around my hair, rinsed it in the pool, and spread it on a steaming rock to dry.

There was no gatekeeper to insult us here, only the heron, which flew off with an elegant swoop of its great wings. I stepped into the pool and sat down facing Francesco, with my breasts at the water line, visible through my wet shift.

I was pleased to find that he had been observing. He hopped on one leg then the other to peel off his hose, uncovering his nakedness, a contradiction of hard lines and rounded contours. He bunched up his clothing to cover his groin, then tossed the garments aside, laughing at himself. I reclined against the warm rocks as he hobbled over the sharp ground on tender feet. Perhaps I had something of my mother in me, priming me for secular love, or perhaps the city had taught me to fear loneliness more than lust, for the man who walked towards me appeared more god-like than human. After all, wasn't Eros a god—the same god Dante knew as Amore?

He dipped an ankle, made a face. "It's cool."

"Only because you've been sitting in the sun."

I stretched out a bare foot to nudge him in. He eased his legs into the pool, while I plucked leaves from an aromatic shrub nearby and dropped them into the water. Soon we were splashing each other like children. Far above us, a peregrine's cry echoed against the cliff as a fowler lowered himself on a swinging rope, wedging his feet into the crevices to hunt for the nest of young falcons. Everything was easy between Francesco and me, with none of the awkwardness there often was in Avignon. Although I knew little about men, I could see that the heat of the pool had a happy effect on him. He clamped his hand on my wrist, pulled me towards him to show how my game had roused him, and spoke some rough Tuscan that made his intention clear.

In spite of my yearning, it was suddenly too much, for I saw and heard, once more, the Florentine—naked, erect, and in a rage—speaking even rougher Tuscan. I was pitched headlong into the terror and pushed Francesco away. When he observed my fear, his ardour cooled. He climbed from the water with his back to me and hopped from foot to foot over the sharp rocks to collect his clothing and yank up his hose. I lay on a flat rock in the sun and fell into a troubled sleep. I woke sometime later with aching temples, to see Francesco's pen working its way across a page. My shift was almost dry. I pulled on my robe and sat beside him until his pen halted.

"I had an unsettling dream that I cannot drive from my mind," I said, "in which you received a letter commanding you to go to Italy. We travelled on horseback with two servants over a mountain pass known for its brigands. At night, we stopped in villages for safety, getting little sleep because of saddle pain. At last we entered Rome, where we were greeted by Italian nobles, who feasted you, robed you in sumptuous garments, and placed a crown of scented leaves upon your head."

"Laurel," he said, "like the shrub growing here. In ancient times, poets were crowned on the Capitoline hill with laurel wreaths. This is dark knowledge that you bear inside you, Solange. I hope it is a predictive dream, since I would like nothing better than to be honoured for my poetry."

I had wanted to put such visions behind me when I left the abbey and was now sorry that I had so artlessly revealed this one to him.

He handed me a sheet. "I've turned my thwarted passion to good use by writing a poem while you lay in your trance, as alluring as the goddess Diana when Actæon spied on her, and almost as unclothed."

With some difficulty, for the ink had run into the wet paper, I read, *Non al suo amante piú Dïana piacque, quando per tal ventura tutta ignuda la vide in mezzo de le gelide acque . . . Diana could not excite her lover more when by a stroke of luck he gazed upon her naked beauty in an icy pool.* Then, after a few more lines about my hair, the stunning confession, *Quand'egli arde 'l cielo, tutto tremar d'un amoroso gielo . . . Even in the hot sun, I tremble with love's chill.* He had finessed the vowels into an erotic pattern of sounds that rose to a climax in *tutto tremar d'un amoroso gielo.* Did he really feel such love for me? Deeply moved, I pressed the poem against my skirt to dry it.

"It is a madrigal, lively and musical. However, I dislike this new paper of yours, Francesco, because it gets wet and rips, unlike parchment." I realized that I sounded peevish, but I was unsettled by how far my shadow stretched across the ground. "It's late and we have a long ride ahead of us."

Full of summer, we had thought the light would last forever, but the sun was nearing the horizon, showing us the direction to Avignon. He was instantly remorseful, and collected his writing materials to stuff them into the saddlebag.

"You have paid a steep price for my madrigal, Solange. Forgive me. I have put you at risk."

Our horses retraced their steps downstream as the evening star rose in the west. We would not get back through the city gates before the Pope's trumpet sounded, yet there was magic in the hour, as if lovers were not subject to curfews or wild beasts. The new poem had made Francesco sanguine and neither of us wished the day to end. We rode for some time, unwilling to jog the mare out of her drowsy pace, until a small chapel appeared between two cypresses, silhouetted by the rising moon.

Francesco leapt from his mount. "I remembered it was here and steered towards it, hoping it was not a ruin. Let us stop overnight, for it is safer than riding across country in the dark and falling prey to roving boars or lawless men."

We opened the door, content to find a floor of polished earth and candles in a small shrine to the Virgin. We would rest in this paradise, then set out at dawn to return to Avignon. As soon as we had stretched out to sleep, Francesco was fingering the hem of my robe. When I did not protest, his hand rose to my thigh, to discover the age marks scored into my flesh.

"What barbaric rite is this?"

"There are sixteen cuts, one for each year of my life before I met you."

"A scholar uses a calendar, not a knife."

"You sound like a professor of law."

"Do I?" He was smiling now, a little too sure of himself. "Then I must try to sound more like a lover." He put his arms around me and pulled me close to recite soft Tuscan verses.

"And this?" I thumbed the scar in the curve of his collarbone, which spoilt the perfection of his chest. "Some barbaric custom that men have?"

"A gift from a brigand on a forest path from Bologna."

I touched my mouth to the sword-bite, then to his lips. Now that I wanted him, I saw in every touch of his, in every word, a kindness. What was there to be afraid of in this courteous man, except that he might talk too much and take too long?

The air was warm and full of night sounds and we were too young to waste the night apart. We could not shed our clothes quickly enough, for our bodies had much to say to one another. When the moment arrived, I yielded with no hesitation. I opened to him willingly and we were soon enjoined in pleasure, sucking joy from one another's flesh. This act, so new to me, so quick, so carnal, was also spiritual, for in that mutual joy our base affections were transmuted into purer metal, as alchemy turns lead to gold. Surely this ecstasis, like being pierced by a flaming spear such as angels carry, was how the soul felt when it pierced the resurrected flesh. A nightjar whirred as it took flight above the chapel and I came back into myself slowly, cautiously, knowing I had been forever changed.

"Does this mean we are betrothed?" I asked, since I had given myself to him without a promise.

His pause was brief, little more than a sharp intake of breath. "Let us say a vow together."

In that sacred place, we plighted our troth. I did not insist on waiting for a witness, for our love had carried everything before it. Such love was for eternity. The moon, now full above, was a chaste observer as our lips sought kinship in the night, then strayed to taste the saltiness on each other's skin. The spirit was truly there in that moment with my beloved as the morning star rose in the east. I fell asleep with his arm as a banner of love across my hip and woke to a wasp sitting on my mouth, stealing the sweetness from our kiss, waiting—but waiting for what?

Seventeen

AT THE START OF holy week, Francesco and I walked towards Notre-Dame-des-Doms cathedral to meet Gherardo and their friend Guido Sette, who had arrived from Bologna to seek work as a canon lawyer. It was the sixth of April in the year 1327 by Francesco's system of timekeeping, which I was trying to use to please him.

When we emerged from rue Saint Antoine, where the money-changers gave way to the Florentine bankers, the northwesterly funnelled between the buildings to drive the city's evil straight at us. Some grit flew into my eye and I stopped to get it out while Francesco stood close to protect me from the wind. In the flow of people coming towards us, I saw Gherardo and Guido and stepped away to a more formal distance. Francesco and I had lain together so many times since our trip to Fontaine-de-Vaucluse that I had bought a good bed for my chamber at the Cheval Blanc. Even so, Francesco wanted to keep our betrothal secret until he found a way to rise in Avignon, though Gherardo and Guido had guessed at our intimacy.

Gherardo loped towards us like a wolfhound, then sprang up to rattle a sign to startle Francesco. Moving was harder now, since bodies were surging towards the square outside the episcopal palace, where Pope John resided. The ritual we had come to see was underway and the red chapeaux of cardinals bobbed in the crowd. However, it was not the holy procession that we had expected, for the city marshal's men held up poles with death-warrants nailed to them. When we saw these, we tried to turn back, but the mob shouldered us forwards. Three Franciscan friars were hanging from posts in the square. It was apparent that they had been flayed alive, since their feet were broken, their backs were scored, and their habits, soaked with their own blood, hung from their waists.

Guido, walking ahead, turned to warn us. "Don't look, Solange. Their tongues have been cut out."

His warning came too late, for I had seen the horror. I burrowed my head deeply into my hood and pinched it closed at my throat.

Gherardo's voice held none of his usual humour. "The Pope is cleansing the city for Easter."

"We must pretend to enjoy the spectacle, or be seen as heretics ourselves," Francesco said.

The church was playing on the people's fear that Christ might not rise this year if heretics were abroad. No longer was it enough to drag the guilty through the streets, then let them moulder in the Pope's jail. Men who had got drunk for the holy day were sobering quickly as they entered the square and looked around. Few women were about, mainly bawds or women hardened by unsavoury work. The well-dressed monks who had dared to show themselves were from the worldly orders, not the spirituals.

The folk parted as sergeants marched through another Franciscan, accompanied by an executioner with a warrant on his pike. Wood had been piled around a stake in the lee of the wind and the sergeants forced the friar to climb on top, then tied him barbarously to the stake with wire. I clutched Francesco, whose arm shook as he steadied me. If we bolted, we would only draw attention to ourselves. A sergeant torched the wood, sending the flames leaping towards the friar, who gave off saying his paternoster in Latin and shouted for mercy in his native Provençal. As yet, the flames were only licking his heels, for the timber was green and smouldering, but some wood-cutters had dragged over a sledge of dry faggots, which they were selling to the spectators to build up the fire.

"I suppose his crime was embracing Saint Francis's vow of poverty," I said. "How can you bear to watch, Francesco?"

Sweat was breaking out on his forehead. "Because I value my life more than that friar's. Do not flinch, for anyone who pities him will join him on the pyre." He paid the faggot-seller for a large bundle. "Help me heave this on to make the fire burn faster."

We threw it at the friar's ankles and the flames blew up his robe. He would soon be out of his agony, for he could not live much longer. I saw why the sergeants had used wire. It was the only thing that kept him upright against the stake. The crowd roared at the holocaust, shouting wild huzzas. I was choking on the fumes from the burning hair and flesh, worse than the smoke from hooves and skin on carcass-burning day. A wave of nausea overtook me and I fell upon my knees with my hands joined at my breastbone, as if in prayer.

"Stand up!" Francesco said. "You will be spotted as a sympathizer."

I had no power to obey, because the crowd came between us, and carried Francesco some distance off. Either my vision was impaired or preternaturally sharpened, for as my eyes fixed on the horror, a thunder-cloud appeared, transforming the sky into a mass of jagged black. God had smelt the burnt offering and was in a rage at the torture of one of His spirituals. He descended in a whirlwind of wrath to fan the fire around the roasting carcass, waiting for the moment to collect the friar's soul. All at once, I saw God suck the glowing red soul into the sky's black vortex, as easily as sucking a flame through a hollow straw.

I was still kneeling in the square, but only a few bones remained tangled in the wire on the stake. The friar's tunic of flesh was gone and all that remained of him was whirling flakes and char. The vision had left as quickly as it arrived. I kneaded my eyes, scrubbing the dirt more deeply into them. Had I seen everything, or nothing? My voice rose, joining the mob's tumult in a nonsense jumble that did not resemble speech. Then a man's voice overshouted mine—a cardinal hailing his distant swordsmen, who flailed their weapons to clear a path towards me. One of the Pope's guardsmen joined them, a man with a leather nose shaped like a falcon's. Again the cardinal shouted, but I could not rise from my knees. How could I stand when everything was swirling and weaving?

Then my friends appeared out of nowhere. Francesco and Gherardo each grabbed an arm to jerk me to my feet. Before I got far, I lost my footing and went sprawling, a sack of wheat thudding to the ground. The brothers grasped my shoulders, Guido caught hold of my legs, and the three stood me up to propel me through the mob. The swordsmen gave chase, weapons held high, with the Falcon at the head of the pack. We slipped through a dodge into an alley, barred the heavy door behind us, and escaped down the ruelle des Chats past Saint Pierre. Our pursuers would have to detour around the Pope's palace and by then we would be well away to the south.

We ran until we were safely in the Jewry. In the vacant streets, the last gust of the dying wind rattled a canvas portière to reveal a pair of exotic eyes, one of the Jews keeping to their dwellings in fear of disturbing the Christians during holy week. When we got through the south door of the Jewry, my rescuers shook off their hoods and slowed their pace.

Francesco stopped beside me, his hands on his thighs as he took deep breaths. "If they had caught you, they would have thrown you on that fire."

He wiped his brow with the inside of his elbow. He had got a good scare, as had we all, and I implored his forgiveness with my eyes. How could I explain what I did not understand myself? He had liked my talent well enough when I had dreamt about the laurel wreath at

Fontaine-de-Vaucluse, but that had been bliss and this was terror. While I had been kneeling next to the scorching fire, I had no power to move or speak—or so I thought. On the last score, I was wrong. It seemed that I had had plenty to say.

"You spoke a heap of gibberish in a cryptic language," Gherardo informed me, full of his usual brass now that we had outrun the swords.

"What sort of gibberish?" I asked.

"You prophesied the fall of the papacy," said Francesco. "According to you, if Pope John continues to persecute the spirituals, God will return in a column of avenging fire to blast him. Today was just a fore-taste of His divine wrath."

Guido defended me. "She is not in danger, for she spoke in riddles."

"There may even be some profit in it," Gherardo said. "When Anne de Panisses told the last pope that she saw God blessing him with a tongue of fire, she received a prize of thirty florins and will likely be beatified."

"What is prophecy to one pope is necromancy to another," said Francesco. "If Pope John dislikes Solange's riddling, he will charge her with heresy and extract her tongue. She has a gift that neither of you comprehend, one that can be perceived as evil as readily as good."

"No one can identify her, for her face was shaded by her hood," said Guido.

"Given a whiff of the Pope's torture chamber, you would betray Solange," said Francesco. "Perhaps I would also. We are none of us heroes, Guido." He looked down the rue de Sainte-Clare. "The little church of the Clarisses is ahead. Let us go inside until the sergeants have withdrawn."

"They may have left already," said Guido. "I will go back to see."

The nuns were coming out of the church after the morning office. We waited for them to return to their cloister and then crept into the nave—quiet and austere, a haven after the turmoil outside. Gherardo lay on a bench and crossed his arms over his chest, pretending to fall asleep.

We were all feeling more frightened than we were willing to admit. While Francesco wandered around the church, I looked for an image of Our Lady to thank for our deliverance, and found a wooden statue of such antiquity that its face was black and fissured. As I knelt to this arcane Virgin, the calming voices of women washed over me and I realized that others were in the apse, praying as earnestly as I was.

They began to chatter, the waterfalling talk of women schooled to reveal their rank with every phrase and gesture. I gleaned that they had been abroad when the auto-da-fé had begun and sought refuge in this church. Now, as they discussed whether it was safe to leave, a young woman came from the confessional in a pale green robe with extravagantly wide sleeves. She hovered in the cool light from the east window, lit a taper to Saint Clare, then crossed herself with delicate fingers. She was my age, with a pearl-studded cap, stitched white-on-white, pinned over her flaxen hair. The ladies swept her like a violet-scented bloom into their colourful garland.

Francesco was at my elbow, watching her. "She is from one of the old Avignon families. There is a coat of arms on her sleeve."

I disliked the note of reverence in his voice. "That is likely the family nose as well," I said, "since it would be better suited to her father's face."

The Avignonnaises passed us, with the maiden drifting a little behind. I was too full of malaise to care about her, but when she approached, Francesco bowed with an arm outstretched, as befitted his rôle as an aspiring poet. His hand grazed the stones, but somehow he managed to keep his head erect and his eyes on her while bowing. His boldness so astonished the young woman that she dropped her gold-trimmed gloves. Francesco picked them up and returned them to her with a few words I did not catch. Their eyes met—perhaps their hands did also?—before the maiden looked chastely aside and quickened her step to catch up to the women.

Francesco's skin had greyed. It was as if he had worshipped at a shrine and I was a heathen intruding on a holy rite. Blackened by char, smelling of smoke and burnt flesh, I was damp from the chase through the streets. My hair was blazing-bright beneath my hood, and in spite of my nightly applications of almond milk, my skin was freckled by the sun.

Francesco said, "She was probably praying for the friar's soul, like many persons of good heart this day. Did you hear her voice? It was lark-song, high and clear. She floats above that common horde like a lark above pigeons."

Hardly pigeons, I thought, for the Avignonnaises had worn dowry belts encrusted with gems and medallions. However, when Francesco spoke like this, it meant he would write a poem, and when he wrote a poem he would read it aloud to ask my opinion of it. This ivory angel had done me a kindness, for her worship would bring him to my bed tonight.

Eighteen

A YEAR PASSED, enough time for my rash prophecy to be forgotten, or so I hoped. Outside the city wall, we had more to fear from brigands than from the Pope's guards, who seldom came this far. And inside the wall, the Pope was rarely seen, only glimpsed on feast days in an opulent barge, which turned west before it reached our gate. Thousands now lived outside the wall—ten thousand, perhaps twenty. Even the city marshal could not keep an accurate count.

By August, my chamber in the Cheval Blanc was so hot that the ink dried on contact with the page. This morning, the cicadas had been whirring in time to my pen-strokes, but now I finished copying a letter for Francesco in a queer vacuum of sound. All at once, the sky darkened and the rain pitched down in a noisy torrent. An orage d'août—an August storm, which might last a few hours or a few days. There was no sense waiting it out. I left for Francesco's house with the rain bouncing off the new wool of my robe. The water hammered the street, flew up, and chased the filth down the centre gutter. Citizens and courtiers were sheltering under merchants' canopies. Handcarts stalled in mud blocked my usual route, so I deviated to the east, my heels sinking in the cart tracks near the Bourg Neuf, a circle of dwellings where prostitutes clustered for their own protection.

The sky was the colour of lead, so profoundly sad it was more night than day. As I walked, a bout of dizziness attacked, brought on by the sudden storm. Shapes moved around me, barely visible in the mist and rain. Three figures raced past—two young boys in pursuit of a pale stag, a gallant creature of fine breeding—and I followed out of curiosity. The frightened beast skittered into the Bourg Neuf and came to a stop, ribcage heaving. When the children noticed where they were, they ran off. The rain was easing and the public women would soon appear. If they caught the stag inside their wall, they would slaughter him for meat. Exhausted, he could not find his way out, so I unhooked my belt, looped it around his neck, and laid my cheek against his chest to quiet him. As his heart slowed, my head cleared. I led him outside the bourg, unlooped my belt, and set him free. He stood motionless, looking towards me, then leapt to freedom, his hooves skimming the rain-washed grasses, as the first line of a poem flew into my head.

When I reached the house of the scholars, Francesco put out a hand for his letter. Instead of giving it to him, I shook the water from my robe, told him about the stag, and pushed aside the papers on his desk to record the lines I had been composing in my head. At last I dropped the pen and he snatched up the poem to read it aloud, beating out the rhythm with his hand.

"I cannot believe you wrote this so quickly."

We sat on the cushions, side by side, to improve my Italian phrasing. This was the part of writing we enjoyed most—tossing verses back and forth, cozening the meanings from each word until the nuance was exactly right. We were developing a mutual language, caresses of vowel and consonant, a tongue that we were in no hurry to master. After an hour, we put the poem aside, having taken it as far as we could. In the weeks ahead, he would work alone, balancing the syllables and accents, revising my verses, scoring out and rewriting, until they had a more literary turn. On the page, my poems were heart-simple, written to please him, whereas his were studied, solemn, with an eye to posterity.

He picked up the fair copy of the letter I had brought. "Today I must present this to Giacomo di Colonna, who admires my Latin writings. I am to help him study the church fathers. He is preparing to take orders and suggests I do the same, because he desires more of my company."

"But surely you don't wish . . ."

He was not listening, for eagerness had overtaken him. "His brother is Cardinal Giovanni Colonna, whose household has swept into Avignon like a whirlwind, taking over several grand houses. You must see what it means to me?"

Why was he speaking like this? After two years, I was no closer to marriage than I was in the chapel at Fontaine-de-Vaucluse. When walking with me in the city, he had become scrupulous about keeping a formal distance from me so that people would not guess our relationship. At such times I felt more like his sister than his betrothed.

"Francesco, you have not forgotten that we are promised to each other?"

His eyes drifted away. Like me, he was probably recalling that we had vowed our love in a deconsecrated chapel with no lawful witnesses. I jerked on his sleeve. "Answer me! Why did you betroth yourself to me if you did not intend to keep your vow?"

"But I do intend to keep it! It was a covenant of love, written in sand and water and blown about the air."

Had all the candles gone out, all the air been extracted from my lungs? My joy was mingled with regret that I had doubted him. He was my own Francesco and always had been.

"Our covenant," he said, "has more validity than a contract between two people who are bound by their fathers' wishes. My thoughts have been much occupied with this of late. Marriage has little to do with

love, and poetry has little to do with marriage. Think how the troubadours sang most sweetly to women who were not their wives."

This was not what I wanted to hear, since I wanted him both to
wed me *and* to write poems about me. As he checked the letter I had
brought, I rubbed my thumb joint where it ached from copying.
Satisfied, he poured on some green wax and pressed his ring into it,
preparing it for Giacomo di Colonna.

"There is something else I have been contemplating." He held up
the letter to admire the Petrarch family seal. "Courtly poetry is never
written to a social inferior. It is always addressed by the poet to a bella
donna far above him in station."

In the days that followed, I carried this pain delicately behind my eyes.
The two words, *bella donna*, had fallen heavily upon me. Very happy he
was with these bons mots, with no care for the barb he had inflicted,
for there was nothing noble about my lineage. In spite of his plan to
take minor orders, Francesco was no monk. In bed, he loved me well
and truly, as I did him. To forbid him my bed would be to punish
myself unnecessarily, for even when he was not with me I retired in joy
each night and rose in remembered pleasure.

On the day before Michaelmas, I was using bâtarde to make
splendid copies of Francesco's poems, which he would give to seigneurs to win favour. As I transcribed the madrigal about my bathing
naked at Fontaine-de-Vaucluse, I observed that Francesco had changed
the woman's hair from red to flaxen. Strange things had happened
to the poems since I had last set eyes on them. The poet could neither
eat nor sleep from lovesickness, a disease that appeared to have
robbed him of good sense as well as rest. Amongst the drafts, I found
a sonnet in which he spelt the woman's name for all of Avignon to
see: *LAUdare et REverire.*

There was no point looking for this paragon in the city, for she existed only in the realm of poetry. Or so I comforted myself until I began to copy the sonnet, *Et se di lui fors' altra donna spera, vive in speranza debile et fallace* . . . *If some other woman desires my heart, she lives in fallacy and feeble hope.* At this line, my heart plummeted. By this second woman, did he mean me? He had gone too far if he expected me to copy this without complaint. I cast it aside and picked up the final poem, the one I had written about the stag. I assessed the damage Francesco had done to it, then sharpened a goose feather to a wicked point with my miséricorde to strike out the worst phrases. However, I could not bring myself to harm the poem and had just begun to copy Francesco's version, when Gherardo threw open the door, whistling a foolish tune. Why did he never knock?

"This looks like a real scriptorium now." He drilled his fingers on the broadsides. "Are these the presentation copies?"

"I am just finishing the last one. Why didn't Francesco come himself?"

Gherardo shrugged and I thought, not for the first time, of the difference between the brothers. Gherardo was a scapegrace, a princely flâneur. So good was he at avoiding any industry that he pursued none at all. He would always be a drain on Francesco. He lifted the lid on a skillet, dipped his finger to taste the sauce, then noticed the well-stoppered jug of ale. Beside it was a single cup. After a moment's hesitation, he poured ale into the cup, and set cup and jug next to me.

This scrap of kindness undid me. My anger evaporated and I felt ill at Francesco's betrayal. "Why does Francesco do this?" I asked. "He has changed my stag to a doe. It wasn't daybreak, it wasn't spring, and I was wet by a storm, not by falling in a river."

"You don't know?" he blustered. "You're the one who's been copying his concetti about a cruel mistress whose eyes burn, then freeze him."

"This poem about the doe is different, more original."

"Francesco is simply observing the conventions of courtly love.

Readers expect the lady to have skin of ivory, hair of gold, brows of ebony, teeth of pearl. Her lips are blood-red. And so it goes, down to her toenails, ad unguem."

"So this one is about the woman also?"

I pushed the jug towards him to loosen his tongue. He took a draught and ran his sleeve over his mouth. Half the drink had landed on his shirt.

"Are you truly ignorant of who this Laura is? You saw her yourself on the day you predicted the downfall of the papacy." He recited glibly,

> *Blest be the hour, the day, the month, the year,*
> *Blest be the season, country, and the sphere,*
> *The very moment and the very place,*
> *Where I beheld her perfect face.*

"Of course!" I reached for the jug and took a pull from it. "The girl he met in the church of Saint Clare, the ivory maiden who smelt of violets. So she is his bella donna!" I had copied the words, but had deceived myself, unwilling to see the truth before me. Francesco probably thought I had guessed long before. "She wore an Avignon coat of arms, so her father will have arranged her betrothal. Francesco would not be able to even see her."

"Is that what you think?" For all his disaffected air, Gherardo was observing me with concern. "Come with me," he said, rolling up the finished poems.

He struck out north towards the city gate with the broadsides under his arm. We cut through the stomach of Avignon, past fishmongers and poultry-men whose throttled chickens danced with flies, to the good quarter of the city, where the noble mansions felt the clean air descending from Doms rock. When we reached a mansion built of yellow stone, Gherardo led me through the servants' gate into the rear of the courtyard.

"Stand out of sight behind the shrubbery, where Checco stands in the morning to watch Laura comb her hair at the window."

He watched her comb her hair at the window? I stared at the house in disbelief. The garden was being readied for the fête of Saint Michel. The master, a man of advanced years, was giving his servants directions about a heavy basket. They dragged it into the shade, while Gherardo lounged at the edge of the garden, trying to catch the steward's eye. As soon as the steward saw Gherardo, he hurried him from view, for the ladies were entering in flowing surcots to pick sugared grapes from the decorated shrubs. At their centre was the pale maiden with the large nose and flaxen hair, wearing a pearl choker around her neck. Her abdomen was gently rounded and her head erect, probably from balancing a psalter on it in deportment lessons. I watched her until Gherardo returned without the broadsides, flipping a purse with satisfaction.

"You have been selling our poems to Laura's father!"

His mouth split into a grin. "Not her father, her husband—Hugues de Sade. They call him *le Vieux*. He's a jumped-up bourgeois, the owner of the de Sade woollen looms. She is the one with the noble blood, the daughter of the chevalier Audibert de Noves, who gave her that nose."

So Laura was married, and to a man twice her age. Gherardo's vulgarity did not change the facts. It sickened me to think that Francesco found Laura even more desirable because he could not have her. He knew that Laura's husband guarded her vigilantly from admirers. That was why the doe's collar was inscribed with Caesar's words, *Nessun mi tocchi. Touch me not.*

"Where did Francesco tell you to take the broadsides?"

"He wanted me to carry them as love gifts to Laura, but why waste good verses?"

Love gifts to Laura? I stumbled backwards, as wretched as a child who has eaten a bellyful of unripe fruit. Was this what lovesickness felt like, a cold sweat followed by a rabid fever? My heartache must have showed, for Gherardo was sizing me up, probably wishing he had not brought me.

"Instead of giving the poems away, I sell them to put provisions in our larder," he said, "like knocking two apples from the same tree. Do not even consider reporting this to Francesco. If you do, I will tell him that Laura saw you spying on her."

We both knew that Francesco's pride would not bear such a thing. Whatever name he gave to me—and I could only fear what it was—he must be ashamed of our connection. This was why he had told me our betrothal must always be written on the sand and air, not parchment. It would not further Francesco's standing as a love poet for it to come out that he had carnal dealings with a flesh-and-blood woman. Worse, if he was humiliated, everything between us—every joy I felt when by his side—would be snatched away from me.

From behind the shrubbery, we watched the entertainment taking place. The nobles and their wives gathered as de Sade gave Laura a beribboned key. When she unlocked the large basket, the four sides fell flat onto the ground to reveal a turbaned youth folded into a human puzzle. First one black arm emerged, then another, then a leg and a second leg. He must have been in pain, but he stood to full height, slowly and proudly, in his blue loincloth, as all the guests applauded.

I suppose it was something to boast of, having a poet in love with your wife in the troubadour fashion, like having an Indian in a box who would unfold himself for your guests for a few coins. However—and this gave me a moment's satisfaction—Gherardo should have taken a closer look at the poems before selling them. De Sade would approve of the sonnet on the taming of the doe, but he would not like Francesco's madrigal about the woman bathing in the pool at Fontaine-de-Vaucluse. De Sade might well wonder what his pale, perfect wife had been up to and tighten the collar around her neck. Perhaps he would even throw her—and her lovesick poet—to the hounds.

Nineteen

WHEN GHERARDO next arrived at the Cheval Blanc with a fistful of poems for copying, I sent them back to Francesco. He even tried sending Guido Sette with a letter, but I told Guido to return it to Francesco. Laura was festering between us, a wound gone septic. I punished myself with his absence for seven days. I *would* triumph over my desire for him. I *would*.

On the eighth day, Francesco arrived, evidently believing that he could cajole me into better humour. He dragged over Luc's chair and spun it around to sit facing me.

"If you brought work, put it beneath those manuscripts. I will do it when I have time."

"These are our poems, Solange, the ones we are composing together."

"Those you must take to another copyist, if you can find one who writes bâtarde as well as I do."

His face was a study—puzzled, unbelieving. "Were you not proud to copy the last poems? Many of them travelled from your heart to my head and back to your pen. And now I am presenting them to the nobles of Avignon."

Had my love only fed his vanity? Certainly, my stomach was no fuller and neither was my purse. "You must begin to pay me, Francesco. I have made Luc a journeyman, but I cannot frank him unless I keep us both employed."

"Pay you for what?" His hand grazed my arm.

"For my copying, of course."

"And the other? Is that free?" He was teasing me. "I will be able to pay you when my friendship with Giacomo di Colonna matures. His recognition sets me in good standing with men of influence."

"And drives a wedge between us," I said bitterly.

"You and I are as close as this"—he wove his fingers together—"but I cannot write about it for the nobility to read. The seigneurs wish to hear a poet paying tribute to one of their own."

"You mean Madame de Sade."

"So that is why you are out of temper. You know the code of amour courtois as well as I do. I write poems to noblewomen as a courtesy to their families. My reputation is growing amongst these rich chevaliers."

Bold, piercing words, since he had yet to find a patron. "Your ambition blinds you, Francesco. Even if you receive great honours, only your name will appear on the poems, not mine. Love poetry is always written by a man, not a woman."

He did not deny it. "I will share all the rewards and praise with you." He walked the legs of his chair closer so he could place a much-folded sheet on the table between us. "Listen as I read this and tell me where the rhythm falters."

It was a worked-up poem, one we had created jointly, a temptation I could not resist. But this was not all he wanted in the half-dark of evening, and in my half-folly, half-wisdom, I gave it to him. I defy any woman to put aside a man who can bring her to the crest of desire and ease her down again. He lay beside me afterwards, and I could scarcely breathe. His arm lingered across my breasts as the moon slanted through the shutters and his fingers throbbed gently, as if mapping out the verses of a new poem.

The seasons drifted by, cold and achingly damp, then hot and sweet, until autumn came round again. Late on Saint Martin's Eve, the wind blew up, banging the shutters on the Cheval Blanc and scraping my ears raw. In the morning, I went outside to observe the damage. Hollowed by heart-rot, the ancient sycamore had broken at the waist and fallen into the canal. It had split the blades of the paddlewheel, justifying the cloth-workers' hatred of it all these years.

Would the mistral blow three, six, or nine days this time? I stuffed the shutters full of straw to keep out draughts, then lit the lamp on my table. Between now and Quadragésime, fifteen weeks by the calendar, Luc and I would need lamplight for copying, as well as a fire to warm our fingers and drive the moisture out of the parchment. At least we no longer had to solicit trade. Merchants and tradesmen sought us out with more work than we could copy.

Even now, a parade of boots sounded on the stairs. The officials of the Worshipful Company of Leather-workers swept in wearing festival gowns so long they dragged. At their head was the bookseller, Belot, who had been the leader of this band of ruffians for as long as I had known him.

I put down my quill. "What do you want, Belot?"

"To inspect your workshop."

"I do not belong to your confraternity," I pointed out. "I asked to join, but you did not let me."

He signalled to his confrères to begin. If they challenged my ability as a scribe, I would counter with examples of my finest work. Most of them had no claim to be literate, let alone scribes. The most talented amongst them was Belot's parchmenter, who ripped the skin from dead calves and cut it into book-sized pieces. I bought my parchment from him to keep Belot at arm's length, paying through the nose for the privilege. Years ago Belot and I had come to an agreement. I could copy for anyone I wished, as long as I gave the binding work to him.

I stood aside as Belot prodded my supplies with his knife, lifting sheets to see what lay beneath. He seemed surprised at the quality of my copybooks, amongst them a good psalter and a decorated book of hours. Codices awaited payment, all bound at Belot's own workshop, for I had been scrupulous. A felt-lined case popped open to expose ink-pots from Paris. Belot dunked a monstrous finger in the grey liquid, smeared it on parchment, and held the mess over my lamp to see whether the ink darkened. Oak-gall, the highest quality, with a trace of wormwood to keep mice away. He sniffed the pot to be certain. When he turned up nothing to use against me, he motioned to the shortest of his confrères, who reached into his gown for a maroon-bound volume.

Belot pawed to the final page. "This is your colophon, yet the book was bound by a Florentine in Carpentras. Is that or is that not the stranger's mark, Rostand?"

"Ouais," the short man agreed. "Mais voilà."

I took it from him to a chorus of sniggers. On the binding, a man and woman embraced in a loggia. Inside were the delicate poems, now smudged by crude fingerprints, that Dante had written about Beatrice. The *Vita Nuova* I had copied at Clairefontaine. I had last seen it when I lent the unbound quires to Francesco, who had promised to guard them vigilantly.

"This is mine. Where did you get it?"

"From a pawnbroker in the Jewry," Belot said, "for a florin."

I could scarcely take it in—Francesco must have pawned my copy, although he knew I had written each word painstakingly by hand. Belot had likely paid less, but I gave him the florin anyway. "Now, leave and take your bloodhounds with you."

His lips drew back around his yellowed teeth. "You have broken our agreement by paying swindlers to do your binding. You have taken bread from our mouths. Has she not, gentlemen?" The chorus of fools concurred and he proclaimed, "You are henceforth barred from copying in the city!"

If I defended myself, the confraternity would trump up another charge, for their real complaint was that I had been charging a lower tariff for better calligraphy. My facility with scripts and languages had brought me work no one would entrust to them, but saying so was no way to win them over.

"Let me beg the privilege, once more, of joining your confraternity," I said. "I will pay back fees for six years, enough to mount your feast of the Virgin. Don't be pigheaded. You won't get another denier if you drive me out of business."

Belot crossed his arms judicially. "No woman can work for us unless she is a wife, daughter, or widow of a guilds-man." This wisdom was cheered by his confrères, large and small. Belot pointed at the shortest, the bookbinder with the bandy legs. "You there! Confiscate her leather goods and let no man sell her more!"

But this short fellow had a mind of his own. He had not washed and combed his hair to visit the female scribe only to have Belot order him around. He spat upon the floor, declaring, "You do not need to be my wife to work for me. You can be my paramour, my leman!"

At this fine offer, the men broke out in whoops and hollers, patted one another festively on the back, and shoved the bookbinder towards me like a bridegroom. I propelled him back, cursing him in the old tongue, which he understood, for he spat some insults at me and led the confrères in stripping my shelves bare of goods, ready quires, and parchment. They broke my table, stomped on my quills, and left in good cheer, carrying away everything of value. I was now blacklisted and no one in the Worshipful Company of Leather-workers could hire me without violating the city's guild system.

As Belot packed off my case of Paris ink, the tinny bell sounded for prayer at the chapel of the Pénitents gris. Outside, the mistral was howling, settling in for a lengthy stay. My livelihood was gone. My scriptorium lay in ruins and everything I had worked for had been swept away. My days as a femme seule were over. Fortune had grimaced and spun her wheel, unseating me once more.

Twenty

IN THE COOL OF MORNING, I hung out the window to listen to the water rushing over the paddlewheel's new blades and watch the dyers' children playing along the canal. My own day began a little later. I worked for merchants in their premises or directly from the street, operating from a stall I could pack up if any of Belot's men appeared. Over the winter, I saw little of Francesco, who had been drawn more deeply into Giacomo di Colonna's circle. In June, Giacomo rode west to Lombez to take up his post as bishop, with his men riding in convoy, Francesco amongst them. Francesco's letters to me were full of banter—long, elegant meanderings of keen observation. I knew that they were written not so much to me as to posterity, and I refolded them to return to him. At summer's end, Francesco wrote to say that the bishop had recommended him to his brother, Cardinal Colonna. He signed his name in the Italian manner, *Petrarca*.

Now Francesco was back in Avignon, and we were to meet in the cimetière des pauvres, for he was wary of being seen at the Cheval Blanc. Inside the entrance to the cemetery, a pig was rooting in the spongy earth to get at a freshly buried corpse. As the sun climbed, the starlings began to fish for termites in the leaf litter and the students emerged from the shanties where they lived. I opened my stall on top of an ancient sarcophagus, as I had done many times throughout the summer. Francesco arrived, boosted me onto the sarcophagus, then sat beside me.

"Have you presented yourself to Cardinal Colonna?" I asked.

"Yesterday, as soon as I returned. His men are fifty strong, one-tenth of the Pope's own court, and have great need of culture. He has made me their companion-at-table."

"You will be a splendid ornament! I am not surprised that your sober habits won over the cardinal."

"I will also be their chaplain. Before I left Lombez, I took minor orders." He said this in a cowardly rush. "Don't glare at me, Solange. I am a minor cleric, not a priest."

The sarcophagus felt cold beneath my thighs. "But now you cannot marry. You have betrayed our vows in the chapel at Fontaine-de-Vaucluse."

He reached for a hand, but I had tucked both away. "That night was long and full of exquisite love, Solange. You expected a betrothal and I did not wish to disappoint you."

This sank in painfully. "Was it only courtesy that bound you to me?"

"You know it wasn't. I wanted you as wholeheartedly as you did me—and I still do."

"Yet you did not hesitate to pawn my Dante book, knowing how precious it is to me. The leather-workers discovered that it was bound in Carpentras and the guild has blacklisted me. You must help me find other work, Francesco. There are many libraries in Avignon and few scribes with colophons as good as mine. You have the power to introduce me, to commend me as a scribe." When his eyes evaded mine, I took a different tack. "Your cardinal requires books for his young men. Could you arrange a commission for me?"

He jumped off the sarcophagus. "I cannot risk all so soon. Wait until I am lodged in Colonna's household." Then, in a burst of remorse, he added, "I will give you all my own copy work and will pay you as soon as I can."

When would that be? Today, the wind was stirring, and at any moment might turn malignant. Soon it would be winter and too cold for me to write outside. Around us, students were sharing free bread from the Pignotte, brushing crumbs off their clothes, tugging down their hats against the chill. Some were kicking chestnuts as an excuse to watch us, which upset me.

"These students wonder what our business is together," I said. "Since you have taken minor orders, we must break from each other. Your love has ruined me, Francesco. No one will marry me now."

"And I cannot marry either," he said. "So we are together, as we have always been, sheltered from scrutiny by my attentions to Laura."

"Do you expect me to believe that you are using her as a blind?"

"Laura is ethereal, like Beatrice. For you, I feel the affinity Paolo did for Francesca."

"Whom Dante consigned to the second circle of hell for their lust."

He laughed. "And what sweet new poetry he made from it—dolce stil novo!" He kissed my knuckles, likely recalling the shape of my bed, its comforting draperies, the nights spent together. "What am I thinking? You must be cold and hungry." He hailed a passing vendor, inspected the pies, and chose one with eels, hot peppers, and garlic.

I took a bite. "This is too strong."

He broke off a piece to taste. "No—it's good. Strong food will give you dreams tonight, because you have a sanguine nature. Perhaps your dream of a laurel wreath at Fontaine-de-Vaucluse arose from the spiced sausage you ate that day," he said slyly. "Giacomo di Colonna thinks Laura is a fabrication, a play on the word *laurel*. But you know the truth of it. By predicting a laurel crown for my poetry, you caused me to fall in love with her."

Could this be true? Had I not only foreseen but also caused their meeting?

He said, "Can you imagine how I felt when I met a great beauty with such a name? You were there at that blessed moment, Solange, as much a part of it as I was."

As Francesco lifted me down from the sarcophagus, his knee pushed the fabric of my robe between my legs and I consoled myself that Laura, for all her spiritual power, would never hold him between her thighs. A jealous husband kept them well apart. Perhaps I was mad, for I still loved Francesco after all his deception.

He held out the rest of the pie. At any moment, he might massage my throat to slide it down and I was just the silly goose to let him. "Does this mean you will return to the Cheval Blanc with me?" I asked. "That is, if you are not afraid of being seen entering and leaving."

In answer, he folded my stall to sling it over his shoulder. All along the moat, men were filling sacks with gravel to stop the rising water. If the Rhône rose much higher, it would push the moat's water upstream to flood the Sorgue canal. Once we were in my chamber, Conmère dove at me, babbling in the old tongue. She ate the remains of the eel pie, then curled up near the hearth, while Francesco observed her keenly. She muttered a charm at him, then some blasphemy, then ran howling back to Perrette's room.

"What did she say to you?" Francesco asked.

"Very little of sense. She becomes disturbed whenever the full moon causes the Rhône to flood." I shivered and tucked my hands into my sleeves.

"Perhaps you feel the same disturbance. After all, you have her blood and bones."

"I thought you despised such superstition. However, I will admit that my fingers and toes are prickling." I drew up my sleeve. "Look at this gooseflesh."

"Lie on that blanket near the fire." He sat behind me, my head upon his lap, and dipped his fingers into a bowl of fragrant oil. "My nurse used to ease my childhood fears this way. Let yourself go into a trance."

"I suppose you need a poem for Cardinal Colonna's table."

A short pause, then an honest answer. "He wants one his music master can set to music." His thumbs, slightly abrasive, circled towards my temples. "Let me guide you into the space behind your eyes."

His fingers travelled across my cheeks, my chin, my throat, then loosened the neckline of my robe to rub my shoulders and collarbones, quickening all my senses. The motion of his hands reminded me that we had not lain together for one hundred days. I felt the easy curve in the back of my neck and down my spine and tried to descend into the miasma that foretold a fit. I knew he was feeding off the excitement. He wanted to milk me of my deepest thoughts, musical phrases he might turn into poems, but the ripe, oily fragrance of my skin was distracting us. Soon my robe was gone and we were entirely together— only his shirt flapping between us—and Francesco was uttering long, hard syllables of pleasure.

When at last we separated, I fell into a heavy weight of brain and limb and woke much later in a wild heat with my arm close to the glowing embers. All was confusion until I realized Francesco lay entwined with me. What seemed to be his leg was actually mine and what felt like my arm was his arm weighing me down. My writing stall was open beside him, with the ink-horn unstoppered.

"Did I say anything in my delirium?"

He rolled over to look at a sheet of parchment. "I wrote down everything you said, but I'm not sure I can make sense of these scratchings."

"Just do not turn this into a poem about Laura."

His breath became laboured, an audible in and out, as if there were miniature workings inside his head that meshed like verge and foliot to create unspeakable complexities of thought.

"Laura is the subject I have been given, Solange." He spoke gently, trying to make me understand. "While I was reading your copy of Dante's *Vita Nuova*, I began to comprehend that the figure of Beatrice held the book together. Now that I have found Laura, she will give unity to all our scattered verses. They will become a song cycle—the canzoniere of Francesco di Petrarca de Florentia. We have twenty good poems now and with your help I will soon have twenty more."

His hand plunged into his shirt, somewhere in the region of his heart, where a bulge rumpled the cloth. He dug it out: a white glove, trimmed with gold and stained with a man's sweaty longing. Between us, all this rare afternoon, had lain this small, impermeable barrier.

"It began with this," he said. "Laura's glove."

Should I laugh, or cry out in anger? "How long have you been carrying that?"

"Since the day sacred to poetry, the sixth of April in the year 1327."

I had seen him pick up the gloves myself in the church of Saint Clare. He must have kept one. All this time, he had been clinging to this fragment of her like a saint's relic, whereas I had given him my whole self readily, pawning myself for scraps of intimacy. What did I have left to offer? Nothing but ideas for his poetry.

Well, now I had one. "Write a sonnet in which you return the filthy object to her. Write it this instant, Francesco di Petrarca de Florentia, or I will do it for you and deliver it to Laura de Sade myself."

Twenty-one

O BELLA MAN, *che mi destringi 'l core, e 'n poco spatio la mia vita chiudi.* What bitter irony! I had taunted Francesco into writing a stunning poem about my rival's bare hand. *O beautiful hand that squeezes my heart, that grips and rules my life.* Skin of ivory, fingers of Orient pearl—he had outdone himself. When he brought the poem for me to copy, he could not thank me enough.

Cardinal Colonna's music master wrote a melody for the poem and Francesco reported that, when it was sung at the cardinal's table, the young men stood up to clap. Afterwards, when the young men met women from Avignon's scant supply, they begged a glove and promised eternal obeisance in the style of Petrarca. Even the city courtesans could sing the lines from *O bella man*. I heard them myself as they strutted with their gloves pinned to their belts to show off their bare fingers. Encountering youths on the street, they hailed them as *petrarchinos* and challenged them to write sonnets in praise of their naked hands.

Francesco's skill with words was now established and the myth of Laura grew with each new poem. All of Avignon knew Francesco was paying court to her, but she was so pale in character that few guessed her identity. Little was known about her except that her husband kept her cloistered and only permitted her to go out attended by her women, who ensured that both lady and poet obeyed the code.

Then Cardinal Colonna chose Francesco as an envoy who could write elegant reports for the cardinal to share with his allies. Something blessed happened: the poems about Laura stopped, and Francesco wrote spirited letters to me instead, full of lively reflections concerning his travels in the north. On his return, he sent a message to say he had been relegated, once again, to civilizing the cardinal's boisterous young men, a numbing task more suited to a chaperon than a man of letters.

On the following day, I set up my stall at the crossroads at which five alleys converged on the place des Études, where Francesco had told me he would bring one of his pupils. I often worked there because the university guilds-men were more hospitable than the leather-workers, who seldom ventured there. The students sat in the dust listening to their masters in the amphitheatre formed by the stone buildings. They had learnt to like a female scribe who knew the ancient authors better than they did and brought me their rented books, which Luc and I copied in tandem. I wrote on the right page with my left hand and Luc wrote on the left, our elbows bumping in the middle unless we kept exact time. Our work was not careful, but it put meat in our stomachs.

Today, the sun was drying the ink too fast. A pestilence had driven the beggars mad, turning them into animals that scratched scales of flesh from their arms. An afflicted man ran past us naked, howling for rain as he dodged the refuse pitched by the scholars. They were listening to the spiritual Franciscan Louis de Montpellier, whose razor-sharp Latin ricocheted off the buildings, travelling straight over the heads of most of the dust-sitters. The students dipped their bread in oil, picked nits out of one another's hair—anything to relieve the tedium of listening to the lecturer. Today their ignorance kept them safe, for with Pope

John ninety years old and in failing health, this Franciscan was striking out with deadly rhetoric.

I saw Gherardo working his way through the crowd, a head taller than most of the men. He often hung about my stall to see if any gamesome students needed help reading the more salacious Latin authors. Sometimes Guido Sette came as well, but today Gherardo had brought Francesco, along with the youth Francesco was tutoring. Both wore the white columns of the Colonnas and the low-slung great belts known as zonas. Francesco's was a bauble compared with the youth's, which was inlaid from tongue to buckle with enamelled medallions.

The youth threw a pamphlet onto my stall. "Copy this and do not overcharge." He left with Gherardo trailing him in a familiar way.

"Agapito Colonna—the cardinal's nephew and his kin in temper." Francesco was leaning against the wall beside me, posing as a client not a friend.

"This is Virgil's fourth eclogue," I said, surprised. "Luc, I will copy this one myself. Why don't you solicit work from the hospitaliers instead. Will your pupil comprehend it, Francesco?"

"I think not, but I must try to teach him anyway." He was now listening to Louis de Montpellier. "The man's thesis is inflammatory. *Less is more*—a heretical position given that Pope John is a known glutton and excessively fond of his vineyards."

"Before you arrived, he was claiming that the peste was caused by the Pope's persecution of the spirituals. It is rash to talk about it here. Can we meet in the Two Ravens later? It has been too long since we have seen each other."

He shifted position so his back was towards me. I guessed that his pride was smarting beneath the Colonna badge, which was too much like livery to suit him. He had left the supervision of his pupil to Gherardo, who was idling near the Colonna nephew. As they talked, Gherardo placed his arm over the boy's shoulder, a compliment the nubile lad seemed to enjoy. He thumbed the edge of his blade like a child eager for battle. Then Gherardo drew his own weapon, likely a rental from the rue des Fourbisseurs, to illustrate some point of swordsmanship.

"See over there, behind the orator—a lurking guardsman, one of the papal guard," I said. "It shouldn't take long for him to pin some heresy on Louis de Montpellier. The man is begging to be apprehended."

However, the guardsman was not attending to the Latin. Instead, he was cocking his head, his falcon nose-protector shoved up on his forehead, as if he was struggling to recall where he had seen me. In profile, he was unmistakable, one of the men who had tried to corner me in the Jewry after I had predicted the Pope's downfall. Then he spotted Gherardo, no doubt recognizing him from that day as well. If Francesco hung about much longer, the Falcon might remember where he had seen the three of us together.

I shoved the pamphlet at Francesco. "Get Colonna's nephew out of this square. It's a crucible today."

While Francesco looked around for his pupil, I folded my stall and retreated into the shadows. I would wait for the guardsman to leave, then lose myself in the crowd. He approached Gherardo and must have questioned him, for Gherardo took umbrage, smacking his blade on his forehead, then saluting his opponent with a feint between the legs that almost castrated him. The Falcon lowered his nose-guard and tapped his blade on his helmet to return the challenge. Gherardo needled here and there with his weapon. Soon they were dancing about each other, putting on a better show than cranes displaying during courtship. The students circled in their long black gowns, heckling, yelling, badgering, so that Louis de Montpellier was losing his battle against the noise. After a few minutes, he cut short his lecture, and wisely disappeared.

A duel was now in progress. The two men scuffled about, raising a cloud of dust and oaths and pushing onlookers into doorways. Gherardo took a run and overshot, gashing the Falcon's leather sleeve—a lucky blow, for Gherardo was no swordsman. A returning stroke caught him across the cheek. Gherardo sank against the wall, the Colonna nephew took his place, and the guardsman had to defend himself, though only an idiot would lift a sword against a Colonna. The students tossed their books onto ledges and threw off their gowns to join the farce. The square became a mêlée of motley garments, eager swords, and hats of every badge and plumage. Somewhere in the dirt and heat was Cardinal Colonna's heir, about to be blooded in his first campaign.

Francesco propped Gherardo against the wall to inspect his bleeding cheek and I emerged from my doorway to hand them an ink rag to stanch the blood. All at once, pounding out of the hot sun, five men on horseback were galloping down the rue des Études towards us, the horses' hooves kicking up enough dust to whiten the buildings. A pack of Colonnas, riding from the north with gleaming spurs, probably alerted by a student seeking a reward. Francesco—at last remembering that he wore their badge himself—stepped into the fight to pull out the Colonna boy just as the white charger bore down upon us.

The rider shouted, "Put up your weapons!"

The man could only be Cardinal Colonna, since his nose was hooked and his shout imperious. The cardinal reached to his hip, grasped the hilt of his sword, and swung it in an arc to bring it out of the scabbard. Then the warhorse cleared the square by kicking its hind legs in a circle, as it had been trained to do in combat.

The cardinal brandished his sword at the scholars flattened against the buildings. "Show yourselves, all you who caused this fight!"

Francesco and the nephew stepped from the crowd. To Francesco's credit, he stood by his young charge. His chin was level, neither tilted up nor down. The Falcon was beside them, his cuirass unbuckled at his waist and his chin bent shamefully to his chest.

The cardinal rebuked him. "As a member of the papal guard, you are charged with keeping the peace not breaking it."

The cardinal's sword arched back into his scabbard. The Falcon had been made a sweating, public fool. As he backed away from the cardinal, his helmet dangling from his hand, he knocked into Gherardo, who raised a rude fist in an attempt to stir the guardsman up again.

The cardinal addressed his nephew. "Step forwards, Agapito Colonna."

The youth held his blade high, exultant. "What sport, Uncle! You should have . . ."

"Where is your silver belt?"

The boy groped around his waist. His zona was missing—no doubt unhooked during the fight by a student who had recognized its worth. The charger's foreleg landed near the nephew. I was close enough to see that the horse was not white after all, but a magnificent grey.

"Why were you in this brawl?" the cardinal asked.

The youth fell to his knees. "Monseigneur, I fought to uphold the Colonna honour in this public place."

Gherardo sniggered and I elbowed him to stop. The less attention we drew to ourselves, the better. The cardinal demanded a prayer book and the master of his horse produced one. When the nephew had the book, the cardinal ordered, "Swear your fealty to me for all to hear."

Francesco, feeling the youth's humiliation, knelt beside him to accept his own share of the blame, and afterwards reached for the book to swear upon it himself.

The cardinal cut him short. "From you, Petrarca, your word is good enough. You will give me a full accounting in my palace. Now, serve me as you are paid to do and help this tyro mount."

Having just stood up, Francesco was made to kneel again so the nephew could stand upon his thigh. The cardinal pulled his nephew into the saddle with him, spurred his charger, and the horsemen fell in behind, driving the students back against the walls. Francesco scrubbed the filth from the knee of his new hose. Then, without a parting word to me, he set off at a brisk pace towards Cardinal Colonna's livrée.

Twenty-two

A FEW MORNINGS after the scuffle with the guardsman, Gherardo arrived at the Cheval Blanc. His swagger was subdued and the scar on his cheek had started to fester.

"Turn your head sideways." I held him by his hair while I poured marc over the wound. When he motioned towards the leather jug, I relinquished it. "You don't usually ask my permission."

"I've got myself in a stew." He took a gulp, then continued talking without any encouragement. "Agapito Colonna liked it well enough, but there were others who objected."

It took me a moment to decipher this. "Such as Cardinal Colonna, or Francesco?"

He appraised his scar in my looking-glass. "Remember the guardsman with the falcon nose whose blade did this? He had me watched until I bedded the nephew. Now the guardsman is blackmailing me. If I don't pay up, he'll take his story to Colonna. You must help me or I'm euchred and so is Francesco. You know how hard he worked to earn the cardinal's approval."

Indeed I did. For all Gherardo's bravado, he was as fearful of hurting his brother's chances as I was. In that, we were allies. I held out a purse of coins, but he shoved it away.

"I have enough to live on for a year."

"So it was you who stole the nephew's zona! Where did you pawn it? Not in Avignon, I hope."

"I sold the belt to a rogue silversmith and kept the medallions to sell one at a time."

"Then pay the guardsman what he asks."

"He wants something warmer, not for himself but for an old cleric in the palais des Papes." Gherardo bit his thumbnail. "He has seen us together in the city and thinks you are our sister. He knows you have the gift of clairvoyance."

"You mean you blurted it out. He has been seeking me since the auto-da-fé. Now you have exposed me as the woman who predicted the fall of the papacy!"

Another shifty bite of his nail. "The guardsman will turn a blind eye to my bedding of the nephew if we aid him in this enterprise. It will be an easy job for you, Solange. The old cleric in the palais is on his deathbed and wishes to talk to the spirit world. Go to him and have one of your visions. He will believe every word."

"You know I cannot bring them on at will."

He shrugged off the difficulty, his mouth working like a bellows. "Just pretend you hear the dead speaking. Say something in that sibylline voice of yours." He spoke more boldly now. "I will come for you at vespers. If you refuse, I might land in the pillory."

Gherardo admired his scar in the mirror and was gone. In spite of his bravado, he was frightened. The last sodomite put on the pillory had been stoned until his head was pulp. Even if Gherardo escaped that fate, the Petrarch honour would be tarnished. The thought of Francesco finding out that I had played some part in it, even so little as refusing to help Gherardo, was too much even to contemplate.

At dusk, I was surprised to find Francesco at my door, full of apology for deserting me after the swordfight. He carried a gift, a trader's cache of precious spices. He lit my tapers, dripping pools of wax on my furniture in which to stand them up, while I heated red wine, stirred in threads of saffron, and poured it into wooden bowls. We drank liberally to celebrate his first visit since returning from the north.

"It is unwise for me to be seen in public with you, Solange. The cardinal knows me as a man of literature—a writer of Latin epistles and sonnets to a high-born lady." Five gilt buttons emerged from a parcel he had brought, then a length of cloth. "You can tell it's from Bruges by the way it is folded. Two ells, as fine as gauze, dyed with cinnabar. The colour reminded me of your hair."

He wound the cloth about my head and shoulders, let it slip around my waist, then spun it off me. My clothes flew off so quickly that neither of us knew who did it. He caressed the birthmark above my knee, his thumb lingering on the lines that radiated outwards.

"The mark of Venus." He rubbed his hands until they were hot, then placed them over my eyes.

I put his hands where I wanted them.

"The mons veneris," he said, kissing me there.

He supported the small of my back to lower me, and entered me gently, as we had joined in the chapel at Fontaine-de-Vaucluse. On that night, we had plighted our troth in the sweet season between the evening star and the morning star. Hesperus and Phosphorus, they were called, different names for Venus. But today I could not lie in my lover's arms until dawn.

When we drew apart, my lips sought the sword-bite near his collarbone. "It's almost vespers. You must go."

"I have a poem to show you."

"Not now. I'll be at your house at sext tomorrow."

"I've moved into Colonna's livrée. You can't go there."

"Then meet me in the nave of Saint Pierre."

As he left, the angelus sang out at Notre-Dame-des-Doms. The lesser bells at other churches followed, each with its own tone and duration, until the air tumbled with bell-song. Gherardo came up the staircase as the Pénitents gris, who were always late, struck their out-of-tune gong.

Gherardo said, "I dodged Francesco alongside the canal. Is that why you are so unready?"

He had brought Perrette, telling her he was taking me to conduct a séance. Soon she was lowering her brazil-red robe over my head and removing her own combs to pin up my hair.

"Leave it down over her shoulders," Gherardo said. "I'm told the old cleric likes a girl with a bit of red in her hair."

While they dressed me, I sucked on the jug of marc like a pedlar. I had been drinking it neat to fortify myself since Francesco went out the door.

"You Petrarchs make use of her too freely," Perrette said. "Why do you try to pass her off as your sister? I have never seen an Italian woman with eyes and hair like this." She reached for the gauzy cloth from Bruges.

"Not that, not tonight," I said.

Outside, I climbed into the dog-cart Gherardo had hired. He had taken unusual care with his own appearance, and even combed the rented hound for fleas. The cart negotiated the narrow streets through the Change, carrying us to the hind gate of the old episcopal palace where the guardsman waited, sniffing at the air with his falcon nose. He had asked for the Petrarchs' sister and he would get her. I consoled myself that he did not know who I really was.

As Gherardo wrangled the dog-cart back up the path, the Falcon disappeared into the darkness ahead, leaving me to follow him along the winding corridor towards I knew not what. He led me up a corkscrew staircase, then wrenched open a studded door. We traversed the inside of the labyrinthine fortifications until we emerged in palatial quarters on the upper floor.

The Falcon showed me into a chamber that was a paradise after the dank passages with torches set too far apart for light. A steward put a glass of strong drink in my hand, then returned to peeling a Persian fruit and rolling the slices in scraped sugar. Here was a blazing fire and burning sconces. From the ceiling hung bed-curtains embroidered with a black falcon, a sinister crest that explained the guardsman's leather nose. Amongst the grim attendants, I saw two médecins, one with a doctor of physic's hood. On an ermine pillow lay an old man's head, shrouded in a cap-and-earflaps such as corpses wore. The senex's eyes were closed, his breath spent, his jaw slack. When I was announced, his eyes flickered and his gums trembled into speech.

"So you are the Petrarchs' sister," he said in Provençal. "I have been seeking you since the burning of the heretic friar. Is it true you can hear the voices of the dead?"

I answered warily, "I have visions, but they are more like fits. I speak in riddles that I cannot hear, as if my ears are stopped with wax."

At this he fell into a kind of stupor, and I looked towards the médecins for assistance. One was holding a flask of urine to the light to inspect its tincture. He poured some into his palm to smell and taste. I went to the table where the doctor of physic was casting a horoscope.

"Why was I brought here?"

"We need someone with the power of Venus to forestall the force of Mars, which is trying to dispatch the old man's life. Try to have a vision to calm him."

"Who is he? What family is the black falcon?"

"The Duèze from Cahors. Give him what peace you can since he is close to death."

I returned to the bedside to hold the man's frail hand. What had my mother said to me in parting? I conjured up her deathbed and spoke her final words aloud. "Go with the good father and do not look back. I will be well where I am going."

This seemed to soothe him, but his ears and cheeks were feverish.

I called for balm-water, moistened an embroidered cloth, and bathed his forehead, neck, and chest to conquer the heat. At last he fell into a deep, nourishing rest. His palsy was gone and so were his attendants. It had been a long night and the strong drink was fermenting inside me. I wanted nothing more than to sleep, and must have said so, for the old man's eyes sprang open.

"Climb into bed, my dear. Warm me, for I am cold."

He drew back the blanket to show me bone-white feet that were knocking together like old teeth. He lay curled on his side because his bed was not long enough to accommodate him from head to toe. I entered the bed and tugged the curtains closed. What harm could come from comforting a dying senex, holding him as a mother would her child?

I woke sometime later to find out, for he was kneeling between my thighs. My skirts were pushed up and he was climbing on me with surprising agility for one who had been moribund a few hours before. Like Priapus, he had revived, his penis now as mighty as a crescent moon. I grasped his shoulders to roll his dwarfish body off me. He would hit the floor like an old jar crashing from a height. Before I could shove him off, a coarse hand parted the curtains and a leather nose appeared. I reached for my miséricorde, but the Falcon scraped his thumb across his Adam's apple to warn me he could easily slit my throat. Clearly, I had been brought here to dispense not mother love, but the carnal kind.

In this room, evil held all the swords. As the old man sucked new blood from my marrow, I stained the ermine pillow with my tears. I tried to think of Francesco sharing Cardinal Colonna's fine table, discussing literature with the great men of the city. What was my sacrifice to his hard work, his promise?

Now that the morning sun was invading the chamber, lighting up the bed-curtains from without, I saw that they were subtly woven with triple crowns. The papal tiara. This was no member of the Curia but the Pope himself: John XXII, whom all Avignon knew to be at death's door.

His attendants drew the curtains and he climbed from the bed, well pleased with his recovery. The doctors saluted him with squat bows and shows of obeisance. They cared little for me now that they had used me, although I had driven back the force of Mars. The flaps on the Pope's deathcap flopped like asses' ears as he danced a little dervish jig, exposing himself beneath his nightshirt. All the hair had been scraped from the back of his legs where they had rubbed against clerical robes all his life. He pissed into the urine flask, splashing the médecin with the renewed force of his stream.

At least no one would accuse me of stealing his manhood with sorcery. I rose in shame—stiff and ill and queasy. I shook all over, humiliated and broken. I could not control my hands, which ran up and down repeatedly to smooth my robe, only serving to press the wrinkles deeper. I caught sight of myself in the pier-glass, as tousled as an overripe peony. I had worn Perrette's robe and might as well have worn her cap with crimson ribbons to broadcast my whoredom.

I hammered on the chamber door with my fists, but it would not give, for the bar was down and the bolt was in the socket. The Falcon stood with his legs spread like a broad gate. He jerked his thumb towards a seat beside the old man. When I did not move, he gestured that he would hoist me up and carry me there if I did not use my own two feet. I sat down beside the Pope and was made to share the meal the minions had laid out, plate after silver plate mounded with nauseating dainties. The Pope fed me lewd purple figs from his left hand, and when my mouth was full of undigested pulp, he grasped my chin to draw my lips towards his greasy face. Full of disgust, I raised my head to look into eyes of lapis lazuli—eyes as bright and familiar as mine had been when they stared out from the Pope's own looking-glass.

Twenty-three

WHEN MY MOTHER was a young woman, this Pope, then a bishop and even then an old man, had frequented her chamber in the Cheval Blanc. From inside her womb, I had seen his dark blue eyes and a face as foxed with broken blood vessels as if a painter had illumined it with carmine. The bishop had mounted her, engendering a child with eyes of costly lapis. At what cost, I finally understood, for as I had been trapped inside her body then, so I had a prisoner inside my own womb now.

Men of science taught that the child took the father's colouring and that the father's semen gave the child its soul. If this was so, my father was a left-handed man with red hair and eyes of lapis blue. Perhaps he was the Pope, but I would never know for sure.

Not long after the child in my womb began to show, Francesco found me sitting outside the Cheval Blanc. Under cover of dusk, we ran back and forth across the plank like children. Francesco did not appear aware that his brother had taken me to the palace and I did not wish to tell him. The fewer who knew of my bed of shame, the better.

Upstairs in my chamber, we opened the shutters to the humid night and rubbed our bodies with cumin oil. The scent collected in our elbow creases, at our collarbones, behind our knees, filling the dark room as amply as our yearning. I closed my eyes, sensing where he was by his heat approaching me, then receding. After we had lain together, Francesco's fingers rested upon my rounded stomach and I allowed myself to wish that I might give birth to his son. At this wild hope, I began to weep. He guessed that I was with child, and snatched his palm from my belly as if it were a hot grill.

I said, "Surely we might have a child?"

"No!" He rolled up his hose so hastily that his thumb ripped it.

"You need a son to carry on the Petrarch name. Many clerics father children to secure their family lines—why not you?"

His back to me, he tied his points, a task I usually performed for him. "My reputation as a poet of spiritual love would be destroyed. What about Laura de Sade?"

With so little thought for me, he pulled on the rest of his garments and fastened his shoes. While he was pawing through the bed-covers for his new tunic, I picked it off the floor where it had fallen. I held it out the casement and, just as his eyes turned in alarm towards me, let it drop into the canal. He reached the window in time to see the expensive cloth, embroidered with the white columns of the Colonnas, churn into the paddlewheel on its way to join the filth in the city moat.

The rage that had boiled up in me simmered just as quickly down. One day I would cry and the next day I would laugh. Was this usual for new mothers? I no longer understood myself. As summer turned to autumn, I palpated my womb, hoping for a well-formed boy, but the mass grew daily, taking hideous shapes that shifted beneath my hands. Sometimes three feet kicked me at once. At other times, the infant's head felt large enough to be two. If only I could look inside my womb, as I had done for others. What if the child was born with eyes of lapis blue? I would be undone for sure. I prayed Francesco would never guess the child was another man's, for such I now believed it to be. The evil of my palace visit had taken root inside my belly.

By All Saints', Francesco's fear of being seen in my company had grown to a deformed anxiety. He no longer visited and his letters were bursting with advice. *Do not venture out of your chamber. Write to me if you have need of anything, but do not on any account seek me out in person. Here are coins to have food sent up from the tavern. Read these books I am sending to divert you.* This was more than any other courtier would have done and I was grateful, in spite of missing him. His servant or Guido Sette brought the parcels, since even Gherardo kept his distance, probably afraid I would accuse him of tricking me. I could not dismiss his part in this affair, for he had used my love for Francesco against me. But how could I blame Gherardo when I had used it equally against myself? I had gone into the palace willingly.

Advent was upon us, plaguing the city with lashing wind and hail-storms. Although my lying-in was still some months away, I was awak-ened at prime one morning by biting cramps. My infant was coming early. The midwife arrived and tried to hurry me by rubbing my pelvis with a smelly ointment. She pricked my thigh to see where the blood was pool-ing and was startled that my birthmark would not bleed. Conmère told her it was a thimble, the sign of the cloth-makers, but the midwife thought her mad. Perhaps Conmère was, but she knew I was in pain and tried to ease it by opening the shutters to unlock my womb.

The midwife closed them just as quickly. "There is malice in that storm."

Conmère cast salt into the fire, then huddled near the hearth. She warmed some wax, shaped it into a wax midwife, and stuck it with the midwife's own pin. The midwife did not flinch, but my pains deep-ened and I cried out in fright, clamping my hand around her wrist to beg her aid.

"Will I die with the child crushed inside me?"

"Not if you bear down when I tell you."

Seven hard pushes and the baby was out. For all my terror, it slipped out easily, for it was tiny and serene. After a short respite, a wave of sharper pains assailed me. The midwife dove her hands back between my legs to tug out a larger infant, which was kicking. I fell back, panting, relieved that I had borne twins, not the misshapen creature with the three legs and enlarged skull that I had felt growing inside me.

The midwife swaddled the two infants, laid them beside me, and wiped her forehead, smearing it with blood. "The boy is dead, but the girl is living."

Then the midwife's face changed and I knew the worst—the girl was now dead as well. I made the sign of the cross on their pale foreheads, though it was too late, for their limbs, though perfectly formed and still warm to the touch, lay motionless. The midwife rubbed salt in their mouths and was about to close their eyelids, when she took a jump back, shrieking, "Their eyes are different colours!"

She shot out of the room, leaving me staring at the tiny corpses. The boy's eyes were brown, the girl's deep lapis blue. Through the open door, I heard her voice ascending from the tavern, accusing me of being a whore who had slept with two men at the same time. She was not far wrong, for I had lain with both Francesco and the Pope that same night. The boy had been conceived under Venus and the girl under Mars. My son was a child of love who gave up meekly. My daughter had lived a few minutes longer. She fought for her life before she succumbed to the harsh wind of Avignon. I took them in my arms, feeling the weight of their small, pitiable forms. I soaked my childbed with bitter tears and slept cradling my infants, until awakened by Perrette binding my stomach to support it. My arms were empty and my children gone. I knew, without being told, that Conmère had taken them to the cimetière des pauvres.

"You slept for several hours," Perrette said. "Drink this to kill any lingering pain."

I downed the potent liquor in one gulp, stood up to test my arms and legs, and found that I felt better when I moved about.

"We must go downstairs to eat," she said, "or the innkeeper will come up to demand the same rent from you as he gets from me."

We ate what the innkeeper put before us. He looked at me oddly, but when I paid him generously, his curiosity faded, as it usually did. He told us that the rising storm had attacked the Pope's towers, loosening the building-stones, and that some of the townsfolk had got it into their heads that God was blasting the Pope for his sins. The door rattled as one of the Pénitents gris entered, filled his jug with ale, confided something to the innkeeper, and hurried out.

The innkeeper collected our trenchers. "The city marshal's men are searching the quarter. You'd better find somewhere to hide."

"Who are they looking for?" I asked.

"The sorcières who caused the storm."

We were too late, for the midwife had returned with two armed sergeants. She pointed at me, testifying that I was the malefactor who had given birth to monstrous spawn with many-coloured jewels for eyes.

Perrette knocked the bench over as she rose. "What do you want with her?"

"We have come to collect you as well," one of the sergeants said. "The devil is at work in this mistral. All the harlots must surrender for the crime of storm-raising."

Twenty-four

THEY TOOK all three of us—Conmère, Perrette, and me. As we were paraded north, we were joined by other women suspected of sorcery, who were being routed from ale-houses by other sergeants. One of the ale-wives stood her ground until a punch split her lip and made her malleable. A serving-girl ran away in fright. A sergeant chased her down, stabbed her twice, and left her body where it landed. We were docile now and moved quickly when prodded.

Once through the city gate, we merged with harlots who had been hauled out of brothels in the Bourg Neuf and the rue de la Madeleine couchée, where for years they had gone about their business comfortably, befriending clerics in the papal court and paying a tax to the city marshal. As we were driven up the rue de la Curaterie, Conmère began to lag. We were now at the rear with only a single sergeant behind us. When a vespers bell sounded, Conmère spat, cursed, pointed to the thunderclouds, and accused *the black pope* of hideous evil. The sergeant went after her, calling her an old poule, a vieille sorcière, and kicked her to make her stumble. A cornered animal, she cursed him in the old tongue. My thoughts were also raving, fed equally by despair and rage. What if the same darkness rivered through me and was called forth not by vision, but by a madness like Conmère's?

We caught up to the group of harlots. At the cross streets, the wind clawed at shutters and hammered doors. The first peal of thunder sounded and I shoved Conmère into a cellar behind a canvas portière. Perrette was leading us like a flagship, her hair and laughter flying in the wind, by the time we reached the Change. The night was slippery with menace, but not slippery enough to keep the poor inside. Behind us, keeping their distance, was a flux of curious people. Some of them carried burnt olive branches to invoke Saint Barbara, whose night this was, to repel the approaching thunderclouds.

Here at the Change, where the grandes rues joined like spokes into a hub, dividing the city into seven wedge-shaped parishes, the city marshal was waiting for us. He jerked his sword up and down to divide the captives into seven groups, one for each parish. This done, he demonstrated what he required of his sergeants by catching Perrette by the hair, calling for a lantern, and pouring the lamp fuel over her. She gave me a toothy smile as she was marched out by two men who kept her at sword's length to avoid getting fuel on their own clothes. She threw her head back, laughing, but as she reached the corner leading to Saint Pierre, I saw her struggling against her captors.

The city marshal ordered his men to march the seven groups outwards from the hub, depositing a fuel-soaked harlot at every bell-tower. Each was to ring the bell to ward off thunder. If lightning struck her, she would go up in flames as a deterrent to the advancing gale. This supreme assault upon the vengeful storm began at once, with the men-at-arms hissing like drovers as they whipped out their herds of women.

My group, the smallest, was the last to be driven out. We were pushed north into the parish of Saint Étienne. At each bell-tower along the way, no matter how broken or unshapely, whether it rose from chapel, friary, or mansion, one of the sergeants doused a harlot with fuel, pressed a blade into her back, and ordered her up the wind-ing stairs. I had just been singled out by a sergeant with a drawn sword, when I heard a scream and spun around to see a bright shout of flame. One woman had been drenched in fuel before the lamp was fully out and had instantly caught fire. The folk bellowed their approval, claim-ing her incineration as proof of sorcery. But had her death mollified the storm? It was unlikely, for the thunderclaps were getting closer and the first stroke of lightning split the sky in half.

My sergeant-at-arms marched me towards Notre-Dame cathedral, my hood torn, my hair scattered by the wind. As we passed the Pope's palace, the row of guards stood ready with their poleaxes, each in his cuirass, steepled helmet, and distinctive nose-piece. A guardsman stepped from the ranks with an ugly smile, his falcon nose-guard as familiar as his leathery face. The Falcon halted my sergeant, pointed at me, belted out an order, then pointed at Notre-Dame cathedral. The sergeant refused to relinquish me. He wanted the satisfaction of escort-ing me himself.

We started up again. This time I had two blades at my back instead of one. Perched on its outcropping of rock, Notre-Dame-des-Doms was taking the brunt of the northerly. This was the Pope's own church, the first to sound the angelus bell. While the two men argued about who was in charge, I walked ahead to the church porch, unhooked the lantern, and extinguished it myself, sparing them the trouble. We were now without light to see by. I doused myself with the lamp oil like a willing scapegoat, but spilled most of the foul-smelling liquid onto the ground instead. The sergeant prodded me into the narthex, staying clear of my oily clothing, leaned against the wall, and gestured to the bell ropes. They hung down the hollow chimney so the canons could spare their legs by ringing the small bells from below, but when I grasped a rope, the Falcon sneered. He unbuckled his cuirass to drop it on the pavingstones, then forced me into the corkscrew stairway. Two hundred steps led upwards to the highest bell of Avignon. I knew

because I had once defied curfew to climb them with Francesco to view
the city spread like a splendid future before us.

A step and a jab from behind with his dagger, a step and a blow.
There were now just two of us, the Falcon and me. Before we had
gone up fifty stairs, he trod on my skirt deliberately to crash me down.
His dagger fell, clanging far below, and he was atop me, pushing my
skirts out of his way. However, the stairwell was tight and he was
having trouble manœuvring his heavy frame into position. These
were fortified stairs, which curved to the left around the pillar to
cripple a right-handed swordsman attacking from below. If he drew
his sword, it would hit the centre pole before it struck me. When his
weight shifted, I thrust him backwards, knocking him down three
steps. Then I scrambled up the staircase, circled past the minor bells,
and aimed towards the largest, the one the folk called the Iron Pope.

At the landing, I paused to ease the stitch in my ribs and surveyed
the great, greedy, angry city—Avignon. It was a city with as many lawyers as churchmen, a city full of assassins and cutthroats. One of those
cutthroats would soon emerge from the stairwell beside me. There was
no need for the Falcon to hurry, for the only direction I could go was up.
I scaled the ladder-stairs inside the spire and stepped onto the narrow
platform that surrounded the giant bell. Up here, the wind was gusting
spitefully, changing directions with such force that I could scarcely stand
upright. The spire itself was swaying, no doubt the reason the canons
preferred to ring the small bells from below. I knotted my skirts to keep
them from flying, supported my back against the grille-work, and spread
my feet, waiting for the bell rope to swing towards me so I could grab it
without plunging down the chimney.

Far below, the mass of people travelling along the main arteries was
a writhing, sinuous being. The maelstrom of bodies mirrored the dark,
swirling waters of the Rhône. I thought I could hear Perrette ringing
Saint Pierre's bell. Several towers around it were already blazing, but
the sacrifice of these harlots had not appeased the thunderstorm. With

each roll of thunder, the lightning forked closer, and I was clinging to the tallest spire of Babylon, the one most likely to attract its wrath.

Necks craned, fingers pointed, and the mob spotted me on my swaying roost. I gripped the grille-work as a lightning bolt jagged past, missing Notre-Dame but attacking Saint Pierre in a blow of light. Saint Pierre's bell clanged fiercely, then flames erupted from the tower. If Perrette had made it to the top to shout her challenge to the thundering skies, she had been silenced. The mob roared, adding her to the count of dead sorcières.

I had no time to pray for her, because the rope swung towards me. I caught it and pulled the bell for all my life was worth. The biggest bell in Avignon, its peals were deafening. I rang to frighten off the devil I did not know and to summon the God I knew too well—the God who had taken my mother and my stillborn infants, the God who created whoring popes and vicious guards. I rang to tell Him to come to get me if He dared. If I was going to die, I would blaze out in a spectacular way, flaming into an inferno.

Another bolt jagged across the sky, lighting up the Falcon, who had arrived on the platform across from me. My robe stank of lamp oil, but he had absorbed almost as much fuel from pressing himself against me. I watched him wonder where the next bolt would come from and saw him turn—his surprise making him almost human—as a tongue of lightning licked his shoulder, igniting him. Kindled by fire, he fell backwards through the open arch. I heard the cries of the mob below and imagined what they saw: a harlot burning all the way down, her arms and legs convulsing, her brains boiling inside the helmet of her skull.

If the folk thought me dead, I would prove them wrong. Feet braced, I yanked the rope backwards and forwards in time to the breath racking up and down my ribs. I pulled and pulled, almost tearing my arms from their sockets, until at last the sergeant tapped my shoulder with his blade. He was teetering on the thundered, broken platform and his moving lips told me that I had rung so hard and so long that my bell was the only one still pealing. The noise had deafened me, but neither God nor the devil had dared to claim me. The sergeant mouthed his plea: would I render mercy for his offence against me? When I had done so, my courage broke. He steadied me on the ladder, then led me down two hundred steps into the narthex, where I saw, rather than heard, the canons pulling the bell ropes to ring the angelus.

The crowd stilled as I emerged from the cathedral porch. It was now the first hour of the fourth of December in the year 1334, Saint Barbara's Day, and I had been awake since prime the previous day. The tempest had passed through, littering the piazza with broken tiles, orphaned shutters, and unrecognizable debris. Massive building blocks had plummeted from Pope John's old palace and whole branches had been ripped from the trees upon Doms rock.

The canons stationed me on the rocky esplanade, where I could be admired from the piazza below. Townsfolk were gathering from all quarters of the city and the first rooks flew down to scrutinize the pickings. I must have looked half-burnt, for the oil on my robe and hair had attracted the flying char from the thunder-blow upon the spire. At least I was not on the cart of corpses the becchini wheeled around the piazza so the scorched harlots could be spat upon and cursed as sorcières. Foragers were surveying the black mess where the flaming guardsman had fallen. His legs were still connected to his trunk by a rope of skin, but his arms and head had landed further off. The men circled warily— prodding the remains for cloven hooves and horns, or the bony spine of a forked tail.

A forager speared the Falcon's burnt helmet and spun it high. "The devil's skull!"

The mob took up the cry. My ears snapped open and my head rang with each war-like shout. But had this puny devil, no more than a man in size, actually roused the sorcières to unleash the violent storm? Even the simplest of scavengers appeared doubtful.

As dawn broke in the east, transforming the loopholes in the city's battlements to insubstantial lace, I saw a sight more vivid than anything yet seen. A stocky man with turnip ears and a leather apron lurched towards me, pointing towards his brazen hair to claim kinship with me. Behind him came a band of men with red hair ranging from brassy carrot to deep umber—the confraternity of weapon-smiths. I knew them as the men who worked in the city's forges, hammering metal into weapons. They had probably spent the night in their little church of Saint Barbara, praying to her for deliverance from the thunder and lightning.

The master with turnip ears called out to me, "Saint Barbara!"

One at a time, his brethren dropped to the ground. They walked on their knees towards me, crossing themselves to north, south, east, and west. They knelt on the first stair, then the second, ascending by painful increments towards me on the esplanade.

"Barbara, our guardian saint!" the master shouted. "You saved us from the sky's artillery. Now bless us and save us from burns in our own forges."

His men repeated the same plea. "Saint Barbara! Bless us and save us!"

Who could blame them for believing that their patron saint still lived? Barbara had been imprisoned in a tower and tortured by fire, which she miraculously extinguished, and as surely as I was gowned in black char, I had been devoured by flames but triumphed over them.

Some of the mob knelt with the weapon-smiths, as eager as they were to find a hero for Saint Barbara's Day. The poor had a memory for such things, though the rich—who were keeping to their mansions—liked to forget them. This sort of adulation was fraught with peril, since I was still only a hair's-breadth from death. I looked for an escape from the esplanade, but the phalanx of canons hemmed me in.

Now I saw why, for the Pope's guardsmen were mustering outside the episcopal palace in their gleaming breastplates and painted nose-pieces. At the second hour of Saint Barbara's Day, the ninety-year-old Pope sailed forth on a barge of crimson velvet, ostrich feathers, and cloth of gold—shouldered by a dozen palafrenieri—to see the miraculous bell-ringer for himself. This was the Pope who had sworn never to mount horse or mule except to ride to the Holy See in Rome, yet had kept the papacy captive in this Babylon for eighteen years.

"Out of his way," the guardsmen cried, clearing the mob with flashing swords.

As the Pope's splendid barge mounted the ramp towards me, the people massed, their faces as dark and severe as their clothing, with only a leavening of courtiers and merchants to brighten them. Yet there was grandeur to them—and they had collected to honour me. Now they honoured their Pope as well. This show of homage from his vassals was humbling even for John XXII. But *who* had blasted his city with thunder and fire, and *who* had saved it from destruction? The mob awaited the Pope's official proclamation.

The Pope's tiara and lapis eyes rose out of the barge and his fist menaced the sky. "Sorcières stirred up this tempest," he decreed with shaky voice, "and were halted by the power vested in me, Christ's Vicar, through the agency of my own visionary, a necromancer with the power for good!"

His gilded staff nodded towards me and his eyes met mine across the esplanade. He recognized me, as well he might, for he had taken me by force in his luxurious bed. Beneath his triple crown was the same woollen deathcap he had worn in his bedchamber. Under the magnificent cope was the same senex, looking like a cobbler in the costume of a grander man. I did not lower my eyes and they were an even darker lapis than his own. Did he fear my power today as much as I had feared his then? The potency I had given to him a six-month past I now took back, sapping his power. He spoke some maundering drivel, then was swallowed by his opulent couch.

The city marshal shouted to the crowd, "The Pope rewards this visionary with a purse of gold!" He made a show of giving me a weighty purse, then ordered the guardsmen, "One of you, put her in the keeping of the captain, who will know my mind."

Just then, the Pope was stricken by a surfeit of bile and his coughing tilted the barge off its axis. The marshal signalled to the palafrenieri, who heaved the barge-poles onto their backs to shunt the Pope at full speed to the battered palace. The officers and guardsmen trotted to keep up, each assuming some other man was guarding me.

The poor flooded the esplanade, scraping the ground for gold threads that might have fallen from the papal garments. I was cloaked from scrutiny by the weapon-smiths, who surrounded me to pick charred scraps off my robe. They walked me through the piazza to protect me from the mob. Although they had elected themselves my citizen army, they had not grasped the marshal's intention, and I was well hidden in their red-haired company. Only now did I feel my breasts aching and my womb cramping with after-pains from my unhappy births. My arm sockets stiffened from the bell rope. Where the street twisted, I was squeezed into a narrow corridor of moving flesh, and eluded the kindly smiths by ducking through a dog-leg. I ran south, supporting my belly with my hands, through workshops and potteries and slaughterhouses until I reached the rear of the Cheval Blanc.

I found Conmère delirious in my bed—the first time I had ever seen her in it. She was complaining that the Rhône had risen so far inside her throat that it was choking her. I rubbed her with sweet almond oil and dressed her cleanly. I slept and woke, troubled by grim imaginings of Perrette's agony, and slept and woke again. Conmère died with me beside her, my tears soaking her filthy, matted plait. Her death was swift, brought on by crouching in a damp, infested cellar, her heart already weakened from carrying my dead twins to their unhallowed grave not long before. There, in the cimetière des pauvres, Conmère also found her resting place, for no hallowed graveyard could be paid enough to take her.

Twenty-five

NOT LONG AFTER I saw Pope John carted towards the palace, he died in state with his cardinals around him, having recanted his heresy about the Beatific Vision. As was the custom, the camerlengo struck the Pope's skull with a mallet and called out to him using his birth name, *Jacques Duèze, are you dead?* When this was repeated three times without an answer, the camerlengo pried off the Fisherman's ring and cracked it with shears. It was buried with the corpse inside triple coffins in the cathedral of Notre-Dame-des-Doms. The Pope's death appeared to be the sacrifice the storm demanded, since a new pope was elected in a single ballot.

These mysteries jumped from mouth to ear along the city's arteries until they reached me in the Cheval Blanc. When the Pope's ring was crushed, so was my link to the papacy. Still, I thought it wise to tame my hair with henna to a disguising auburn, for I had almost died. Fortune had spun me up, then spun me down, where I was safer. At Noël, when the new ring was cast for Jacques Fournier, it bore the name Benedict XII.

Twice born, I opened my window to dedicate myself anew to life, and my soul leapt under the bold moon. I would much rather embrace Francesco than join the martyrs, where mortal arms would never enfold me. He had fled to the Vaucluse to speed his writing in seclusion. From there, I received beautifully composed letters, the latest announcing that Pope Benedict had summoned him to an audience on Mardi gras. How much did Francesco know of my ordeal and fleeting glory? Nothing, I hoped, since I wished to put it all behind me.

On Mardi gras, I walked along the rue de l'Épicerie, which was brisk with trade. Here were turnips, celery root, sacks of glistening rice, and traders calling out the merits of fish, wine, and foreign cloth. A black cat sprang in front of me, a dancer with white paws. The weathercock was motionless and the air was redolent with winter spices— mace, cumin, and cinnamon bark that reminded me of Francesco's skin. I could sense his presence in the city as I had sensed his palm travelling a breath above my naked flesh.

A pedlar held up a mask of silver wire, twisted delicately into feathers. "Try it on, madonna?"

His smile was too broad to bestow on a woman of good family, but was it not a day for masquerade? Today, the sun itself was made of filigree. After some banter that we both enjoyed, I bought the mask and tied it to my belt. I felt a pinch through three layers of fine cloth. Gherardo, in pattens and baggy hose, standing beside me.

"Your laughter is bouncing off the buildings, Solange. I suppose you are also meeting Francesco at the Two Ravens." His grin was sheepish. "It is good to see you after all these months."

How did he always charm me so readily? "So you have come out of hiding, Gherardo."

He squinted at me. "What happened the night I conveyed you to the palace? Where did the guardsman take you?"

I was in the mood to forgive, and would make it easy for us both.

"To the Pope's bedchamber, where I cured him of his fever. Where were you during the thunderstorm, Gherardo?"

"Cowering in the Vaucluse with Francesco. He has our mother's fear of winter storms."

Then the brothers knew little of what had gone on, which suited me. About the rest, Gherardo was incurious. As we walked along the rue des Fourbisseurs, Gherardo clacking in his pattens, one of the red-haired smiths hailed me from his munitions shop, "Saint Barbara! Have you had any more visions? Do you need an honour guard for carnival?"

It was the master, the man with the turnip ears. Gherardo looked at me oddly, but I waved the master off and hurried Gherardo away from the workshop. At the Two Ravens, we found Francesco with Guido Sette. Francesco had slung his cloak over the only proper chair, which he offered to me, allowing his hand to graze my head covering, the cinnabar cloth he had brought from Bruges. Five months had passed since we had been together. I leaned back against his cloak, glorying in its familiar scent, and whispered that I was glad to see him.

Before he could respond, Guido said, "Tell us, what is Pope Benedict like?"

"As austere as we were told," Francesco said. "The opposite of Pope John. Half his age but twice his size. He welcomed us in an old Cistercian habit. By contrast, all the men of letters, all the artists, were overdressed. The nobles were ingratiating themselves, strutting in their regalia like the Pope's camel and his bear. He gave only modest rewards to the cardinals who voted for him and is packing all the useless clerics back to the provinces."

"What will Benedict do with Pope John's vineyards?" Gherardo asked.

"From what I saw, he will drink them dry. We Italians have been deceived in Benedict, for he is in no hurry to return to Rome. He will build a new palace in Avignon to replace the damaged one. It will be the greatest monastery in Europe, a cold Cistercian fortress to keep his enemies at bay. And he is in a hurry. Eight hundred workers will be employed."

"His French allies will be glad," I said. "So will the labourers and guilds. Those of us who live here will benefit as well."

"I have already," Francesco said, "since he has awarded me a canonry in Lombez."

Guido and Gherardo hauled him up to perform an Italian dance step from their Bologna days, but I could not wish Francesco good fortune. How could I, when he would be more frequently absent from the city? He was moving up in the world of diplomacy, a world that had never welcomed me.

"You already have a post with Cardinal Colonna," I protested.

"As an errand runner and nursemaid to his nephews. At any rate, I need not give that up. I will divide my time between Avignon and Lombez."

Gherardo did another dance step. "Pope John must have appointed you before he died," he blurted out. "This is Solange's doing . . ."

My ears were smarting. "Gherardo, stop!"

Guido looked from Gherardo, to Francesco, to me. "What does he mean? What did these Petrarchs make you do?"

Francesco swirled the brackish liquid in his tankard. "I would like to know the answer as well, Gherardo."

Gherardo wagged his tongue back and forth to relax his lips. "Pope John requested our sister. How could I refuse?"

"What took place, Solange?" Francesco asked.

I could not admit that the old pope had forced himself on me, for the shame would be excruciating. How little could I get away with saying? "I found the Holy Father in an illness, amidst his doctors, and managed to give him comfort."

Earnest for once, Gherardo said, "I took her there myself."

Guido stared at him. "Are you a half-wit? Would you have given your real sister to him?"

"I had no choice," Gherardo said calmly. "Pope John's guardsman was blackmailing me for having carnal relations with Agapito Colonna."

At the mention of Cardinal Colonna, Francesco pounded the table so hard the tumblers leapt. He strode to the wall, and smashed his fist through the wattle and daub, breaking the skin across his knuckles. Gherardo and I sank into ourselves, while Francesco smacked his fist into his palm, again and again. Then, sucking his broken knuckles, he righted the stool and sat down. What had angered him most—his brother's misdeeds or the risk of Cardinal Colonna discovering them?

At last Francesco spoke. "It was a dangerous ruse, Gherardo— dangerous for us all, but mostly for Solange. If we are asked where our sister is, we must say she has returned to Italy. I see you have darkened your hair, Solange, and bought a new robe, but not one so fine as to attract attention. This way you can lose yourself in the city again, a citizen of Avignon."

Gherardo smirked. "And a necromancer who drives off lightning storms. There are men in this town, swarthy guilds-men with hair redder than hers, who know her well by sight."

"You have done too much harm with your loose tales," said Francesco. "Solange's fame died with Pope John and it must stay that way. Now, go, both of you. I need to talk to her."

Prudently they fled, but I was bristling. I had heard the lawyer in Francesco, concerned more with preserving his reputation than mine. "You want me to slide back into anonymity to shield yourself," I accused. "Or perhaps you are jealous that I am recognized by other men."

"Being admired is a two-edged sword, Solange. The mob is fickle and might easily turn against you. One misstep and you will be in the papal prison. This new pope led the inquisition against the Cathars. He sentenced countless heretics to death. I want you alive, not dismembered and hung on the city gates. *Alive.* Do you hear, Solange? I cannot love a dead woman."

With these words, he regained my affection in an instant, for only half my heart had shut him out. Now that we had moved closer, his eyes rested on my belly, which had been swollen when he last saw it.

"Are you a mother now?"

I could not find the words to tell him there had been two deaths. "The child was stillborn."

"I am sorry." He gulped from his tumbler.

"The boy was yours, a beautiful, well-formed child who should have lived to give joy to us both."

His head fell into his hands. His eyes, when he finally lifted them to mine, were red. Now I did feel sorry for his grief, although it was a shadow of what my own had been. We had both lost a child we could have been proud of, a son who could have worn the Petrarch coat of arms. I had lost a daughter as well, a double grief, so deep I could not speak of it. He grabbed my hand and gripped it, a link to the pain that neither of us could fully share in words.

"I thought of you frequently in my seclusion in the Vaucluse," he admitted. "It is a lonely place, conducive to writing prose, but not so much to poetry. For that I seem to need you near me."

At this admission, our hearts lightened, though neither of us could manage a whole smile. "I would like nothing better than to see your new poems," I said.

He fingered the mask that dangled on a ribbon from my belt. "Your silver visor shines like moonlight. Will you wear this to some Mardi gras revels? Perhaps one of your admirers will escort you."

"Do not mock, Francesco."

"If you'll wear your mask for me, I will take you to one of the city's finest livrées."

I hesitated. "You cannot wish to be seen in public with me."

He held my chin to study my face. "You are handsome enough to display anywhere, and tonight Cardinal Colonna is hosting a musical fête. It is the last evening before Lent," he coaxed, "a night we have often spent together."

Twenty-six

A S DUSK FELL, Francesco led me into a courtyard created by buildings of various heights and styles. Each grand in itself, they had been connected into a palace by Cardinal Colonna. Banners of bright cloth flapped above our heads, night-flowers released their fragrance, and liveried servants offered fortified wine and savouries. Everything, even Francesco's ravaged knuckles, looked intriguing through my filigree mask. Musicians were playing a clear, sweet melody. I had sometimes heard a new music seeping out of Avignon's livrées, but none so deeply stirring, so profoundly moving, as this, since it was the first time Francesco had invited me to an assembly.

Courtiers arrived—proud men in fur-lined gowns with silver zonas—whose visors were tied to their arms, like Francesco's. The men remained in the courtyard while the noblewomen, in flowing garments that signalled their wealth and lineage, ascended the marble stairs towards the open gallery. Could I never dress in fashion? Although my mask was like the other women's, I had worn a robe of rosato, a noble colour, only to discover that the Avignonnaises now favoured pastels. Cardinal Colonna emerged from an arch arm in arm with a bishop, saluted Francesco, then crossed the courtyard to greet the dignitaries. The bishop, a singularly large man in a tent-sized habit, came straight towards us.

"The poet who is afraid of thunder!" He clamped Francesco's hand in his own and bobbed it up and down.

Francesco kissed his friend three times on the cheek, then drew me beside him. "You have heard me speak of Giacomo di Colonna."

"The eminent bishop of Lombez." I tipped my forehead in deference. "Francesco tells me you are like a brother to him."

"Your Latin is almost as good as mine," the bishop said. "This must be your scribe, Francesco, the one with the extraordinary penmanship. What a profusion of chestnut hair! And what startling blue eyes. More French than Italian, I believe. Greet some of my brother's guests while I show her the Colonna tapestry." The bishop took my arm to steer me into one of the grand buildings. "You must call me Giacomo when no one else is listening. I admit to great curiosity about you."

I gave him a wide smile, for we were alone now. "Since your name is Giacomo, perhaps you can explain something about Italian men. Why do so many of their names begin with G?"

Giacomo laughed—an open-mouthed bellow. "I like you, my dear. Francesco reports that you have the most stimulating effect on him. He says you provoke him to write his best poetry. You must know that Francesco covets being made poet laureate. He even hinted to my brother, the cardinal, that he might nominate him!"

"How did your brother respond?"

"He grunted and ignored Francesco. He is good at grunting, my brother. Now, observe this cunning doorway. My brother has been collecting buildings since he moved his household here. Fifteen have been joined into this palace, which is the equal of any in Avignon. See this decorative frieze? The craftsman is from Florence."

"Like Francesco," I said, running my hand over the tiles.

"Yes, my brother has also collected Francesco—a brilliant acquisition, for he is ascending like a comet. We will go up here." He stood aside to let me proceed him up a stairway and into a grand hall, where musicians, dancers, and jesters had been painted on the wooden beams. Along the walls, trompe l'œil arches were supported by columns. "The family symbol," he said, tapping one of the painted columns. "The artisans hate it. There is only so much they can do with a stiff, manly column. Now, here is what we came to see, the Colonna history." He described each scene in the large tapestry for me, skipping modestly over his own heroism at the San Marcello church in Rome to dwell on his brother's investiture as cardinal. Servants were ferrying elaborate platters past us into the banqueting hall. The bishop plucked two pasties from the top of a roasted heron, one for each of us. "Sweet and fresh. We are saying farewell to meat in style, for every type of game and flesh is here."

He escorted me down the marble staircase as if I were a favoured guest. Perhaps it was a masquerade to fool the guests into believing that he, like most bishops, kept a courtesan. The torches had been lit in the courtyard and braziers drove off the Lenten chill. I looked in vain for Francesco while the bishop sought out his nephew Agapito, whose charms had lured Gherardo into such a bed of trouble. The cardinals were dressed like seigneurs, the chaplains like knights, and the youths, who lurked beneath the arches, sported smaller versions of their father's arms. Foreign courtiers congregated in the middle, where their conversation rose and fell in Italian, Spanish, and Flemish. An acrobat twisted in the air, landed, and did handsprings across the marble pavement. In the midst of it all was Cardinal Colonna, his bearing erect, his voice loud, as he introduced Francesco—who seemed to have forgotten I was there—to this great man and that.

A tabor was struck, the musicians took their places, and the noblewomen hung over the balustrade above us to listen. A gypsy dangled a vielle impatiently until the courtyard quietened, then whipped the instrument to his shoulder to fiddle wildly, joined by a timorous flute, then bells and bagpipe. After a time, the carnival instruments retired and a musician plucked his lute. A youth began to sing, his voice neither bass nor tenor, but something in between.

"*Pace non trovo, et non ò da far guerra,*" he sang. "*E temo, et spero. Et ardo, et son un ghiaccio.*"

I took in a long breath, then lingered on the exhalation. I glimpsed Francesco's tense face across the courtyard and wished myself beside him, though I could not catch his eye.

Bishop Giacomo was holding my elbow gallantly again. "*Fearing and hoping, burning and freezing. Caught in a snare, blind and mute, hating and loving, laughing and weeping.* Have you guessed the author?"

The sonnet was superb, exquisitely set to music and exquisitely sung, but I had never been so torn between admiration for Francesco's gifts and anger at his subject. While the lute echoed the theme, I said, "This poem is quite new. Francesco has never spoken so frankly of his worship for Laura."

"A great lyricist, yes, but a buffoon to waste himself on this tug-of-war. It vexes me to see such vast talent tied up in agonizing knots."

I liked the bishop's opinions as much as I liked him. The song over, the performers gestured towards Francesco, who bowed and was recognized by the courtiers. Francesco raised his palm towards the Avignonnaises, and the gallery erupted in activity as the ladies pushed one of their company to the balustrade. Pale-skinned with a cap of pearls, the masked woman had the straw hair that troubadours called flaxen but I had always thought was limp and ugly.

"So that is Laura," said Bishop Giacomo. "I was mistaken. She is not just a pun on *laurel* after all."

Around me, the men—courtiers, churchmen, dignitaries, fools every one—seemed to be coming to the same conclusion as they praised her pallid beauty. They begged her to reveal her identity, their requests ascending harmoniously. Assenting at last, high above them on the gallery, Laura removed her mask to reveal her face. In the courtyard, the talk buzzed and swelled, until the men identified the crests on her sleeves as the de Noves lozenges linked with the eight-pointed sun of the de Sades.

Now Laura surprised us all. Even to my critical eye, her fluttering gloves, edged in gold, held a poetry of movement as she signalled for the guests to be silent. She took off one glove and held up a pale hand. Without any accompaniment, she sang Francesco's lyric *O bella man*— her voice pure, disciplined, and flawless. When the song ended, she dipped her knee to the listening audience. Did Francesco still think her voice was lark-song, or was he now comparing her to a nightingale? I could not see his reaction, since he had positioned himself to face the gallery.

Bishop Giacomo whispered, "It is Madame de Sade. Laura is a real muse, not a figment of his imagination. The face is divine."

Laura his muse? Waves of angry red swamped my vision. "But her nose is unfortunate."

The bishop laughed. "Her husband is now gripping her elbow like a grandfather. With that scowl, he does not need a mask. Hugues de Sade must do better than that with the seigneurs watching him. Look at the crowd around our poet now!"

The guests were elbowing up to Francesco, who did not even glance in my direction. The noblewomen flew down the marble steps to celebrate his triumph in quick, shrill exclamations. De Sade came down the staircase with Laura displayed on his arm, her sleeves flaunting her rank and title, though her smile was forced. Beneath her elegant surcot, her gold *this* and silver *that*, I detected the covert bulge of a new infant, though Francesco probably saw only the ivory complexion and delicate feet, not the ripe female form between.

De Sade dropped his nose a notch as he neared Francesco, a begrudging nod to the artist all were honouring, then wheeled his wife off by her elbow. The musician resumed playing. This was the signal for jesters and tumblers to leap from the arches, and for the tabor, vielle, and rattling drum to overtake the lute with a fervour that prompted even the proper Avignonnaises to lift up their heels to dance with the Italians.

Bishop Giacomo shouted in my ear. "What a spectacle! How will Francesco handle this attention? If he secludes himself to write new poems drooling over Laura, it will have an odious effect on his disposition. He will become more monkish and you and I will be deprived of his generous friendship. Madame de Sade may be his muse, but he is better served by you, for you can quench the desire you awaken." His gaze settled on me. "Yes, I know the nature of your relationship with him. Your eyes are watering, my dear. Wipe them quickly with your sleeve."

After a few more dances, Cardinal Colonna invited his guests to sweep up the marble staircase to the banqueting room. Soon the courtyard had emptied except for the musicians, and Francesco noticed me standing alone. He hesitated, looked around him, then came towards me. I grasped how it was: he had brought me here because I was masked, deserted me when the courtyard was full of nobles, and reclaimed me now only because it was empty. Had he enlisted Bishop Giacomo's help to keep me entertained? Woven into Francesco's tunic, I saw the Petrarch arms, although the Colonna column overshadowed them. My father, even if he had been a pope, had not bequeathed me so much as a bastard falcon to sew upon my sleeve.

"What did you think of my new poem?" Francesco asked.

What did I think? I had loathed seeing him swear fealty to Laura. However, he had invited me to my first assembly and I hoped to attend many more. If Francesco could raise himself with the cardinal's help, I could raise myself with Francesco's. "You have pleased important men tonight," I conceded.

He looked at the knuckles he had smashed in the Two Ravens. "But what am I? A medallion on Colonna's belt. A poet who composes lyrics to entertain his guests. I need to break from the cardinal to write what has never yet been written. While the guests are at dinner, I will show you something."

We went through a darkened arch and up a low-ceilinged staircase. At the landing, he unlocked a vaulted chamber with manuscripts spread across every shelf and table.

"The cardinal's library. Look for yourself—not a single book authored by Francesco di Petrarca de Florentia!"

He waved a hand dismissively over the largest collection of manuscripts I had ever seen. I fingered one after another while he sat sullenly on top of a table. The room was not just a library—it was an atelier. An array of the finest tools sat ready on the widest carrel. One librarian-scribe would work there, with room for a second at a smaller, unused carrel.

"I would give anything to be a scribe in such a library. You promised that you would commend me, Francesco."

"I grant you have the skill, but no prelate would employ a woman." When he saw that he had hurt me, he added, "Solange, use your wits— these manuscripts are for the cardinal and his nephews. Did you never think what books rich men collect? Many of these are secular. Look at this . . ."

I examined a page that illustrated the workings of the human body: on the right a naked man, and on the left a woman. Did they represent Adam and Eve, or the denizens of Avignon's brothels? The mask bit into my flesh like a reprimand: you are neither of this house nor of these people. I still carried a whiff of lamp fuel from the night of thunder. Tonight had shown me that Francesco would never recommend me to a well-placed cleric or chevalier. Nothing I could do, not wearing the finest cloth, or speaking several languages, or being his favourite scribe, would earn me the status Laura was born with.

"This is a more worthy book." He thrust his hand into his shirt to dig out a small volume. "One that has much affected me, Saint Augustine's *Confessions*. When I have finished this, I will lend it to you."

I had already read the *Confessions* and knew that Augustine had turned his back on his loving mistress to become a prurient cleric.

"I would rather read Ovid's *Art of Love*," I said. "Remember how we took turns reading it aloud?"

The *Confessions* snapped closed. "Solange, you must listen. If we continue in this way, we will cling together in hell like Paolo and Francesca. If I am to write well about Laura, I must drive lust from my thoughts." He shoved the book inside his shirt, like armour to protect his heart.

"And how will you do that?"

He went to the window. When he was certain that no one was below to see us, he drew me beside him to point to the giant white dome in the night sky some leagues to the north.

"I shall climb that barren mountain. Mont Ventoux—the tallest of the Dentelles."

Twenty-seven

Five times planned and five postponed, the Ventoux climb took place the following year. Francesco set out on horseback with Gherardo and two servants. They arrived at Malaucène on Saint Mark's Eve, rested a day, then rose at dawn to ascend the windy mountain from the north. Gherardo took the steepest, most direct route, but Francesco, carrying the *Confessions* as a penance for his lust, took a gradual, easier path. He found Gherardo awaiting him on higher ground, well rested and amused, for what had looked like snow from the foothills was the barest stone. On the descent, they lost their footing in thin-soled boots that sharpened every rock, and reached the base at moonrise. Back at the inn, Francesco wrote one of his formal letters, evoking each moment of the climb with a poet's clarity.

All this I learnt when Francesco brought the letter to the Cheval Blanc with a request for a fair copy. He insisted that I read it while he sat opposite, observing my face.

"Why do you ask me to copy such a vexing letter?"

"Because your bâtarde is superlative. You know I will pay you the going rate."

But it was more than that. It was a coward's way of telling me that, like Augustine, he wished to put his carnal past behind him. I shoved the sheet beneath my other copy work and let Francesco find his own way down the stairs.

Spring arrived, then summer, with its jeering heat and constant whine of cicadas. It cheered me that in spite of Francesco's resolve to tame his flesh he could not stay away from the Cheval Blanc. He would slip in before curfew to lie in my arms, then talk long hours into the darkening night. As soon as curfew ended at dawn, he let himself out, invisible even to the dyers along the canal. Our lives had fallen, once again, into a comfortable pattern, but I wanted more. Sometimes, I could scarcely breathe from the fierceness of my love for him.

All his talk about Saint Augustine had given me an idea. I knew that before Augustine had converted, while he was still a slave of passion, he had fathered a son on his mistress. He had such regard for the boy that he raised him in the church. All men wanted sons to carry on their family line—why not Francesco? His lust was wholly mine and I would make it serve me. I had grieved for my dead twins long enough and desired another child—a son who would bear the Petrarch coat of arms. In such a way, I would latch on to Francesco Petrarch, man of letters, so firmly that he could never shake me. The closer I could ally myself with his growing fame, the more I would secure my future.

But how could I conceive? Ludicrously cautious, Francesco now brought rue to crumble into my wine against conception. Autumn arrived, but I was no closer to becoming a mother and my frustration was acute. On the day of little Saint Dionysius, who was always getting himself confused with Dionysius the god, I was in the nave of Saint Pierre singing vespers when Francesco whispered in my ear, "Come with me. You say these same psalms every week."

We walked along the rue de la Balance towards the river and the odour of fish entrails, stopping to raid a tree for some green figs the size of a baby's fist. He went into a shop, emerged with a jug of vernaccia, pulled out the stopper, and took a long pull. We sat on a low wall side by side. It was the rich hind part of the day, with a sky like yellow cream fresh from the cow.

"These are the figs that are ripe when green." I bit into one, fed him the rest, then bit into another.

"The shopkeeper saw you and asked me whether you had seen any more visions. He was as unkempt as a neglected horse. You are too well known by such men, Solange. You must be more discreet."

"These men are harmless. I am often recognized in the low streets along the river and canals."

Was he ashamed of me or fascinated? He seemed unsure himself, vacillating from one to the other. He took another pull, splashing the drink over his mantle.

"This is unlike you," I said. "What is wrong?"

"I have made no progress on the anthem to Italy that Cardinal Colonna insists that I compose. All I have is a title, *Italia Mia*. I am desperate to see Rome, but the cardinal will not send me there. I have written so few lyrics that I will be forgotten before the decade is out. You have seen the most recent ones. What is wrong with them?"

Were his ears drunk enough to hear the truth? "They are trite, Francesco. Even Mont Ventoux was not large enough to wedge itself between Laura and your sterile passion for her. A glimpse of her at a window, a brush with her at an assembly, a nod or a glare—they feed your lovesickness. The sky lights up when she smiles, darkens when she frowns. Does the sun have so little to do in poetry? Doesn't it need to ripen crops or cure the hay?"

"My poetry does sound foolish when you sum it up like that." With his mouth on the jug again, he looked like his brother.

"Give up Laura," I ventured. "She is drying up your verses and you as well. Do you think drinking that will help?"

"It might help engender poems." At last, a smile from him. "After all, it stimulated Dionysius, the god of wine and fertility. And vernaccia is the favourite drink of popes."

Who father many sons, I thought. I tipped the jug to drizzle some of the spirits down my own throat, warmed by the thought of children being fathered. Since Francesco would never give me permission to have a child, I must act on my own and ask forgiveness later. Tonight he was mine, by what miracle I did not know, but how to get him near a bed? We walked towards the Rhône with frequent stops to lighten the jug. Near the bridge, we found a fisherman selling live eels from a basin.

Francesco dangled a thick one by its tail. "This size?"

I pointed to another, giggling. "That one will fit better." Francesco inserted the eel head first into the half-full jug. "It won't take long to drown," I said.

We sat near some pilings at the river's edge until the city quietened and we heard the Pope's trumpet shout the curfew. From now on, the city watch would be vigilant. The moon was rising and the night sounds began—an angry squirrel, or a nightjar flying with its mouth open to capture clicking moths?

"The gates are closing," I said, "but we can walk around the wall to the Cheval Blanc."

"I cannot stay there overnight again."

"You've stayed there often enough. No one in the tavern cares."

"*I care.* I wish it were otherwise, Solange, but it is this way."

We stared at the drunken eel in the glass jug and listened to the *slap-slap* of a boatman's punt about to slip its rope and escape downriver. A pouch dangled from the zona at Francesco's waist. Bitter rue, I guessed. So he did want to bed me, but where?

I caught an idea, leapt up. "Let's go out on the Rhône."

We scrambled through the swamp grass, almost sinking into a quagmire before we reached the punt, which was filled with green rushes. He untangled the rope and I climbed in with the jug, wedging it so it would not roll, then stood on the till to pole us out of the mud. After a few shoves, Francesco got aboard as well, wet to his middle. He felt around his waist for the pouch, but it was missing since I had untied the laces to rid us of it.

Soon the river was too deep to pole, so we sat beside each other, taking turns with the single oar to keep the craft moving in a straight line. From the poplars alongside the river came the *chink-clink* of roosting blackbirds. The river seized the punt and drew it into the channel faster than we wished.

"The current is too strong," he said. "Unless we steer towards the bank, we'll get carried down to Arles."

Eventually, by rowing and drifting, we approached an island about a quarter league downstream. We aimed at a poplar overhanging the river, went past it, and missed three of its fellows, until only a single tree was left, the last on the island. As we approached the tree, I stood on the till to pole us to shore. With a tremendous lunge, Francesco caught a low branch and pulled us into the shallows, knocking leaves over the water's surface.

"We'll moor here," he said, his hair sticking to his forehead in sweaty clumps, "and make our way back at dawn."

While we were fighting the current, the light had dimmed from twilight to evening to full night. Once we had secured the rope, we lay back in the punt as if this was where we had been aiming all along. The moon was high, the air mild and warm. How many more nights would Francesco spend with me? Even now, winter clouds were moving in. He extracted the dead eel, sliced some rounds, then squeezed the rest back into the jug. After we had eaten, he drew me into his lap, and cradled me in his arms while I traced his ribs with my fingertips. As my fingers crept lower, his belly tightened. Each breath rising to his chest was quicker than the last.

He stopped my fingers with a kiss. "Why can't I master my lust? Even before I come to you, I imagine how we will be, together. And you can no more restrain yourself than I can. I believe you thrive on it. Saint Augustine would say . . ."

I leaned over the gunwale, already knowing Augustine's low opinion of women. "I want more than desire from you, Francesco. I want to be one with you in spirit as well."

"I can never give you everything you want from me."

Perhaps this was true. I let my hand trail in the river, and inhaled the scent of weeds and marshland. Slow, black—but far from still, the water was sucking down the fallen leaves. A whorl of spume drifted past, got caught, plummeted into the depths. "This whirlpool is making me dizzy."

"It is the autumnal equinox today. Stare at the circling water until you feel its pull."

He had said the words too eagerly. I knew now what he was after. "I don't wish to incite more visions, Francesco, for they are troubling beyond their worth."

The whirlpool forgotten, I somehow had got upon my back, my spine nestling in the soft rushes. Francesco bunched up his mantle and tucked it beneath me. In his eyes, I saw our unborn son. My skin pricked, my skirts rode up, and my thighs fell open, begging his hips to push against my own. My indwelling spirit rose, arched upwards to the night, and fell upon the sharpness of desire. An owl shrieked, a child quickened, a tear shook from my eye. A feral scent drifted past—fox, or more likely stoat.

We lay quietly afterwards, unwilling to be parted. Then, cajoling and caressing, he began to speak the Italian of his native soil, the same words over and over, guiding me into illimitable darkness, into my mind's fecund whirling loam. An idea arrived, but I could not grasp hold of it—too slippery and dark it was for me. But I had spoken aloud, for I could see by his face that I had brought out of that furtive depth a daimon phrase that pleasured the poet in him. Beneath the sheltering branches, I uttered a stream of lyrical nonsense, muddled with the old tongue. What did I say? Enough, for his brow furrowed with the strain of remembering until he could capture it in verse.

He rolled on his back beside me, his fingers still holding mine, but his mind transported elsewhere, probably to a new poem. As the branches sagged into the river, the boat swayed, and the eel sloshed in the vernaccia. It made me think of the eel pie that Francesco had fed me in the cemetery. Had he intended tonight's eel as a stimulant also? He knew that strong food elicited disturbing visions in me. He so seldom allowed impulse to guide him that I suspected that he had planned this séance for the equinox, when day and night were of equal influence, because he needed raw ideas for verse.

Still, what did I mind? I, too, had taken what I most desired and I was now carrying Francesco's seed. I would bind him to me with a son who carried the Petrarch name, for in Francesco's eagerness to get a poem from me, he had forgotten the necessity for the pouch of rue that had dropped into the murky shallows. Instead of the bitter herb crumbled in vernaccia, I had savoured the slippery and most fertile eel.

Twenty-eight

RICH WITH LAND, the convent of the Cordeliers was sheltered from the Sorgue canal by a thick wall of trees, where I had arranged to meet Francesco on this wintry day, the shortest of the year. The sacristan walked past me, ringing a hand bell to call the nuns to prayer, without violating the rule of silence to ask if I had lost my way. The gardener turned the soil cleanly with her spade, drove it into the ground, scraped the earth from her hands. Here, in this chaste peace, I was overcome with longing for Clairefontaine and the faith that had comforted me as a child. Here, like Luke's sinner, the Magdalene, I might be forgiven for conceiving a child out of love.

I entered the chapel so I could listen to the nuns chanting their psalms in the adjoining church. The old Avignonnais buried their dead in private chapels like this, while in the cimetière des pauvres, pigs rooted up corpses too shallowly interred. As I crossed myself for my two babes and Conmère, boots scuffed behind me—Francesco, his eyes adjusting to the poor light, his palm resting on an eight-pointed sun cut into the wall, as if it had rested there before. I recognized the bold mercantile crest of one of Avignon's wool companies. This was the chapel of the de Sades.

The gardener's shoes knocked along the gravel path until her round face appeared in the chapel doorway. "Madonna Laura?" she addressed me. "Ser Petrarca?"

I cringed at the gardener's mistake. After her pupils dilated, she would see my hair—the colour of Rhône wine and as untameable as the river when its currents were winter-fierce.

"It's all right, Sister," he said. "This is my scribe. We won't disrupt your midday prayers." He gave me a sharp push into the garden, steering me towards a stone bench in the trees alongside the canal. "This is where I intended us to talk."

"You've been meeting Laura in that chapel."

"She has been gracious enough to meet me in this convent. I know you do not understand, Solange, but if I do not glimpse her or hear her voice, my poems have no substance. You told me yourself that they were trite." He unfurled a sheet of paper. "Be honest—is this one any better?"

I read the poem while he waited, eager for my opinion. The vigorous new canzone praised a woman's eyes that sounded like mine, except they were not blue but tantalizingly vague in colour, *soavemente tra 'l bel nero e 'l bianco*, neither black nor white. In short, they were dull grey, like Laura's.

"It's a fine poem," I said, "but you've rushed the words together. You have enough here for several poems, not just one."

He read the lines aloud, rehearsed metaphors, asked for my advice on vowels and rhymes, even admitted that my trance had given him the heated distillate from which he had extracted phrase after phrase of purest song. Having stolen an alchemist's word-hoard from me, he saw nothing wrong in using this plunder to clothe and feather his bella donna. The praise was nauseating, but these days everything nauseated me. The cloth-dyers' vats. The odour of the haunches crackling on the tavern's spit that wafted up through the floorboards. Even the cheap ink that I used to copy documents for everyone except Francesco. Because I was several weeks with child.

"You will soon have something else to occupy your mind. Like half the prelates in the city, you have fathered a child out of wedlock. I am carrying your son, Francesco." I was expecting an argument, but got none. He reached over to hold my hand. Having lost one son, he seemed more willing that I might bear him another.

"How do you know it is a boy?"

"I felt his soul enter his body on the fortieth day. He was conceived the night we took the punt out on the Rhône."

He sat quietly a moment, taking the news in. "I hope this child lives longer than the last one. I would be loath to know another son of mine had died."

My son arrived in cherry time. He was big and I laboured at his birthing. His cry was strong, his soul very much his own. Overjoyed, I sent for Francesco, eager to share the perfection of our child, from his spiky black hair to his small wrinkled feet. Francesco scrutinized him, as if searching for the Petrarch lineaments in his olive skin and prominent nose. Satisfied, he lifted his son to the window, so he could hear the angelus.

"We will call him Giovanni," he said.

I agreed, hoping my son would soon receive the surname Petrarch, although Francesco was deeply troubled about the birth, afraid it would sully his reputation. Indeed, a few weeks later, Gherardo tumbled into my chamber to look for Francesco, announcing, "I have been at Saint Agricol's, where the talk is that *the grand Petrarch has fathered a child on a common mistress.*" Then, noticing that I was as distressed as my crying son, he added, "I am sorry, Solange, but that is what they are saying."

A look of torture creased Francesco's features. "Who was there, Gherardo?"

"Cardinal Colonna, for one. He defended your honour, denying that such a thing had taken place. However, others came forwards, the poet Jean La Porte amongst them, who were happy to confirm the rumour. The worst of it was that Hugues de Sade was there with Laura, who was startled by the revelation."

Francesco's shoulders knotted and he rubbed the back of his neck. Word would travel through the nobility, the upper clergy, even the papal palace, until Avignon herself laughed at her favourite poet for no more fault than being human. Hope leapt inside me, in spite of the humiliation, in spite of Francesco's pain. This pressure—this fear of public opinion—might speed him towards acknowledging his son, and I wanted nothing more than for Giovanni and me to live under the same roof as Francesco.

The months passed and Francesco visited us infrequently. Sometimes he did not even remove his outer garments, staying only long enough to check that Giovanni was healthy and to dry himself at my hearth. It was not so much that Francesco scorned us—for his letters were kind and apologetic—but that Laura was furious and he was distraught.

"No man can be content," he wrote, "until he rests in his grave."

How had his distress swelled so quickly to thoughts of self-murder? As the months passed, the poems he sent me to copy showed Laura's ill humour growing, verse by verse. She refused to see Francesco, and not even the beauty of his son, for Giovanni was thriving, could distract Francesco from that wounding blow. The whole fantasy he had created—how he had met Laura, admired her from afar, spied on her combing her golden hair, returned her glove—was now forced to embrace her jealous wrath.

From this came a canzone frottola, blistered and fretted with pain, which he sent to me to copy. *Chi non à l'auro, o 'l perde, spenga la sete sua con un bel vetro . . . If a man cannot have gold, then he must quench his thirst with a glass of something cheaper.* I was *bel vetro*, an insult so vulgar I refused to copy, even read, his poetry for days. But when I was able to face the canzone again, I found myself admiring the raw, scalding lumps of twisted feeling. I could imagine the blottings, re-visionings, cross-outs, and additions—the number of sheets devoured! He had unleashed a creative force so tortured that he needed a different glass to pour it into. He had progressed beyond Dante's *dolce stil novo* to stony rimes about a stony-hearted woman. I took up my pen to tell him so, praising his poetry as *rime petrose* and encouraging him in this important new direction.

With Laura shunning him, his aversion to the city grew. According to his letters, it was full of cutpurses, coinsmiths, foreigners, the begging poor and the arrogant rich. At Fontaine-de-Vaucluse, near the rock pool we had bathed in, he found a house where he could write in silence. His letters praised the healthy diet, the noble peasants, the salubrious atmosphere. I wrote to tell him that when Giovanni was a little older, we wished to live there also, so Giovanni could flourish in the country air, as I had done at Clairefontaine. Some of my hopes I kept to myself for the present. In the Vaucluse house, out of reach of the city's guilds, I would be able to set up a scriptorium. With Francesco's help, I could earn commissions from other learned men to create belles-lettres that I would be proud to sign.

Even in Avignon, even without Francesco, everything gave me pleasure: the morning coolness after a summer night, the scent of clean pressed linen, the jabber of children at play. I nursed Giovanni to sleep in my arms, dreaming of his chasing geese and finding berries in the straw. When he cried, I stroked the fontanelle on his skull where the bones did not yet meet, or held him at the casement to watch the paddlewheel, or walked along the canal jiggling him over my shoulder so he could see the cloth-workers at their trade.

Francesco sent letters from the Vaucluse for me to copy—dangerous, embittered letters in which he urged Benedict XII to return the papacy to Rome. I made the copies in haste, warning Francesco that Benedict was sending roots deep into foreign soil. I told him that I sometimes carried Giovanni as far as Doms rock so he could peer down at the hundreds of workers demolishing the Pope's old palace and rebuilding it, wing by wing. The tour du Pape was growing from the dungeon, with its nine-foot-thick walls, to the treasury, the camerlengo's chamber, the Pope's own bedchamber, the library, and the châtelet at the top.

I, too, was building—a bastion of love—for I knew that Francesco must soon acknowledge his son and his son's mother. Giovanni could now push a stool to the window to watch men pulling hand-carts, boys riding donkeys, and friars crossing the plank below us to seek refreshment in the tavern. He was not quick to learn but grew into a happy child, eager for a romp, who wanted only to be fed and pampered.

Twenty-nine

ONE AFTERNOON when Giovanni was three, I returned to my chamber, coated with the mud and stench of the city, to find my servant Des-neiges lying on my bed, fingering some coins. Francesco must have given them to her, for he was reading Augustine's *Confessions* to Giovanni, who was pretending to listen, his eyes big and round, though he could not understand a word.

"Maman!"

Giovanni jumped down on his chubby legs to point at his doll, perched on a shelf high above his head. I guessed that Francesco had put it there, since he thought it an unsuitable toy. I lifted Giovanni to rescue it, and kissed him under his ear as I set him down. The child had borne enough and so had I. For three years, I had been coaxing Francesco to share his country house with us, but we still lived in the filth of Avignon. Whenever I asked, Francesco would reply that it was too hot, or too cold, or too windy for the boy to come just yet.

"Des-neiges," I said, "take Giovanni along the canal to play."

After they had gone, I tried to find a soft beginning. "Why don't you discuss your poems with me anymore? You used to be so eager for my ideas that you put me into trances to steal them from me."

"A man cannot think in such a noisy chamber."

"Giovanni is now talking. He needs a father who will listen to him."

"We will become better acquainted since it is time for him to learn his letters."

"You scarcely know his age, Francesco."

"Giovanni must be weaned and have his curls cut off. He must learn his rôle in life."

"What rôle? The love-child of a poet and his mistress?"

Francesco adjusted the hang of his silver zona. "He's destined to be a canon."

This hit me sidewise. "Even if he's as little suited to it as you are? You, who beget children you will not acknowledge?"

"He will be suited to it if he is my son."

"Who else's would he be?"

"Men go in and out of the tavern as if it were a stable."

"For the new harlot in the next chamber, as you are well aware!"

"My son cannot be raised in a brothel. You know the truth of it, though you feign otherwise."

This pierced like a shard of glass. I had been betrayed by Francesco, by this city of men, by this church that turned honest women into courtesans because canons were forbidden to marry. "He lives here because you have provided us no other home. You have made him a bastard."

"That's a hard name for a little boy, Solange."

"You have given me no better name to call him by."

"When the time is right, I will have Giovanni legitimized."

This was what I had been wanting, for Giovanni had need of his father's love. "Will you take us to the Vaucluse then?"

He glanced towards the door, eager to be gone. How much longer would he make us wait to share his pastoral retreat? I recalled our excursion to Fontaine-de-Vaucluse. A day hot and windless, a night cool and full of odd, compelling sounds. In the neglected chapel, we had exchanged our sacred promise.

I tried again. "Why do we speak in anger, our best selves forgotten? I only wish to see more of you, Francesco. Put your vanity aside and take us with you. In the quiet of the Vaucluse, our betrothal will be as good as a marriage. We won't be subject to scrutiny as we are here. With your help, I could set up a scriptorium. Perhaps we could have a daughter . . ." An unattractive pleading had crept into my voice. "I know you love me, Francesco."

"With my flesh, but not with my soul. That belongs to Madonna Laura." He looked tired, as if he had explained it many times before without me hearing. "If I'm to pursue fame, it must be now. I have received an invitation from the Roman Senate to be crowned poet laureate in Rome."

"You have much craved this recognition! Remember my predictive dream so many years ago?"

"How can I forget? It was the day we bathed in the pool at Fontaine-de-Vaucluse. Now I must return to my house there to write my coronation speech in solitude. This is the greatest task I have yet faced. You must see that this comes first?"

Yes, I did see. All else was secondary to this great ambition, which I cursed myself for fostering. He would rise so high that he could never reach down his hand to pull me up beside him.

He was rubbing his neck, trying to find the words he needed. "I must turn my back on the past. I have been weighed down too much of late."

He meant Giovanni and me. Eyes stinging, I escaped down the stairs, but tripped part-way and rolled head over heels. I picked myself up to stumble across the plank and along the canal, my skull ringing from the fall as I searched for Giovanni.

I could not find him—not near the paddlewheels, or moat, or anywhere Des-neiges might have taken him to play with the dyers'

children. I ran down the alleys, checking the impasses and open doorways in the quarter, believing that I saw Giovanni in every begging,
motherless child, until I had no will to deceive myself any further.
When I returned home, hours later, sodden with rain and blasted by
cold, my chamber was empty. Des-neiges's corner had been cleared of
her few worldly goods.

I did not understand until I noticed something else—something
that caused me to collapse on my knees in bottomless despair. Giovanni's
little mattress was lumpy, although I had smoothed it that morning
with my own hands. Before Francesco had taken Giovanni, before
Giovanni had been torn from everything he loved, he had escaped from
his father long enough to hide his doll beneath his mattress so that his
father could not find it.

I was kneeling on the floor, clutching the doll so hard that the
buckwheat was bursting from a seam, when I observed that Francesco
had left his *Confessions* of Saint Augustine. Had he dropped it in his
rush, or left it for my edification? A strangled sob came from my very
gut. I grabbed the loathsome Augustine and skimmed it across the
floorboards with such force of rage that I drove a splinter deep beneath
my thumbnail. I rocked myself back and forth, mourning the loss of
my beloved child as the blood spurted eagerly from my thumb.

Thirty

I WAS REDUCED TO a cold hearth and a smoking lamp for company. At first, a stifling languor overtook me, an inability to think or even care whether I could think or not. Then gusts of wild imaginings attacked—and I ran mad. What day was it? My book of hours, by which I told the time, was face down in the papers on the floor. Had Giovanni been injured? Was he still alive? Sometimes, while he had slept, I feared that his breath had stopped. I would touch his quickly beating heart and be reassured by breath as soft as thistledown. Even now, his scent was on his linen and his cry rang in my ears. Fear chased me mercilessly, preventing me from taking any rest. My only relief was in mindless copying—one word, line, page after another.

The door banged open and Guido entered in his canon lawyer's gown. He built up the fire, threw open the shutters, and winced at the squalor.

"What have you found out, Guido? Where is my son?"

"With Francesco."

"But where? At Fontaine-de-Vaucluse?"

"Not there. Some distance off, in a secluded place. Francesco will not tell me, but I will try to find out for you."

This was not enough—this relief, this joy that Giovanni was safe. I wanted to know more, but Guido was descending to the tavern. When he returned with bread, thick soup, and a flagon of wine, I waved the food away. "I don't care about myself. Tell me more about my son."

He sat near me to examine my thumb. "This is festering, Solange."

I looked at it without much interest. Enflamed by the splinter, the thumb had swollen like a wasp's nest on a branch. Guido held my wrist with one hand and picked up my miséricorde with the other.

"Scream if you like," he said, "but do not jerk, or you might lose your thumb."

He split the skin with the knife, then drew his fingers up my thumb, removing the case of dead skin, filled with pus and the rotting sliver, in one pull. The new thumb beneath was red and half the size. He bandaged it with gauze, and tied the ends snugly.

"Keep it bound even if it throbs." He reached into his gown. "Francesco sent this for you."

I snatched it from him: a child's handprint pressed onto the paper. Smeared, as if Giovanni had been wriggling while Francesco took the print. The letter with it assured me of Giovanni's well-being, but the same cruel ink, the same cold pen, announced that his father intended to keep and raise him.

I cried for my lost child, clinging to Guido in desperation, weeping harder because of his kindness. After a time, our embrace became more sensual and Guido gave me to know, by pressing himself against me, how I had aroused him, asking me wordlessly to ease his own swelling. How could I refuse? I was not made of adamant or stone. I did not wish to condemn him to lovesickness, for I knew its pain. He undressed me reverently, kneeling at a shrine long venerated from afar. After we had consummated this strange, needful love, he filled a tub from the hot kettle and sponged me with soapy water. Then he combed my wet hair, dressed me in a clean shift, and fed me the soup, one spoonful at a time. I asked him to sleep beside me to chase away the suffocating cauchemar of deep night.

And so Guido Sette became my lover, but whether he cured me or I cured him I do not know. Perhaps he purged the madness attacking me, or perhaps I saved him from dying of lovesickness. Certainly, our lovemaking rekindled my will to live, for at heart I was a woman still, with a woman's desire and a woman's strength.

I washed Giovanni's doll, stuffed it with clean buckwheat, and sewed it new clothes. I kept the brush with Giovanni's hair, so that when he came to collect it at the general resurrection, we would be reunited for eternity. Until that day, I would be busy. My mourning was over and anger was now my fuel. Francesco was lost to me, but I would fight to regain my child by any means I could.

A few days before Mardi gras, Francesco's admirers gathered on the Rhône's main wharf to send him forth on his sea journey. His years of punning about Laura as his laurel wreath had finally borne fruit, for he was setting off to Rome for his coronation as poet laureate. I was on the wharf, but did not show myself until the Colonnas, up early to bestow large wishes and generous purses on Francesco, had taken their leave. I had not seen him since he had abducted Giovanni.

I approached Francesco and spoke quickly, so he would not turn away. "Take this for good fortune on your journey."

I gave him his cherished copy of Augustine's *Confessions*. He was so moved that he almost took my hand, but thought better of it in that public place. Why had I wished him well? Because I wanted his permission to visit my son. I looked around the wharf, but could not find the small person most dear to me.

"Where is Giovanni?"

"He is in good health in the country, far from the city's corruption." Francesco's voice was low and rational. "Your part is over, Solange. You nurtured your infant, but now I must educate my son."

Under my arm I was carrying Giovanni's blue jacket and his doll, for I had hoped—against all reason, I realized now—that my son would be brought to see his father off and I would capture him from his nurse's arms. Gherardo and Guido were undeceived by my pretence of good cheer. They moved to either side of me to prevent me from any rashness that might embarrass Francesco. Eager to leave, Francesco embraced his brother, then Guido, then entered the flat-bottomed barge, which would take him to Marseille to board a galley bound for Italy. The three of us, the truest of his friends, sat leadenly on the riverbank until the current seized the barge. We were acting as if shriven for Lent and embarking on forty days of fasting. Perhaps we were, for Francesco, who had been our meat and drink, was gone.

In misery, bereaved of my beloved son, I handed Gherardo the doll and mended jacket. "Will you give these to Giovanni?"

Gherardo held up the jacket, then wrapped it around the doll and shoved it back at me. "He has much finer garments now."

"I must see him, Gherardo."

"He lacks nothing in his daily care."

"Where is my child?" I shouted.

He picked blades of wet grass from his hose. "Francesco has not told me. He considers me a bad influence on my nephew. Do you think I would prevent a boy from reuniting with his mother? My own mother was everything to me. Noblemen usually care little for their bastards, but I will say this for Checco. He may be high-handed, but he writes his son's name as Giovanni di Petrarca de Florentia."

The name I had wanted my son to bear. Giovanni Petrarch, a poet laureate's son. Warmed by this thought, I admired a Lenten rose blooming in defiance of the cold. If I did not cripple myself with despair, I might find a way to hold my head up once again.

"It does not seem like carnival this year with Francesco away," said Gherardo. "However, it is a good time to be absent from Avignon, with Pope Benedict ill and the preferiti gathering to elect a successor."

At last Guido spoke. "Francesco has betrayed you for fame, Solange. You have sacrificed more than anyone for his success."

"As you say frequently," Gherardo said, cracking his knuckles.

"With Francesco in Italy, Solange will have little copy work and little income."

This was true. Since I had few coins put by, I must look for another vocation.

Gherardo was smirking at Guido. "I suppose you will keep sniffing at her while Francesco is away."

My ears stung. How had he discovered my intimacy with Guido? "There is no need to tell Francesco."

"I don't blame you for avenging his cold-heartedness by bedding his friend," said Gherardo. "Guido has been made a fool of as usual." Gherardo leaned on Guido's shoulder, forcing him to sit back down. "Good friend, one thing we can agree on—my brother is a blockhead where women are concerned. The laurel is going to a poet who has spent years skulking after a noblewoman who rarely speaks to him."

"It is well he knows that other men desire Solange," Guido said. "Why not tell him?"

Had I really been driven by vengeance? Sometimes Gherardo's ravings had a kind of wisdom to them. "Guido," I said softly, "we cannot continue as we were that day. I was overcome by grief, but I need to rise above it. You are finding favour amongst the notaries and might soon become a papal lawyer. We must be friends henceforth, not lovers."

Guido burst out, "Are you fool enough to love Francesco still?"

I looked at the doll in my lap, still wrapped in the small blue jacket. "I have learnt that it is possible to love and hate the same man. Francesco's worth is above Avignon or even Rome. The Romans are honouring him more for his Latin letters than his poetry. One day they will be collected like Cicero's. He will change the face of literature forever. Much can be forgiven a man of such greatness."

"Generously said for one who has been spurned," declared Gherardo. "I believe you love my brother more than I do, for you seldom find any fault in him. But then, we seldom find fault in you. We're both in love with you, aren't we, Guido?" That said, he stretched out his long legs and smirked a preposterously large smirk.

I stood up, then stepped over his legs to get past him. "If that is the case, then you must both help me get my son back. Guido, you know the law. You must represent my interests for me. How must I begin?"

Palais des Papes

1342–1348

Thirty-one

BY THE TIME I reached rue des Masses, the four men carrying my litter towards the Dominican friary were flagging. It was Pentecost, the thirty-third anniversary of my birth, and Benedict XII was dead. Once the camerlengo had smashed the Pope's ring and buried it with his corpse, seventeen cardinals elected Pierre Roger of Limousin. The old pope's tight-fisted ways had pushed the conclave to choose a noble with princely habits, who would be crowned this day in the city's largest friary. Ahead, a feral pig was gobbling offal from the centre gutter. Soon it would be caught and roasted, the cook denounced for thievery, and the thief dragged in chains to lose a hand or tongue. I hoped my own fate would be kinder, for I had hired the litter to carry me to the coronation in the guise of an invited noblewoman.

As the litter turned into the rue Calade, a glut of men slowed it down. I tapped the roof. "Advance as far as you can."

I was carrying the legal papers that Guido had drawn up. He had put off his canon lawyer's gown for a palace notary's and found out how I must proceed to get Giovanni back. I had to petition the new pope directly, and to do so, I must get close enough to deposit the slick vellum in his hand. However, if the guards smelt me out as a threat to the Holy Father, I might grace the inside of the papal jail instead. Hidden in my belt was my miséricorde, in case I needed to protect my honour or my life.

The city's labourers and craftsmen, forbidden to mount their usual Pentecost festivities, were attempting to procure work by brandishing their tools: scissors, cleavers, awls, and wine-thieves. As my litter advanced, I heard two carpenters speculating that the new pope would favour the rich and squeeze the tradesmen. Why should Pope Benedict have gilded nails in his coffin, when they could not get work hammering iron ones?

My litter-bearers were halted by the crowd. Two red-haired smiths, in their iron-toed boots and leather aprons, shoved their faces into my litter with great joyful grins of recognition, asking, "Where do you go?"

"To see the coronation from one of the viewing stands," I answered.

The litter-bearers hoisted my box onto their shoulders to jog it forwards. The weapon-smiths used their brawn to clear a path for me through the rough fellows of other trades until we joined a row of similar conveyances creeping towards the friary. Here, where the street curved, the courtesans broadcast their calling as loudly as did the tradesmen, wearing their white caps with crimson ribbons as the law dictated. The great machine of the church was changing direction and the clerics sent packing by the previous pope were streaming back into the city. A thousand had already arrived to beg gifts and benefices from the new pope—a thousand clerics in need of beds and food and women. The innkeeper of the Cheval Blanc had already taken in five more harlots and raised my rent to try to force me out.

My litter was set down at the friary gate and a sergeant in the new pope's colours inspected me. I held out a Latin document that said no more than was safe to say, that I was a citizen of Avignon.

"Go forwards," he said, impressed by the fine script, though he was holding the document upside down.

My litter stalled, was set down once more, then hoisted up again, as the people eddied and swirled into the courtyard. My stomach was objecting to all the ups and downs and sidestepping. Around me, I heard Italian spoken. Lawyers, goldsmiths, and moneychangers—who could afford zonas and bright, saturated dyes—were taking their places beneath the three keys of Avignon.

As we crept along the north side, I heard Provençal. The noble families were entering the shady pavilions beneath their flying balda-chins, the heraldry resplendent: roses, chevrons, besants d'ors, rampant lions, eagles. In a mob of noblewomen in a viewing stand, I saw a dark head wearing an archaic crown of laurel, my first glimpse of Francesco since he had been summoned back to Avignon. He was swathed in a gown of regal velvet—without doubt, the one King Robert had given him for his coronation in Rome. As he bowed to accept the congratula-tions of the Avignonnaises, I saw the flutter of the de Sade banner and witnessed the stiff neck of Laura de Sade bend to acknowledge his elevation to poet laureate. Her eyes, the courtly grey so impossible to capture in verse, welcomed the honoured poet to her sphere. Soon all of Avignon would know the very hour and day that Laura forgave the poet Petrarch for begetting a son on a common woman.

I sank back into the litter to hide my face as I was shouldered past. We came to a halt at the largest pavilion. Here floated the banners of the Pope's kinfolk and allies, forty strong, that trumpeted his blood lineage against opposing claims by Italian cardinals who would have returned the papacy to Rome. A sergeant-at-arms opened the litter door. This time, the Pope's azure band spoke for me, because I had paid to have his coat of arms sewn upon my wide sleeves and sweeping hem.

"The Pope's niece?" The sergeant did not wait for me to answer. "Up there with the others!"

I struggled on foot towards the platform of richly ornamented women. All the seats had been taken, so I stood in the cruel sun with-out a sheltering canopy while the rank and file of papal functionaries marched past, followed by squires and knights in battle armour, then the city marshal, the camerlengo, and the grand penitentiary with his ferula. Visible at the rear of the procession was a plush barge accompanied by seventeen cardinals balancing their red hats on spiral poles. These were the members of the Sacred College, the grand seigneurs of Christianity, only a fistful of Italians amongst a score of French.

But whoever was in the palanquin, it was certainly not the new Pope, Pierre Roger, for he was riding a white mule led by the dukes of Normandy and Burgundy. The Pope was escorted to Saint Peter's chair, the high seneschal of Provence emerged from the barge to kiss the Pope's slipper, and the people roared their approval of this pageant. One ritual speech followed another until the head of the conclave, the Gascon Raymond Guillaume des Farges, held up the gold tiara embedded with a massive carbuncle. He lowered the crown upon the Holy Father's head and arranged the lappets on his neck.

Having stood through all these Latin tributes in the heat, I was perspiring. The dukes and dauphins were kissing the new Fisherman's ring. After them would file viscounts, noblemen, and knights, and those who defied the sumptuary laws to pass as such, each paying homage with the hand-kiss, the baisemain. I had now had my fill of seigneurs and sovereign princes with their heraldry and reeking perfume. Once they had moved forwards, I must fall in behind to get to the Pope before the men of arts. I wanted to stay well ahead of Francesco so he would not see me.

My temples ached and my elaborate robe was sticking to my skin. The only woman in the line of noble vassals, I progressed in increments towards Saint Peter's chair, until at last the Pope loomed on the dais, smiling genially as if we were kindred spirits in our outsized costumes. He looked like a Limousin farmer, with a broad forehead and jaw planted with a crop of stubble. Rattled by the heat, I lurched towards him, fell heavily on my knees on the dais, and dropped my petition in his lap. Immediately, some functionary's arm stretched out to toss it into a basket with a multitude of others. I tried to steady myself by staring at the Pope, but the sun was in my eyes and everything had shunted out of kilter. Was the Pope peering at me, or was I peering at him?

He held out his gloved hand so I could kiss the colossal ring. "My dear, there is no need to kiss my feet. Although I am God on earth, I am a mere servant to beauty."

The cardinals, archbishops, and bishops laughed uneasily and the Pope smiled an elongated, lopsided smile. As my lips neared the Fisherman's ring, a blinding ray of sun threaded through his tiara, skewered the red carbuncle, and stabbed my eyes. The tiara split into three, each crowning a separate head. The middle spoke Provençal, the left Italian, and the right Latin, all striving to be heard over the others. Even more disturbing, the voices were all mine. I was babbling nonsense, the worst kind of prophetic nonsense about God crowning the Pope with Pentecostal flames. How long did I talk? I did not know— long enough to irritate the men lined up behind me, but at least I had not spoken in the old tongue. A petition whistled past my ear. Another grazed the Pope's cheek, flung by one of the disgruntled friars marooned behind the men of arts.

The Pope lifted his hand, his fingers tight as soldiers, to calm the multitude. "This prophet has spoken fair. We have witnessed God's fire, the tongues of flame that blessed the apostles at the first Pentecost. My predecessor did not know how to be pope, but you will find me over-flowing with generosity. I have decided to be called Clement, the sixth pope of that name, and will be full of clemency towards my people." The applause rose, then subsided. "No man who seeks a favour will leave my city empty-handed as long as he observes the rule of law!"

The cardinals knelt hastily in vassalage, the dignitaries scrambled to make obeisance, and Francesco was borne forwards in a wave of literati as eager as the sweaty friars to glimpse the Pope and his new prophet. Francesco could see me kneeling at the Pope's feet and he seemed agitated, as if recalling his warning that one day my riddling tongue might be torn out in the Pope's dungeon. I tried to stand, but my legs were too weak to hold my weight, and the Pope signalled the Limousin guards to remove me from the dais. As they bore me off, I heard some of the cardinals seizing upon my vision of divine flames as a providential sign, and as the guards carried me past the French allies, I heard the opinion amplified into an anthem of praise for their new pope.

Thirty-two

I WOKE IN A mute black space. Perhaps a torture chamber. Rolling on my side punished me with a seasick belly and a stab of pain behind my eyes. I felt for my miséricorde and found it still hidden in my belt, where I had ready access to it. A gaunt man drew the curtains that hemmed me in. So I was in a bed. He introduced himself: Gasbert des Sept-Fontaines, a médecin sent by the Pope. The chamber was small but well furnished, with a single window, too small to climb through, and a single door, blocked by two of the Pope's elite guards. A jail, then. But a comfortable one.

My mouth tasted metallic. "Is His Holiness displeased with me?"

Sept-Fontaines widened his eyes. "Why would he be? Yesterday you brought the nobles to their feet, the cardinals to their knees, and spoke three languages more fluently than his brother speaks his native tongue. Like a wise sibyl, you were enigmatic. Each man has taken what he wished from it. The French are proclaiming that your prophecy legitimizes Clement VI's right to the throne and the Italians are spitting bile because it encourages the Holy Father to reside here instead of Rome."

Sept-Fontaines bled me, funnelled tasteless fluids down my throat, and spooned in jellied pap, talking all the while. From him, I learnt that two hundred casks of wine had been drunk at the coronation banquet. The Pope's guests had devoured a hundred cattle, a thousand sheep, five hundred pints of red sauce and five hundred of green, and finished off with fifty thousand tarts. I had missed it all and so had this médecin, who had drawn the short straw of tending to me.

"Am I in the Dominican friary?"

"In the Pope's palace, at the base of the tour de l'Étude. The Pope's Limousin guards carried you themselves. Mary of Egypt could not have been more tenderly transported."

Hours later, my laboured sleep was broken by two women jabbering in the same accent as the guards. An old voice, brittle and unpleasant, and a soft, youthful one. I peeked at robes trimmed in ermine and sable, outlawed to all but members of the court. The clementine roses on their sleeves were red, unlike mine, which were white. How could I have made such a mistake? I shut my eyelids and pretended to be asleep.

"Aliénor, look at that hair," said the younger woman. "As abundant and shiny as a chestnut. Who can she be?"

Aliénor rustled off my blanket to finger my robe. "This is English wool, but she looks more like a city harlot. She should be taken to the repenties of the Magdalene and confined there."

"Could she be the woman rumoured to be Francesco Petrarch's sister? Observe how strange and tranquil her face is. Do you suppose she is having a vision?"

"Let us find out. Visionaries do not bleed."

As a needle pierced my toe, I breathed into my back, willing myself to take the pain. I concentrated on the mattress, which was tufted and springy. Feathers, not horsehair. What were they doing now? Staring at my foot?

"No blood," the younger said.

Gasbert des Sept-Fontaines entered, followed by shuffling servants and the aroma of roast game. "What is this—a conclave? Leave us, for the Pope has sent a haunch of venison from his own table to enrich her blood." The women swept out. "You may open your eyes. The jackals have gone."

"Are they the Pope's kinfolk?"

"A sister and a niece, although many of the palace women called kin are really courtesans. As you will learn, beds in the palace are more for entertaining than for sleeping. Only the Pope seems to know who is blood and who is water."

Two days after the feast of Saint Jean, the servants took my garments, and returned them cleaned and brushed. Just as they had finished putting the final layer of clothing on me, a brutal knock sounded— the captain of the palace to collect me, Aigrefeuille by name, his armour studded with three stars. Had I been gowned for public show or for the pillory? The captain escorted me into the labyrinth of corridors, up staircases, and through long halls linked by massive towers. In every chamber stood hostiarii—guards, stewards, doorkeepers, ushers—in papal livery. We emerged in an antechamber weighed down by late-day gloom, where Pope Clement sat in the only chair amongst a cadre of his officers, their faces grim and sceptical. An inquisition, then.

A fur-lined cloak appeared with an old dignitary buried inside. The camerlengo, I guessed, from the chain that snaked around his neck. His voice was formal, pitched to the corners of the chamber, where men with dark faces and darker clothing lurked. "You are familiar with Francesco Petrarch?"

What did this mean? I did not rush to answer.

He spoke louder. "Are you a member of his family?"

Beside me, the captain muttered, "Is he blind? Can that hair grow on an Italian head?"

The camerlengo persisted for the Pope's benefit, since he was observing me attentively. "I ask you again, are you Petrarch's sister?" His hand went up, down, right, like a lazy man crossing himself.

I took one breath, another. "I am not."

"So we surmised." He scored his point in the air.

"But she *is* clairvoyante," said the Pope. "That is no deception."

The camerlengo bowed. "Your Holiness, her vision at your corona-tion is not in doubt. It is God's choice of instrument we question. Why such a woman?"

The captain spoke, impatient to get on with it. "You have been seen at Petrarch's side in the city."

"Carrying his quills and parchment, yes. I was his copyist for a time." At the vulgar laughter from the rougher men, I looked at the Pope, appealing to his gallantry. "Is that an offence in Avignon?"

"There is no charge against you," the Pope said, his eyes leaping from man to man. "Did any one of you say otherwise?"

Several of the Pope's officers looked down. Whatever they knew—and I feared the worst—they were reluctant to air it in front of Clement VI.

Another man resumed the interrogation. From his accent, coat of arms, and new marshal's cloak, I knew the speaker to be Hugues Roger, the Pope's brother. His jaw wide, his hair like wind-blown straw, he had the same coarse features as the Pope but none of the Pope's courtesy. "Cardinal Colonna recalled Petrarch from Rome. What was the reason?"

"So he could attend Pope Clement's coronation, I presume," I said. "I have not spoken to him since his return."

"Do not dodge! How do the Italians intend to use Petrarch? What is his rôle as poet laureate? Surely you can speculate on that."

"Give her time, Hugues." The Pope rose from his chair. "My brother means, should we be wary of Petrarch, my dear?"

I considered. "You have a poet, Your Holiness, by the name of Jean La Porte. At your coronation, he was dressed as opulently as Francesco Petrarch was. I understand he has already written a tribute to glorify my vision of the flames descending at your coronation. Petrarch plays the same rôle, but on the Italian side."

Hugues Roger kicked a screen beside me, making me jump. "You mince words. Is he a poet or a threat?"

"More of a threat because he is a poet," I said. "The Italians will employ his eloquence to persuade the Pope to return the Holy See to Rome. But surely you expected that, Your Holiness."

The Pope acknowledged this. "What if I offer him a priory in Pisa? Will he take himself there?"

"He might, for he is a man of honour. However, he can write diatribes from Tuscany and might write more frankly there."

"This is true prophecy!" The Pope threw out his arms, compelling his officers' agreement. "This woman was sent for a purpose. See how she wears the clementine roses upon her robe, but in white, a more saintly colour?"

They would soon discover, if they hadn't already, that my relationship to Francesco had been more intimate. "Your Holiness, may I approach?" I spoke for his ears only. "I have a son, Giovanni. I have petitioned you to have him recognized in law. I pray that you will grant me my request."

The Pope's hand swept the men away. "Leave us. All of you. *Now.*" At this sharpening of his tone, the officers scattered for the door. "Hugues, you must go as well."

The others left, but his brother whistled hollowly and landed on one of the window seats with a thud. "You cannot be left alone now that you are Pope. Your safety is in my charge as city marshal."

"Hugues," the Pope said in exasperation, "I believe you would suspect the Magdalene herself!" Steering me towards another window seat, he inquired, "Whose son is it, my dear?"

"I was betrothed to Francesco Petrarch. In my allegiance to him, I bore his child, but he abducted my son and cast me aside. As a femme seule, I put myself in your hands, Your Holiness. If you help me to regain my child, I will repay you with my loyalty." The softness in my voice said more, as *his* softness had invited.

Hugues Roger stood, knocking dried mud from his riding boots onto the painted tiles. "Why should he trust you?"

The Pope forestalled him with the hand that bore the enormous ring. "I will do all I can for your child without making a foe of Petrarch. That I will never do, for his voice carries to men of letters across Europe. Hugues, get your men to find her a title, something that restores the dignity this poet stripped from her."

Hugues Roger's boots sounded through the next chamber and the Pope slid closer on the window seat. "Now, describe for me—how do these blessed visions come to you, my dear?"

"With a speed that catapults me into a deep void. They arrive in pain, and when they go, I remember little of them. This can scarcely be called a blessing, Your Holiness."

"Visions come from God, the most clear-seeing of all."

"If they do, He sends them for you, not me."

This earned me a smile. "Then you will have them and I will interpret them. What is a Pope without a prophet by his side?"

Eight days went by before I saw Clement VI again. I was saying vespers when he entered my chamber, followed by a dozen armed canons wearing long cassocks and pectoral crosses. Behind them followed the old camerlengo, out of breath and in ill humour, and hiding both poorly. My maids retreated, their eyes lingering on the parade of men. Apparently, the Pope had begun to say the office in the chapel, when he changed his mind and forced the canons to bump down the flights of stairs after him with all the holy paraphernalia.

I rose, but the Pope waved me back to my prie-Dieu. "Since you were not in chapel, I came to join you in your prayers." He listened to me chant the final psalm, which his canons duly repeated. "Why do you say vespers by yourself?"

I stood to greet him. "I have no church to say them in."

"You must use my chapel—were you not told as much?" He snapped his head round to command his men. "Where is the camerlengo?"

Today the camerlengo was buried in a different cloak, a syrup-yellow lined with fox. "As the vicomtesse de Turenne"—he crossed himself hastily—"you are the Pope's niece, with access to his private chambers. Sleeves are being embroidered for you with the Turenne arms."

The Pope said, "You chanted the psalm from memory. But even if you have mastered the psalms, you need a psalter. Give her mine."

One of the canons relinquished a magnificent psalter with reluctance. Pope Clement was staring at me in a more than pleasant fashion. Suddenly, he flipped his hand, communicating an order to the camerlengo.

The camerlengo said, "Out, out—only one needs stay as guard. A table chaplain, someone discreet. Nicolas, you."

On his scabbard, the youth displayed the de Besse arms, a branch of the Pope's family. His hand rested on his sword hilt, twitching slightly. I had no doubt he would be fast, if necessary. I turned a few pages of the psalter, catching the scent of wild irises, then laid it on my bed. "I know the value of your gift, Holy Father, because I was trained as a scribe at the Benedictine abbey where I was raised."

"We have that in common," he said affably, "for I was a child oblate at Chaise-Dieu. I might from time to time offer you my company, if you are willing."

I dipped my forehead in agreement, since it was not a question. He had disrupted vespers to seek me out, forcing his canons to troop down the tower stairs en masse. While I was so high in his thoughts, there might be time to strike a bargain. I was in for a denier, why not a sou? "When I am not needed by Your Holiness," I suggested, "I might be of some use in the library."

He embraced the idea. "Daily, we acquire books by right of spoil that have to be restored. As well, you may commission new books to refresh my ears at the close of day. Perhaps you will read to me even now?"

A thin book appeared from a fold of his cassock. It was a fine rendering of the Song of Songs, which he was pleased to show me sitting beside me on my bed. Bed-coverings of fur arrived and sweet wine with trays of delicacies. Nicolas de Besse kicked a hassock into a corner to slouch on and the camerlengo bowed himself towards the door without turning his back upon his sovereign.

The Pope read his favourite verses, his voice a nightingale's building to a tremor. His robes were scented with balsam and lemon. And his breath—had he been chewing frankincense? Next, it was my turn to read to him, marvelling that I was closer to the Pope's ear than any of his kindred. I felt a surge of power, then something more sensual. What was it worth to touch a pope?

Gentle and patient, he was in no rush to enjoy me, but at last, his hand caressed my waist with a determined pressure. His were the arms I must fall into, and I found them sweet and welcoming. All of a sudden, his face flushed and his breathing quickened. Then the book fell and so did he, a heavy suffocating weight across my chest. In one blow, my ribcage flattened and the air in my lungs was forcibly expelled. A sword clattered on the tiles and Nicolas de Besse was there, rolling Clement off me. De Besse laid him on his back to loosen the jewelled pin at his throat. His face enflamed, his torso quiet, Clement scarcely seemed alive.

"Let us send for the doctor," I said.

"And have all seven arrive? Better to let him rest than to listen to the physicians argue over how to treat him." He retrieved his sword and inserted it into the mouth of the scabbard. "It will pass shortly," he said, "with or without the doctors' physic."

"What causes such a fit?"

"There are seven theories, one from each doctor. A growth inside, or gravel, or sweating sickness, or the French pox. It comes on when he cannot rule the nobles, or win a debate, or bed a woman. It always happens on the first night with a new niece." He jiggled his sword up and down in its sheath to make his point.

So there had been other nieces, which explained why the Pope's servants were so adept with pillows and wines and savouries.

De Besse drew his sword half-way out and sighted down the blade. "Tell no one about this seizure. If it is known, a crisis of faith will ensue."

The implication was clear. If I told, I would die of something quick and sharp. The sword clinked back into the scabbard and Clement's lips moved soundlessly to call me to him. His face was less flushed and his breathing more regular.

"There is no need to speak. I will not reveal your secret." I ran my hand across his brow, a stroke that silenced him and caused his eyes to water. I straightened his cassock and lay beside him, spreading the same fur to cover us both.

Thirty-three

A FEW DAYS LATER, the Pope summoned me. I climbed the first flight of stairs with fear and the second with intention. At the turning, a small window gave onto the Pope's garden, where his ménagerie was kept, and I saw the Barbary lion. This fragile insight led me upwards, for I could not go backwards to the Cheval Blanc. There were one hundred steps from my chamber at the base of the tour de l'Étude to Clement's bedchamber in the tour du Pape, the most heavily fortified tower in the palace. From now on, I learnt, I must climb to him. When all his wooing was done, and all his love made apparent that first month, Clement had wooed me not as the Pope, but as a man. I lay in his arms with equal pleasure, for I was no more a saint than was any other woman, and more than a twelve-month had passed since I had lain with Guido.

Over the summer, the number of Italians in the Curia shrank. On Saint Matthew's Eve, Pope Clement created eleven new cardinals, only one of them Italian. Each kissed the Pope on the mouth and received a sapphire ring. The Pope's brother, three cousins, and two uncles were elevated, and another uncle became archbishop of the richest see in France. With nepotism in such favour, I hoped to reunite with my son, and sought out Guido in the thicket of papal functionaries, where his talent was commending him. But as much as he tried, he could not hurry my petition to reclaim Giovanni. It lay so deeply buried that we must wait for due process to unearth it.

As the nights grew into autumn, so did my eagerness to return to the Pope's bedchamber, where it was always summer. Musicians played new compositions, the fireplace radiated heat, and guests had their pick of liquors and sweetmeats. Clement sat propped up on the papal bed and his officers stood to conduct business or sat beside him to converse more privately. The prelates whispered to me, stroked my garments, laughed at my wit, admired me with their eyes, as I advanced towards the Pope, who savoured me through his men's appetites. At a finger's snap, the prelates withdrew.

Only Clement's watchdog, Nicolas de Besse, remained with us. This was not the time to ask the Pope about my petition for my son. Nor did I wish to, for another niece would be eager to rest her head upon the ermine pillow. Since the papal bed was too short for us to stretch out fully, we embraced sitting up, then turned sideways to plea-sure one another. His desire keen and quickly satisfied, his manners courtly, Clement was always regretful to dismiss me to my chamber. As I left, his stewards rushed in to sit him up, for the Pope must sleep upright in case God called him in the night.

In that first winter, I dreamt of Giovanni running towards me, reached for him, and woke, my arms empty. At first light, my steward carried in a round loaf, fragrant with coarse salt. I broke off lavish chunks to dip in oil from the Pope's own olive trees. Since I must bear life without my son, why not bear it in luxury? When Giovanni returned to me, we would live here together, wanting for nothing. In the Cheval Blanc, cold and hunger would have been my compan-ions. Here, I could enjoy a man's touch again—after all, I was hair and flesh and bone, such parts as other women were made of. And I had an education better than most men's, which Clement did not find offensive.

I had won the librarian's trust by repairing damaged books, which I read greedily, and was already commissioning works myself. After the library, my favourite room was the hall Clement had dedicated to the new sciences, where the hourglass and the calendar ruled men, not the book of hours. Today, few men of science were in attendance, since it was Mardi gras. I found Clement with the court astrologer, who had been working on a map of the heavens based on his astrolabe sightings in an attempt to explain the misalignment of the planets.

"Tonight," the astrologer was saying, "the sky will be darkened by a supernatural event."

If this was true, it would explain why the Rhône was surging, which might result in crop failure and famine for the people. A cardinal's skullcap bobbed towards us. Hugues Roger, snapping some parchment impatiently as he bounded to Clement's side. Being the papal whip had made his temper vile. He had none of the polish schooled into Clement in Paris, where he had been a familiar of the King. Their voices clashed, one ebony, the other ivory, then Hugues Roger lunged at me to thrust the letter beneath my nose.

"Is this written by Francesco Petrarch?"

The handwriting was crabbed and tight, and utterly familiar. Francesco had made no effort to disguise his authorship. It would be dangerous for me to lie. "It is his penmanship and style," I admitted.

"This is a foul attack on the Pope, my brother."

The Pope was not as hasty. "It is so clothed in superfluity, Hugues, that we cannot decipher what it means."

Hugues Roger snapped the letter under my nose again. "What does all this rhetoric signify?"

The Latin was hard going while my thoughts were jangling. "He composes in this elevated way when he feels strongly."

"Was it written to you?"

I looked at it and discarded the notion with relief. "It is not addressed to anyone."

Hugues Roger smacked his mozzetta against his thigh and put it back on crooked.

"I told you, Hugues," Clement said. "She does not correspond with Petrarch."

Hugues Roger's finger poked at the sheet in my hand. "Who is this *unyielding star?*"

"Cardinal Colonna, who leads the Italians."

"Yes, yes—I see that now." He was angry at himself for missing it. "And the *nodding oarsmen?*"

"The new French cardinals," I said. "*Remos agunt inexperti.* Like all Italians, Petrarch distrusts the French."

"Why does he uncork such vitriol?"

"A sense of duty to the papacy."

"By condemning the head of the Christian church? Calling my brother the sick, blind captain of a capsizing boat? How did he discover Clement's malady—tell me, how?"

I looked at the letter again. "He refers to an abstract malady, uxoriousness. He accuses His Holiness of being too fond of his new consort. This flesh-eating fish likely refers to me. Petrarch fears I am devouring the Pope, who suffers from excessive love."

"A dog-fish," mused Hugues Roger, trying to locate the phrase with a dirty thumbnail.

Clement appeared satisfied. "Now I will take you into my confidence, Vicomtesse," he said. "Rumours of my last illness flew beyond the palace and letters arrived from abbesses, nobles, and royal heirs to promote their candidates for the next pope. Such rumours threaten to break my grip upon the Holy See, but I know they do not come from you. You have proven your loyalty and I shall prove mine. From this day, you will be rectrix of the papal Comtat, and any man"—he transfixed his brother with a forthright glare—"who questions your rôle in my household will be a mortal enemy."

A rectrix—why not? An empty title, but better than some of the names the papal officers were calling me. Clement tucked my hand into the crease of his arm and led me across the hall to see what new physic the surgeon Jean de Parme had underway. De Parme was slithering to the summit over the other palace doctors, a snail climbing over the shells of other snails. Lately he had persuaded Clement to try treatments that made me uneasy. De Parme had strapped a patient to a chair today and laid a carpenter's brace and trepan-bit on a nearby tripod. The surgeon told us that the man suffered from fits similar to the Pope's. The man's head was immobilized by wooden cross-bars, his hair was shaved, and the sections of his scalp were identified with Greek letters.

De Parme pointed at the sections one by one. "This area controls the liver, this one controls the spleen, this one the gall bladder, and this the lungs. Each organ is the seat of one of the four humours: sanguinity, choler, melancholia, and phlegm. In this skull, the four are so out of balance that the vapours have built up excessively." He tapped the patient's cranium to locate the thinnest bone. Then he blew on the trepan, pushed it into the skull to anchor it, as a carpenter would push it into wood, and began to drill into the bone. The trepan whined and a cloud of bone dust took to the air with a putrid odour. "This will relieve the pressure that causes the swelling."

Clement asked, "Does the man feel any pain?"

"Not at all, Your Holiness. This bone is less than two deniers thick." The bit perforated the skull and de Parme lifted the trepan, flicking it with a finger to show how hot it was. "That hiss is the vapours escaping. Now he will be free of seizures." The patient emitted a muffled, strangled noise. "See how the poor man feels the good of it immediately?"

A peculiar fluid oozed from the wound and I tried to turn the Pope away. "Clement, the man has been drugged. Give me your word you will not allow this Parme to work his arts on you."

Clement was too fascinated to be drawn off. He was soon hard in conversation with the surgeon and would be for some time. On a night like this, the Pope would not invite me to sup at his table. I would have only the company of books and the crushing loneliness of the dark, papal citadel. When I returned to my quarters, I found a new steward, with a freshly shaved tonsure, arranging dates in a pyramid on a silver salver. It was Gherardo, with skin as yellowed as a capon's. Several teeth had rotted since I last set eyes upon him. He picked up a gold goblet, weighed it in his hand, and put it down.

"How did you get in here, Gherardo? You are no palace servant."

"No, Solange. But then, you are no countess from Turenne." His mouth split into a grin.

This was true, and should Gherardo reveal that I was from the Cheval Blanc, better known as a stew than a tavern, I would be at worse risk than he was. Clement had asked few questions about my origins. There was a league of comfort between a tavern scribe and the Pope's prophet—a comfort I had become accustomed to.

"What news have you brought me of my son? Where is he?"

Gherardo extracted a date from the pyramid, causing the others to tumble. "I would tell you if I knew. Francesco still won't let me near Giovanni. I am too vulgar for his son."

We had that in common. I thought of the dog-fish in Francesco's letter. "That letter about the blind captain of a listing ship—did you bring it to the palace?"

He spat out the date stone, and helped himself to wine. "Francesco told me to deliver it."

"So Francesco wants the Pope to read his jeremiads! I should have guessed."

"Bibamus papaliter," he toasted, sucking back the Pope's good Beaune.

Let us drink like a pope. With drink, Gherardo would become malleable, and I might learn something of use from him. Indeed, he was already waxing philosophical, his trouble spilling like sewage from an open sluice. He spread himself across the table, face buried in his arms.

"You cannot know what love is, Solange. It claws a man's chest, ripping skin from him like the peste."

I poured myself a goblet of wine and sat on a chair beside him. His tears were real, for they were dampening the table at an alarming rate. He told me that he still loved Cardinal Colonna's nephew, who had just been made a bishop and was living in the palais. Gherardo had bribed a servant for his livery jacket and hunted down the Colonna youth in the labyrinth. One night of love was all Gherardo wanted, but the nephew had called him a sodomite and threatened to summon the guards. Gherardo had been truer to his noble lover than his lover had been to him. He was not yet stone, for tears could not flow from a senseless object.

"Francesco wants me to live with him in his Vaucluse retreat so the country air will cure me of my liking for boys, but I would go mad there. He avoids Avignon, calling it a sty and a sink, and digs the soil like a peasant. He is writing a secret dialogue between a sinner named Petrarch and Saint Augustine in which the saint wins all the arguments."

My breath came out in a rush. "So he has stopped writing sonnets to Laura?"

A soulful burp. "You could as soon talk a rabid dog out of its foaming. It is ink for his quill."

"At least he is celibate."

"But his mind is wanton." Gherardo dug inside his shirt for some crushed papers. "I brought these for you. Checco wants your opinion of these poems, though he won't lower himself to ask. Look at this one—he craves Laura's company at night. And this—full of self-loathing, as though he had been intimate with her. I suspect that, between these two poems, Laura finally weakened and invited him into her bed."

This was such folly I did not bother to refute it. I spread the poems across the table. They were autograph drafts, so far advanced in art that I almost forgave Laura for inspiring them. I could taste my lover's sweet mouth, feel olive fingers mapping the bones beneath my skin. The pain of longing for Francesco returned. Why had I squandered love when it was mine?

Gherardo could not be stopped. "It is not just Laura who haunts him. Now that you are the sheath for the papal sword, he's lusting for you again. His quill has become his phallus. He bloats up until he's purple, then flagellates himself in overwrought concetti. He'd be better off bedding a boy to give us all some peace."

His tongue had lost none of its sulphur. Why did I let him work me like this? "Gherardo, remember where you are."

"In the chamber of the Pope's *niece*." The smile of a palace gargoyle. "Yes, dear sister, I know very well where I am. In the fortress of the Avignon popes. Watch yourself, for it is rumoured that the last niece died from eating ground emeralds stirred into her food."

It was not the first time I had heard such harrowing tales. We were both quiet for a moment. "What will you do?" I asked.

The scar whitened across his cheekbone. "Only one person can help me now."

Did he mean himself, or me? I studied the dregs in my goblet, considering how to get him out of Avignon for my own sake as well as his, for he endangered us both.

The bells for compline had rung some time ago. The palace was emptying of human noise, since tonight most of the prelates were attending Mardi gras fêtes in the city. The servants would soon be gone as well, for it was useless to forbid them the ancient right to celebrate carnival. By now, the astrologer would have progressed up the tour de la Campane with his astrolabe and map of the constellations. Clement and his counsellors would take seats on the roof, where they would witness the metaphysical event and argue over its meaning in Latin.

I would have enjoyed the speculation, but Clement had not sent one of the Limousin guards to fetch me. I had spent much time alone of late. Perhaps his taste for me was souring, because I had not had a vision since his coronation.

My chamber door was swinging closed. I put my head into the stairwell, my voice echoing, "Gherardo, where are you going?"

"To the dyers' quarter. If you have the courage to escape from this mausoleum, come dance with me along the rue du Cheval Blanc as we did last year."

Thirty-four

T HE PALACE WATCH did not challenge me, even though I was
without my customary escort. Clement had become a benign
tyrant, a grand seigneur who forbade me to go outside the palais on my
own, but it was Shrovetide, when anything might happen, and the guards
opened the double portcullis for a coin. Although I had no lantern to hold
up, the moon was full and I knew the streets and byways better than anyone.

The alleys were seething with dark forms surging towards the
twelve gates in the old city wall. I liked slipping my leash and walking
amongst the folk once more. I felt the force of the mob as I headed
towards the rue du Cheval Blanc, where I had agreed to meet Gherardo.
The gates were guarded after curfew, but the guards were common
yeomen. Tonight, they were drinking liberally and turned bleary eyes
on the slurry of humanity issuing out of the city. Only those foolish
enough to carry lanterns, as was the law, were marked down in the
record book for the city marshal's inspection.

The canal was full, the water skimming over the top onto the
marshy ground. Here in this sublunary realm, where the Pope could

not enforce his curfew, a dark power welled up. There were no men of science, no dissectors of the truth, only peasants illuminated by the fickle moon. The folk were bent on enjoying themselves before being shriven on Ash Wednesday for the forty days of fasting. A vast fire was already burning and the fête du quartier was underway, a black sabbath by the looks of it, for a pig was boiling in its grease and more animals were tethered. There would be a mass-bouffe and a few sacrifices before pointed sticks would fish the boiled pig-meat out of its cauldron.

Drummers and acrobats led the dancers along the rue du Cheval Blanc. Ahead, I saw Gherardo, back in his own clothes with a wineskin fastened to his lips. The harlots had come out of the Cheval Blanc to enjoy the fête. Here, also, were liveried servants, who stood out against the dull backdrop of peasants, churlish apprentices, and dyers who could not afford to wear the purple that stained their own arms. Few of the people had bothered with masks and in the half-shadow, half-light I might be one of them again. I caught up to Gherardo to ask for a turn at the skin. Our talk of Francesco and my lost son had depressed my spirits. Tonight I felt like escaping into the world these people inhabited, but Gherardo refused to give me any drink. Instead, he handed the wineskin to a mountebank as they staggered off together, arms linked, into a passage.

All at once a pall fell over the sky, and I remembered the astrologer's prediction. The folk pointed in horror as the surface of the moon became mottled, then blood-red. A giant unseen orb traversed the moon until the entire sky swelled with hellish red. An old weaver shrieked in langue d'oc that the devil had drawn his altar cloth across the moon. Reeking with fear, the folk cried out that the moon was dying and the whole world with it. Ignorant of eclipses, they believed they were about to die unshriven and plunge headlong into hell. Mothers wept, causing panic in their children, and ox-like men stood on the lip of the canal, ready to leap in to extinguish the hell-fire. One man held two infants in his arms, prepared to fling them into the water to spare them from the flames, and others were dragging their children to the brink to do the same.

Gooseflesh erupted along my arms and I tried to marshal my thoughts into some order. The sky was now so black it no longer held even a smudge of colour. How long had it taken the moon to darken? I knew from the court astrologer that it would take an equal time to lighten, but the terrified would drown themselves before the moon reappeared, since few of the folk along the canal could swim.

I stood on one of the planks across the canal, lifted my hands to command their attention, and shouted, "None of you will perish if you do as I tell you. Say ten paternosters, one after another, and before you say the tenth, the moon will return."

I started chanting a paternoster loudly. The woman next to me joined in, and so did the next, and the next, and so did all the men, until all the jumpers were chanting, the children most eagerly of all. Gradually, the sky became a field of chevrons, pulsing red on black, then black on red, like the patterns that sometimes appeared on the inside of my eyelids. On the ninth paternoster, the fat red moon appeared on top of the teeth-like crenels of the city wall.

A man yelled, "The moon is back! The devil swallowed it, then spat it out!"

The jumpers left off chanting to crow at their good fortune and the musicians picked up their instruments to pluck them with gusto. The folk celebrated their escape from hell by throwing more fuel on their fire. A goose was hauled up a greased pole in a basket and the brawniest of the climbers, who finally made it to the top, earned it as a prize. A reveller chased down a striped cat, normally thought to bring good fortune. The youths nailed it to a post and took turns butting it with their heads.

What issued from the pipes, psaltry, and tabors could not be called music. It came like a disease from the gut of the poor, a dark, wounded joy. The thigh-slapping rhythm made my feet twitch with old memory and I danced until every bone felt alive and only thinly clothed in flesh.

I sensed the tug deep inside my womb, for though I was born under the sun at Pentecost, I bled each month when the moon was full.

The mountebank who had gone off with Gherardo limped out of the passage towards the fire, his lips tinged with phosphor. Long in the tooth, but short of brain, he seemed known to the mob, for they encouraged a stinking he-goat to ram him cruelly. The man was bleating gibberish—wild accusations of aiguillette, castration by Satan. Two men demanded that he prove it, goading him with pointed sticks. He ripped off his cloak and his tunic then, egged on by the mob, his shirt, his hose, until he stood naked with a saintly pallor, exposing the split and empty purses dangling between his legs. The cry went up that the eunuch was the devil's catamite and the folk spun him around until he crashed against the boiling cauldron, splitting his head open and falling lifelessly into the flames. Howling at the loss of their pig-meat, the mob threw wood upon the blaze to speed it, then tossed the battered cat on top of the dead eunuch, as another of the devil's party.

The smoke blew at me, cloaking me with ashes. It stank of the burning offal and horns on the street of the butchers. My nose remembered the burning flesh of the friar at the auto-da-fé. Saint or catamite, they smelt the same. I sank back into the mob, belly-sick, despising myself for speaking the same rough tongue. The goat hobbled off, pursued by revellers with sharpened sticks, and Gherardo reappeared with a sober mien, as if he had expelled a mess of bile.

"What was in that wineskin you shared with the eunuch?" I asked.

"Greco laced with wormwood oil. I meant to drink the skin myself, but he grabbed it from me and downed most of it."

"Then he took your death upon himself, for he was pushed into the fire. Why do you associate with such knaves, Gherardo? You have exiled yourself from Avignon with such behaviour."

"And you, Solange—why do those men lurk about you? Those red-haired barbarians on the far side of the fire are carrying pikes. Why are they in this quarter tonight, if not for you?"

"They are only weapon-smiths." I drew my cowl over my forehead. "I'm sure they do not recognize me."

"Look at your feet. You are wearing palace shoes! I heard those smiths saying that you cast a spell over the moon to make it taste so bad the devil spat it out. The more they glorify you, the more they give you dangerous powers."

"You are in danger here as well. There is nothing left for you in Avignon."

He hugged me with surprising force. He was still a strong man in spite of the toll rough living had taken. "You've been a true sister. Francesco is a fool for casting you aside. When he and I climbed Mont Ventoux, I chafed at his authority and headed up the steeper path. Checco said I was always looking for the short way to the top, like our mother, whereas he was destined to follow our father's long, prudential route. I suppose he meant it as a rebuke, but he was right."

"Where will you go?"

"To a quiet place to find a man with willing arms."

There was a glint in his eye—a tear or a wink? I watched him set out towards the south, a knight armed only with chicanery. Wherever he was headed, I knew it would not be on the via prudentiæ. When I lost sight of him, I turned north to follow the dark alleyways back towards the fortress on the rock.

Thirty-five

CLEMENT ENTERED HIS bedchamber in the early morning after the eclipse, bone-chilled from his deliberations on the palace roof. I held out a drinking cup with wine I had spiced myself, having arrived only shortly before him. He dismissed his weary officers except for Nicolas de Besse, who crawled onto his pallet with one eye open, like a pedigreed hound. I told Clement I had ventured to the carnival, taking the risk of being chastised at once rather than in the weeks ahead. He asked me to describe the revels for him. When I got to the part about the moon reappearing on top of the battered fortifications, he became thoughtful.

"This is a sign that I should strengthen the broken city wall."

From the palace roof, Clement had seen the dancers snaking along the rue du Cheval Blanc outside the city wall, a fortification so breached that only a fosse marked its jurisdiction at one point. By the light of the carnival fires, he had seen the dwellings erected outside the gates to house the overflow of people, and the bourgs that had been shambled together to ward off mercenaries and brigands. To protect his people, he told me, he wanted to erect a new wall to triple the city's size, spreading his wing over thirty thousand souls. The new ramparts would extend beyond the Mardi gras fires, bringing the outlaw lands into the city, the mob under control of their primate.

In the wake of the eclipse, raging currents swelled the Rhône until the arches of Saint Bénezet's bridge cracked under the river's displeasure. The city was under siege from the Rhône to the west and north, from the Durance to the south, and from the Sorgue canal, which was spilling over its banks in the southeast. The unpaved streets were spongy, the water ankle deep and rising. Only Doms rock, where the cathedral and palace stood, was dry. Had the contrary moon whipped up the flood, or was it the devil's hand at work? Panic grew, until the guild-masters, the heads of the confraternities, met behind closed doors. They came forth in their regalia to proclaim the eclipse a bad omen for the papacy. The flood, they announced, was only the precursor of greater evil.

On the second Sunday of Lent, Clement gave a sermon in Notre-Dame-des-Doms to subdue the people's fears by declaring that the eclipse was a favourable sign for the papacy. The very moment Clement VI emerged from the cathedral porch, a nimble mason dangling from the spire yelled down, "Most of your city is under water! We will all starve."

Unruly apprentices of every stripe and colour brayed at the Pope, stomped their wet boots, and cursed the dry and richly clothed nobles progressing from the cathedral towards the palace for the debate on the eclipse's meaning. Between the brewers and the hatters stood the raucous weapon-smiths, swatting their leather aprons and clanging their pikes. Recognizing the master by his turnip ears, I deviated from the palace women to speak to him. The smiths greeted me as Saint Barbara, their intercessor—the prophet whose sugared words poured nightly into their pope's ears—and crossed themselves with flying thumbs. Several knelt to beseech me with makeshift prayers, attracting Clement's eye. When he made an about-face, the convoy had to halt, for it could not go ahead of the Pope.

Clement drew near, his fur-lined cope skimming the rocky ground beside me. "Vicomtesse de Turenne, what do these red-haired men want from you?"

What should I tell him? Whether I deserved the smiths' affection or not, this was a chance to shine before Clement's officers and family. My status as a prophet had spun up at his coronation, then tumbled. If it fell too far, I stood to lose my footing in the court. Even now, clinging to Clement's sisters was a new niece with tight brown curls, who was as unrelated to them as I was.

I pitched my voice for others to hear. "Your Holiness, the weapon-smiths think I drove off the eclipse and saved the city. In their simple faith, these men believe I am Saint Barbara, their patron saint, come back to life."

"You spoke to them. What did you say?"

"That I owe my powers to the highest authority, the Pope."

Pleased, he gestured that I should progress with him along the rocky path towards the palace. The audience chamber was filling with nobles, merchant-princes, bishops, and cardinals in chapeaux rouges. Telling the prelates from their notaries was hard, since their cloaks were as short and their sleeves as long and fluted. The Pope's Barbary lion reclined on the dais, restrained by a slender, golden chain. At Clement's command, I took the chair to his left and surveyed the audience of standing men. At the front were Cardinal Colonna and Cardinal Ceccano, swords slung militantly over their great robes. Between them stood Francesco in his laurel wreath and velvet gown, sizing me up impertinently. Behind him was a conclave of Italians, well girded with silver zonas, who had brazenly shunned the Pope's sermon. This brigade of overdressed thieves outshone the audience chamber, which was severe. Its massive beams and stonework reflected the previous pope's character, not Clement's love of ceremony, since he knew what was due to him as monarch of the church.

Clement banged his ferula for the debate about the eclipse to begin.

He had stated his own views in his sermon to avoid the risk of debating in an open contest that gave no advantage to the Pope. The papal squires distributed copies of his sermon, and the Pope's allies would speak in his stead. Hugues Roger sat at Clement's right, but notoriously lacked diplomacy in speaking. Therefore the camerlengo began, declaring that during the eclipse the planets had aligned favourably to the French Pope—the words Clement most wished to hear. The camerlengo unrolled a sheepskin with a city plan that showed the new city wall the Pope would build to protect his people. As the man who ran the papal finances, his opinion should have carried weight, but his speech was long and tedious.

The debate now passed to the other side. Francesco di Petrarca de Florentia stepped forwards for the Italian lobby. I had been waiting for him to make his move with an uneasy mix of dread and anticipation, because I had not seen him since Clement's coronation. He snapped open a broadside with one hand and held it out in front of him. As he read his speech, I admired his strong profile. Riding his stallion from Fontaine-de-Vaucluse at Colonna's beckoning had honed his body to masculine perfection. His gestures were broad, his voice more deep and charismatic than in his youth.

"This disastrous eclipse is a sign that the Pope should vacate Avignon. The city does not belong to the King of France, much less to Pope Clement VI, although he now possesses her. Her true lord is Robert the Wise, King of Naples and Sicily and Count of Provence." The crowd acknowledged the jab, since the opulent gown the poet laureate wore was known to have been King Robert's. "This ruinous flooding"—Francesco's voice tapped higher with each word—"is punishment for the Pope's infidelity to Rome."

Clement was twisting in his throne, consulting with his advisors on either side, for he had no desire to forfeit the vast revenues of his western territories. Scenting mutiny, he was steeling his clemency with anger. None of his foes understood Clement's love of Avignon. He wished to guard his people. How could he do that from afar? He had never spoken of going to Rome, even in private moments. I had been privy to his most fervent hopes and this was not amongst them.

As Francesco spoke, Cardinal Colonna refused a copy of the Pope's sermon that a squire offered him. With the cardinal was a wolfhound dressed in a Colonna jacket. A dog of good breeding, it lounged insolently beside its master, attending to Francesco's balanced sentences—until the Barbary lion stretched and yawned, magnificently. The wolfhound slipped its jewelled collar and charged, head down, towards the dais. Sneaking behind the lion, it planted its well-bred teeth in the beast's hindquarters. The lion reared, yanking up the dozing stable-boy at the end of the chain. The wolfhound plunged through the arch, heading into the cloister with the squires in pursuit. The Limousin knights gripped their sword hilts, a broth of soldiers coming to a simmer.

Clement pounded his ferula and bellowed, "When your dog is caught, Colonna, it will be castrated. And you—if I smell a whiff of treason—you will be excommunicated!"

Of course the Pope could do no such thing, since the rules of debate precluded it, and his advisors counselled him to sit back down. Francesco had been rotating his broadside, and looked up to see what he had missed. One of Colonna's hands trailed an empty leash; the other was on his sword. Cardinal Ceccano was also ready to draw his weapon, a threat in black beside Colonna's red. Francesco leaned towards them, doubtless reminding them of the rules of debate, but Colonna snapped an order at him. Francesco shoved his speech into his gown and held up his palms to silence the uproar. My ears itched, for I knew that this would be worth listening to.

Francesco now spoke ex tempore. "Your Holiness, Cardinal Colonna is one of the supporting columns of the papal edifice." He gave the audience time to catch the pun on *Colonna*. "The cardinal is as necessary to this court as Jupiter is to the solar system."

Clement swung his gloved hand with the Fisherman's ring towards his court astrologer, who took up the Pope's case unsteadily. "I challenge this assertion. When the moon was darkened by a hostile force, Jupiter was afraid to show its face, because it feared the moon's superior power."

By the moon, the astrologer meant me, as his sweeping palm made plain. Surely he did not expect me to speak? Apprehensive, I focussed on the few women in the audience, country nuns in Benedictine habits, the only pious sight in the packed chamber.

Now the Fisherman's ring swung in my direction and the Pope addressed me. "Vicomtesse de Turenne, all of Avignon knows of your wisdom at prophecy. Will you not say what this eclipse prefigured?"

I took my place beside the astrologer, rustling loudly in my heavy silk robe. I was Clement's prodigy and must perform in public for him. Bedecked in the finest goods the eastern trade routes offered, I was being asked to prove that I had earned them other than in his bedchamber.

"Holy Father . . ." I felt my way cautiously. "The eclipse signalled that the Pope has wisely betrothed himself to this city. The moon triumphed over the dark forces that besieged her, prefiguring that Avignon's strengthened battlements will repel the Pope's enemies."

The French stamped their boots, which stirred up the Italians. Cardinal Ceccano raised his fist and jerked it hard against his other palm, a vulgar tribute suggesting where my true skill lay. Hot with shame, I stood my ground. Francesco was looking at me in a way I did not like. Indeed, every man in the room seemed to be contemplating doing something with me in private.

"Your Holiness," Francesco said. "This *niece*, this Countess of Turenne, this rectrix of the papal Comtat"—he sharpened his tongue on my titles—"witnessed the Spirit descend at your coronation. She predicted that a three-headed pope would ascend Saint Peter's throne, signifying that your adulterous reign will end in division unless you return to Rome, your lawful bride." He was in full stride now, his arms as lively as his voice. "Unless the excesses of your court are checked, it will grow the seven heads and seven crowns predicted in the Book of Revelations." He jabbed a finger towards me. "*I saw a woman sit upon a scarlet-coloured beast, full of names of blasphemy, having seven heads and ten horns. And the woman was arrayed in purple and scarlet colour, and decked with gold and precious stones and pearls. And upon her forehead was a name written, Babylon the great."*

Only one man in Avignon could have quoted this verbatim and only the most obtuse in the crowd missed the point of his barb. Why did Francesco feel such animus towards me? Although the response was wild, Francesco was not finished. I had not recovered from his attack when he launched a new spear at me.

"Your Holiness, only the ignorant believe this woman saved the city by summoning the moon back after the eclipse. And as for saving it from flooding? A hundred men with buckets could do so faster. Place no more store in prophetic harlots and turn your face from this Babylon towards imperial Rome."

I fought to regain my composure as Ceccano elbowed Colonna and the Italians jostled Francesco in appreciation. Even the French cardinals were ignoring the Pope's ferula, which he was banging against the floor, enraged that a superior orator had trampled his case on home ground. Reluctantly, the audience obeyed the call to order. Clement glared at his astrologer as if it were his responsibility to prevent all natural disasters. When the astrologer, who was perspiring, could not rally, the camerlengo tapped his heart and began crossing himself. Would Clement be drawn into the debate? He was known for his skill at oratory, but speaking impromptu was not his forte. Clement consulted his officers— Hugues Roger, the camerlengo, and the captain of the palace—then flipped his glove to signal that I should retaliate.

I was still recoiling from Francesco's assault when the Fisherman's ring signalled me. That brilliant flash revived me. I turned my humiliation to anger and my anger to the Pope's cause, gathering the shreds of our case. "The cardinals may be glorious planets, but they are controlled by the Pope, the sun. The sun rules the solar system as the head rules the body and as the lion rules the lesser animals." I knew, as soon as the argument was out of my mouth, that it was blunt. It was like raising a sail on an unstable craft in a mistral. The wind and the river showed no mercy.

"The Pope might well be the sun," Francesco agreed, enjoying himself, "but the papacy revolves around Rome, just as the sun revolves around the earth and as a lion quakes at the bite of a dog."

The Pope's case capsized and the Italians threw their hats into the air in triumph. The Florentine bankers surged around Francesco, slurping praises on him, and the Tuscan youths slapped him on the back. His forehead ashen, Clement stared at the bare walls of the audience chamber as if Pope Benedict's severe décor was to blame for the liberties taken by the foreign courtiers in it.

Hugues Roger's gaze scoured me, landed upon my Turenne crest, and glanced off scornfully. If I did not wish to be stripped of my Turenne lands, I must play the vicomtesse. There was no strength in hiding behind the Pope's skirts. If I was discredited as the Pope's prophet today, I would be fed ground emeralds tomorrow. But how to get the crowd's attention? I looked for the bucket in which eels were soaking in vernaccia to soothe the lion when he tired of ceremony. The stable-boy had fished one out and fed it to him after the wolfhound's attack. Now I held up a dripping eel until the lion roared, then threw it into his mouth. Once a few heads jerked my way, I fed the beast another. After a third I had every eye upon me and began.

"The Italian dog cannot intimidate the king of beasts, the Pope! Francesco di Petrarca de Florentia speaks of cardinals by using symbols, as poets ought, but consider—for you are men of reason not mere poets—how cardinals actually behave. The feuding of the Colonnas, the Orsinis, and other nobles has made a blood-bath of the Italian states. The Pope's life would be worth sweet salt amongst those barbarous tribes—at most, a peppercorn. Let him remain safely cradled in the arms of Avignon!" I extended my arms, in their bright Turenne sleeves, to emphasize my point, then shouted over their cheers, "Ubi papa ibi Roma." *Where the Pope is, there is Rome.*

My appeal to reason had transformed the listeners into savages. *La Popessa!* they screamed, pounding one another's shoulders. Citizens and foreign courtiers had enjoyed the debate equally, although it had ended in a draw. No longer caring a whit about the eclipse's meaning, they were hungry for the Pope's famed hospitality and lavish board. With three blows of his ferula, Clement closed the debate and stepped from the dais to lead his parade of guests towards the Grand Tinel.

Thirty-six

FRANCESCO SWEPT towards me in his great robe, part of the group of Tuscan youths on their way to the banquet. One of the petrarchinos snatched the laurel crown from Francesco to perch it jauntily on his own head. Soon the youths were laughing and tossing the crown from hand to hand to try it on themselves.

"Francesco di Petrarca," I hailed him. "Although you think little of Pope Clement, you might find his library worthy of your praise. Would you care to visit it?"

He halted, scanning my face for anger, which I suppressed with difficulty. I wanted news of my son and this was the surest way to get it. He could not resist such an invitation, as I knew. I took him to the library, gave him an hour alone with the books, and found him sinking into a rare work by Cicero when I rose from my carrel.

He let the pages drift reverently closed. "So this is where the vellum is being hoarded. These books are not here for the cardinals or their sons, who have inherited little taste for literature."

"The volumes on this wall are for the Pope's own use. This is one I commissioned." I fanned the leaves of an illuminated manuscript.

A gesture dismissed it. "A bedchamber book."

"Yes," I said, meeting his eyes, "such as you and I once read to each other."

This nettled him. "Is the Pope amorous after granting benefices and indulgences all day?" Louder now, insistent, "How does the Pope perform in bed?"

I did not shift my eyes away. "Like a Benedictine."

Taken aback, he stared. "That was unforgiveable of me. I wish the words unsaid." He looked contritely around the shelves and carrels. "I see your hand in this great enterprise, Solange. I have heard that you have attracted scribes from Paris and Flanders to work in the scriptorium. You have achieved your desire of commanding a remarkable library."

I handed him a slim volume of his own poems, penned in my finest script with decorated initials. His years of shifting words here and there had fashioned an exquisite harmony in the patterning of vowels. "Forty poems by Francesco Petrarch that will stand the test of time," I said. I wondered whether he was still breathing.

At last, he lifted his eyes from the volume. "You have chosen better than I would myself. I have written few poems of this worth of late. Will you lend me the book?"

This is what I hoped he would say. "I will, if you lend me my son."

He extracted a square of parchment from his velvet gown. It was a portrait of a boy, aged about five, with Francesco's eyes and hair. I could scarcely see him through my tears.

"I meant in the flesh," I said. When Giovanni came to court, he would run happily into my arms as I saw him do each night before I fell asleep. But what would the child see? Would he recognize his own mother?

"That cannot happen."

"I have waited patiently these three years."

"Hardly patiently. You have used Guido to heckle me for news."

"Is Giovanni in Carpentras with your old tutor?"

"So you have been searching for him there? The boy has a better hiding place. Your servant Des-neiges is with him still and he learns apace with his own tutor."

I had indeed been looking. Guido had sent men across the Sorgue basin. They had followed Francesco to Fontaine-de-Vaucluse and back on his new horse. Either he was too clever for us or he saw little of the boy.

"Your rôle in his life is over," he said. "I do not wish my son corrupted by the court."

"By the Whore of Babylon, you mean. You must be fatigued with hauling such dung for your Roman masters. But you didn't speak only for Colonna today. You spoke for yourself."

"It's true. I meant to warn you."

"In the most public way."

"Do you deny your position in the palace? You are an odalisque, une horizontale. Look at your sleeve. You wear the Pope's brand."

"This is the coat of arms for my lands at Turenne."

His mouth was grim. "Which you will never be allowed to see. Be warned. The Pope's men will drag you down as swiftly as they raised you up, for you have been privy to their secrets."

"And you have grown envious and petty. You visit court to beg favours like the others, repaying the Pope's generosity with insolence."

"You refer to his gift of Pisa. Well, Pisa came to naught."

"Then he will give you another benefice at my behest—unless it would rankle for you to be in my debt?"

"Why do you persist in thinking ill of me? I admit I went too far in the debate. Forgive me, I did not wish to hurt you quite so deeply."

"But you *do* wish to hurt me? You admit as much?"

"You are the Pope's consort. More than anyone, I wish that you were not. You are the most desired woman in Avignon, but you neglect your own heart."

"What does that mean—that you would have me back? Lead me to Giovanni and I'll give up all of this." My hand swept across a thousand of the finest books in Christendom, but he shook his head. "Then let Giovanni live with me in the palace. He will learn from the scholars, read books that you will never read yourself. Clement will treat him kindly."

"Like his Barbary lion? He would be on display as you were in the audience chamber—the love-child of the Countess of Turenne." He became grave. "Even now our son's life may be in danger. For Giovanni's good, I will ask the Pope to legitimize him. The world being what it is, our rivalry is inescapable. But in this matter of Giovanni, you and I must agree. Legitimization will protect his life and remove the stain of bastardy."

As soon as he said the words, I knew them for a truth. Clement would never allow me to raise another man's son in the palace. That was why my petition had fallen on deaf ears. Clement had most likely blocked it without telling me. I was so distressed I could scarcely speak. "It would break Giovanni's ties to me."

He spoke softly. "They are already broken. He thinks his mother is dead."

"You cannot have told the child this!"

"It is kinder to stay dead than show him who you actually are," Francesco reasoned. "He could never hold up his head amongst men."

Certainly Giovanni had little future as the son of a femme seule, even one who had risen to my rank and titles. Some part of me had known this all along.

"I wish to leave Cardinal Colonna's service and go back to Italy, to my father's town of Florence. They expelled him with a price on his head, but now they wish to pay me honours. I will accept them for Giovanni's sake. He will stand on my shoulders as I stood on my father's. The further I take him from Avignon, the safer he will be. Shall you give us fair wind?"

"You've left me no choice, since I want Giovanni to be out of harm's way." I reminded myself that although many noblemen fathered children, then washed their hands of them, Francesco was acting with integrity. Giovanni would be raised in the manner I had always wished for him. My son would wear the Petrarch arms in pride.

"Now let us be friends," he said, "since Fate has decreed we can no longer be lovers."

His look was full of regret, as though he was put out with Fate, her decrees, and everything about her. When I extended my hand in friendship, he pressed it against his heart. A hand's-breadth away, his soul tugging at mine, he was easy to forgive. We gazed at each other for many minutes, knowing we might never be close enough to touch again. I had discovered my own way to his heart—and he still had one.

At last, I let go. I went to the library door and locked it with my key from the inside. Francesco threw off King Robert's velvet gown, spread it across the floor to cushion us, and drew me down beside him. Soon he was unpinning my hair as he used to do. Once a few jewels were unfastened, the strands tumbled in a glossy heap. I rubbed my hands to heat them, then touched the sword-bite in the hollow of his collarbone. Now something less spiritual came between us. He, too, was feeling it. From underneath his cloak of honour sprang up a full, well-muscled appetite.

My lips neared his, then withdrew. "I still have some power over you."

"And I over you."

His hand ran along my inner thigh, reclaiming territory ravaged by his foe. No one had made such a claim as his upon my flesh. Even when I had been with Clement, I kept my inwardness sacred to Francesco. Beneath my fingers, as I undid his points, his leg muscles tensed. He had been celibate too long and I had learnt a thing or two about pleasing men since I had last lain with him. I stripped off his hose to caress the belly of each thigh, and when he was naked to my eyes, I clothed him with my hips. He rolled me over, his hands supporting my back, then he rose up and entered in sweet plunging glory.

After we had both surrendered equally, we lay on our backs, taking in great greedy gulps of one another's air. Now that his eyes had fallen closed, I felt for my miséricorde and snipped some of his dark hair—a souvenir that might prove useful, like the angel Gabriel's feather that the Virgin plucked during the Annunciation. After a while, he began to stir. His palm swept the floor as he groped for his hose in the daze of a man whom pleasure has taken unawares. Celibacy had loosened its grip upon him. He was now easy about the eyes and would be easier in his poetry, too, not so tightly bound in figures. I wrested his gown from beneath my spine and held it out to him, the nap of the velvet so crushed that it might never spring upright again. There was nothing left to say. Only the key spoke—two revolutions in the lock, a *clank*, a push—and he was gone.

Lust, enflamed by intimacy, had triumphed over Francesco's resolutions and I conceived on that second Sunday of Lent in the year 1343. The moon was new, her most fertile phase. I gave Francesco a gift of joy and took from him what he could never reclaim—another child to replace my son. However, when I searched for the shank of his hair, it was missing. Either the draught had blown it into the scraps and threads that the scribes had dropped on the tiles, or Francesco himself had stolen it.

Thirty-seven

I RODE IN PROCESSIONS behind Clement VI, sat at his left in tournaments, and rinsed my fingers in his silver bowl. I plucked off the hood of my falcon to send him soaring through the air. What did I care if the Avignonnaises whispered behind gloved hands? Even when Laura was amongst them, I did not wish to change my state for theirs. I had pricked my hand and dropped the blood into spring water. The drops floated, telling me that I was carrying a daughter.

Now I followed Clement's canopy through the porte des Infirmières towards Châteauneuf-du-Pape, my hair erected to such a height that it rivalled the Pope's three-crowned tiara with its cross. The people lining the way had waited for hours to see us. The more outrageous my surcot, the more the folds of rich cloth rode up around my belly, the more they loved me. I kept to my horse in the beating sun until we made our first night's stop at the bastide de Périgord. In the morning, our cavalcade continued to the Pope's summer palace on the right bank of the Ouvèze, having collected a Florentine ambassador who called Clement *Notre Seigneur* and asked questions when he was least wanted. I guarded my tongue around him, for he was a parasite who wrote things down and conveyed them to his countrymen.

After a week at Châteauneuf-du-Pape, we rode to the bastide de Gentilly at the invitation of Cardinal Ceccano for the dedication of his new chapel to Saint Martial, Clement's favourite saint. We were met by sixteen cardinals, plus counts, bishops, damoiseaux, captains, chevaliers, down the line to écuyers wearing spring livery branded with both Ceccano's magpie and Clement's rose. Half the cardinals were related to the Pope. Even musicians could be bought and sold, for one of Francesco's friends was leading a motet sung by the Pope's young nephews, future bishops with runny noses. In the audience chamber, I watched the seigneurs of both land and church filling their cups at a fountain spewing five colours of wine, from deep grenache to the clearest Saint Pourçain. A tenor began to sing from behind a screen. A woman's voice joined in, like oil anointing skin. They clung together, calling and answering, rising and falling in a suggestive rhythm.

Two noblemen strode across the hall, their silver belt tongues slapping their thighs. They paused near me, not bothering to hide their scrutiny. "What a quantity of gold and ermine is loaded on her person," the shorter said, in a Paris accent. "Surely Avignon noblewomen do not bare their breasts so boldly?"

"That is one of the city's spectacular harlots," his companion replied. "The Countess of Turenne. The Pope finally got himself a courtesan who can read and write. She is as rich as Crœsus from selling fiefs, the few the Pope did not give to his family."

"How much power does she wield?"

"More than most cardinals. Watch her work the Pope. To see her fawn, you would almost think she cared for him."

I spun towards the welcome sight of Guido in his palace notary's gown, pushing his beaker beneath the fountain's spouts, one after another, until he had collected all five wines. I embraced him discreetly, then drank some of the pinkish fluid in his cup. "If you can tolerate this mixture, Guido, you will make a good archbishop. What news do you have of the Petrarchs?"

"Gherardo walked eighty miles south to Montrieux, where he has found asylum."

"In the monastery? An odd place to wash up, but he will be calmer there. Has Francesco taken Giovanni to Florence?"

"Not yet. He's not been able to shake free of Colonna. Each time I see you, Solange, your garments fit tighter. I suppose your strutting makes the Pope feel virile, but you are also provoking the Italians. It irritates them to pay you homage. Where will it lead? Are you sure you know?"

"You tell me, Guido. You are Italian. What does Annibal Ceccano intend by all this overarching splendour? He bullies the Pope to return to Rome, yet has built three châteaux here himself. Everyone seeks Clement's favour, even those who attend me in the guise of friendship."

"Did you know Francesco refused to compose a tribute for this banquet? Instead, he has shut himself up at Fontaine-de-Vaucluse to write tirades about the court's wickedness. Sonnets, I think."

I seized his arm. "Did you bring them with you?"

"Why would I?" He shrugged. "He is also writing eclogues about the Pope milking his flock to glut his treasury and anonymous letters in which he calls you Semiramis, the sultan's consort, whose stallion has hooves of gold."

I suppose the bargain was a fair one—furious new writings in exchange for the infant I had taken from Francesco without his knowledge. But *hooves of gold?* "When you next write, tell him I am with child by the Pope. Let us see what he can make of that."

"So that is why . . ." He gestured at my belly. "You are dancing at knifepoint, Solange. What if the Pope objects?"

I asked myself the same question as a knight escorted me into the banquet hall, where I took my place at the Pope's left. Clement had not yet noticed my condition, but if Guido had observed that my garments were snug, so might others. Clement and I cleansed our fingers with rosewater and ate generously of the roast meats, only to discover there would be two more courses. In the first intermezzo, the Pope was given a battle-horse worth four hundred florins. In the second intermezzo, he received a sapphire ring and one of topaz. My clothing shrank course by course, until, after nine flights of dishes, divided into threes by intermezzos, the chef quickstepped out with his thirty cooks in time to our handclaps.

When this debauchery of ear, eye, and stomach was over, Cardinal Ceccano escorted us to a gallery with a view of the meadow. Ceccano's knights showed us their prowess in close combat and youths sparred with long-swords, while marriageable young women paraded in their heraldic sleeves. Ceccano leaned over the Pope's shoulder, rounding his back to share a lewd observation, although I was within hearing. I straightened, spreading my fingers boldly across my thickening belly. Catching on, Ceccano swerved his eyes from me to the Pope and back to me again, attempting to stir up enmity between us.

"Petrarch was right," said Ceccano. "This courtesan has cast a spell of uxoriousness that keeps you besotted in your Babylon."

"Indeed she has." Clement's face went soft, no doubt sizing up my roundness, counting the months, recalling the times I had come to his bedchamber of my own volition. He gestured towards my fecund belly, raising his voice for others to hear. "See how I send out shoots in spring? In this year of the eclipse, this is proof that the Pope is well rooted in the soil of Avignon."

He kissed me full upon the lips, as he did when appointing a cardinal, then removed his sapphire ring to place it on my finger, a deliberate insult to his host, who had just presented it to him. This was so remarkable a show that the French cardinals stomped their heels, drumming their approval.

"Now, Ceccano, listen to your pope. Your palace is fine, but mine shall be finer. I shall turn Avignon into Nova Roma, a queen armed mightily against her foes. She will have a new jewel in her tiara, a magnificent palace with an audience chamber of such surpassing size and luxury that no man will ever again question whether the Pope will remain in Avignon."

Annibal Ceccano was simmering. "For my next entertainment, Your Holiness"—he pointed across the meadow to a tableau that was assembling—"I have invited the masters of your city guilds to attend the evening's revels. As a mark of courtesy, I have erected a bridge across the Sorgue to shorten their way."

We watched as the guild-masters dismounted, adjusted the hang of their festival robes, and manœuvred into their proper rank and order. When the bridge was overburdened with human flesh—two dozen guild-masters bowing towards the Holy Father—it let out a thundercrack and gave way. The bridge twisted sideways, broke into two, and dumped the worthy burghers in the river. This was no bridge of merit made from seasoned wood, but a sham—a manifest folly that Ceccano had built expressly to deceive and he laughed coarsely while the victims paddled like dogs to the bank. They had come by no harm, yet I felt for their damaged pride and ruined linen, since it was an unkind way to make sport. Fattened by the banquet, despoilt and fawned over, Clement was also laughing, though more weakly than his host.

But then he stopped. Abruptly, his hand lifted and fell, signalling the termination of the revels. Silence radiated outwards from his throne: first the cardinals stilled, then the bishops, then the musicians, then the young noblewomen and the youths, who sheathed their nimble swords with scarcely any clatter. The bastide, even the birds above it, fell ominously silent, for when the Pope rested, so must all his vassals.

I was shown to a bedchamber decorated with sinister magpies and delicate clementine roses. A sickening beat sounded on a tabor as Clement entered like a bridegroom in an escort of cardinals and lackeys. Thankfully, Clement had as little stomach for this jockeying as I did. His palm flipped to dismiss the men. The servants removed my stiff outer garment and we were left to share a bed but little else, for we were too ill with ceremony for more.

At dawn, a heavy fist attacked the door. Nicolas de Besse leapt from his pallet beside our bed, shot open the bolt, and Hugues Roger banged in, announcing, "A body has washed up against the weir."

Clement threw his legs over the side of the bed and dropped his head between his knees. "Not one of my cardinals?"

"A guild-master who pitched into the river when the bridge collapsed. He became entangled in his heavy robes and drowned." Hugues Roger marched around the great chamber, cutting the edges of his turns sharply. "The guild-masters are blaming the Pope. The cursed Italians have tricked you into falling out with your own confraternities."

I rose from the bed. "Your Holiness, you need those guilds to construct your palace."

Hugues Roger halted in front of his brother. "This is well said. If they band against you, they will strangle the construction of the new wings."

I said, "Give all the masters a length of fine cloth to replace their spoilt robes, along with some furs above their station for their wives."

"That may salve their humiliation, but not mine." Clement lifted his head. "I have been caught in the snare of my own vanity. Where is the corpse?"

"Our Limousin knights have dragged him to a borie. After he is stripped of his clothing, he will be buried like a serf."

"No," said Clement. "Tell the knights to claim his body honourably. The man must be paid every homage, the best wax candles, the whitest shroud. Not in Avignon, where too much notice might incite rebellion, but in Ceccano's new chapel, where this misadventure belongs. Give Ceccano my instructions, then hasten to the widow to tell her yourself, most gently. Do not bribe her, Hugues, but with charm and plain speaking, do all that can be accomplished. I will ride to the city in penance. Arrange for thirteen paupers to be at the eastern gate, so I can kneel to wash their feet before I enter."

The brothers clasped hands—one ebony, the other ivory. Then Hugues Roger strode out, as full of purpose as his brother. Clement called for his steward to dress him and I withdrew into the antechamber, where all my gluttony came up into a pail a servant held for me—one course after another, until all nine had made an appearance. The girl whisked away the pail before the smell of it made me retch up my very guts.

Dressed in a simple priest's cassock, Clement mounted his white mule to ride the straightest route to Avignon, with as many dignitaries as could be persuaded to follow him. There was no upholstered barge with canopy to glorify our progress. As we neared the city wall, we learnt that the guild-masters had passed this way earlier, crest-fallen, wet, and in ill humour.

People were congregating outside the porte des Infirmières, their mood hostile, their behaviour truculent. Whipped into a sense of general injustice, they had come to witness the Pope's penitential return. Someone pushed an ass in front of the Pope with a sign saying, *Make me a cardinal too*. Troublemakers pelted us with petitions wrapped around rocks, then with rocks alone, and then anything hard within arm's reach. When the Pope's guards fell behind, a prankster smacked the white mule on the rump, causing it to bray, but Clement kept his seat, and once the folk were close enough to see his face, as dusty and streaked with sweat as theirs, they let him pass without harm.

But I was different. Even in a modest surcot, my hair covered by a wimple, I was taunted crudely. Some shouted *la Popessa* and some *la poule*. Ahead, dangling from a gibbet, was an effigy—manifestly big with child—gowned in a scarlet robe. The effigy's towering coiffure was a mockery of mine at Ceccano's banquet. But at least I had not been strung up in the flesh. I hoped that Clement had not seen the coarse placard slung around her neck, *Whore of Babylon*. Petrarch's words had a habit of spurting through this city like flames through hollow straws.

My guard retreated, the mob howled, and the lane became a mass of jumping flesh. A sow galloped between the legs of my palfrey, causing her to shy. A bucket of slops flung from an upper window splashed over me. At last, someone acted. The papal almoner trotted up on a squat grey pony to scatter coins, which cleared the mob out of my path. One of my guards climbed to the effigy to cut it down and the rest chased down the three worst troublemakers, then dragged them into the crossing, where the points of daggers prodded them to confess. With the heat of the steel at their backs, they would not be long about it.

I spurred my mount forwards to close the gap between the Pope and me. Ahead, just inside the gate, stood the thirteen paupers, clad in their own rags, their feet and toenails filthy. Even at four paces, they had a ferocious smell, but Clement did not buckle. I heard him confess as he inclined his forehead, "I am a sinner amongst sinners." If any man would bear God's yoke, he would. He climbed from his mule without assistance, knelt before the paupers, and reached for the sponge to bathe their feet with his bare hands.

Thirty-eight

I ALSO WAS FEELING the heat at my back. Believing in my own powers, I had flown too close to the sun and been singed. I sought out Hugues Roger to ask what had become of the prisoners, wanting to forgive them and thereby gain forgiveness for my own excess. He took me to Renaud de Pons, master of the palace jail. His skin thorny and his breath foul, he was from hide to hair a complete villain. He whistled a cheery hornpipe as he walked us to the torture chamber. The knaves had been tortured to extract confessions, then killed because they had nothing to say. The leader had been dismembered first. His head, limbs, trunk, and bagged entrails sat in a river of blood, waiting to be nailed to the city gates to warn against further treason.

I pressed my forehead against the wall to blind myself. "Even if they made that effigy, it was no more than I deserved for my pride."

De Pons snorted. "Do you want them to hang you from a gibbet?"

Hugues Roger guided me into the corridor, away from the butchery. "Henceforth, you must stay within the palace."

"I would rather have the freedom of the city."

For once, he did not growl at me. "Any attempt on you is, ipso facto, an attempt on the Pope. He is most secure inside the tour du Pape. That Florentine ambassador is spreading scandal about the counterfeit bridge—*le pont postiche*, he calls it—that dumped the guild-masters in the river. His confrère Francesco Petrarch has learnt that you are carrying Clement's child and is dipping his pen in vitriol again."

"At least my loyalty to Clement is no longer in doubt."

His jaw twisted. "No, I'll give you that. You've managed to convince my brother that the child is his. I will move you into the family apartments, where you will be better protected."

My garments and jewels weighed on me like winter livery. What I most wanted was to choose my own companions, to go into the city at will, to buy my own goods in the marketplace. But that was not possible, and as long as Clement believed my child was his, she would be safe—and so would I.

My daughter quickened on the eightieth day, the day her soul entered her body. Fœtus animatus. In bed with Clement, I shifted his hand to my belly, but he could not feel the life inside. He now spent more time with his master mason than with me. His plans for the new wings were being translated to stone: firm, white blocks from the best quarries. As the tour de la Garde-robe rose, the Italian opposition grew. Every piece of masonry, every stone and nail, every fortification, was an insult to the Romans. Jean de Louvres and Matteo Giovannetti were imported to direct the work, but the hundreds of men who dragged the blocks on sledges, dressed them with mallet and chisel, then winched them into place were from our seven parishes, and soon Clement was easing back into their favour.

In the étuves at the base of the new tower, my sweat mingled with Clement's in the aromatic steam. This caldarium was Clement's idea and he sat next to me, counting the age marks I had cut into my thigh.

"Why did you stop at seventeen?"

Because I met Francesco. But I could not tell Clement that.

"This looks like a chalice," he said, touching my birthmark. "You have borne one son and will bear another. Your new son will be a citizen by right of birth. When he is fifteen, I will appoint him bishop of the city."

I felt a flat-footed blow inside my womb—the kick of a girl, not a boy. I moved his hand and this time he could feel it. "And if God chooses to give us a daughter?"

"I will make her a dynastic marriage. I was once betrothed myself. As a young clerk, I fell in love and fancied myself a troubadour. However, I could not get the girl with child, so her father voided the agreement and took his daughter back. That was when I espoused the church instead. Soon I was an impetuous young monk at the University of Paris, as sterile as a mule." He gave me time to apprehend his meaning—that he knew he hadn't got me with child—then tapped my belly. "I assume this one is Petrarch's as well. I approved his petition to legitimize your son since Petrarch is a thorn in my side and it will hasten his departure. Does he know he fathered this second child?"

"No." At least I could be honest about this.

"It must be kept that way. I do not object to being thought the father, for there is no greater fool in Avignon than a prelate who cannot get a courtesan with child. But if you divulge the truth, prophet that you are, countess that you are not, I must cast you out."

He took me—in the heat and sweat of the caldarium, my back against the lead bathing tub, my eyes fixed on the clementine rose sculpted in the vaulting—more roughly than he had ever done. I had risked his affection and my life for a moment's pleasure in his library and could not gamble on his forgiveness another time.

In the days ahead, Clement toiled at his sermons in his new study, soothed by his two gardens, the one outside his window and the woodland fresco painted inside to remind him of his Limousin birth-place. When his sermons were too plain to suit his ear, he asked me to bring books from the library so he could steal from others, even Petrarch, to feather his texts with borrowed plumage. And now, more of Francesco's writings were coming to light, in which he did not spare the Pope. In a new sonnet, he preached that *From this impious Babylon from whence all shame has fled, I too have fled to save my life.* It was as if each man wanted to be the other, for as Francesco's poems soared into sermons about the cardinals' vices, the Pope's sermons slipped indecently into rhyme.

Félicité slid from me easily, embracing her destiny without com-plaint. The astrologer cast her horoscope, pronouncing her birth auspicious. Mighty planets, he told the Pope, had contested at her engendering. Her little heart beat wildly beneath my fingers, two beats for every one of mine. I kissed her fontanelle, and vowed to guard her better than I had her brother. One day, I hoped, we would both take up residence on our lands at Turenne, where the wind blew free of clerics' perfume.

Clement presided at my daughter's baptism in the small chapel, twelve royal feet by twelve royal feet, which jutted like a pious after-thought from the banqueting hall. A few canons attended, a few boy choristers, but it was no ceremony to speak of. Clement looked toler-antly at Félicité until she shrieked on being dunked into the font. My servant rushed her away and her cries diminished down the corridor. Behind me, the sound of velvet creeping against velvet: the niece with the tight brown curls, who had added ermine to her wrists and throat. In the boil of women in the palace, she was rising to the top like scum, eager to interpose herself between the Pope and me. Instead of follow-ing my child as I wished, I went to Clement, who was running his hand over the new coat of plaster.

"I must choose a subject for the frescoes," he said. "Matteo Giovannetti is ready to paint this chapel."

"Why not dedicate it to Saint Martial to rival Ceccano's chapel at Gentilly," I suggested, knowing he had a soft spot for French saints. "He was a Limousin like you, and if Saint Peter is pictured giving Martial his rod, it will vindicate the Pope's residence in Avignon."

He allowed himself a smile. "Your advice is both timely and political."

"You could be the model for him." I ran my hand across his stubble. "Yours is the chin of a saint, especially with those black hairs on it."

He caught my hand and held it tightly. "Your laughter echoes in these stark corridors. I have missed you at my side, Countess."

With each day, I found new ways to stay there. Although Clement had washed the paupers' feet, he was still smarting, for reports of papal luxury were migrating along the trade routes of Europe. In penance, he pledged to increase the supply of grain to the Pignotte, and within six months the almshouse was giving away twenty thousand loaves a day. Even so, Clement's banquets did not cease, for he did not want the dignitaries to take their appetites to enemy tables. The number of men residing in the palace grew to four hundred, four hundred and fifty, five hundred. Women navigated the corridors in garments with ties and clasps that served no purpose except to delight the eye. Their provenance as murky as my own, they crept into antechambers and forged alliances in bed. Even the new camerlengo left his door ajar to view the palace nieces, his counting board heaped with the wealth of spoil from prelates too spiritual to father heirs.

Before long, Félicité was begging words from me as other children begged sweetmeats, and thus she grew clever but thin, strong inside but frail outside. Each night she fell asleep in my arms, tickling her nose with a feather until her hand fell quiet. In the day, I mended rare books and commissioned new ones, parcelling out the gatherings to the scribes. To be near Félicité, I often worked in my chamber, where we listened to the steady chinking of the masons' chisels outside. One by one, the old buildings were demolished, the rock was levelled, and the workmen shouldered away the debris in paniers. As the new wing rose, stone by chiselled stone, Félicité learnt to recognize each man by his hat and girth and named him in a child's fashion. Dust, mud, noise, and blocks of limestone—she re-enacted each day's labour with pebbles and sticks inside our chamber. I now lived two lives, one as Clement's consort and one in the labyrinth where I raised my daughter. The less seen of Félicité, the better. Although I kept her away from the public chambers, I took her frequently to the Pope's ménagerie to feed the animals.

In summer, we found an orphaned crow in the garden. We mothered it, kept it warm in a woolly box, and dripped milk down a ribbon into its beak. Soon it was tottering about our chamber like a drunk bishop. When Félicité released the crow in the garden, one of Clement's nephews caught its wings and pinned them under his feet. Félicité tossed a rock at him to make him stop, but hit the gargoyle on the Pope's fountain instead, chipping its ugly flaring nostrils. As a result, the children had to appear before Clement in the audience chamber, who chose to make an amusing example of them to the day's petitioners. Félicité was crying, for she was not yet four—too young to tell a genial Pope from a harsh one.

The boy chorister, who was twice her age, argued his own case against her. "Your Holiness, this girl is a sorcière like her mother. That crow is her familiar. So are the rocks, for she commanded them to take to the air to attack me."

The ingenuity of this delighted Clement, who called his nephew to his knee to rub his hair, then forbade Félicité from entering the papal garden. As he gave his judgement, he scrutinized her tearful face, since I had allowed him few glimpses of her over the years. Was he looking for Francesco's features, or plotting a betrothal between the nephew and Félicité? To secure titles and lands, Clement had made alliances between even younger children. When my daughter returned to me, I pushed her head into my skirts and ran her from the chamber.

I knew what he had seen. At birth, Félicité's hair had been a papal gold like Clement's, but it had now darkened. Her skin was cream skimmed from the top of milk, deepening towards olive as each day passed. I started to wash her complexion with almond and her hair with camomile, which only made her eyes look blacker. Her maid began to comment on her appearance. Before long, our servants would whisper that a swarthy man had fathered my child, perhaps an Italian. Someone—the camerlengo, the French allies—would delve into Clement's past, and unearth a series of mistresses without children. They would conclude the Pope was sterile and accuse me of whoring with another man. Clement would be forced to discard me. I might be jailed in a tower like Saint Barbara, or roasted in the hot baths like Saint Cecilia. And what would become of my sweet daughter?

In late autumn, the wind vibrated the waxed membranes over our windows and our door rattled. I woke one night to discover Félicité sitting up in bed beside me, chewing on the corner of her blanket because she thought that the nephews were breaking down the door. She huddled next to me until first light, picking apart the wool of her blanket while I read to her from our bestiary. She had never seen a pasture, or a sheep, or an old woman carding and spinning wool. The only animals she knew were the monkeys, lion, camel, and the other exotic beasts in the Pope's ménagerie, which was now denied to her. That day, I knelt to the Virgin to implore her aid, then boiled a root of Our Lady's Candle together with a small destroying angel to make a numbing potion. On this night, All Saints' Eve, there would be merrymaking by the folk and my servants would not return until day-break. Félicité and I ate a simple meal: a roasted beet, stewed celery stalks, and a basted fowl. Then I poured the potion into her goblet with the serpent handle.

"We will be sorcerers together," I told her. "Drink this, and when your maid returns, you will have disappeared."

Instead of drinking, she snapped my miséricorde out of my belt tongue to admire how neatly the ivory pieces fit together to disguise the weapon. "Will I need your secret knife?"

"No, my sweet. You will be safe where you are going."

"What are the words?" She asked this question each time she looked at the phrase carved into the ivory.

"*Amor vincit omnia.* Love conquers all." I held out the goblet and her small hands gripped the serpent.

"Will it hurt, Maman?"

"No more than a fever. This tastes sweetly of honey."

She stirred after nocturns, breaking out into a sweat. I sponged her, then nestled her in my arms, rocking her to comfort us both. When her tremors worsened, I waited for her heart to slow. It was now safe to send for the old surgeon Jean de Parme, since he could do nothing to help her. Félicité was lying quietly in my arms when he arrived. Seeing the pain written on my face, he squeezed my shoulder to console me. Just as he bent to examine Félicité, she went into a spasm in my arms and he moved back. Then she fell motionless. He pronounced her dead of a putrid fever, because of her clammy skin and cloying breath, and ordered me to bury her at once. He scuffled away, afraid to touch her. My daughter's face was the colour of béchamel. So was mine, for I had truly gone through hell and could no longer stifle the violence of my sobs.

I bundled Félicité's tiny corpse into the contagion shroud I had made ready. The night watch raised the portcullis hastily, crossed themselves, and retreated in fear. I carried her through the dark alleys to the priory of the Poor Clares, where I laid her gently beneath the ancient Virgin in their church. I spared only a glance for the wooden Magdalene weeping at the foot of Christ, for I did not wish to be seen. If I took shelter here with Félicité, as my heart counselled, or lingered to weep over her even for an hour, I would endanger both of us. I removed the contagion cross from her shroud and loosened the top to reveal her sweet face. Inside the shroud, where I had told the prioress to look for it, I placed a purse with gold florins sufficient for an oblate's dowry.

Thirty-nine

ON ALL SAINTS' DAY, I knelt in Saint Martial's diminutive chapel to pray for my daughter, my eyes fixed upon Martial's soul being borne upwards by two angels towards the azur d'Allemagne heaven that Giovannetti had just painted. Even though the tapers had melted into a lump of wax, Clement was still dry-eyed, as if Félicité's death had solved a problem he was struggling with. The choir-master sang a lachrymosa—a single syllable hammered to vibrating gold wire, then another, then another. The boy choristers opened their lungs, their voices clean and pure, their hearts genuinely heavy, and then the brief service was over.

At midnight, when Clement had fallen asleep, I left his bedchamber by the circular staircase hidden in the wall. I was not returning to my own chamber, as usual, but leaving the palace by the postern gate, the one the servants used. When I reached the priory of the Poor Clares, I sought out the prioress, who was waiting for me. She had discovered Félicité in the church before prime as I had arranged. The shroud had kept Félicité warm and the potion had worn off, doing her no harm. She had been sitting up with the gold florins in her hand, waiting to give them to the prioress, as we had planned. Now fed and fondled, Félicité was asleep in her bed in the lay dormitory. She had died to danger and been reborn to safety. My tears in the chapel had been crocodile, for I would never have harmed my beloved child.

Before giving Félicité the potion in the serpent cup, I had told her, "You must be brave. We will play a trick on the palace by pretending you are dead. When you wake, you will be in a sheltered place with kindly nuns."

"Yes, Maman, it will be a good joke. We will be sorcerers together. Only, let me play with some new children, for I am tired of the Pope's nephews."

Now the prioress took me through the cloister and up the staircase to the dormitory, where I found Félicité in bed. After I had knelt to thank the Blessed Virgin for her aid, I tickled Félicité's nose with a feather.

She stood on the bed and leapt into my arms. "Maman! I knew the serpent would protect me."

My voice stumbled as I explained that the priory must now be her home. Her eyes stood out like coals and her hair stuck up like thistledown.

"What ails your throat, Maman?"

"Only a little frog."

"Fais vite, let him jump out!" She pushed on my cheeks to expel the poor creature.

She was a wise little girl, older than her years, and knew there had been much to fear in the palace. She led the way into the garden in her night shoes. Here, under the fallen leaves, she showed me the late-bearing strawberry plants and picked the berry she had saved for me. When the bells rang for nocturns, we watched the Poor Clares walk in pairs past us to the church. Although they belonged to the Franciscan Order of Poor Ladies, their fine brown habits were trimmed in fur. The gossip trickled down the column as their eyes assessed me: a well-made robe without blazons, a silver belt with a carved ivory tongue. A merchant's wife who had borne a child in disgrace? Was she visiting at such an hour to evade her husband? As the prioress passed, she tapped my arm and laid her finger across her lips. My secret would be secure with the Clarisses.

Félicité and I listened to the psalms, then her soft hands clung to me as I took my leave. We kissed eyes, noses, ears, and mouths. She remembered her vow to be brave, saying, "Only, come again soon, Maman, and we will whisper in the night."

In the priory of the Poor Clares, Félicité became as nocturnal as a black-eyed owl, sleeping only an owl's sleep until I arrived from the palace to wake her. She fell happily from high to low estate for she was a sanguine child. Remembering how I had loved Clairefontaine, I asked that she perform small chores. Soon she had a plot of frost-bitten earth where she could sow poppies in the spring. Before long, she had a friend. The Poor Clares called Anne-Prospère *la petite misère* because she was of phlegmatic humour, but she was as welcoming a companion for Félicité as Elisabeth had been for me. Anne-Prospère told me that her father disliked her, so her mother had given her to the nuns to keep her out of his sight. In the day, when I yearned for Félicité's hand in mine, I took solace that I was not the only mother who had chosen the priory as an asylum for her daughter.

After the frescoes of Saint Martial's life were finished and the chapel had been dedicated, Clement turned his attention to the beatification of another of his favourites, Yves de Bretagne. It was soon after Yves had been canonized—for the devil's advocate failed to vilify him in the canonization hearing—that a letter arrived for the vicomtesse de Turenne, palais des Papes, Avignon. A pilgrim riding hard from the south who sought urgent audience with the Pope had carried it. I recognized Gherardo's bold hand at once.

My dear Countess,

I write to you as one much changed, whose day is filled with labour and singing the offices faithfully to Our Lord.

I have found refuge in this harsh order, with its fierce rule of silence. Here, our hands do the work of our mouths. I have prayed and slept and eaten in my solitary hermitage. I have worked in the fields until I have collapsed in exhaustion. Can you imagine how difficult this silence has been for me, for whom talking is life? I came to crave the offices of the day, when we opened our mouths to sing, more to one another than to God. My nostrils hungered for the censer, hungered for the sulphurous wick of a candle, hungered for the pungent smell of love denied.

For four years, I did not touch the flesh of another man except the novice I shaved. I caressed his head like a lover, learning every bump in his skull (and which body part it controlled) as if it were my own. I admired his ear as a sinner does the orifice of his confessor. When I was done, he shaved me, prolonging the exquisite torture. We spoke only with our fingers, yet this was the deepest love that I have ever known. When finally my hands strayed into forbidden paths, he could tell no one, since his mouth was stopped by vows.

For we were now monks. I had foresworn my past life (so far as it could be foresworn by one such as I) and had embarked on the long, penitential route up the mountain when the atra mors came north to punish us. The tale came to us through a sailor begging confession, who had been in Messina harbour when a plague ship arrived from the Crimea groaning with the dead and dying. His merchantman set sail on the next tide, putting in to Toulon with a diseased crew. He travelled north by land, to seek shelter with us at Montrieux. He was the devil's man, for his tongue and urine were black. Near his genitals was a lump like an

apple, and rotten eggs lurked in his armpits. He died spitting
poisonous blood into the prior's ear.

Two days later, the prior died in my arms and I carried him
on my back to his grave. Soon there were more monks struck
down than monks to tend them. When there were only three left,
we shrove one another, then dug a pit large enough for three. We
tied a rope to a sling filled with earth and ran it through a pulley,
so that it needed only tugging to release its cargo into the pit. We
made a vow that the last one to die would climb in alive and tug
the rope, to join his brethren under the rich, autumnal earth.

When the first man died, we dumped him in the gaping
hole. We slept in one bed, unshaven. When my lover died, I
dragged his body to the pit to roll it over the edge. I released the
goat, the sheep, and our milking cow to forage in the fields and
walked naked to my grave. I was not depressed in spirits, for my
life had come to a just end. I climbed into the pit, lay down on
top of my bloated, stinking brothers, and reached for the rope to
drop the cradle of earth upon my head. The monastery dog sat
by the grave, observing me with alarm.

To say that a vision stayed my hand would be an act of pride.
Visions are granted only to the pure of heart like you, Solange.
But for the first time in two score years, I thought of another
first, myself second.

If I died, who would feed Fidèle? In his stupid loyalty, he would
squat by my grave until he died of thirst. I climbed out and filled a
kneading tub with water from the well. With Fidèle at my heels, I
dragged it to the grave and climbed back in. He sat on his haunches,
cocking his head at me, his tail wagging at this game. I lay down on
my deathbed and closed my eyes to enjoy the blessed repose.

I could hear Fidèle's soft, red tongue lapping the water. My
hand reached for the rope, then hesitated. I had only postponed
his death. Now he would die of slow starvation, not of thirst. It

flashed upon me that his wagging tail must be a Sign. I did not quibble that the medium was an unlikely one for God to use, for this Sign was followed by a Voice.

"Get up, Gherardo," the Voice commanded. "You will not get out of work so easily this time. Get up, you lazy beast, to feed your hound. Your field needs tilling. Gather your livestock back into the fold and run this priory by yourself!"

And so I did, taking the quick, easy way out of my grave by scrambling up the steepest bank. I did not want to give God time to change His mind.

I tilled that field and another. Since then, God has vouchsafed to me poor wanderers, bereft in soul and body, speaking foreign tongues, who have walked over the hills to escape the plague cities. Here they have found a home, digging and hoeing in return for my vast stores of wine and foodstuffs.

I must go now and perform lauds in my out-of-tune way, for Fidèle and I keep the Carthusian offices here. He is all men to me and I all dogs to him. I would not trade him for the noble wolfhound that was once the pride of Cardinal Colonna. We have made a pact to die as brethren, but I trust that God will keep us alive until He has exacted a just measure of industry from me.

Beware, dear Countess, of sailors bearing tales from Toulon, for the plague is coming north.

A servant of God in Montrieux-le-Jeune.

Vacate et videte quoniam ego sum Deus.

The pilgrim carrying Gherardo's letter brought others addressed to Pope Clement VI that told a similar story. I listened in apprehension as the pilgrim begged the Pope to pray for his own city, Aix, and to open the gates to all the refugees toiling on foot or by ox-cart towards

Avignon. Panic rode before them, for they were said to be travelling under a plague-cloud of biblical dimensions that was advancing one league a day. Even now, the lookouts on the palace towers thought they could see, to the south, the black sirocco carrying the plague towards us.

Just before Epiphany in the year 1348, Clement sat in his half-finished audience chamber, listening to cases and portents about the plague. In my chair beside him, I anchored my tongue, for too much prophecy was already in the air. Every delegate was allowed to speak in turn, both rich and poor. A nobleman complained that his cask of wine had turned to vinegar. A beggar displayed the miraculous blood spots on his tattered cloak. A savant spoke of auguries in flood and famine and proclaimed that the eclipse had been a portent of the horror now travelling northwards. A village priest swore that the plague was God's punishment for wickedness. Avarice, lust, gluttony—he rhymed off the court's sins, including the Pope's incest with his niece. Had this simple man read the eclogues Francesco was writing from Italy, in which the Pope appeared as a drunkard and the cardinals as goats?

As the corps of refugees trudged closer, the citizens demanded that the gates be barred, but Clement was adamant that his city would house all those who sought its shelter. I was visiting Félicité inside the Poor Clares' priory one night when the gatekeeper alerted me that the first refugees, more than two hundred strong, had stepped on the rue du Cheval Blanc. I left quickly, keeping ahead of the migrants as they dragged themselves, cowls pulled over their foreheads, up the rue de la Curaterie, then the rue allant du Puits des bœufs, driving fear before them until they reached the papal square. I was too late to get back into the palace, since the guardsmen, in their breastplates and polished helms, had formed a human barrier to prevent the migrants from entering. Their march halted, the men threw their robes into a heap, lit the fire, and circled the smoking mess, beating their naked flesh with tails of rope.

I watched them from across the square, where a mob was gathering. Some people were ringing hand bells to dispel the deadly plague cloud. Others were accusing the flagellants of being Jews or Jew-haters or plague-carriers or, in a muddle of fear, all three at once. They were soon joined by other knaves, who had armed themselves with cudgels, clubs, and pikestaffs to give the visitors a thrashing. Every chamber-pot and close-stool was making it his business to take the law into his own hands.

The migrants' scourges hit their chests then backs, their right shoulders then left shoulders, foreheads then thighs, with a nauseating *whack-whack, whack-whack*. By dawn, their whips were red and their blood was flowing from open wounds. One man fell on the ground, his tongue swollen like a dog's. I approached to pick up his water flagon. A few drops remained, which I squeezed on his tongue. He had a pungent odour and black patches under his skin, but as far as I could tell, none of the carbuncles Gherardo had reported. Then, as he rolled over, I saw it—nestling in the pit of his arm—a black plague-egg. I ran the gauntlet of mocking knaves to get to the mercy barrel across the piazza, but when I attempted to fill the flagon, a rogue kicked the barrel and it rolled down the slope, breaking the spigot. Before I could say an Ave Maria, all the water sprayed out on the ground. The flagellants were now a stupefied mass staring at the wasted water with glassy eyes.

A steady drumbeat signalled the approaching men-at-arms. The new city marshal, one of the Pope's nephews, was finally making an appearance with the captain of the palace, Aigrefeuille, in his star-studded armour. Their gauntlets flew this way and that, flashing their ancestral crests as they gave orders, until they had persuaded the flagel-lants to leave the square with promises of clothing, bread, and ale.

The plague-stricken friar I had touched leapt up as if resurrected, to join the flagellants who were snaking off. The city knaves now aimed themselves at me, making a great racket, in which I heard shouts of *Saint Barbara!* I saw how it must look to them: as if I had raised the friar from the dead. The coarser men taunted me, full of unspent energy and sour drink. One took a swipe at me with a knife, drawing blood.

Another plucked some hair from my head and held his trophy aloft, swearing it would ward off the plague.

Some red-haired smiths collected around me to tug at my sleeves and hem. Instead of chasing off my attackers, they joined in, using their clumsy weapons to cut pieces from my robe. I was spun from man to man as a source of relics, and when my blood dripped on the earth, they mopped it reverently with scraps of my robe or filthy sponges. How had it come to pass that my life was no longer my own, but the property of such men? Those who had worshipped me as the miraculous bell-ringer on the tower, their own Saint Barbara who could drive off thunder and eclipses, were on the point of turning me into a martyr themselves. I clutched the hilt of my miséricorde, ready to plunge it into my flesh before they did it for me. My vision blurred into a delirium of pulsing reds and blacks. Was this a malfeasance of the earth, or the result of the surrounding horror and stink and noise?

How long had I held my knife before the sun rose from behind the palace? I hid it in the tongue of my belt just in time, for at my elbows were two Limousin knights in full armour, their weapons reflecting light and order. Never had I greeted them with greater joy. To my shame, I shrank from my dark roots and became, once more, a creature of the light.

Forty

T HE TEETH OF THE inner portcullis bit into the earth behind me, and the knights' fingers dug into my elbows. I was not so much being rescued as force-marched to a reckoning. Once I was dressed more cleanly, Hugues Roger collected me. He fell in step with me, showing his knees in a short hunting tunic. He must have ridden hard to get there, because his hose was streaked with dust.

"Why did you expose yourself to that jacquerie in the piazza? You should not have left the palace. And to touch a diseased friar? For a supposed clairvoyante, you are remarkably short-sighted." He gave me a sideways jab into the salle de Jésus. "Here's my brother waiting for you. Try not to cause him any more pain."

Word of the mystery in the piazza had travelled quickly, for the new camerlengo's robes flew out darkly as he stormed in, trailing Guy de Chauliac, the most recent court surgeon. More boots were scraping across the tiles. Advancing were Clement's nephews, Nicolas de Besse and Guillaume de La Jugie, followed by the men who had married into the family, then the uncles, cousins, officers, and Limousin nobles.

Nicolas de Besse wore his new cardinal's mozzetta, but few of the others had been given time to put on their robes of office. Notwithstanding the haste, seven cardinals stood before their pontiff, all members of the family. The men talked in bursts about the need to protect the Pope, cursed and commiserated about the pestilence, and reached a decision quickly.

Hugues Roger spoke for them. "Clement—Your Holiness—we have decided that you must retreat to Châteauneuf-du-Pape until the disease abates."

"I will not seek asylum while my city is blackened by contagion."

Hugues Roger threw up his hands, then snapped them into fists. "You cannot come and go like a commoner!"

The surgeon steepled his fingers so that his thumbs grazed his heart. "If you will not retreat, Holy Father, you must keep to your private apartments and see only those examined by your doctors. Banquets and audiences must be postponed. For her own protection, the Countess will be sent into the country."

Clement was brusque. "The Countess will remain here with me."

The men were about to argue, when a herald came in at a run to report that the diseased friar and several of the flagellants had died in an almshouse outside the wall. More troubling, three of the city's own Carmelites were dead and others dying.

"The Carmelites are hermits," Captain Aigrefeuille said. "They cannot have been exposed to the flagellants."

The runner said, "A few days ago, they accepted a novice from Aigues-Mortes."

"Throw in bladders of wine, then nail the cloister shut," Aigrefeuille said. "Let it become their tomb."

Clement lifted his gloved hand to silence the captain. "There will be other plague houses. You cannot board all of them up. De Chauliac, how does it spread?"

"It is thought that the poisonous vapours enter by the mouth and nose."

"Then we will build fires in the streets to drive the vapours off," said Clement. "Where is the new city marshal? Tell him to bring me the parish maps. We will need to enlarge the cimetière des pauvres."

Clement and his officers worked through the day to organize alms and relief. After the evening angelus, the Pope appeared at his new indulgence window to speak to the clerics, merchants, and guild-masters called to assembly in the courtyard below.

His final instructions were, "Every doctor in Avignon, from the Jews to my own physicians, must attend the plague-stricken at my expense. Each of my churches will become an infirmary. The priests must attend every man, woman, and child with the peste to give them the last rites."

A man in a brown cowl hollered from the courtyard, "They are dying faster than they can be absolved!"

The Pope replied, "Then every priest from curé to cardinal must remit their sins without hearing their confessions."

"How many cardinals do you see here?" the loud-mouth yelled. "Most are packing up their households! Sauve-qui-peut."

Save yourself. Others picked up the cry, pushing a sea of cowardly flesh towards the bottleneck of the double portcullis.

On the morrow, when the herald returned, he was told to stay in the grande cour, so he would not breathe on anybody's face. He broadcast his news from below. The refugees from the south were finally crossing the Durance. Half had died on the journey, but the survivors, who were coughing up black blood, would soon be at the city gates.

We never saw the runner again. Another replaced him, then another, as each was infected and succumbed. The wealthy Avignonnais fled to their ancestral houses in the country and Clement's allies barricaded themselves at Villeneuve across the bridge, thinking more of their own

selves than of the general doom. Soon everyone with the means to escape
had done so, leaving the diseased and poor inside the city wall. Palace
servants who fell ill were stripped of their livery and sent to their homes.
If servants had the misfortune to die inside the palace, their corpses were
shunted out at night or shoved into the largest mouth of the palace drain,
the égout souterrain, to wash towards the Rhône.

Without Félicité beside me, the hours slowed and my food tasted
flat and bitter. Each day, I climbed the corkscrew stairs to the palace
roof to strain my eyes for the flag on the Poor Clares' bell-tower: white,
the agreed-on signal to tell me that Félicité was well and God was still
capable of grace. The Poor Clares had barred their gate and cloistered
themselves so they would not contract the plague. They were of noble
blood and loved their comfort more than succouring refugees. For this
I was glad, because the disease had been shut out also.

As the weeks passed, the Avignon death toll mounted. At first it
was said that a thousand people died in a month, then a thousand a
week, then a thousand in a single day. The sick and needy clung to the
Pignotte, scooping up the hard loaves that the Pope's bakers threw out
the windows at them to avoid contamination.

Then, just before Shrovetide, the branches of the Sorgue flooded
the alluvial plain to the east of the city. The mistral blew fiercely for
three days, then six, then nine. I crept onto the palace roof and sheltered behind the parapet to watch the wind-lashed waters of the Rhône
batter Saint Bénezet's bridge, and push the waves into the moat. The
dyers' canal, now unable to feed into the moat, was running over its
banks to swamp the dwellings of the workers. Some of them were
already camped across from the palace on Doms rock.

What I saw next alarmed me even more. The white flag at the
priory of the Poor Clares was hanging by a prayer. A gust flattened me
upon the roof. When the mistral eased long enough for me to stand
upright again, the flag was gone. I scrambled into the stairwell and down
the steps, to find Clement's stewards rushing between the garde-robe

and bedchamber to clothe him in his amice, alb, stole, chasuble, and cope. I was in the procession when the Pope rode his white mule to the riverbank to consecrate the expanse of the Rhône, blessing it by breadth and length, so that the plague victims tipped into its currents would be remitted of their sins.

Having seen the bloated corpses for himself, Clement sat next to his fire, reading dispatches and giving free rein to his natural fears. His humours were out of alignment, veering gloomily towards melancholy. But who was I to belittle his terror, since it was as much for his people as himself? I lived with my own fear, for the Poor Clares had not hoisted their flag since the mistral.

One night in my own bed, I shook myself out of a paralytic state and went to Clement's bedchamber. I emerged from the hidden staircase to find him propped on the short papal bed, his lips stained red by courage-giving wine. His jowls were grossly enflamed, his skull was bandaged, and his eyelids were bruised. He told me that waking alone and falling prey to apprehensions, he had sent for his old surgeon, Jean de Parme. I lifted the bandage to see what was beneath. Jean de Parme had drilled a hole, which now oozed fluid into the flimsy gauze.

Clement was enunciating more precisely than usual. "It is only a small hole to let the ill humours escape."

I crawled beneath the fur coverings to comfort him. "Did the drilling hurt?"

"Very little. The vapours made a malevolent hiss as they shot out."

We lay together, his hand idling on my thigh, going nowhere, until he fell asleep and I rolled to face the window. At dawn, a rare burst of sun penetrated the deep embrasure, exposing the much-scraped parchment of his skin. I was growing old as well and did not relish looking in the pier-glass as much as formerly. Soon I might wear the guimpe and mantle of a mature woman.

But not just yet. I was pulling on my azure robe when in came Hugues Roger with the surgeon de Chauliac, who seemed to have taken command of the fight against the plague. Hugues Roger was hitching up his belt as if he had dressed in haste. After them arrived Captain Aigrefeuille of the pointed stars, with the jailer Renaud de Pons. Five or six other men, all vital to palace operations, entered the room. The servants spilled out of curtains to begin the morning routine and the old steward threw a brick of antimony and arsenic on the fire. The odour was perverse, but Clement believed that it drove off any plague fumes that rose this high.

"Knot faster," I told my maid, who was fastening my sleeves. I had very nearly been caught sleeping like a servant.

De Chauliac approached the bed. He surveyed the Pope's tranquility and his puffy face, then peeled the gauze back to inspect the lesion. From this, I gathered that de Chauliac had encouraged the trepanning of Clement's skull. He applied his fingers to Clement's armpits and groin, searching for growths, then palpated his bladder for stones, a humiliating exercise repeated every morning before the surgeon proclaimed that the papacy was in good health. But why had de Chauliac brought the captain and the jailer with him?

The old steward robed the Pope while de Chauliac's bony fingers examined me through my clothes, prodding along my collarbone, beneath my arms, and deep between my legs, where plague-eggs might be lodging. He pushed up my eyelids with his thumbs, looked at one eye, then the second.

De Chauliac made a smug bow, one hand at his navel, the other at his back. "Holy Father, observe how the Countess sweats. She is carrying the plague."

This was absurd. "I have no symptoms," I protested. "I may be moist, but so would any woman swathed in layers of linen, wool, and sendal."

Again he spoke to the Pope, not to me. "When she went out amongst the flagellants, she drew contagion into her as a lightning-rod draws light. She is the source of the ill humours that have been unsettling you.

The servants complain of a dark miasma issuing from her eyes. You must turn your gaze from her at once." He snapped his fingers for Aigrefeuille to step between the Pope and me.

"If I had been infected by the flagellants," I said, "I would have died several weeks ago."

My maid threw herself at the surgeon helpfully. "On that night, she left the palace at the darkest hour. I followed her through the postern gate to a brothel."

The words fell heavily upon my chest. She might have followed me into the alleyways behind the palace, even past a brothel, but no further. However, to prove my innocence, I would need to confess that I had gone to the Poor Clares' priory and Aigrefeuille's men would unearth Félicité. Since she was already thought dead, her life would be worth a toss of salt. Once Clement had taken it in, he would be forced to put me aside, as he had warned me years before.

Aigrefeuille said, "Your Holiness, the Countess has wilfully endangered your life."

"What would happen to Holy Mother Church if you fell ill?" the camerlengo asked. "The death of the Pope would sink the city."

Only Clement and his brother showed any pity for me. Hugues Roger was knocking the dust thoughtfully from his hose. "I have been talking to the ironmongers, that peculiar guild of red-haired men who are working on the palace. They used scraps of her garments to soak up her blood during the riot in the piazza and swear these devotos have protected them from the plague. What if there is some truth in this?"

Clement swivelled hopefully. "Then she has kept the disease from me, not brought it."

"If this is true, Holy Father, it is necromancy," the surgeon said. "Consider that she touched the dying friar, but did not die."

"You also touched the plague-ridden and are alive," I countered. "I am a prophet, not a necromancer."

The surgeon's rebuttal was quick. "A prophet who has not prophesied since the eclipse."

But Clement would not be put off. "If tokens of her blood and clothing ward off pestilence, her charisms go beyond prophecy to the miraculous."

"My dear Pope," the camerlengo said, "you must stop looking for saints under every bed-sheet. Think how much it cost us to canonize Saint Yves, yet nobody takes him seriously but you."

The camerlengo and the surgeon gathered Clement into their conversation and walked him from the chamber. The other officers followed, circling him with their iron will.

Hugues Roger stayed with me in the bedchamber. "Clement has received another vicious letter by Francesco Petrarch. This time he signed it. He says that the Pope's doctors are charlatans who are trying to kill him and reports a blow Clement took to his skull that sharpened his memory. You must have told Petrarch about the trepanning."

"How could he have heard of it in Italy so swiftly?"

He looked at me sharply. "You were not aware? Jean de Parme drilled Clement once before."

"Then Petrarch heard about it some other way. All the Tuscans know one another's business. Any one of them could have told him." Guido, I thought, though I did not say it, or any of the other Italian notaries.

He relented. "Yes, I see that now, but you cannot blame me for suspecting. You come and go too freely. Who can tell how many men you sleep with—where, or when?" His eyes lifted my hem to dine on possibilities. His pity gone, he planted his hand on my breast, his oily palm a lubricant to something more. When the back of my legs hit his brother's bed, his knee spread them apart. "This is not the only ermine pillow in the palace."

We had both been faithful to Our Lord, the Pope, but now that Clement must cast me aside, I saw what Hugues Roger was wanting:

the right to claim the spoil. "No," I said. "I will go to my estates in Turenne." At his laugh, my gut knotted.

He twisted my arm to rip off the sleeve with the Turenne crest, and stuffed it into his shirt. "This will go to the Pope's new consort."

He left to follow the Pope, who was progressing towards the ante-chamber in his band of officers. Clement's force spent, he had simply let me go. I was not surprised to discover that he loved Avignon more than he loved me. He would be safe here, with his iron chancellors, waging his war against the peste. I would make it easy for him. I did not chase after, but took a last look towards the library, where I still had projects underway.

I walked slowly and thought fast. I had no friends to aid me. I could not turn to Guido, for any alliance thus revealed would injure him. If I got through the double portcullis, the guards would hunt me down until they snared me in an inn or tavern. I would be tossed into the torture chamber, where even the Pope's fondness could not save me from his jailer's gusto for extracting limbs from sockets. No man would lower his eyes as my soul passed out of me. If by chance I escaped the net being dragged for me, the folk would clutch at me, begging me to defend them from contagion. I could never wander freely on the streets of Avignon. Once they recognized me, they would yank my clothing from me, piece by holy piece, then tear out the hairs on my head, my nails, until I was stripped of every token that could be used to stave off the plague.

At last, this tortured thinking blew me into harbour. I had a duty to stay alive to protect Félicité. Martyrdom would save no one and would certainly give me no pleasure. In my bedchamber, my maids were already pawing my garments. While they were gossiping over my state robes and fur-lined cloaks, fancying them theirs, I put a few things into the alms-bag at my waist. I pointed myself towards the latrine tower as if answering the call of nature, but darted, instead, into the garde-robe, where visiting prelates left their outerwear, along with bribes for the officers. I drew a red cape from a hook and put it on. The cardinal who had hung it there had also left his chapeau rouge, which would shade my face from scrutiny. I lacked the spurred boots, but the bribe I had picked up—a fat partridge in its cage—was genuine. I walked purposefully, judging the best direction.

As soon as Aigrefeuille realized I had bolted, he would ring the alarm and bar the gates. The drums would sound, two long, two short, until every guardsman was deployed. To the north, a huddle of guards were already laying siege to the latrines. A guardsman ran past me with a pole-axe to break through the wooden door. When they found the sanctuary empty, they would assume that I had dropped into the pit that contained the excrement below. They would soon be occupied with throwing dice to decide who had the odious job of lowering a rope to slide down it.

That is, unless they noticed something odd about the cardinal now strolling through the Grand Tinel, or heard a discordant note, for the partridge was becoming restless. I climbed into one of the window seats with a view of the garden and unlatched the cage to release the partridge from the window. The bird plummeted, remembering its wings only moments before it hit the saffron crocuses. First one cook came out of the kitchen to puzzle over the squawking bird, then the others followed, then the cooking boys, wiping greasy hands on their tunics.

While they were chasing after the partridge, the kitchen would be empty. I ran through the dressoir, down the stewards' passage, and into the lower kitchen, where I found the great table spread with animals being dismembered for the Pope's next meal. I removed my outer clothes and hid them. A short flight of steps led to one of the mouths of the égout souterrain that carried the waste water directly to the Rhône. I remembered seeing its size when it was being built—large enough for a child, too small for a man. I tipped in a bucket of cooking fat to grease the drain, then slid in, head first, before I could pause to weigh my chances of making it to the river alive.

The Vaucluse

1348

Forty-one

HE WATER CHANNEL narrowed as it left the palace, then broadened into a uterine cave that swilled with kitchen waste. I grabbed on to a passing cabbage, wormy but buoyant, to keep my head above water. The channel became a chute, faster, with scarcely enough air to breathe. Then the roof disappeared and I was shooting through an open sewer towards the Rhône. Once in the river, I fought my way up through the foaming water, to meet the eyes of a bloated corpse that was eddying near the shore instead of negotiating the currents to Arles. I drifted after it beneath Saint Bénezet's bridge, until my feet touched mud. I slithered into the vegetation to pull myself onto the bank, where several plague corpses had beached themselves near a plague fire.

I emerged from the marsh, river-blackened and unrecognizable. A crowd was gathering around the large fire. Some ritual was in progress and I dove back into the reeds to watch unseen. A group of labourers—with iron-toed boots, with red hair, weapons-smiths to the man, for this was Saint Barbara's stalwart band—were dragging a woman who looked like me along the tow-path. It was my maid, wearing my robe of seven reds, her saucy look wiped off by terror. I had often seen her lusting after this robe, which I had hated since Gentilly. I watched in horror as they threw her onto the fire, shouting names such as *Saint Barbara, la Popessa*, and worse. As the flames licked her shoes, she protested her innocence fiercely. The fire ran up the inside of her leg and I imagined the searing pain, hoping that she died before her soft white innards curdled like burnt cream. It was a high price to pay for the theft of my clothing and I pitied her from my heart. She had taken my death upon her shoulders, sparing me.

At last, the flames died, the crowd dispersed, and the beggars sifted through the embers for charms against the plague. As I went past, holding up my collar to hide my face, some lucky fellow retrieved a hand, a choice relic from which a profit could be made. I was walking along the rue de la Balance, keeping clear of doors branded with red crosses, when a horn announced the arrival of the becchini to heap the day's cadavers on their cart. Two servants prodded a distended corpse out of a dwelling with long sticks, while a horrible lament—pain, or grief, or both morbidly entwined—came through the open door behind them. I took the rue de la Palapharnerie du Pape, staying outside the ramparts as long as I could, then aimed south on the rue de Sainte-Clare to the priory of the Poor Clares. The gate was barred and the sacristan, the sternest of the nuns, sat as its keeper. When she did not recognize me, I collapsed against the iron grille in a wretched bundle of wet filth.

How long had I huddled there? I heard whispers, but when I looked up, the sacristan was gone. Something dropped on me—a chunk of bread shoved through the grille-work that joined the other chunks I now noticed on my robe. The whispers turned into giggles and a tiny finger beseeched a kiss. I wept with joy at the sight of Félicité's dark eyes. My daughter was alive and well! I kissed nine more fingers through the grille, then her nose, then the bulge of her small cheek. Soon her new friend, Anne-Prospère, was also poking her fingers through the iron webbing to beg my kisses.

The prioress rushed towards us, gesticulating wildly, her wimple askew. "Do not touch that plague victim!" Her hand thudded on Félicité's shoulder, then Anne-Prospère's, propelling them back towards the cloister.

"Grant me asylum with my beloved child," I implored. "I am in mortal cold."

Only then did the prioress realize who I was. "You consigned your daughter to my priory, made me her guardian in your stead. I will not expose her to contagion by letting you enter."

"I am desperate for sanctuary and this is the Franciscan Order of the Poor Ladies. I am not carrying the plague, for I have been washed clean by the twice-blessed Rhône."

"The disease has already taken one of the nuns in my care," she said. "I sent the servants home to their families and we are so crippled without them that we cannot even bury our own dead."

In her red, tearful eyes, I saw my chance. "Which of your nuns has died?"

She wavered. "The herbalist, but no one has gone near her."

"With a plague corpse in your midst, you will lose more of your nuns. Such corpses are said to exhale pestilential fumes that infect the healthy. Push it out with poles and lay it here for the becchini."

"You will not trick me into opening my gate," she said. "Besides, she must be buried in our church as befits our order."

"If you take me to her body, I will bury it for you," I bargained. "I know how it is done."

She turned the key in her hand hesitantly. Just as I lost hope, she fumbled it into the lock and pushed it home with a decisive *clack*. I got through in an instant and put some distance between me and the gate. After I had scrubbed myself in the lavatorium, the prioress let me embrace Félicité and spend a blissful hour with her in the warming house.

Now I had to fulfil my part of the bargain. I found the dead nun in her herbarium. Several of the Clarisses huddled at the doorway, pinching their nostrils and uttering prayers. The herbalist had stripped herself naked to warn the others against touching her sores. She was so bloated that she appeared to have four breasts, two in front and two cankerous lumps in her armpits. A young woman was coming from the cloister with a shroud across her outstretched arms. By her stride and the speed of her approach, I saw she had some backbone to her. She was wearing gloves and had brought a pair for me.

"I am Angière de Bédarrides, Anne-Prospère's sister."

About twenty years of age, she was not in the brown habit and black veil of the order, but a fitted costume of patrician blue. She told me she had been visiting the priory when she heard the cry that the plague was running rampant in this quarter and chose to stay behind the grille when it came down.

I examined the jars on the herbalist's shelves, peering and sniffing until I found angelica water to sprinkle over the nun's face and a bag of quicklime, which I dusted over her body. When we had positioned the shroud beside her, I lifted her shoulders and Angière lifted her ankles to roll her into it. We tied the ends and manœuvred the corpse onto a barrow to wheel it inside the shrine of Saint Clare. I adjusted to the damp, musty stone dressed by the stonemasons' chisels, then absorbed the power of the workmanly church. Here, in this little church, Francesco had first caught sight of Laura. I let Angière go ahead while the memory, with all its bitter fruit, engulfed me. After it passed, I went into the Lady chapel, with its cracked wooden statue of the Virgin, where the Clarisses had pried up a paver with a crowbar and dug out the soil beneath. They now stood beside a shallow grave with a pile of earth heaped on the opposite side.

While the prioress recited the words of the psalm, *De profundis clamavi ad te Domine*, Angière and I wheeled up the barrow and tilted it to slide the corpse into the grave. The lady nuns took up spades and shovelled in the earth like brawny ploughmen. After they left, I removed the gloves and shook out the folds of my robe. Although I was missing my Turenne sleeve, the azure fabric had cleaned up enough for the pintucks and embroidery to show.

"You are the Countess of Turenne," Angière said. "No one who has seen you at the Pope's side could ever forget you. I was at Gentilly when Pope Clement gave you a sapphire ring. It was the day that my father consigned me to misery by betrothing me to the seigneur de Bédarrides."

The old Avignonnais did not throw their daughters away on men beneath them in station and Angière had married into a good family, as her dowry belt confirmed. I asked, "What do you mean by misery?"

"I believe the poets, who say there is no love in marriage. The seigneur de Bédarrides is a cruel man who married me only to beget sons. I hid in this priory so he would not know that he has quickened my womb. I beg you to help me dislodge this child I am carrying. It is said that the palace women are skilled in such matters." Her voice was firm and her forehead creased with purpose. "I can only get free of my husband if I convince him I am barren. I do not fear what needs to be done."

"As the Pope's consort, I did not intend to lead young wives astray. Is there no one else to turn to? Surely your mother . . ."

"She is ruled by my father. If he finds out, he will beat me, then return me to my marriage bed. The best my mother can do is give me to this convent as she did Anne-Prospère. My sister will remain cloistered all her life, yet my mother knew unimaginable love. I believe you know her: Laura de Noves."

That was why Angière looked familiar, for her eyes were as grey and her hair as flaxen as Laura's. The plague had made strange bedfellows of us. This time, when the memory of Francesco rose, I did not try to quell it. "It was in this church that your mother met Francesco Petrarch on the sixth day of April in the year 1327."

Angière looked into the vault, taking it in. "I wondered if it was here."

"The day has been celebrated in the finest love poems ever written. *The very moment and the very place where he beheld her perfect face.*"

"Indeed they are exquisite. I helped my mother hide them from my father. She did not bow to Petrarch's pleading until, just as her beauty began to fade, he appeared at Pope Clement's coronation in his poet laureate's gown. She saw you there—voluptuous, free, desired by all men. I believe that she gave in to him then and that Anne-Prospère came from a night of love they shared soon afterwards."

A night of love. Had Laura finally enjoyed his fingers' poetry upon her skin? Francesco had claimed his love for Laura was only spiritual. Why had I believed every word he uttered while we lay in one another's arms? He had deceived himself most of all, believing the lies of his own poems.

"Laura and I sheltered our daughters in this priory for the same reason," I said, "for we both associate it with Francesco."

"Were you not his mistress before you were Pope Clement's? My mother said you were."

"Félicité is also Francesco's daughter, though she does not know it. I suppose that is why she and Anne-Prospère make such good sisters."

"My mother hated you for your hold over Petrarch."

"We have been yoked together, we three, for over two score years."

"I have lived under his shadow as well. My mother hired a tutor to teach me Italian so I could read his poems to her."

I could not believe what I had just heard. "You mean that Laura cannot read?"

"She can neither read nor write."

"I'm sure that Francesco does not know it. He has written two hundred poems about her!"

"I doubt we saw half that number. It distressed her to learn there were apologies and love words she did not see. And now, she has so lost her beauty that she is fearful of Petrarch casting eyes upon her, yet ill with wishing to see him all the same."

What use was beauty—especially faded beauty—if Francesco Petrarch no longer praised it? "Tell your mother she need not fear. I do not think he wishes to see either of us again."

"I believe she knows, for she has given up on life. She is wearied from confinements, yet my father will not stay away from her bed. The whole house is in an uproar until she lets him in. I do not wish to be bound to my husband as my mother is. Will you free me of this child I am carrying?"

The seigneur de Bédarrides did not deserve this fine young woman. I would do what I could to help her. We returned to the herbarium, where I pulled out stoppers to smell the contents of the jars until I found the pungent wormwood I was seeking. A distillation of artemisia, its most potent form. As I poured the green oil into a vial, I splashed some on my hand.

"Now make a solemn promise. Go home to your mother. Inform her that Francesco Petrarch has left Avignon, never to return. Tell her about the child in your belly and give her time to change your mind. Promise me that you will hear your mother out." I waited for her to nod, then closed her fingers over the vial. I trusted Laura to find a way to free Angière from her husband without injuring her child. "The potion must only be inserted internally—do not take it any other way. Tell your mother it is poisonous by mouth, but not who gave it to you."

Angière tied the vial to her dowry belt with a strip of cloth. "Look after Anne-Prospère for me. It may be some time before I see her."

"She will be another daughter to me, even as you are. Go carefully, Angière. Stay away from the corpses laid out for the becchini." I kissed her brow, so much like Laura's that it pained me.

The gate was being keenly guarded by the gatekeeper. At the rear of the garden, a mound of earth was heaped over the fig tree's roots to protect it from frost. From this height, I boosted Angière up the priory wall. She hung off the other side with only her fingertips showing. Once her fingers let go, I heard her feet drop softly onto the ground beneath.

After Angière left, I took on the herbalist's duties, consulting her herbals to remind myself how Conmère had mixed remedies. This was a way for me to prove my worth and earn sanctuary here. In spite of all our care, several died, including the sacristan and prioress. Without them, the nuns blundered through the divine offices. I no longer worried about being put out on the street since I was the only one who could lead them through the psalms. Then, just as the first shoots appeared on our almond tree, the deaths stopped.

We kept the gate barred for our safety. In April, when the nuns had run out of spices to relieve the tedium of their cooking, Angière scaled the priory wall on a ladder held by one of her sisters. When I saw her perched on the top panting heavily, I brought a chair to ease her down, for I was glad to see she was big with child.

Chastened by her mother's valour, Angière had indeed changed her mind, and returned to the priory to give birth to her infant. She told me sadly of her mother's fate. Laura had collapsed in despondency upon hearing that Petrarch had gone to Italy for good. When Angière told her mother that she wanted to dislodge the child, Laura had confiscated the vial of poison. On the third of April Laura became gravely ill and on the sixth of April she died. In her will, she gave Angière one florin and promised her to the nunnery of the Poor Clares so her husband could not get at her. Thus, two women were freed from their marriage vows. Angière told me that Laura died of the plague, but I knew that the plague did not strike a single member of a family where there were more to feed on. No—Laura had drunk the wormwood oil I had given to Angière, as I had hoped. Weary of life, Laura fell eagerly upon the vial and welcomed her release. Her death on the sixth of April—the sacred day on which Francesco had met her—told me that she had chosen to die.

Angière reported that Laura's burial happened in a rush because of the pestilence. There was no time to tie crêpe bows on lemon trees. She was hastened into the ground in the de Sade chapel, where her dead children were buried. I had wished Laura gone so many times and by so many different means. Now she was truly dead and I rejoiced, but only inwardly, because Angière was mourning for her mother.

My revenge over Laura was as sweet and fragrant as the priory's almond blossoms after the severe plague winter, but I could not scrub the stain of wormwood from my palm, for no matter how much Laura welcomed death, I had done her no kindness. I had killed her and stolen her daughters from her.

Forty-two

ANGIÈRE LAY IN the infirmary with a pillow beneath her knees. The heat was murderous, yet she was giving birth. The shutters were open to ease the burden from her womb, but so far the infant had not budged. I cooled Angière's brow with water from the bottom of the well and splashed my own face and arms. I could not bring myself to peer inside her womb, in case some evil might be lurking there. I wished there were someone else to attend her, someone who did not love her as I did.

Félicité and Anne-Prospère played knuckle-bones at the threshold, where the Clarisses clustered to worry and cross themselves. They brought the last of the sugared almonds, knitted soakers, every thing of luxury we did not need. Finally, the novice pushed through them with a flask of distilled liquor from the cellar. I pressed it to Angière's lips to ease her pain, then took a swig of the fiery brew and asked the novice to assist me. With her help, I tied a rope to the beam for Angière to pull on, but still her groans were mighty enough to split the tiles on the roof.

My legs were trembling when the infant finally shifted. I tugged the baby free—a well-formed baby girl. I rubbed her with sweet almond oil and pressed my lips to her fontanelle to pray for her and Angière. Only then did I let in the Poor Clares, each noisily claiming the right to hold the infant first. The little girls climbed onto the bed, rendered dumb by the perfection of the baby's toes and fingers. When the tiny creature made a feeble cry, I gave her to Angière to suckle.

All pain forgotten, her face glowing, Angière held the baby to her breast and the infant's lips closed over the nipple. "Solange, you must be her godmother. I'll call her Laura, for she has my mother's hair."

As soon as the plague moved north, we opened the priory gate, to learn that one-third of Avignon's courtiers and citizens had died, leaving many dwellings empty. The city's value had fallen so low that Pope Clement bought it from Queen Joanna, granddaughter of King Robert the Wise, for a scant eighty thousand florins. Now that Avignon was Clement's lawful property, he pledged to restore her former glory. The stonemasons' chisels had resumed sizing blocks for the new perimeter wall that would protect the outlying poor from mercenaries.

I wrote to Guido to beg news of Francesco and my son. Although Florence had been ravaged, Guido reported that the Black Death had bypassed Parma, where Francesco was a canon living in a garden house more ample than his retreat in the Vaucluse. Now eleven, his ties to me severed by law, Giovanni was being tutored by the scholar Moggio de' Moggi. My joy was absolute, for though Francesco and Giovanni were far from me, they were together and had survived the plague.

Other letters arrived gradually, which we read to one another in the cloister. Angière's sister wrote that Angière's husband, the seigneur de Bédarrides, had died just before the plague withdrew. Angière creased the letter to sail it into the rosebush, where it settled jauntily on the briars.

She pulled the pins from her hair to toss it about her ears. "Wash my hair for me? I no longer need to wear it coiled like a matron."

The two little girls helped me fill a tub with hot water. We added camomile to bring out the flaxen colour, stirred up a frothy brew, and dunked Angière's head until she came up laughing. While I brushed Angière's hair dry in the sun, Félicité watched a sparrow bathing in the water we had spilled.

"How did the prioress's soul get inside that bird?" Félicité asked.

The sparrow was now on top of the rosebush, combing its wings with its beak. Satisfied that its feathers were dry, it began to preen and warble. It did indeed look like the plain brown prioress, whose presence we so missed.

"Who told you that it did?" I asked.

"The nuns." She leapt up to chase after Anne-Prospère.

When the midday gong sounded, the Clarisses roused themselves to walk to the refectory, leaving their needlework and letters where they fell. Angière retrieved her letter from the thorns and smoothed it out to read the rest.

"My sister says that she saw Francesco Petrarch haunting our mother's grave in the de Sade chapel."

Laura again. Would I never be rid of her? "Perhaps your sister only saw Laura's wandering spirit."

"It was no ghost," Angière said. "Petrarch's defilement of the tomb was real enough to offend the Cordeliers, who are paid by my father to sing orisons for my mother. They sent a runner to alert my father, but my sister intercepted the message and went to the chapel to halt Petrarch herself. Apparently, he had received a letter in Parma about Laura's death, mounted his horse, and ridden straight through without stopping. My sister writes that he was saddle-mad, clawing at the tomb and weeping like a madman."

I was ashamed that my own elation at Laura's death had made me forget what Francesco would feel. I imagined Francesco weeping over a pavingstone that looked like all the others, carrying death inside him as real as the corpse that had been rotting for months beneath the chapel floor. "Most likely he was driven mad by grief," I said. "How did your sister make him stop?"

"She says that he became calm as soon as she appeared, perhaps confusing her in his troubled mind with Laura. Of all my sisters, Gorcente looks most like our mother and was wearing her seed-pearl cap."

Where had he gone? Back to his house in the Vaucluse, I guessed. His old servants would nurse him until he was strong enough to ride back to Parma and our son. I hoped that, like a sleepwalker, Francesco would remember little. He would stop composing poems about Laura. Although it pained me that he had not sought me out, my daughters were safer without him knowing about them. My duty was to keep them safe from evil, including high-handed fathers. Someday, when Francesco could no longer threaten to take the little girls from me, I might tell them that a sublime poet had fathered them.

In the weeks that followed, I turned my attention to restoring the priory to working order. We had no servants, no priest to confess us, and no obedientiaries to lead us. Worse, we would soon have an empty larder. We had survived the plague summer by eating dried foodstuffs, but our stocks were dwindling. It would soon be Michaelmas, time to buy stores for winter, but when the prioress had died, so had the key to her reckoning system. From what I could tell reading her accounts, the Poor Clares had no income. The prioress had been selling off priory lands and now there was nothing to sell but the priory itself.

The Poor Clares were as little endowed with common sense as with money. Franciscans they might be, but they spent their days like noble-women, gossiping or doing needlework in the shade or sun, according to the season. Amongst the chattering, ineffectual Clarisses, I often found myself longing for the silence and intellectual rigour of the Benedictines.

I was trying to decipher the record books in the prioress's house, when I heard two of the nuns quarrelling outside my window over a misshapen loaf of bread. Drawing my miséricorde from my belt tongue, I said, "If you give me the loaf, I will halve it for you."

"It is all right," the youngest replied, relinquishing it to me. "She may have it all. You mean to shame us by showing yourself as wise as Solomon."

"Since you take my meaning so well, make another batch of bread. Make loaves for all the sisters this time. Make them evenly round and put leaven in them so that they will rise!"

They tucked their hands into their fur-lined sleeves.

"What is it now?" I asked.

"Our salt cellar is empty and there is no more flour."

I had been locked up with the priory accounts too long. If we were out of flour, we would soon be out of food, since the weevils had infested the other grains. It was time for me to leave the priory to take my daughters to a better place. I made the announcement to the Poor Clares after a spartan meal in the refectory.

"The priory of Saint Clare is without income," I told them. "There is no more fuel and the cellar cannot feed you through the winter. We can live without meat, but not without bread and salt."

They sat in silence, as if they all had indigestion, and perhaps they did. Outside, the wind hummed disconsolately, producing an irritating vibration in the wall.

"You must choose between returning to your families, if the plague has spared them," I said, "or following me where destiny calls me. I have written to the abbess of Clairefontaine to beg asylum for us, but I can wait no longer for her answer. Tomorrow, my daughters and I set off at dawn. If you wish to come, you must straighten your backs to carry your own goods upon your shoulders."

Forty-three

WE LEFT THROUGH Porte Magnanen, and followed the moat beside the city wall until it became the canal. Here, beside the cloth-workers' paddlewheels, I saw the sign of the Cheval Blanc, where I had sought refuge in my fifteenth year. As we walked along the canal, it widened into the Sorgue, which became swift and clear as the city fell behind us, although the Pope's fortress refused to shrink, when we looked back, for some time longer.

Trailing behind me in a disorderly line were eleven Poor Clares, one novice, two little girls hopping and skipping, and Angière with her infant in a sling across her chest. We followed the Sorgue upstream past bourgs, past farmers' fields, until it turned north, and we parted company. We stopped frequently for Angière to feed baby Laura and for the Clarisses to rub one another's feet. When we had walked the friars' path deep into the Vaucluse, we encountered the Sorgue a second time, and I glimpsed the distant cliff where the river surged from the black cavern of Fontaine-de-Vaucluse.

After another half-league of walking, a cloud shifted to reveal the Clairefontaine bell-tower with its ironwork cage. At last, the walled abbey came into view, and Félicité and Anne-Prospère began to run. Both were five, my age when I had first come to Clairefontaine. Here, Félicité would grow swift of foot and strong of limb, learning to sleep through the night. The Benedictine discipline of mind and body would nourish my daughters as it had nourished me. The high gates swung open to reveal twenty-four Benedictines in order of rank, headed by the ancient sacristan with her hands wringing her holy book, who was overwhelmed by our noise and disarray.

Elisabeth was the first to speak. I knew who she was at once, for my paternoster beads dangled from her bony wrist. "We bid you welcome to the abbey. The plague has so reduced our numbers that we have need of helping hands, even ones as soft as these."

Although few words were spoken, our welcome was blithe. The Benedictines put their fingers to their lips to silence the Poor Clares, then signalled that they would be well fed in the refectory in spite of the hour. Elisabeth washed my hands in the lavatorium, as was due an honoured guest.

I kept my voice low. "I am pleased to see you, Elisabeth."

She dried my hands with a linen towel. "You must call me Sister Martha." Her eyes veered away, tracking the obedientiaries through the cloister. They were not going into the refectory with the others, but towards the abbess's house, perhaps to decide what to do about me.

"I beg you—do not let Mother Agnes turn me out."

"Mother Agnes is dying of old age," she said. "She refused to believe you died in the plague and told us you would come, even before your letter arrived. She has waited for you so long she is living off her own flesh, taking nothing by mouth."

Elisabeth gestured that I should follow her to the abbess's house. Mother Agnes had proven stronger than the plague, but was now in a state of grace, propped at a slant in bed and ready to breathe her last. I straightened my back against the doorway, trying to stop my body from shaking as I took everything in. Mother Agnes was frail, yet there was an immense presence in her. Elisabeth joined the obedientiaries pressed along the inner wall. Each awaited her instructions holding the sign of her office: Elisabeth with her cellar keys, the sacristan with her testament, the choir-mistress with a sheet of music, and the infirmarian-vintner with a bleeding bowl. Many I had known were missing, felled by the passing years or by the plague. Sister Raymonde must have died, for the gardener was new, as was the stockbreeder, the beekeeper, and the chambress.

Mother Agnes called Elisabeth to her. "Sister Martha, your task is to continue my life's work."

She gave her the key to a battered ledger on the writing table, the boards so warped that the leather cover had split. Elisabeth bowed her head, her face thin and anxious, and I wondered why she had received such an act of penance. The abbess continued through the other obedientiaries, her voice weakening as she assigned tasks to each.

At last, she asked, "Where is Solange?"

Either her eyesight had dimmed, or she did not recognize me. I dipped my knee, realizing too late that the gesture spoke of the vanity of court. Even the azure of my robe was an effrontery in the midst of black habits with grey veils. I sank to my knees beside her bed, my lips blundering through a half-remembered prayer. She had mothered me, counselled me, loved me. I hoped she had not heard of all that I had been. How much of my fame had swum upstream to the abbey? She pushed my head into her lap with the strength of death in her, as if she meant to humble me.

"I have been waiting for you." She removed her chain of office and kissed the seal. "My daughters, kneel to your new abbess."

Caught off-guard, I could only manage a single word: "No." Even though the chain hovered, I did not raise my head. "I do not wish to become a nun, much less an abbess. I came to offer myself as the abbey's librarian." Perhaps she could not hear, for she dropped the chain heavily onto my collarbones. Tears stung my eyes, cleansing them of the grit of Avignon. "Lift this burden from me," I entreated Elisabeth, but she did not move, nor did any of the nuns.

I lifted the chain from my own neck, lurched to my feet, and hung it from the bed-hook, where Mother Agnes could see it. However, she had closed her eyes and folded herself inside the bed-covers to die. My courage buckled and the obedientiaries guided me into the study to minister to me. The chambress sat me on a chair so she could wash my blistered feet, Elisabeth brought me wine, and the infirmarian began to bleed me to balance my humours. I rested my eyes on the abbess's map, still nailed to her wall, while the nuns went in and out, discussing the quality of her breath, which was now as troubled as a rasp crossing iron. Then, all at once, the rasping from the bedchamber stopped and the infirmarian jerked around. Her bowl and lancet clattered onto the floor, spilling my blood. I pressed a cloth on the wound and went into the bedchamber to find the obedientiaries swarming around Mother Agnes. As the last pulse drove through her, they raised their eyes to witness her soul's escape and joined their palms in lamentation. After four score years, Mother Agnes had given up her ghost to God.

That same day, the abbess was carried into the church on a bier in her heraldic splendour as Agnès de Clairefontaine. Every nun was in her appointed place and the servants, monks, and villagers crowded the public area behind the screen. The sacristan reminded us that the abbess's forebears had founded the abbey on their ancestral lands and that their sons had fought in the crusades, then the abbess was laid in a tomb carved with the Clairefontaine arms. Although I had rejected her chain of office, I carried her brother's sword with Saint Peter's toenail shining in the pommel. When the mourning bell ceased, I climbed the church tower to stand beneath a clean, unclouded sky to strain my ears for the greater tones of the bell at Notre-Dame-des-Doms, three leagues away.

A half-year had passed since I had tasted butter and cream, and twenty-four years since I had tasted a fat capon roasted over faggots from old vines. The obedientiaries at the high table plied me with all the goodness of their order: their olive oil, their wine, their dried fruits stewed in honey and fresh fruits preserved in spirits. The nuns' deft fingers signalled the merits of each dish to their guests, for they still observed the rule of silence in the refectory. They had silenced the Poor Clares by placing them between mute Benedictines, though the abundant food would have done that by itself. Even the two little girls were subdued. Although Elisabeth sat beside me, she guarded her words as if they were gold florins. She was listening so intently to the sacristan's reading of the Life of Saint Hildegarde that there was nothing for me to do but eat.

After the funeral supper, the chambress assigned each of the Poor Clares a bed in the lay dormitory, which had space for my daughters as well. I was left until last, then told—to my dismay—that the only vacant bed was the one the abbess had died in. To postpone going to bed, I went into the church. The sculptured portal of the Benedictines, the graceful columns, the stained glass were like nectar after the spartan church of Saint Clare. My nostrils pinched with the familiar scent of beeswax mingling with damp stone. I ran my palm across an ashlar block to locate one of the masons' marks that I remembered being there. I knelt before the wooden altarpiece to seek Our Lady's counsel. Throughout my life, I had been a fair-weather worshipper of Our Lady, asking for favours but seldom begging forgiveness after I had sinned.

Black mourning stoles lay over the top of the icons and the wooden triptych. I had often stared at this triptych as a girl. In the left panel was the young Virgin with the angel Gabriel. In her, I had once seen my own mother. In the centre panel, the crucified Jesus was remote and skeletal. His mother was older here and smiling wisely because she was in on the secret of the resurrection. The right panel showed the jubilant risen Jesus in a garden. The woman holding the alabaster jar had dark blue eyes and wild, tangled hair, the colour an exuberant red. This was the other Mary, the flamboyant Magdalene.

As I looked at the three paintings, trying to make sense of them, I felt faint from the bleeding earlier. My lips became numb, then my tongue, then the numbness crept down my left arm into my fingers.

The skin on my forearms quivered into gooseflesh, as if feathers were sprouting, and circles jagged across my vision. The Virgin plucked one of Gabriel's wing feathers, the feather turned into a suckling baby, the baby squirmed on the Virgin's lap, and his chin grew wiry, black hairs. The two Marys blended into one gigantic female, gloriously big with child, who blotted out the tiny, pompous Jesus. I was talking aloud, saying only-God-knows-what. I had once spoken with the tongue of an angel. Perhaps I still had something of the gift. A door slammed and a draught sucked through the church, banging the side panels of the triptych closed. I wondered who had been creeping about in night shoes and what she had overheard me muttering in my delirium.

If this was a sign, what did it mean? Perhaps only that the rich dishes of the head table did not agree with me after the months of meagre food. I was ill all that night in the abbess's bed, running a fever, clammy one moment, shivery the next. At daybreak, Elisabeth brought in an opiate to sedate me, but the sweet odour made me queasy and I pushed it away. The obedientiaries entered the bedchamber behind her. The sacristan took down the chain of office and held it out to me with a serene look, as if she knew the outcome, like the knowing Virgin.

"You are forgetting that I have not taken my vows," I said. "Any one of you would make a better abbess than I would. Your chastity is a much finer thing than my belated celibacy." In spite of my protest, they did not shift their feet towards the door. What could I say to dissuade them from this scheme? Far from condemning me for my sins, they were eager to hear more. "One of the children who arrived with me, Félicité, is my own daughter."

Elisabeth muttered to the sacristan, "I told you the child was hers."

What other rumours had reached Elisabeth's ear? Certainly, she had guessed something of my past, more than the others, who were whispering almost as foolishly as the Poor Clares. I had no wish to itemize more sins to convince them of my unworthiness. Why should I name the great men I had lain with? I wanted to keep my past a secret.

When the bells called the nuns to vespers, I left the abbess's house to watch them rising from their tasks, brushing earth and flour from their hands, deserting their handwork to go gladly to choir. I walked into the fields in the setting sun as the owl flew out of the pine's yoke to scan the earth for mice. Burrs and foxtails and the thorns of trailing brambleberries caught at my hem. What business had I wandering about an abbey under the swollen mass of the rising moon?

That cool, wordless moon had plucked me out of the tinderbox of Avignon just as she plucked words out of tongue-tied lovers. Yet she was not as chaste as poets believed, for her pull on the blood was strong. Her power over the sublunary realm was fiercely carnal. Even now, she called me to her own offices. I was still fertile. Why should I become a celibate nun? I had no desire to become a barren sister barking at the full moon, chanting faint hymns and chafing at the abbey's bonds.

"Why do you keep bothering me?" I yelled at the big yellow globe. "What do you want from me?"

Then I remembered that I was a mother and looked around to ensure that no one was creeping about in her night shoes. Ahead, wormwood moths were collecting in a pool of moonlight on a bough, then sparking off into the dark with an eerie phosphorescence. I had given birth to four children, two of whom had lived. I, too, had been born of woman. On the eightieth day of my life, my soul had entered my body. Now, beneath the moon, I was once again that luminous spirit inside a ball of flesh. Expelled in a river of blood, I had slithered out between Maman's legs, slipping onto her great bed, gathering speed until I came to the end of her silken cord, which yanked me back like a palace bell summoning a truant servant. I was sniffed at by an impertinent snout, licked by a cat's tongue, peered at by an old moon of a grandmother. I had begun the soul's journey from bloody birth to bitter death. This was so docile I could scarcely call it a vision. My soul had simply fluttered to the surface to remind me that it dwelt within and that it had needs I could no longer ignore.

The abbey buildings had shrunk since I last surveyed them. The cracks in the infirmary had lengthened and the stones were green with mildew. The foundation had been laid for the new infirmary, but the work had halted. There was a whiff of feral stoat outside the scriptorium. It, too, was sadly tumbled, for discipline had not been enough to keep the walls well mortared. After a time, I gathered courage to go inside, where I found the desks knocked over and mouldy folios scattered across the pavingstones. The shattered window was letting in the draught. When I was last here, the Florentine had attacked me, propelling me outwards into the world of men.

I drew my miséricorde and squinted at myself in a piece of broken glass. I sheared my hair close to my scalp, letting the red hairs drop through my fingers onto the stone floor. The winter stubble left upon my head was as grey as a Benedictine veil. I walked to Sister Raymonde's gardening shelter, my scalp cold and my eyes moistening with remembered love. Inside, I lit a candle and said an orison for her soul. Her last specimen, an unusual blue wort, had dried where she had left it on the workbench, but curiously, one of her brushes was still wet. Nearby lay cakes of madder and woad, along with pea-sized lumps of vert de flambe and saffron, brushstrokes still visible on them. What had Raymonde been drawing? There was no parchment to be seen.

In her old hiding place, I found a record book. Here, too, were others, strapped to the underside of the bench, a life's work that awaited the return of a disciple who knew where to look. The last leaf of the last journal was marked *Midsummer Eve 1348*. On it she had drawn the blue-eyed wort with a note that it opened at night only when the moon was full. She had named it *belle-de-nuit* and written another name nearby, *Solange*. I leaned against her chest in memory and breathed in the scent of newly furrowed earth. I had so much I wanted to say to her. Why had she died just a few weeks before I returned to Clairefontaine?

I was not the only one who had visited this shrine. Indeed, someone was approaching even now. I heard the cry *who-looks-for-you, who-looks-for-you-all,* then a step, too soft to be Raymonde's restive spirit. The candle guttered as a waif entered, her fingers tinged with saffron.

"Maman?" Félicité said. "Are you unhappy?"

"No, my sweet. You bring happiness with you." I lifted her onto my lap to hug her, enjoying her stillness for a moment before she wriggled out of my arms. She weighed no more than an owl, and like an owl, she was fond of wandering under the moon. I kissed her ear. "From now on you must explore the grounds in the daytime, not by yourself at night. Hold my hand and I'll take you back before Anne-Prospère wakes to find herself alone in bed."

Forty-four

O N   T H E   S A M E   D A Y that I became a nun, I became an abbess, responsible for the health of forty souls. I professed my vows in the chancel and the abbot presented me with my crosier and seal of office. I was grateful to Mary Magdalene for taking this path before me. It was a comfort to know that I was not the only woman who had slept with powerful men en route to the veil. I had barely reclaimed my birth name, Solange Le Blanc, when life wrested it from me, for Elisabeth insisted that I take the name Marie-Ange, as the old abbess had wished.

Now the abbess's chain of office swung from my neck and her ink-pot sat at my elbow. My motley scalp was warm beneath a grey veil trimmed in white. I counted the hours by the divine offices, not the hourglass, and the days by the saints, not the calendar of science. My only astrologer was that common astrologer, the barnyard cock, whose duty was to rouse me at daybreak. I wore my silver-and-ivory belt, because an abbess should show her power to the world, and on my finger I displayed the Pope's sapphire ring. I was making plans, since I had no intention of leaving my daughters' fate—or the fate of any of my nuns—to less loving hands.

My first act as abbess was to draw my miséricorde to whittle a quill. I found Mother Agnes's account books in better order than her properties. She had secured the abbey's plate and lands by letting the buildings fall into disrepair, but with no honey to sell or commissions for the scriptorium, we had no ready income. To restore the abbey to its former prestige, I would need to twist a lion's tail. I wrote a letter to Pope Clement VI, signing it vicomtesse of Turenne, abbess of Clairefontaine, in which I asked him for an endowment for the abbey that would surpass the worth of its ancestral lands. I asked for eight thousand florins, one-tenth the amount Clement had paid to buy Avignon from Queen Joanna. For less than it cost to make an honest woman of his beloved city, he could keep me at a distance from his palace.

I pressed the sapphire ring into the sealing-wax to admire the papal coat of arms. Once Clement had grasped that I was still alive, he would see the wisdom of paying the ransom I demanded. He would not wish his sleep disrupted by my ghost returning to Saint Peter's short, cramped bed. What power had enabled me to escape the fire that had consumed me in my Gentilly robe? He was always eager to believe in the miracles and charisms of saints. Perhaps he would fear that I had reassembled my bones by al-jabr and clothed them, in an act of sorcery, with flesh.

Three days later, a horse galloped into the cloister, soaped by exertion, with the gatekeeper chasing after hotly. The Poor Clares swarmed and gossiped, while the Benedictines looked stern and kept their silence. The Pope's emissary leapt down, as fatigued as his mount, and tied the reins of the huge animal to the pommel as the nuns retreated out of range of its hooves. The emissary's purse rang with gold to buy me off and his saddlebags held the rare books I had demanded from the palace library. When I recognized the slim volume of Francesco's poems that I had compiled, I gladly relinquished the papal ring and signed the release the emissary slapped onto his sweaty thigh.

My booty would restore the fame of Clairefontaine. If my daughters did not wish to take up vocations in the abbey, I would provide dowries so they could marry worthy noblemen. Perhaps one of my daughters would choose to live in Francesco's house in Parma and avail herself of the great world offered there. When the time was safe, I would tell him who they were and their relationship to him. Anything was possible. My wingspan was broad enough to cover them wherever they went. But one daughter I would keep with me for all time, for each day I saw more of my beloved Francesco in Félicité's dark eyes and hair. She was my heart—my Francesca.

After I had locked the new books in the armarium and attached the key to my belt, I took Félicité to dig up my mother's perfume bottle and my garden of delights, my hortus deliciarum, which I had hidden so many years ago. She carried them to the pasture, where we lay on our stomachs to enjoy my abbey stories with the misshapen creatures I had drawn to illustrate them. The nuns with their habits soiled from tilling vegetables and herding cows. The sisters treading the grapes, tipsy from sampling last year's vintage. A friar's ribald tale curling into a nun's welcoming ear. A dead Benedictine settling into rigor mortis in her coffin. The abbey as a world unto itself, a microcosmus. All the while, even when laughing at my childish drawings, Félicité kept a good grip on the perfume bottle.

When we reached the end, she asked, "Will you die, Maman?"

Not *when* I would die, but *if* I would—a startling question. Death was indeed hovering closer, although I was only half the age of Mother Agnes when she died.

"We will all die," I said, "and I will die before you, for I am older."

"I will wait for you to fetch me as you did in the priory of Saint Clare."

I kissed her wet lashes. "My soul will fly to yours like an arrow."

"Like a mother to its baby?" She rubbed her nose against mine.

"Yes," I said, rubbing back. "The perfume bottle was my mother's. If you look carefully, you will see dried traces of her tears."

She held it beneath her eyes, then mine, for both of us had begun to weep, then hid the tiny bottle beneath the other treasures in her alms-bag.

"Now you must come to get your tears," she informed me. "And your mother must collect hers. What is it called again?"

"The last busy day, when we will all be together again. Now, that is enough seriousness for one day. Let us make you a book of delights of your own."

Perhaps she had inherited Raymonde's love for science. Or mine for poetry—befitting a child conceived in the finest library in Christendom. Upon her thigh, a shadowy mark was growing, similar to mine. It might yet turn into a thimble or a chalice, even the mark of Venus. In good time, her destiny would be revealed.

All Saints' Day was almost upon us. Our haymaking was over and we were gathering and crushing the vintage. Soon it would be blood-month, the time for slaughtering. When our harvest was done and our salt, fish, and spices laid by, I would put each Poor Clare to apprentice with one of the Benedictines. After the lady nuns were trained, they could choose to stay or return to their own priory, though I hoped they would remain so I could guide and watch over them.

My new scriptorium would rise on the bank of the fast-running Sorgue, where our labours would be soothed by the rush of the river chasing stones. It would be built from the best limestone, with a glass window, not oiled parchment, for each scribe. I intended to make the scriptorium as active as it had been at the height of Benedictine learning, with the finest library along the branches of the Sorgue. Angière had consented to be my first apprentice, for even now she had a good black-letter. When Félicité and Anne-Prospère were older, I would train their stubby fingers to love copying, as mine had done.

The little girls were never to be found when I wanted them. Everything was new to them: hives guarded by stinging bees, green apples that hurt their bellies, a hedgehog darting out of cover, swallows skimming over the corn, the scent of wet hay after the rain. Glad as I was that Félicité was no longer so frail and that Anne-Prospère was no longer la petite misère, I must still lay down rules for them to follow. It was enough to ask the disciplined Benedictines to put up with the disorderly Poor Clares, for they were like salt and sugar. To ask the Benedictines to indulge my daughters, as well, was unfair. They skipped about the abbey, causing havoc wherever they went. They let the goats into the gourds and stole eggs from my henhouse to tame a wild dog. They mimicked the nuns' hand signals by sticking their hands between their legs and giggling when they wanted to make water. And they could not comprehend the rule of silence—even in the refectory where it was sacrosanct while the sacristan read the saint's life from the falcon's nest above our heads.

Such mischief could not go on. It was time for them to learn the daily routine of the abbey. I was forced to that conclusion while we were singing an antiphon during sext. The choir-mistress was leading. *Unde lucet in aurora flos de Virgine Maria*, she sang. The last note wavered, miraculously drawn out as if held by a martyr with perfect pitch, a sacred note too high for profane ears. Was this the music of the spheres, the ineffable harmony of planets in their orbits? As the antiphon resounded from the groined vault, the note heightened into a scream. The choir-mistress clutched her head and clawed off her veil to see what had fallen on it. The flash of two dark heads above the singers told me that the little girls had been playing in the upper stalls and amusing themselves by dripping hot candle wax onto the choir nuns below. They ran out the door, dislodging the wild dog that was lying in the sun. As they escaped, a shaft of sunlight illuminated Félicité, piercing me with dread. No longer thistledown, her hair was as bristly as a hedgehog's. What if she had inherited, through Francesco's seed, some of his brother Gherardo's rapscallion nature?

This reminder of Francesco was my undoing. As the choir-mistress resumed her angelic singing, my thoughts drifted in a more carnal direction. I recalled the pleasure of lying with Francesco thigh to thigh, spinning to the world's swift tune. I prayed that in the general resurrection, in that great synthesis of blood and bones when bodies reassembled, Francesco's soul would be drawn to mine so we would taste the transporting joy that we had known in our youth. Just as destiny had divided us, it would bring us together, joining us in one another's arms for the rest of time. I imagined a laurel wreath clinging victoriously to my brow as I embraced him in the ecstasy of our resurrected flesh.

When the office was over, I found the little girls in the cellar, sliding back and forth on the floor. Elisabeth did not look up from recording the stores in her ledger. Why had she been avoiding me since I returned to Clairefontaine? She was wasting away, but I could not make out what was wrong with her other than too much piety. She had insisted that I become the abbess, but after I had taken on the rôle she had woven a hair shirt of privacy around herself. Was she still bitter that Mother Agnes had favoured me? The names we had been given, Marie-Ange and Martha, separated us even more. A kitchen Martha should be fat and merry, but she was taking after Saint Elisabeth, who had delusions and died from fasting. Where had the Elisabeth of the frogs and insects gone? Where was that whimsy, that fire that had warmed our cell when we were children?

I felt unwelcome in her cellar, but I was the abbess, after all, and I could see that the sack of rice was almost empty. "I will need to inspect the levels for winter," I told her. "All our supplies must be stored by Martinmas."

Still Elisabeth did not say anything, only turned her back to pry up the lid of a wooden box with a crowbar. The nails shrieked, the little girls shrieked louder, and the cellar vaulting amplified the noise. Why had I been so high-handed? Perhaps if I trusted Elisabeth to do her job, she would warm to me in time.

"Come away, mes petites. Sister Martha has work to do." I grasped Félicité's hand to lead her off. Wherever she went, Anne-Prospère would follow. "If you wish to yell, you must go into the fields where the nuns cannot hear you. After Martinmas, I will give you both some duties around the abbey."

"Don't worry, Maman. Sister Martha likes us. Her name is really Elisabeth." Félicité extracted her hand to skid across the floor. "Watch this." She danced on her high toes, then squealed again.

"Look, Fée," said Anne-Prospère, holding a fig by its stem. "Look, Maman." She plunged the fig into the last of the honey and ate the dripping fruit.

My pleasure at being called *Maman* was brief because I was puzzled that Elisabeth had not objected. It was normally as hard to get honey from a cellaress as it was to get blood from a turnip. Félicité dipped in a fig also, smiling like a gargoyle. I gathered the girls' sticky hands in mine, led them to the door, and set them free outside. I came back into the cellar, expecting an explanation, but Elisabeth continued to ignore me. She finished inspecting the box and noted the entire contents in her ledger, without a single look back in the box. Only now did I remember her prodigious memory for the words of the psalms.

At last, she straightened up, wiping her hands on her scapular. "You will be shown the list of supplies when it is ready. I will take the mule cart to Avignon before the weather changes. I will be gone three days."

Such a flood of speech! She wasn't asking my permission, but she was opening the door a little. We were sisters once and perhaps could be again. "I will draw you a map of the friars' path so you can follow the safest route."

"I have a better map in here." She tapped her head. "When the abbess travelled to Avignon, I accompanied her, and when she became too weak, I went on my own. Sometimes I saw you there, but you did not recognize me."

I could not control my face, a mixture of surprise and dawning shame. "Even when I resided in the palais des Papes?"

Another crate shrieked as she dug the crowbar under the lid of a box and forced it down. "Especially then."

Forty-five

THE BRANCHES OF the Sorgue had begun to flood the Vaucluse basin. Our cellar was full for winter and our firewood stacked in cords to season. In the comfort of the abbess's house, between compline and nocturns, I had time for reading and casting back over memories. I had lived fully, loved and been loved, borne children both live and dead. Here at Clairefontaine, within hearing of the bell of Notre-Dame-des-Doms, I would remain, nurturing my daughters until I died in my great bed, with my nuns kneeling around me and my familia of servants mourning.

But death must wait, for I had much to do. One of my duties was to answer letters that came from afar. Addressed variously to the abbess of Clairefontaine, or the Countess of Turenne, or la Popessa, they found their way to me, begging for scraps of prophecy. I drew my lantern close, for earlier that day a letter had arrived in the hands of a passing friar, who had carried it from Italy for a fee. I had slipped it into the inner layer of my habit so that Elisabeth, who was lingering with curious eyes, would not see the wax seal. All day long, I had felt the vellum picking up my skin's warmth beneath my shift. I retrieved it now—translucent from the heat and moisture of my flesh.

The letter was addressed to me in Francesco's lively hand. What did he want from me after so many years? I imagined him writing the letter in Parma, swathed in his coronation gown, with a well-bred hound sleeping loyally beside him. I cut the stitches eagerly, then slid my knife beneath the green wax to unfold the sheet.

> To Solange, in your hermitage,
>
> Now that you have come to rest in the Vaucluse as you once hoped, I return to you in spirit to recall old pleasures and discover new ones. You will be happy to learn that I am writing poetry again. At first, Laura came back to me in dreams to dry my tears with her hair. Unworthy of the parchment I wrote them on, I scraped off the words. Then, one night, I dreamt of Laura as I first saw her in the church of Saint Clare. These fresh poems, now scattered across my table, have remarkable new conceits. I will send a handful today and will convey more by trusted couriers as I finish them. If you find infelicities, do not spare me, for I trust your eye and ear more than my own.
>
> You will be surprised to know, after all the pain I have caused you, how often I caress you in my thoughts. As I fall asleep, I see you bathing naked in the fountain of the Sorgue. I dream of returning to you, but fearful of being roused by your great beauty and becoming a thrall to lust again, I content myself by writing poems about Laura, hoping posterity will share your approval of them.
>
> I write this at prime as the moon angles in its descent towards the earth. How many winters are left to us? How many summers? Take up your pen and write with me, for the future is in our hands. Remember your prediction that I would be

crowned by laurel leaves in Rome? Prophesy for me once more,
my love—will men still read my poetry when you and I are dead?
   Your own Francesco

My own Francesco, returning to me in spirit. My longing for him
flooded back and the zeal of love reclaimed me. He was caressing me
in his thoughts, thinking of me as he fell asleep, succumbing to my
power even at this distance! But when I reread the letter, I saw something more: his fantasy of Laura, so resilient that it now embraced her
death. Anger swamped me, black and red waves striking at the very core
of sanity. Poisoning her with wormwood had only made him cling to
her morbidly. Worms were battening on her decomposing flesh, but it
was no good to tell that to a poet. Could I never loosen Francesco's grip
on his rotting prize? I grasped the hilt of the Clairefontaine sword with
Saint Peter's yellowed toenail and felt my courage swell. But how could
I smite my rival, when she was already dead?

I spread Francesco's new poems across my table. In spite of the
blottings, the poems were sublime, harvested from the deep imagery of
grief. Here and there, he reached too far or dropped a syllable. Even as
he was squeezing these drafts onto the free fold of the letter, he had
crossed out and replaced words. He had much need of my help.
Without it, he would be condemned to altering words, moving verses
from one poem to the next, then poems from one place in the cycle to
another, despairing of finding perfection.

I imagined how our letters would fly back and forth as I encouraged him to trust his heartbeats to pace the lines. No one had written
of love so well, not even Dante. Francesco was purifying the Italian
tongue—what did it matter in the long run of time that Laura was the
inspiration? These poems would alter the way men wrote hereafter. By
guiding him, I would claim this beauty for myself and for my children.
When the songbook of Francesco di Petrarca de Florentia was complete, I would copy it in my finest hand. With my signature as a seal of

authority, it would make its way along the trade routes of Europe, earn-
ing admirers everywhere.

Let history worship at Laura's sepulchre, if it chose, and choirs of
nuns sing fruitless orisons. A great poet might have worshipped her,
but only maggots enjoyed her now. Now that Francesco could not
have me, his desire was flaming up. My body, too, hungered for more,
but first we must endure this earthly fast. When I first lay in Francesco's
arms, I thought heaven well lost for mortal love, but I was learning
the value of the immortal soul. Like Héloïse after she became a nun,
I would enjoy an ardent correspondence with my Abélard. I had just
settled myself at my table to begin a letter, when I heard Angière's quick
step. In her hand was a copper pan.

"May I share your fire? I've been helping Cook think up ways to
use our surplus of apples. Apple confit, apple cider, apple butter. These
are baked with cream. I brought a spoon for you as well."

We sat side by side, passing the pan back and forth as we ate. "It is
the winter solstice, an evening for contemplation," I said. "The night
hours are twice as long as the day's. I feed on these silences in the Vaucluse."

"Your thoughts seem to weigh more heavily on you here than they
did in Avignon."

"I have forty daughters now, not four. I do not wish to lose any of
the souls in my keeping."

"That is unlikely, since the Clarisses have settled in so well." Her
spoon clanged into the empty pot and her eyes met mine forthrightly.
"Now, Solange, do not play abbess with me. When I came in, a smile
was teasing your lips and I saw you hiding the letter that arrived today.
I was the one who told the courier where to find you. Shall I guess
whose seal was pressed into that green wax?"

My lips were curving like a child's. "Francesco is asking for my
opinion of his new poems. What harm can it do?"

"While I was waiting for the apples to bake, I remembered where
I had last seen that coat of arms. It is on this."

Angière laid a small object on my knee and peeled back the linen covering. I almost knocked it away in repulsion: a dried finger with an overgrown nail, such as sorcières used to curse their enemies or raise violent thunderstorms from the night air.

"Whose finger is this? Do you expect me to perform some necromancy with it?"

"Only if you wish to bring Petrarch back to you. Look more closely at the ring. Just before my mother was lowered into the de Sade tomb, my father opened her shroud to prove that the plague had not deformed her. He pulled off her glove to kiss her hand as a show for the funeral guests and was enraged to see this love-token from her poet. He could not wrench the ring over the swollen knuckle, so he cut off her finger in front of us all."

We both stared at the finger, imagining Francesco presenting the ring to Laura, then Laura deceiving her husband by wearing gloves to hide it. Angière pointed out the dark strands twisted into the silver of the ring.

"Not only is that Petrarch's coat of arms, that is his hair. This ring rightfully belongs to you, Solange. You are a better muse to him than my mother was. Now I will leave you to enjoy your memories of him in private."

She left as she came, in a burst of quickness, our spoons rattling in the pot. When the wind banged the door, I rose to fasten it and shoot the bolt. I sat back in front of the fire to examine the finger. The ring would not come off because Laura's skin adhered to the inside, gluing them together. At the resurrection, every soul would collect its body and any scattered parts thereof, even scraps of skin and hair like these. But I had no intention of letting Laura's soul attract Francesco's like a lodestone drawing iron. His verses had made her immortal—that was enough. I would not let them be united for eternity. I twisted the ring to loosen it, twisted and tugged until I freed it from the finger. Then I tossed the finger into the hottest part of the fire, watching with satisfaction as it shrivelled.

I scraped Laura's dead skin from the ring and placed the ring on my own finger. In wearing it, I was guilty of no more than profane idolatry. When the last trump sounded, Francesco's soul would be compelled to return to my corpse to collect his hair. But first, I must be patient until my eyes rolled in their sockets, the flesh fell from my finger, and the ring spun upon bare bone.

Forty-six

IN THE MORNING, I dressed in brilliant light, for the shutters had flown open before daybreak. The gusting wind had cleared the dark clouds and I inhaled the resin from broken pine branches. I put on my fur-lined cloak to inspect the abbey to ensure that the nuns were at their customary tasks. Then I carried my writing materials to the cloister and settled into my carrel in the morning sun. I dipped my quill to write my first letter to Francesco to advise him where the lines were clumsy in his new poems and how he might repair them.

But these fine thoughts were anchored to a scratchy quill running short of ink. The ink-pot itself was dry, for I had left it unstoppered overnight. I went down the cellar steps to hunt for the new bottles of ink and found them next to Elisabeth's cellar records. The ledgers were all neatly labelled, except for an old one hidden behind the others, with covers so warped they had split the dark red leather. Elisabeth had left it unlocked. If she had been recording more than our inventory of stores, this book might bear a clue to her unhealthy piety. I unsnapped the tarnished clasp and the book swung open near the end. I began to read.

Now here is the true legend of Saint Marie-Ange, who saw
visions when yet within her mother's womb. The Holy Ghost
descended at Pentecost to bless her birth in Avignon in the year
1309. Suddenly there came a joyful sound and the newborn saint
stood erect, hair ablaze, and spake in tongues. Her prophecy
confounded devils and delighted sages. While in her ecstasies, she
apprehended not with mortal eye and ear but through the eternal
soul. When not above five years of age, this glorious saint
dedicated herself to the sacred Benedictines at Clairefontaine-on-
the-Sorgue, called *claire* for the clarity of its waters and *fontaine* for
the fountain of the Sorgue. Soon afterwards, she saw a *unicorn*,
that is, Our Lord, resting his head in the lap of a lady in a *closed
garden*, which is to say the Virgin's intact womb. Thereafter, she
had a vision of an unborn calf with seven black spots, a dread
augury that seven popes would rule in Babylon-on-the-Rhône.

A saint's life—an odd book for Elisabeth to keep in her cellar. Even
odder, the words resonated sharply with details of my life. I had seen
Mother Agnes bequeath this battered ledger to Elisabeth when she was
on her deathbed. With a thundering heart, I recognized the scarlet ledger,
darkened by years of handling, in which the abbess had recorded my
youthful visions. For much of my childhood, it had sat on the abbess's shelf
as a symbol of her hope that I would bring renown to Clairefontaine. As
I continued to read, the cellar's creeping damp gave me a rash of shivers.

When the age of majority was upon her, Saint Marie-Ange
did not take the easy way by becoming the virgin bride of Christ,
but took the hard way through the mortification of this world.
When the devil accosted her, she struck him down, her face
aflame with just ire, saying, "Begone, sting of sting, dung of dung,
poison of poison." She saved the city of Avignon by driving back
the artillery of thunderstorm and lightning, and forced the Pope

called John, who was but a partridge trussed up in priestly spoils, to recant his heresy about the Beatific Vision.

Just as grapes are trod and crushed before they are brought to the barrel, so Saint Marie-Ange must needs be harried and threshed in this world before she is brought to the granary of heaven. She was examined in the presence of cardinals and princes, and the truth of her auguries upheld by Pope Clement. The poet laureate could not cast her down, though he blasphemed her as the Whore of Babylon, her cup overflowing with the lewdness of her fornication. With sagacious tongue, she drove back nail for nail.

Now as to her miracles and charisms, wondrous to record. She had a chalice on her flesh, which did not bleed when pricked. Never befouled, her immaculate womb conceived felicitously as did Saint Anne's. She became the first amongst women in the city of Avignon for her wealth, for her beauty of form, and for the pretentious splendour of her attire. She commanded the moon, drove back the flood, and saved the Pope from the plague, which she miraculously repelled.

At last, rising in her volupty in the flames of martyrdom, this twice-born saint renounced the stew of Avignon, for she deemed all the joys of this life to be as excrement. When her feet stepped through the narrow gate of Clairefontaine, the abbess gave up the ghost, crying, "It is accomplished." The chapter knelt and with one voice elected her their new abbess, but she pushed away the cup until the skin hung upon her bones and all the hairs fell from her head, like a whore penitent. She is now hailed far and wide as the Sibyl of the Rhône and is consulted for her miracles by pilgrims and for her apt prophecy by popes and kings and even poets.

At the end, she will be taken up in a column of fire, with body and soul intact, like Mary of Magdalene and Mary of Egypt. At the second coming, she will sit in glory in the Choir of Angels and Martyrs, far above the lowly corps of resurrected mortals, who will only gaze upon her from afar and never more defile her with their impure touch.

This was the last entry in the ledger, but many had preceded it. At the beginning, the handwriting was Mother Agnes's, page after page of plain, workman-like lettering in stark contrast to the enflamed words. Latin phrases twisted and embellished childhood events so that I hardly knew myself. Even when I escaped the abbey, the abbess did not falter. She never gave up her belief that I would be a saint like Hildegarde of Bingen. The more she heard of me from afar, the more she struggled to seek a purpose to my life.

This was not just the abbess's work, for I could see Elisabeth in it as well. As the abbess had aged, Elisabeth had become her legs, travelling to Avignon more to fill her ears than to fill the abbey's cellar. Towards the end of the ledger, Mother Agnes's penmanship became shaky, then was replaced by Elisabeth's heavy, black Provençal. Here was the Elisabeth of my childhood where I least expected to find her, the Elisabeth who had tried to capture souls in goblets. Certainly, her whimsy had been put to strange use, for she had written a *Life of Saint Marie-Ange* that had the power to destroy me. I had forgotten how hard her punches could hit. She had documented a case for my sainthood, turning herself into the advocatus Dei, God's advocate, in a trial for canonization. The church's most recent saint, Yves, had been as flawed as I was, but his worshippers were dogged. Led by a God's advocate as zealous as Elisabeth, they drove back all contrary evidence until the devil's advocate was crushed, and Yves, poor man, was canonized with gusto by Pope Clement himself.

Now I saw where destiny had been leading me. This was to be my final battle: not the fight against Laura, not even the bloody battle of death itself, but the fight for how the world would know me hereafter. Was I to be remembered as a bloodless saint having her Life read to nuns eating in the refectory, or as a woman who had lived and loved?

If Elisabeth succeeded, I would be elevated to the choir of saints, where I would see the Blessed Face of God and be denied all human love thenceforth.

Before Elisabeth could present her case for canonization to the Pope, I had to die. Here in this abbey, Elisabeth and I were rivals once again, outwaiting and outsmarting each other. If I burnt the scarlet ledger, she would write in another one and hide it in a more secret place. Instead, I needed to live long enough to bury the ledger with her in her tomb.

But what if I died before her? By outliving me, she would control my destiny, unless I could outwit her. I pushed the ledger back into its hiding place, chose a bottle of the best ink, and carried it into the cloister. I settled into the carrel with my fur-lined cloak wrapped around me and Francesco's ring displayed upon my finger. I had not come this far to let Elisabeth's piety defeat me now. I skewered a fresh sheet of vellum and took a moment to savour its heady scent, for I was about to write the most important document of my life. I sharpened my quill and dipped it generously in ink.

My daughters,

Today I begin my tale to turn you into the devil's advocate— the keepers of my destiny. If you are reading this, I am dead, and you must take arms against Elisabeth, my foe. To equip you for this battle, I will write my own Life to set the record straight, a livre du voir-dire in which my sins speak loudly in their own defence. Safeguard this story and guard against all false biographies. Do not let the wrath of love, nor fire, nor the sword, nor devouring age conspire to destroy this book.

It is time I told you of my birth, and my betrothal to Francesco Petrarch and the events that followed, to prove that I have led a full and carnal life. My sins of harlotry and pride cling greedily like scraps of flesh on bone, but I have worse sins to confess. I am guilty of killing Laura. By drinking the wormwood oil that I gave to Angière, Laura poisoned herself, as I intended. Most of all, I am guilty of a love that outlasts death. Can I be blamed for desiring to see my lover's countenance more than the Blessed Face of God? I have loved my poet too long to let him slip between my fingers now.

I first heard my mother's heartbeat from inside her dark, surrounding womb. It mingled with my own heart's rhythm, then changed to a harsher, more strident beat. It was then that I had my first and most famous vision of a man kneeling in a purple cassock and biretta. I could see him as if I were looking out a window made of glass. He was framed by curtains that fell in crimson folds around my mother, who lay beneath him on the bed. His face was as clear to me as the blood vessels inside her womb, his skin foxed with a tracery of veins. I looked straight into his eyes and they were as hard and blue as lapis lazuli . . .

Acknowledgements

I am indebted to all the authors who have enriched the legends of Petrarch and Laura and of the fourteenth-century period known as the Babylonian captivity, when the popes resided in Avignon instead of Rome. I was greatly inspired by visits to the historic centre of Avignon, a UNESCO world heritage site. Most of all, I owe a debt to Francesco Petrarch, who wrote remarkable poems about Laura, as well as a few about the mysterious woman who was the mother of his two children. In creating Solange, I found poetic licence in Petrarch's advice to his friend, Philippe de Cabassoles, the bishop of Vaucluse: "If true facts are lacking, add imaginary ones. Invention in the service of truth is not lying."

As well as reading medieval authors such as Petrarch, Dante, Boccaccio, and Chaucer, I consulted a variety of historians and biographers, and made use of Jacobus de Voragine's *The Golden Legend* in the translation by Ryan and Ripperger. I thank *The New Quarterly* for first publishing Gherardo's letter from Montrieux-le-Jeune and acknowledge, with great appreciation, grants from the Canada Council and the British Columbia Arts Council, and a research grant from the Access

Copyright Foundation. I am very grateful for the ongoing support of my agents Dean Cooke of The Cooke Agency, and Suzanne Brandreth and Ron Eckel of The Cooke Agency International. Special thanks to Kristin Cochrane, Lynn Henry, and the expert team at Doubleday Canada and, above all, to my dedicated editor, Nita Pronovost, whose belief in *Muse* has never faltered.

Many people have supported me in the writing of *Muse* over the years. I thank them sincerely for their generous comments, especially my writing group June Hutton and Jen Sookfong Lee, fellow writer Paul Headrick, and friends Lynne Neufeld and Mary-Ann Stouck. Keir Novik, Karen Novik, Tom Emerson, and Bonnie Lumley boosted me up and cheered me on, and Alexi and Tilly have been a boundless source of joy and inspiration. I would also like to thank the North Shore librarians, my network of supportive friends and relatives, and the lively coterie of fiction writers who make it a pleasure to live and write in Vancouver. Above all, my love and appreciation go to my husband Orest, for his unwavering encouragement and constant faith in me.